26 Jan

2008

008

ALLEY URCHIN

In 1870 Emma Grady has spent seven years as a convict in Australia. Now, having earned her ticket of leave, she is still bound by chains of honour and friendship. Yet Emma lives for the day when she will return to England, to face those who cheated and betrayed her. And to Marlow Tanner, the man she loves—and whose tragic child she had borne and then lost.

Emma struggles to make something of her life in Australia despite the sinister presence of her employer's evil son Foster. His determination to 'have' Emma leads to dark and terrifying consequences.

Will Emma ever be reunited with Marlow? Even is she finds him, will he still love her? And what of the child lost to them both? Emma is plagued with fears but her love for Marlow never weakens—and can never be fogotten...

Alley Urchin

Josephine Cox

WINDSOR
PARAGON

First published 1991
by
Macdonald & Co (Publishers) Ltd
This Large Print edition published 2006
by
BBC Audiobooks Ltd by arrangement with
Headline Book Publishing

Hardcover ISBN 10: 1 4056 1160 X
           ISBN 13: 978 1 405 61160 2
Softcover ISBN 10: 1 4056 2147 8
           ISBN 13: 978 1 405 62147 2

British Library Cataloguing in Publication Data available

Printed and bound in Great Britain by
Antony Rowe Ltd., Chippenham, Wiltshire

Dedication

For all their steadfast love and support, my thoughts go out to my two lovely sisters, Winifred and Anita.

Life hasn't been easy for them, but they can always find a smile, bless their hearts.

Not forgetting my seven brothers, Sonny, Joseph, Bernard, Richard, Billy, Harry and Alec.

They could never be described as angels, but our late lovely Mam would have been as proud of them all as I am. (Keep the meat an'tater pies hot, lads!)

Foreword

The research for this book took me to Australia and Singapore, where I travelled many miles and talked to countless numbers of people. As a result, not only did my research prove to be fruitful, but became a labour of great joy. Everyone went out of their way to help, advise, and 'dig up' relevant documentation and information which have proved invaluable.

My husband, Ken, and I spent many long hours browsing through material under the artificial lights of libraries, and in museums and archives. We also traipsed many miles on foot in the tiring heat of Australia, a magnificent land. We saw wonderful buildings which were built by the convicts themselves in the Port of Fremantle, the most striking (and ironic) in my opinion being the prison which was to house them. One particular building which will live forever in my nightmares is the formidable Victorian-style lunatic asylum. This has, fortunately, been preserved as an arts centre and museum. But a one-time padded cell is kept almost exactly as it was, when the inmate might be dragged, screaming, into its dark and grim interior.

To stand inside that cell, to see the narrow iron bed and the high beamed walls, with the only light coming in through a tiny barred window, is to feel real terror. It was the most unnerving experience of my life. The atmosphere seems to have been absorbed into the very fibre of the walls—to touch those walls is to feel the presence of those wretched souls.

When, quite shaken, I emerged from that dank and dismal place, it was to be told by the curator, 'If the poor convicts weren't insane when they locked them in . . . they certainly were when they let them out!' (I, for one, was not about to argue with that.)

Below are mentioned a few of the many people who went out of their way to help in my search for the human story of what might have taken place there so many years ago. Australia is a vast and beautiful land, whose people rightly feel a great sense of pride in it. But picture the unfortunates who are wrenched from home and family, then taken on a long harrowing journey across the oceans to the other side of the world, not knowing whether they might ever again find freedom, or be returned to the bosom of their family. What paradise for them?

Lorraine Stevenson (Archives), Town Hall, Freemantle WA
Sunita A. Thillainath (Librarian), Fremantle WA
Mary Faith Holloway (Custodian), Prison Museum, Fremantle WA
Ralph of Ralph's Cafe, Fremantle WA
Gloria McLeod, Daglish WA
The Port Authority Officials, Fremantle WA
Chamber of Commerce Officials, Fremantle WA
The old Darwin fella in the Cafe—Good on yer, mate!

My love and thanks to Ken who, as ever, gave me constant support and was a wonderful companion.

Part One

Australia 1870

Ambitious Dreams

When night moves in
To hide the sun,
When enemies rally
And your strength is done,
When your weary heart
Longs to be free
Think of me, beloved,
Think of me.

J.C.

Chapter One

'If it takes a lifetime and if I am driven to follow you to every dark corner of the earth, I mean to have you. And I *will*. Mark my words, Emma . . . for you'll find no escape!' Though delivered in barely a whisper, the words struck deep into Emma's heart. The half-smiling, taunting mouth was so close to her face that she could feel the warm breath fanning her skin. 'You *will* learn to love me, Emma, I promise you.' The voice was trembling with passion and, as before, it was charged with a deal of arrogance. There was something else besides. Some deep, dark obsession, something akin to desperation. Or insanity.

'*Love* you!' Emma's stout heart was fearful, yet her grey eyes glinted like hardened steel as they bore defiantly into the leering face above her. Even though she would have denied it to the world, Emma could not deny to herself that she *was* afraid. Ever since that fateful day some seven years before when, along with other like wretches she had stumbled from the convict ship, Emma's every instinct had been disturbed by the covetous manner in which Foster Thomas had brought his gaze to rest on her.

As always, Emma put on a brave front. Drawing her trim form upright and squaring her small, straight shoulders, she told him, 'I could *never* love you, Foster Thomas. Never! The only emotion you raise in me is one of disgust.' Yes, of repugnance and loathing too, thought Emma, being painfully aware of his close proximity as he stood his ground, determined that she should not pass. She saw him as everything vile in a man. Oh, it was true that he had about him the compelling quality that might easily turn a woman's head. He was a fine figure of a man—tall and lean, with wayward sun-bleached hair atop a bronzed handsome face. There was a certain attraction in the coarseness of his manner, yet when the occasion suited him, he carried an air of elegance and devastating charm. But those eyes: only the eyes betrayed the truth of his nature. Small they were, and calculating; murky-blue in colour as the ocean, yet more deep and dangerous, and ever watchful, like the quick, darting glance of a lizard.

For what seemed an age, he made no move. Instead, his smile grew more devious, then, raising his hand, he made as if to stroke Emma's long chestnut hair. But, being somewhat startled by a sudden intrusion, he angrily lowered his arm and swung round to face the intruder. 'You!' he snapped, glowering hard at the homely young woman silhouetted in the barn doorway. 'Haven't you got work to do?'

'Course I 'ave!' came the chirpy reply, as the irrepressible Nelly strode into the barn, quickly dropping the wooden bucket from her arm to the floor. 'Yer surely don't think I've been sitting on me arse all morning, d'yer?' Then, before he could lay the yard-broom across her shoulders, as she knew he would, she added quickly, 'Old Mr Thomas sent me ter fetch yer. He said yer was ter come straight away, on account of it being most urgent.' She manipulated her plain, kindly features into an expression of alarm. 'The poor old thing

4

were having a real fit about some'at,' she said, nodding her head so frantically that her frilly cap tumbled into the dust at her feet. By the time she bent to retrieve it, Foster Thomas was gone, after first asking, 'You say my father wants me right now . . . this very minute?' To which she replied with suitable anxiety, 'Ooh yes, Mr Thomas, sir. This *very* minute!'

'You little wretch,' laughed Emma, as she and Nelly watched him stride away, both knowing full well that he was being sent on a fool's errand. That rascal Nelly, thought Emma, as she lovingly put an arm about her friend's shoulders; she knew every trick in the book. Brought up in the East End of London, she was a Cockney through and through. Since an early age, Nelly had been forced by circumstances to fend for herself, and she was a past master at it. It wasn't the first time she had made a timely intervention on Emma's behalf. Though Emma knew only too well that Nelly could take care of herself, she was constantly afraid that, one of these days, Foster Thomas might take it into his head to get rid of Nelly once and for all.

Emma knew it would be an easy thing, because all that was necessary was for the Governor to receive a formal complaint against the prisoner Nelly, and she would be punished, assigned elsewhere, or both. So far, Emma had stalled such a move by appealing to *old* Mr Thomas, Foster's father, who was after all the employer to whom both she and Nelly had been entrusted since being brought to these shores. With his wife in ailing health, Mr Thomas senior had been thankful for the labour supplied by the two female convicts, and was never too mean to say so—both to them, and in his regular reports to the Governor.

Emma respected and liked him. He was a hard-working and shrewd man of business, having built up his trading post from selling the few items he brought with him when he first arrived in Western Australia as an early settler many years before. He was a good man, and his wife a good woman. Emma thought they deserved a better son than Foster Thomas.

'Oh, Nelly . . . I wish you'd be more careful.' Emma hoped this little episode wouldn't bring trouble down on their heads. 'You know what a vicious temper he has, yet you will keep going out of your way to infuriate him.' Much as she understood Nelly's unselfish motive and her first instinct was to thank her, Emma thought that better purpose would be served by showing her disapproval: 'I'm quite capable of looking after myself, you know.'

'Yer bleedin' well ain't!' came the indignant retort. 'I saw him . . . with his filthy paws all over yer. What! The bugger's lucky I didn't clap him on the back o' the neck wi' a shovel!' Her angry brown eyes twinkled at the thought. 'Randy bleeder,' she went on, at the same time retrieving her wooden bucket and leading the way to the inner recesses of the big barn, where she proceeded to gather up the numerous eggs which had been laid here and there. When Emma pointed out that Foster Thomas was *her* problem and said, 'He's sure to cause trouble for you, when he finds you sent him on a wild goose chase,' Nelly was quick to assure the concerned Emma. 'Old Mr Thomas'll cover up fer me. He's done it afore.'

Exasperated, Emma shook her head, rolled her

lovely grey eyes heavenward and laughed out loud. 'What *will* I do with you, Nelly?' she chuckled. Whereupon, Nelly laughed heartily, 'Send me back ter England.' She added with some gusto, 'The sun don't cook yer brains there, and there's more bleeding pockets ter pick.'

Quickly now their laughter subsided, when a shadow came between them and, looking up, they saw the large, ungainly figure of Mr Thomas. His face was unusually stern and, as he stood unmoving with his two large hands spread one over each hip, Emma saw the frustration in his dark, round eyes which were usually kind and smiling.

For a long, awkward moment, no one spoke. Feeling uncomfortable beneath his accusing glare, Nelly cast her eyes downward. Emma however met his gaze with an equally forthright one, until, seeing that there was no immediate explanation forthcoming and that, as always, he was hopelessly outnumbered two to one, Roland Thomas took his hands from his hips, plunged them deep into his pockets and allowed the whisper of a smile to creep over his craggy, kindly features.

'What a pair of baggages you are,' he said good-humouredly. Then, to Nelly, who had raised her merry brown eyes to smile at him, 'You've got that bloody son of mine running round in circles . . . me as well!' Of a sudden the smile slipped from his face and his voice held a warning: 'You're playing with fire, though. Be careful, Nelly, because though I say it as shouldn't . . . that son of mine is a bad lot!' His eyes were now on Emma, as though willing her to convince Nelly that she was putting herself in danger, 'Be warned. Don't antagonise him.'

'But he were pestering Emma again!' protested Nelly, afterwards falling quiet when Roland Thomas stepped forward, his concerned eyes never leaving Emma's face.

'Don't worry about me, Mr Thomas,' Emma promptly assured him, 'I can look after myself.'

'Look here, Emma'—his voice was quiet now, and on his face a look of anxiety as he told her—'I'm no fool and I'm not blind.' His gaze lingered on her face for a moment. 'Stay out of his way as best you can. Keep a good distance between you.' Having said that, he turned away to leave them to their duties.

It was a moment before both Emma and Nelly recovered from the seriousness of the warning they had just been given. The first to speak was Nelly who said, in little more than a whisper, 'Well, I'm buggered! I ain't never seen old Mr Thomas so harsh.'

Neither had Emma, and her every instinct had been aroused. Was there something going on that neither she nor Nelly was aware of? An idea wormed itself into her troubled mind, and swiftly, Emma thrust it out. No. Surely to God, it couldn't be that Mr Thomas was about to turn over the business to his son! No, he would *never* do that . . . would he? Oh, it was true that Violet Thomas's health had gone steadily downhill these past months, and it had been a source of much anxiety to her husband. But knowing his great passion for the trading business he had nurtured all these years, Emma couldn't believe that Mr Thomas was about to let go of the reins. And certainly not to his son Foster . . . who had never shown an ounce of interest in the business; except, of course, in the

8

money it provided him with, to waste on grog and gambling. Yet there was something . . . definitely something: she was sure of it.

'I'd best get these eggs inside . . . afore the buggers are cooked!' Nelly remarked, at the same time slapping Emma heartily on the back as she passed. 'Roll on three o'clock, Emma . . . and we can put our feet up, eh?' Then, turning just once before she went from the shadows of the barn into the baking heat outside, she added, 'The buggers don't worry me, dearie, and they shouldn't worry you.' Emma smiled to herself. She admired Nelly for her fearlessness, yet she also saw it as being foolhardy. When the two of them had been exiled from their homeland, Nelly's sentence had been less severe than her own. Now, seven years on, their roles were reversed and, while Emma had earned her ticket-of-leave through good conduct, Nelly's rebellious attitude had put back the day of her freedom even further. Yet even though she was her own worst enemy, Nelly was a warm, loyal and steadfast friend, whom Emma loved like a sister. And, though the Governor had told Emma that her ticket-of-leave gave her at least the freedom to choose her own employer and place of work, Emma remained alongside Nelly in the Thomas trading post. While her friend was forced to stay, then so would she. Emma shook her head and chuckled softly, 'The way she's going on though . . . we'll both be old and grey before we get the chance to make our way in the world.' Afterwards she sighed, and turning her attention to the task in hand, at the same time subconsciously noted that the stock of small oil lamps would need replenishing.

Emma loved her work here, and she took a great pride in all of her duties. Mr Thomas himself had remarked on more than one occasion, 'You're a born trader, Emma . . . you've got a real knack for it.' Emma was grateful that she had been assigned to the trading post, for she did feel so much at home, serving the customers, making up the orders and keeping the books for Mr Thomas. It wasn't so very different from being a clerk at her father's cotton mill in Lancashire. Sometimes, when the sun had beaten down mercilessly all day and the stream of customers continued from early morning to closing, when Emma's feet ached and her back felt as stiff and uncomfortable as the ladder she might have to run up and down a dozen times a day, Emma was glad to crawl back to the small room she and Nelly shared, at the back of the stables. It was a hard life, with each day as demanding as the one before. But Emma poured herself heart and soul into her work. Mr Thomas was a good employer and lately, he had been shifting a good deal of the more confidential duties on to Emma's shoulders, so that, besides keeping the stock-book up to date, she was often responsible for the accounts ledger, and even for cashing up and securing the takings.

One particular evening, Emma had overheard a raging row between Mr Thomas and his son Foster who, she knew, bitterly resented his father's increasing dependency on her. Afterwards, she had respectfully pointed out to Mr Thomas, 'I don't want to be the cause of bad blood between you and your son.' His immediate reply was to inform her of two things. Firstly, that he was obliged to spend as much time as possible with Mrs Thomas, who 'is a delicate and refined creature who unfortunately does not enjoy good health', and secondly, 'if she had been able to bear me another son . . . or even a daughter of *your* calibre, I might be fortunate enough to lean on them. As it is, Emma . . . I have a worthless son who thinks it more natural to take rather than to give.' Here, the weariness melted from his craggy features, and in its place was a great tenderness. 'Then, I have you, Emma. And though the hand of fate was so cruel as to condemn you to this land a convict . . . I can only bless my *own* fate, for having deigned that you should be assigned to me.' On this last word, he had turned away before Emma could see how deeply he had been affected by the vehement row with his son, and the added burden that Emma might decide to seek employment elsewhere, which, having earned her ticket-of-leave, she had every right to do. Some time later, her heart filled with compassion at this good man's dilemma, Emma made it her business to explain to him that she would not desert him. He spoke not a word, but touched her gently on the shoulder and when he turned away, it was with a brighter, more contented light in his dark eyes.

Thinking about it all, Emma later reflected on her assurance to him, which amounted to a promise. She thought also about her determination not to desert Nelly. As she dwelt on it more deeply, it became apparent that she was enveloped in a prison other than the one to which Her Majesty's Government had despatched her. It was a prison within a prison, made by her own hand, and one which by its very nature would thwart her plans towards absolute freedom and her eventual return to England. This above all else burned fiercely in

Emma's heart. She knew with every breath in her body that her day *would* come. That wonderful exhilarating moment when she would embark on the ship which was destined to carry her over the oceans to the other side of the world. To England! To the 'friends' who had cheated and betrayed her. And, with God's help, to Marlow Tanner . . . the man whose child she had borne and tragically lost. The man she had loved then, and whom she had loved every waking moment since. Oh yes, that day would surely come. Until then, she must count the hours and be frugal with every penny she earned. Above all, she must thank God for the love and devotion of a dear, dear friend, and count herself fortunate to have the confidence, loyalty and trust of another. She wouldn't let them down. Not even in the face of a no-good like Foster Thomas.

Some two hours later, Emma had completed the laborious task of taking account of all stock, both in the general store and in the huge outer barn, which doubled as a warehouse. Afterwards, when coming back into the small office at the rear of the store, she put the heavy ledger on to the bureau and commented to Mr Thomas, 'That consignment of goods from England is overdue. Another twenty-four hours and we'll likely be sold out of candles, boots and general harness. And another thing, Mr Thomas . . .' Emma quickly finished her final entries into the 'Urgent' page of the ledger, before emerging through the office doorway and into the store. There she assured herself that Mr Thomas was attentive to what she was about to say. Then, taking off her dusty pinnie, she replaced it with a freshly laundered one from beneath the counter and continued, 'I do wish you

12

would think about what I said some time back . . .
about taking up a lease on one of the more
substantial warehouses on Cliff Street. That old
barn isn't secure, as well you know it, Mr Thomas,
and there's a lot of money tied up in the goods
stored there.'

'Oh, Emma!' Mr Thomas raised his finger and
thumb to tickle his mutton-chop whiskers absent-
mindedly; it was a peculiar habit of his whenever
he seemed slightly amused. 'Do you think we're
about to be robbed?' He chuckled aloud and,
bending his back, he grasped the corners of a box
of carbolic soaps with his two hands. He swung the
box upwards, before bringing it down in a flurry of
dust, on to a shelf he had just cleared. 'Or mebbe
you've got a notion that some rascal creeping
about at night has the intention of putting a match
to it, eh?' He chuckled again. 'You're a little
scaremonger, that's what you are,' he declared with
a broad and confident smile.

Emma was not amused. Nor would she be
dissuaded from pointing out the errors of
continuing to store valuable goods and equipment
in such an insecure and vulnerable place. 'There
are "rascals" enough who might well put a match to
anything, if it suited their purpose!' she reminded
him. 'You know as well as I do that there are
certain unsavoury characters in Fremantle who
wouldn't think twice about razing that barn to the
ground, after helping themselves to a good deal
first.' When Emma saw that, at last, she had his
serious attention, she went on quietly, 'Oh, Mr
Thomas . . . I'm not saying as they would, but
you've seen the strangers about of late . . . diggers
and bushmen . . . some new to the area, and some

13

looking even rougher than the worst convicts sent to break stones on the road. Wouldn't it make sense to house your more valuable goods at least, in a small secure lock-up on Cliff Street?'

Pausing a moment longer in his work of setting out the blocks of soap in a fetching grey display, Mr Thomas played one lip over the other, biting first at the top, then at the bottom, while he quietly pondered Emma's suggestion. Wasn't she right after all, when the goods were hard come by, and cost a fortune to ship out from England? Then, once out on the high seas they were at the mercy of every wild storm and natural disaster that a ship might encounter on its long voyage. She was right! Emma was right. Some of the stuff . . . shovels, pickaxes, and good working tools were going out as fast as he could get them in. There had been guarded murmurs about little pockets of gold being found here and there, and that was no doubt the explanation. All the same, merchandise was an increasingly valuable commodity hereabouts, and a person could never be too careful.

'You do see why I'm so concerned?' asked Emma, her shrewd business instinct telling her exactly the thoughts going through her employer's mind. 'I can arrange it . . . if you'll trust me to do the job right,' she offered, knowing only too well that his mind was lately taken up with his wife's unfortunate illness. Emma felt sorry for Mrs Thomas, who had never gone out of her way to make friends, was a very private person and, unlike Mr Thomas, kept both Emma and Nelly at a distance. The only person who enjoyed her confidence, other than Mr Thomas himself, was the blacksmith's spinster daughter, Rita Hughes.

14

Rita pampered her every whim and saw to her every need, for the small weekly payment of a few shillings. Emma suspected that Nelly was right in her observation that 'Rita Hughes has one eye on Mrs Thomas . . . and the other firmly fixed on *Foster* Thomas'! Adding, to Emma's disapproval, 'Though if yer ask me, she's well past it and gone sour.' When Emma protested that that was a cruel thing to say, Nelly was quick to point out, 'Huh! T'would be even *more* cruel if he took a fancy to her! What . . . a fella the likes o' Foster Thomas would mek her life a bleedin' misery.' Emma had to agree.

Emma was convinced that poor Mrs Thomas had withdrawn into herself on account of her husband and son forever being at loggerheads. At one time she had doted on her only son. Now he showed little interest in his mother, and she showed none in him. All the same, Emma suspected that her heart was quietly breaking.

'I tell you what'—Mr Thomas's voice cut into Emma's thoughts—'leave it with me, Emma. I'll bear in mind what you've said.' Beyond that he would not be drawn. Except to promise that the shop takings would not in future be kept upstairs in his room for up to a week at a time, as had become the habit of late. Emma did not agree with his belief that such large sums of money must always be to hand. 'The captains of the pearl-luggers want always to be in and out in a hurry, and, if I'm to keep up with the competition to buy the best pearl-shell in, then I need to have cash to hand at any given minute.' It worried Emma. But this was his trading post, not hers, and she mustn't forget her place.

Neither Emma nor Mr Thomas could have known how tragically Emma's fears were about to be realised, before the hands of the clock had turned full circle!

*   *   *

'Sat'day's my favourite day!' exclaimed Nelly, leaning over the ceramic rose-patterned bowl which was rested atop a cane-bottomed chair. 'Once we've reported to the authorities we'll have the rest o' the day . . . and all tomorrer afore we're back in the shafts.' She gave a loud 'Whoopee!', punched her fist in the air for the sheer joy of it and, scooping her two hands deep into the bowl, she splashed the water on to her face, neck and ears. 'I fancy a fella!' she chuckled through a mouth full of water while peeping at Emma out of one cheeky brown eye.

'Away with you!' laughed Emma, who was patiently waiting for her turn with the bowl. 'If you intend walking along the jetty with me, you'd best curb your urges for a "fella". The way you're going on, my girl, you'll be marched to the top of the hill, where you'll be clapped in irons and thrown in a prison cell, so every poor "fella" will be safe from your clutches.' When, mockingly holding her wrists together and limping as though shackled, Nelly started towards her, at the same time making an eerie wailing sound, Emma grabbed up a towel, held it out before her and, amidst much laughter, launched herself at Nelly. In a minute the two of them were rolling about the floor helpless with laughter. Then a kick from Emma's leg sent the cane-bottomed chair into such a violent swaying fit that the water in the bowl slopped first over one side, then the other. Convulsed by new fits of giggling, Nelly and Emma made to grab the chair, causing it to overbalance completely as the bowl shot forward to empty its entire contents, drenching them both. 'Bleedin' Nora!' shouted Nelly, scrambling to her feet and proceeding to shake herself like a dog. 'I'm bloody soaked!'

Subdued by the initial shock, Emma got to her knees and looked up at Nelly, all the while coughing and spluttering, her long chestnut hair hanging limp and bedraggled over her shoulders. When she saw Nelly's outrage and witnessed her frantically shaking her long skirt while at the same time swearing and cursing enough to frighten hardened criminals, Emma thought of her own ludicrous position and an old saying sprang to mind—'Oh dear God, the gift to gi' us, to see ourselves as others see us.' In a minute she had fallen back to the ground and was laughing out loud.

'Yer silly cow!' yelled Nelly, throwing the damp flannel at her. 'I only wanted a cat-lick . . . not a bleedin' *bath!*' Whereupon she too began roaring with laughter. It was quite some time before they had regained their composure sufficiently to clean up and refill the bowl with fresh water for Emma's wash. Unlike Nelly, Emma preferred to strip down to her camisoles for a thorough scrubbing and, having rolled about the floor, then been doused with dirty water, Emma took longer than usual at her daily ritual.

Some time later the two of them emerged from the stables. Having discarded her grey work-frock with its over-pinnie, Emma looked delightful in a plain blue dress with a small bustle on the skirt and crisp white frills about the cuffs and neck. Her thick chestnut hair was well brushed and drawn into a shining, most fetching coil at the nape of her neck. Her face was bright and lovely and her strong grey eyes brimmed with the steadfast confidence that set her apart from others.

Nelly, however, did not present such a striking picture. Oh, it was true that her thin brown hair had also been brushed with vigour. But, being under closer scrutiny of the prison authorities, and on more than one occasion having earned the punishment that dictated her locks be shorn, her hair did not enjoy the length that might cause it to lie smoothly against her head. Instead, it stood up and out in little wispy bunches which gave her the odd appearance of having just received a fright. Not being one for dainty things and 'feminine fripperies', Nelly was therefore proud of her heavy buttoned boots which came up to her calf. At one time, when Emma had pointed out that there was no need to wear such clumsy, uncomfortable things in the heat of the summer sun, Nelly had been adamant that she would wear nothing else. 'I'd wear an even *longer* pair if I could get me hands on 'em,' she retorted; 'I ain't having no bloody snakes nor spiders running up *my* legs!' However, she did gratefully accept a brown calico dress which had, until recently, been Emma's best one. It was of the very same style that Emma was wearing now, except the frills at the cuffs and neck were black instead of white. Also, Nelly was some inches taller than Emma, therefore the ankles of her boots were visible to the world, even though Emma had twice let the dress hem down for her. But, all in all, she was presentable and, as she put her arm through the crook of Nelly's elbow, Emma cared not who might look down on her friend. The prospect never worried Nelly either!

'Mind you're not on the streets after the curfew bell!' the duty officer warned, simultaneously noting down their intention to stroll along to Arthur's Head. As they hurried away, he took his eyes from the book and fixed his suspicious gaze at Nelly's retreating figure. 'I wouldn't mind betting a week's grog that *you'll* be in trouble before long, girlie . . . it's about that time,' he chuckled, shaking his head and leaning back in his chair to take a long choking draw from his clay pipe; he was soon engulfed in great billowing clouds of smoke.

Following the old tramway route, Nelly and Emma sauntered along at a leisurely pace . . . down Henderson Street, along Essex Street and down towards the bay. 'This is the time of day I love best,' said Emma, shielding her eyes with the back of her hand as she looked upwards to where the seagulls soared above them. In spite of the fact that she was imprisoned in this vast, sparsely-inhabited island of Australia, Emma could not help but be deeply drawn towards its primitive beauty. There was an awesome savagery about it that struck at the heart and inspired the mind. It was a land of turquoise seas and vivid blue skies which merged together on the horizon, creating a sense of greatness and eternity. No mere human eye could ever hope fully to comprehend the vastness of it all, for in every direction the sky stretched, never ending and seeming to engulf those insignificant specks below, who both feared and marvelled at its majesty. Immediately inland from

19

Fremantle to Perth, the landscape was sandy and gently undulating, relieved here and there by weird and wonderful trees, patches of shrub and rapidly growing signs of denser civilisation, with a number of the original timber and bark-roofed buildings being constantly replaced by the more permanent brick and stone buildings. There were also a number of splendid examples of architecture, such as the round-house and other buildings constructed by the convicts. The lunatic asylum, the road-traffic bridge and their own prison were such landmarks.

There were creatures here such as Emma had never seen before—kangaroos, brilliantly coloured birds, and even camels brought in from the desert countries. Most were friendly, but there were those which were not, such as certain snakes and spiders. Also a number of the dark-skinned natives whose resentment of the white man's intrusion on their shores was not entirely appeased. And everywhere the nostrils were assailed by the fresh pungent smell of the sea, so marked as to be almost a taste on the tongue.

Intent on appearing friendly towards a group of aborigines, two of whom were dressed in their traditional kangaroo-skin boukas—the other, a young male, wearing European trousers—Emma was startled by Nelly's jubilant cry as her attention was drawn in another direction. 'Look at that . . . the buggers are naked!' Whereupon she gripped Emma by the arm and propelled her in the direction of Bathers Bay. 'They're *naked*, I tell yer . . . bare as the day they were born. We've got to get a closer look, gal!' she told Emma in an excited voice, her brown eyes laughing, mischievously. 'It's been a while since I saw a fella in all his prime an' glory!'

Sure enough, Nelly was right. As Emma stared in the direction in which Nelly was rushing her at great speed, she too saw the group of swimmers in Bathers Bay. There must have been upwards of ten men, all shouting and frolicking one with the other, and all stark naked!

'Nelly!' Emma forced them both to a halt. 'We can't go down there. *You* can't go down there.' She saw the defiance in Nelly's eyes that told her the temptation was much too great to resist, and to hell with the consequences. Yet Emma was equally adamant that they would about-turn and make off in the opposite direction. 'Don't be a fool, Nelly,' she told her. 'You were warned that if you were brought before the Governor just *once* more, you'd be thrown in the lockup.' By this time the men had seen them, and had grown even more excited and rowdy. 'Come on, girlies . . . take a look, we don't mind,' one of them yelled, clambering from the water and brazenly displaying himself. Whereupon the others laughed encouragement that they 'needn't be shy.'

In a minute, Emma had succeeded in dragging the reluctant Nelly away and out of sight of the bathers. 'Cor, bugger me, gal,' protested Nelly, 'it wouldn't have hurt to watch from a safe distance.' Emma made no comment. Instead, she hurried towards South Bay. Once there, she sat down in the sand, with Nelly sitting cross-legged beside her, irritatedly clutching up fists full of sand and throwing it into the air, where the light breeze caught it and deposited it back into their laps.

After a while, when Nelly's attention was taken

with the lapping of the water against the sand, Emma lay back, settled herself comfortably and closed her eyes. Of a sudden she was back in England, and her heart was gladdened by warm, if painful, memories. The image of Marlow filled her being and she was standing beside him on the colourful barge which had been his home. Oh, how plainly she could see him: that strong lithe body so often stretched to breaking point in his labours at the docks. In her mind's eye, Emma ran her fingers through his thick dark hair. She lovingly returned the smile from those black passionate eyes which had always seemed to see right into her very soul. Now his arms were about her. His warm tantalising mouth brushed her hair, her ears and, in one exquisite moment, he was kissing her with such ardour that made her tremble. With a shock, Emma sat up to find that, even in the heat of the evening sun, she was shivering violently. Both Nelly and she had been disturbed by an intruder.

When that intruder stepped forward, it was with a feeling of disgust that Emma recognised the tall handsome figure of Foster Thomas. He was not alone. Quickly, Emma got to her feet. 'What do you want?' she demanded, at the same time shaking the sand from her skirt and casting her angry grey eyes over his two rough-looking companions. One was tall, painfully thin and had an old jagged scar from eye to ear; the other was of medium height, stocky with a dark surly expression. Both had thick bushy beards, both wore flat wide-brimmed hats and chequered shirts, with dark serviceable trousers. 'Swag men,' thought Emma, as she met their arrogant stares unflinchingly.

Foster Thomas twisted his mouth into a crooked smile. 'Me and the blokes . . . we reckoned you and Nelly might be glad of a little company,' he said with a low laugh, at the same time reaching out to rest his hand on her shoulder. As he leaned forward with the intention of encircling Emma's tiny waist with his arm, the smell of stale booze on his breath was nauseating. His deep blue eyes were little more than slits as they bored down on her, betraying his lecherous intentions and instantly putting Emma on her guard. 'You're drunk!' She spat the words out vehemently, at the same time twisting away from him with such speed and agility that she caused him to lose his balance. When the two bushmen thought it so amusing that they began sniggering and pointing to Foster Thomas as he struggled to remain upright, the smile slipped from his face and was replaced with a particularly determined and vicious expression. 'You little bastard!' he snarled, lurching forward to grasp at Emma's swiftly departing figure.

In her indignation and urgency to get away, Emma lost sight of Nelly. Pausing to look back, she was horrified to see that her hapless friend had made no move to follow her, but instead was shamelessly taking delight in having all three men dance attendance on her. Foster Thomas, in particular, was handling Nelly with a deal of intimacy, which was greatly intensified when he saw that Emma was hurriedly making her way back towards them.

'What in God's name are you thinking of?' Emma demanded of Nelly, whom she thought seemed to be as intoxicated as the men when she began blushing and giggling at Foster Thomas's over-amorous advances.

'*This* girlie knows how to be grateful for a man's attentions,' he sniggered, holding Nelly closer and winking knowingly at the other men, who appeared to be thoroughly enjoying themselves.

'That's right,' rejoined the stocky fellow, sidling up to Emma and running his tongue round his dry lips. 'Like a dog going for a chop,' thought Emma as he stood, legs astride in front of her. 'Now then me beauty . . . how about you showing me what *you're* made of, eh?' In a minute he would have had her fast in his grip, but in that same instant Emma had swung her arm out sideways and, before he realised her intention, had brought her fist across his ear with a resounding thud. As he staggered back, his hand clapped to his throbbing ear and a string of foul language issuing from his mouth, the second man ran forward to lock his two arms about Emma and swing her bodily into the air. 'She's got spirit, has this one!' he laughed. 'She'll do fer me!' No sooner were the words out of his mouth than Foster Thomas had landed his fist in it. 'Take your filthy bloody paws off her!' he yelled, as the fellow released Emma and, confronting his assailant with a furious expression, he invited in a low growl, 'So! *That's* the way, is it? . . . C'mon then, me bucko . . . let's have it out!'

In a minute the two of them were locked in combat, the one pounding his bunched fist time and time again into the other's stomach, and the other with his fingertips digging into his opponent's fleshy eyeballs with every intention of gouging out his very eyes. The third fellow, having miraculously recovered, was hopping up and down, screaming encouragement, first to one, then the

24

other. Nelly did the same.

Never one to miss an opportunity, Emma lost no time in grabbing hold of Nelly who, by the degree of resistance she put up, would much have preferred to stay and watch the fight than run away with what she considered to be the cause of it. 'Ye slapped him good, Emma!' she cried, jubilantly lashing the air with her fists. 'Fetched him a right bleedin' clap aside o' the ear, y'did.' She was beside herself with excitement, and though Emma made every effort to remain above it all, she could only sustain her indignation as far as the old cemetery, when she paused, breathless, against some unfortunate soul's headstone. 'Oh, Nelly, Nelly!' she said, the smile already creeping into her eyes and lifting the corners of her mouth. 'I'm supposed to be the sensible one, who keeps you on the straight and narrow.' The smile broke into a small laugh.

'And you *do*,' Nelly assured her, pausing to catch her breath from the fast and furious pace with which Emma had propelled her from the fracas on the beach. It's just a bloody shame that being kept on the "straight and narrer" don't allow fer a bit o' fun! Just now and then . . . I might like ter throw caution ter the wind and join forces wi' the devil.' When Emma rightfully reminded her that in encouraging a grog-sodden lout like Foster Thomas she was doing just that, Nelly retorted, 'Handsome devil, though, eh?' And in her twinkling brown eyes was a deep thinking expression which Emma had not seen before.

Nelly's remark both astonished and disturbed Emma very deeply. But she made no comment, other than to say it must be coming up to curfew time and they should be on their way.

No sooner had Emma made the observation than the curfew bell rang out, warning all bonded persons that they must be off the street. Emma hoped she and Nelly would not be challenged by an officer because, while she herself was able to show her ticket-of-leave, Nelly was already under suspicion, and being caught out even one minute after curfew could well cost her dear. As the two of them hurried towards Thomas's store, Emma led the way round the back streets, fearful that at any minute an officer would come upon them. Every now and then there would ring out the challenge, 'Bond or free?' as others, less artful, were stopped in the busier streets adjacent. Only when Emma had manoeuvred Nelly on to the porch of the store did she breathe a sigh of relief.

'You really do play fast and loose with the law, don't you?' came the thin, tired voice from a wicker chair in the far corner where the trellis was much higher. Mrs Thomas was very rarely persuaded to come and sit out of an evening, but, when she did, it was on three conditions: it had to be past curfew 'when the criminals amongst us are safely out of the way'; it had to be almost twilight so she could sit in the shadows; and, her high-backed wicker chair had to be positioned securely in that particular corner where the trellis was highest, so the shadows would be that much deeper. Now, when her voice piped out on the sultry evening air, Emma gave a start . . . her heart still beating fast from the fear that she and Nelly would be stopped after curfew.

'Oh, Mrs Thomas!' she gasped, putting her hand to her heart. 'You gave me a fright.'

'And you gave *me* a right turn an' all!' joined in Nelly, whose face had gone an odd shade of parchment.

'Well now, I am sorry,' laughed Mrs Thomas, and Emma likened the sound of her laughter to the soft tinkling of the water in the Leeds and Liverpool Canal back home; that gentle, delightful sound that was made with the smooth passage of a laden barge as it gently churned up the water beneath. But then, everything was 'gentle' about poor Mrs Thomas. She was a tiny pathetic creature now, sitting in that high-backed chair like a duchess of old, or a china doll who was much too frail and exquisite to play with. Emma thought that Violet Thomas must have been a very beautiful lady when she was young, for she had finely sculptured bones and long delicate fingers. Her hair, though snow-white now, was still rich and thick with deep attractive natural curls, which even the scraped-back and severe hairstyle could not disguise. Her eyes were large and soft, as blue in colour as the sky, but they were filled with sorrow, always heavy with pain, and something akin to tragedy perhaps, a kind of deep inner suffering almost as though, even when the finely etched wrinkles on the face were lifted in a smile, the eyes remained haunted.

'Are you all right out here on your own?' questioned Emma, not liking the idea of leaving her seated here alone. 'Where's Mr Thomas?' she added with concern, at the same time coming closer to assure herself that the thin little figure was encased in a blanket, for there wasn't enough fat on Mrs Thomas's bones to keep her warm . . . sunshine or not. She needn't have worried though because, as always, Mr Thomas or Rita Hughes had taken good care of the lady's needs. There was a rug carefully draped about her legs, and a soft shawl wrapped about her small shoulders.

'Please . . . go to your beds.' The long, fine fingers waved into the air in a gesture of dismissal. 'Mr Thomas will be here presently, and I would rather you didn't fuss.' Her voice was sharper now, and the words came in short, tired little bursts. Emma sensed that, as always appeared to be the way, she and Nelly were not wanted by Mrs Thomas. That invisible barrier, which she so cleverly created, had been drawn up between them. They were being sent on their way and, not for the first time, Emma suspected that it was because they were convicts. Although Violet Thomas had never made or intimated the slightest complaint of such a nature regarding the two assignees who worked about the house and shop and who resided in the room behind the stables, her strong condemnation of 'the criminal element thrust among us' was well known. Emma therefore went out of her way not to antagonise her employer's wife, and she implored Nelly to do the same.

Emma would have liked to have been on closer terms with Mrs Thomas, because she knew her to be a lady, and she also felt something of the other woman's deep desire to go home to England 'to live out my days under a cloudy sky and to sup afternoon tea in a more genteel atmosphere'. Many times she had been heard pleading her cause to her husband and, as many times, Mr Thomas had been heard to promise, 'Soon, Violet, soon . . . When we've made our fortunes, for I'm sure you

28

don't wish to starve under a cloudy sky, do you now, eh?' His wife never gave an answer, nor did she make any response within his hearing. Instead, they seemed to converse less, to drift further apart, and to execute a strange verbal dance whereby each might broach a subject close to their hearts; he of his store and business, she of England and her desire to return. Then the other would nod, smile and make meaningless noises, after which a great painful silence would envelop them, as they each retreated into their own precious dreams. Emma thought it sad that they could not find it in their hearts to share the same dream. However, she sympathised with Mrs Thomas's obsession to return to England, because Emma herself had been possessed of that same obsession ever since being so cruelly and unjustly taken from her old homeland. Yet she had never once allowed this obsession to become so deeply rooted that it ravaged her entirely, as was the case with Mrs Thomas. Emma had deliberately thrown herself into her work, always striving towards that ultimate freedom which she knew must one day be hers. In so occupying her mind and thoughts, she had deliberately suppressed her heart's desire, always aware that it was futile to dwell on it too deeply in the early years. Now though, with seven years of her sentence behind her, the realisation of once more being in charge of her own destiny was in sight.

Day and night, Emma's thoughts had begun to dwell on her freedom. Her heart would tremble at the prospect and her spirit was charged with such great anticipation and excitement that there were times when she could hardly contain herself. At these times, and often in the dark small hours when she was unable to sleep, she would get up from her bed to pace back and forth across the room like a caged creature. After a while, when the desperate emotions retreated and other, more tender, emotions flooded her heart, she would go to the window and gaze out across the moonlit sky. Then tears would flow unheeded down her face. Thoughts of home would storm her senses, pulling her first this way, then that, until she could hardly bear it. 'Oh, dear God,' she would murmur, 'will it ever come right for me again?' She longed for Marlow's arms about her, but even if in three years' time by some fortune or miracle there was the money and freedom to return to England, how would she find him? And, if she *did* find him, would he still love her? After all, she had deliberately spurned him in favour of another man even though, unbeknown to Marlow, it was for his own protection. Then there was the fact that she was a convict, charged and marked with a terrible crime. Oh, and what of the child she had borne him, and which was lost to them both? How could any man forgive her? The torture never ended for Emma. But she prayed that it would one day, otherwise there was no reason to go on.

'Emma!' The voice cut sharply across Emma's turbulent thoughts. 'Mrs Thomas has a mind to sit out a while longer. You and Nelly get off to bed.' Mr Thomas had returned from inside and he was quickly aware that his wife was becoming agitated by the presence of the two young women. 'Off you go,' he urged as Emma bade his wife a good night. 'Go on . . . go on. I'll see to her when she's ready to go back upstairs.'

'Miserable old bugger, that Mrs Thomas,' remarked Nelly, pulling off her clothes and getting quickly into her own narrow wooden bed. 'Anybody'd think we'd got the bleedin' plague . . . the way she starts panicking every time we get within arm's length of her!' She was greatly peeved and Emma's reply that 'we must make allowances for her' made no difference to Nelly's mood. 'Well, I ain't mekkin' no allowances for the old sod,' she retorted, blowing out the candle which was on the cupboard by her bed. 'It were *her* sort as pushed me into crime when I were a kid. Look down on yer, they do. Won't give yer no work, in case yer cut their throats at the first opportunity!' Then her mood quickly changed, she told Emma to 'sleep tight . . . mind the bed-bugs don't bite', and was soon fast asleep, the gentle rhythm of her soft snoring seeming a comfortable and homely sound to Emma as she lay in her own bed.

There was no sleep in Emma just yet, only a strange sense of quiet. Sometimes, she wished she could be more like Nelly, because nothing worried her for very long. She had no driving ambitions, no real grudges to bear, and no one person in her heart who could tear it apart. Here Emma checked herself. How did she know whether Nelly secretly loved anybody in particular? What about the way she enjoyed Foster Thomas's attentions today, and what of the remark she made about him being 'a handsome devil'? The very possibility that Nelly might be quietly attracted to that man filled Emma with dread. Indeed, it was too horrible to contemplate, for Emma truly believed that such a man as Foster Thomas would take the greatest delight in destroying someone as devoted and vulnerable as Nelly. Emma prayed that, if Nelly really did feel a certain attraction towards him, she would never let it be known to him, or he would likely take her to the depths and *leave* her there.

With this disturbing thought in mind and with the intention of warning Nelly the very next morning, Emma leaned over in her bed to blow out her candle. She closed her eyes and forced her mind to more pleasant dreams. Of a sudden Emma realised how tiredness had crept up on her. She was ready for sleep.

*   *   *

'Emma, wake up . . . *please* wake up!'

'What is it, Nelly?' Emma was not yet fully awake, but pushing back the coarse grey blanket from her face, she lifted her head and screwed up her heavy eyes to look on Nelly's frightened face. 'Have you had a nightmare?' she asked, not being sufficiently awake to be certain it wasn't she who was suffering the nightmare.

'No, no!' Nelly continued to poke and shake Emma until at last Emma was sitting up against the pillow, her eyes almost blinded by the light from Nelly's candle, which was presently thrust only an inch or so from her face. 'There's some'at going on over the store . . . noises there were!' She was obviously in a fearful state.

'Noises?' Quickly now, Emma got up from her bed and began dressing. 'What *sort* of noises?' she asked, suddenly wide awake.

'Funny noises . . . like scraping and thumping . . . and'—here Nelly hesitated, looking at Emma through the candlelight with big frightened eyes—

32

'I could'a sworn I heard somebody scream.'

Emma paused as she pulled on her boots, and glancing up towards Nelly, she said in a serious voice, 'You stay here. I'll take a look.'

'You bloody *won't*, y'know!' came Nelly's indignant retort. 'Not without me, you won't. I ain't staying here on me own!'

'All right then. But put out the candle. There's no sense in broadcasting what we're up to, is there? Besides . . . if you've been imagining these "noises" and such, and we're caught creeping about in the dark, we'll look a right pair of idiots and no mistake.' A quick glance told her that Nelly was barefooted and wore only her dress over her nightgown.

'I ain't imagining it, Emma. I heard strange voices . . . I just know there's some'at funny going on!'

'All right, Nelly. We'll take a look, if it'll put your mind at rest. But mind you keep quiet. Promise? Or I will leave you here!' Emma was under no illusions that, given just cause, Nelly could make herself heard from one end of Australia to the other. On securing Nelly's firm assurance that she would creep behind 'as quiet as a church-mouse', Emma patted her gratefully on the shoulder. 'Good girl,' she told her, taking the brass candlestick from Nelly's trembling hand, and after blowing out the light, she placed it down on the bedside cupboard. They didn't need a light to show them the way, for they had trodden it often enough. In any case, there wasn't much in this room to fall over, there being only one cumbersome wooden wardrobe, a tall chest of drawers, two narrow wooden beds, each with a little side-cupboard, and a small oblong rag-peg rug between the beds. Emma had thought it a grim little room when she had first seen it, with its one tiny window overlooking the dirt yard between the stables and the store. The Thomases lived in the four large rooms above the store, and the windows of the big bedroom looked down over the stables. Many a time, Emma had noticed Mrs Thomas seated by her bedroom window, gazing out at the skyline with a look in her eyes that was almost desperate, and her heart bled for the poor creature. She had often thought that if *she* were in Mrs Thomas's position, nothing on earth would prevent her from going home! But then she was reminded of two things. Firstly, Mrs Thomas was in very poor health, and secondly, perhaps even more important, it was obvious that despite their deep differences on the matter of which country was now home, she loved her husband and would never contemplate leaving without him. It really was a sorry state of affairs, and one which seemed irreconcilable.

Opening the door with some caution, Emma peered into the darkness. Surely Nelly must be wrong? She could hear no 'noises' of the kind described. Indeed, everything appeared perfectly normal for the early hours. The two grey work horses were quiet in the stable and the only sign of life in the sultry heat beneath the moonlight was a lone furry creature who scurried by their feet. 'Jesus!' Nelly cried in a loud whisper. 'What the devil were that?' When Emma told her to be quiet while she listened, Nelly murmured, 'Sorry,' at once taking up a better grip on Emma's shawl and shuffling closer behind. 'P'raps I never heard

34

nothing after all,' she loudly whispered in Emma's ear, 'p'raps I were imagining things . . . like yer said, Emma.'

'Ssh!' Emma had come to a stop against the end of the stable wall, pausing for a moment before crossing the open yard. 'Look there, Nelly,' she murmured softly, at the same time raising her arm to point upwards towards the Thomases' bedroom, 'see that?'

'Cor, bugger me, gal!' gasped Nelly. 'The light's on! They *never* leave the light burning . . . on account o' Mrs Thomas can't sleep when there's a light burning. There! Y'see, Emma . . . I told yer there was some'at going on, didn't I, eh? I told yer!' She was silenced by Emma's hand being pressed hard over her mouth, after which the two of them crept stealthily towards the back of the store. There was a loose wall board some three feet off the ground, which Emma had often stressed should be made more secure, but which was never on the list of Mr Thomas's priorities. Emma was thankful for his neglect of it, as she now eased it aside then carefully clambered in, helping the reluctant Nelly in behind her. 'Bleedin' hell!' Nelly whispered, regaining her balance and straightening her skirt to her bare ankles. 'What the devil d'yer reckon we're getting usselves into, Emma gal? I don't mind a fight . . . not bad wi' me fists, I can tell yer. But I like to see the enemy coming a mile away.'

'Nelly, be quiet!' Emma was afraid that if there were intruders in the store, like as not Nelly's gabbling would put them on their guard, and the blighters would come at them in the dark like bats out of hell. 'Not another word,' she instructed, standing still as a statue and straining her ears for the slightest sound. There! There it was, muffled, yes . . . but unmistakably a man's voice, and raised in anger. Emma felt Nelly stiffen behind her and for a moment she was afraid of her calling out. But Nelly remained silent as Emma concentrated in an effort to distinguish the voice. She couldn't make out what was being said, but two things she was certain of: that voice did not belong either to old Mr Thomas *or* his son Foster, and, it was *not* a friendly voice! Strange, thought Emma, it couldn't be a business caller, not at this unearthly hour. Why, it must be two in the morning! The doctor then? Was it possible that Mrs Thomas had been taken badly and the doctor had been called out to her? Yes, that was possible. Yes! That was it, Emma was certain. But then she reminded herself, if it had been the doctor, then they would surely have heard his pony and trap, for old Dr Shaw liked the folks to know when he went about his business, especially when he was brought from his bed. No! They would have heard him slapping at the reins and driving like a fiend. Emma had come through the back store, round by the office, and was now almost at the foot of the stairs that led up to the Thomases' living quarters. If not either of the Thomas men, and not the doctor . . . who then? Her heart was beating against her ribs like a caged bird trying to get out. In the dark with Nelly pressed close behind and God only knew what was up in front, Emma felt suffocated. The heat was oppressive and the beads of sweat which stood out along her back began to break into tiny rivulets, which trickled irritatingly behind her shoulders. What should she do? Should she creep out again, and raise the alarm? No, she couldn't risk it, because the minute he knew he'd been tumbled, the intruder would either be away like sheet lightning, or, even worse, in his desperation, he might harm the Thomases. Emma couldn't risk such a thing.

Her mind was working frantically. Emma felt her way towards the rack which held the shotguns. She knew every inch of this store like the back of her hand, but she never thought such knowledge would prove so very useful. In a matter of minutes, she had the shotgun and ammunition in her grasp. In another minute, she had the gun loaded and ready. When Nelly indicated that she also wanted a gun, Emma thought better of it. 'No,' she whispered, 'one of us who can't shoot straight is more than enough. You stay down here.' When Nelly vigorously shook her head, Emma saw the futility of such a suggestion. 'All right . . . but stay close, and keep a sharp eye out. We've no idea who it is up there . . . it could be a friendly visitor, but somehow I don't think so.' By the fearful look on her face neither did Nelly.

As they inched their way up the stairs, Emma thought they would never reach the top, so long and painstaking was the journey. Only once did they pause, and that was when there came a small cry, followed by Mr Thomas's voice. Again, because the bedroom was situated at the far end of the landing and the door was obviously closed, it was not easy to distinguish what was being said. But it was plain to Emma that the cry they had heard was that of a woman, and Mr Thomas's voice had seemed to carry a tone of desperation. She was never more sure of anything, but that the

37

Thomases were under threat with, no doubt, their son lying in a drunken stupor somewhere. Emma also believed that there was no immediate help other than herself and Nelly. Clutching her small hands tightly about the shotgun, Emma went stealthily on, her heart in her throat, and a prayer on her lips that she wouldn't have to shoot anybody! The thought of such a possibility made her tremble and her throat was as dry as a dirt-track road.

With every step they took along the darkened landing, Emma was in dread that she or Nelly might bring their weight to bear on one of the loose creaky boards hereabouts. At last, they were at the door and, pressing her ear to it, Emma listened. The conversation coming through the chinks in the ill-fitting door was enough to confirm her suspicions. First came the stranger's voice, which Emma felt sure she had heard somewhere before, and it was threatening.

'My patience is fast running out, Thomas! You've had time enough, I reckon. There is money stashed away here . . . I'm sure of it! But you've hidden it well, I'll grant yer that.' Then there came the sound of a scuffle. 'I mean it, Thomas . . . I'll break her bloody neck!'

'Leave her be, you bastard!' Mr Thomas cried out brokenly. 'Leave her be. I'll show you where the takings are.'

Emma chose this moment to throw open wide the door and to confront the intruder. 'Let go of her!' she yelled, thrusting herself into the room and quickly taking stock of the situation. She was right. The tall thin fellow with the scar, who now quickly took his hands from round Mrs Thomas's throat, was the same bushman who had been with Foster Thomas down on the beach that day. As he raised his arms in the face of the shotgun, Emma was puzzled by the arrogant smile which seemed to turn the whole of his features downwards. It took only a split second to see that, though relatively unharmed, both Mr and Mrs Thomas were in a state of shock. Mrs Thomas was bound hand and foot in a chair to Emma's right, and Mr Thomas the same, but nearer to the window. The astonishment at Emma's sudden intrusion was evident on both their faces and, even as Emma opened her mouth to issue the instruction, 'Untie them, Nelly,' she saw the astonishment slip from Mr Thomas's face, and in its place came another, more desperate expression.

Emma saw his neck stiffen and his head reach forward. She saw his mouth open and, even as his first word of warning split the air, Emma understood. But it was too late! The very last thing Emma heard before it seemed like the world fell in on her, was Mr Thomas yelling, 'Watch out!' and Nelly's broken scream as she came running towards her. Then the gun was snatched from Emma's hands and a shot rang out. The last that Emma saw before her senses slipped from her was the tall bushman's evil smile as he lowered his arms, and the sight of Mrs Thomas's wide-open terrified eyes before they snapped shut, and her grey head fell sideways to loll against her shoulder like that of a rag doll.

As Emma was sucked deep into the black yawning chasm which engulfed her, her mind began to play tricks, and she saw another limp and lifeless body. It was the body of a young man who

39

had idolised her, but whose love she had not been able to return. It was the body of her husband on the day of his tragic death. The sight of it had made her cry out then. It made her cry out now. But it wasn't his name that fell from her lips as she slipped, unconscious, to the floor. It was another name: the name of Marlow, the man she had lost forever. The man she could never forget.

Chapter Two

'Tell me she ain't gonna die, Dr Shaw.' Nelly's brown eyes swam with bright tears as she leapt up to meet the grim-faced doctor. 'Please . . . I couldn't bear it if Emma were to die!' Of a sudden she had her face bent to her hands and was sobbing. 'She won't die, will she?' she kept saying over and over and even Mr Thomas, who had also been anxiously waiting for the doctor to return from Emma's bedside, had to lift his hand surreptitiously to his face, where he quickly wiped away a tear. When he raised his dark eyes to study the doctor's face, as though he might see the light of hope in it, his own suffering was plainly written in the folds of his aged features and in the weary stoop of his thickly set shoulders. It was there also in the anguish of his voice as he spoke to the doctor. 'What of Emma?' he asked, and he thought how cruel it would be if the Lord saw fit to take Emma's life. The whole town was still buzzing with the story of how Emma had bravely confronted the robbers in an effort to save her employers, in spite of the obvious danger to herself. Why even the

Governor had been so filled with admiration at her loyalty to the Thomases that he had passionately pursued an absolute pardon for her. Unfortunately the recommendation had been rejected on the grounds that, if Emma had not been carrying the shotgun, Mrs Thomas might still be alive.

In the four days following the incident, neither hide nor hair had been seen of Foster Thomas. His distraught father had sent out messengers far and wide, seeking to inform his son of the fatal, if accidental, shooting of Violet Thomas, and that she would be laid to rest in the churchyard on the morrow. So far, the whereabouts of Foster Thomas remained a mystery. With the passing of the days old Mr Thomas had suffered a whole range of emotions. First, there was the grief for his departed wife, and the cutting knowledge that her body would be put to rest in a land which she considered to be alien to her. He had knelt beside her in the tiny chapel, asking her forgiveness time and time again. He had paced the floorboards till all hours of the morning and there were times when he had a mind to put an end to it all and join her. Then he was swamped with guilt and the awful knowledge that, because of his reluctance to hand over the takings, his wife had been put through an ordeal which resulted in not only the loss of her life but perhaps Emma's as well. In the beginning he had felt a desperate need to have his only son by his side; he was anxious, for the sake of his wife's memory in particular, to heal the rift between himself and Foster. In spite of his every instinct, Roland Thomas was prepared to give his son fresh opportunities to prove himself for, of a sudden, he felt the weight of every one of his fifty-nine years. He had thought it was time to relinquish some of the burden on to the only other person who carried the family name. Was it not true that Foster was his own flesh and blood, after all? And wouldn't it have gladdened Violet's weary heart to see father and son working together? Oh, it would! Dear Lord, how he yearned to be able to put the clock back! He could have been more compassionate, more sympathetic to his wife's unhappiness. He might even have been more tolerant towards his son.

But when the days passed and there was no word from his son, Roland Thomas began to realise that he would be the only family to grieve at Violet Thomas's grave. They had a son, yes . . . but he neither knew his parents, nor cared for them. The need to be reconciled with such a son became less and less in Roland Thomas's grieving heart. Instead, he began to believe that he would not care if he never saw him again. Turning from those who were past all hope, he brought his attention to Emma. Dear, loyal, hard-working Emma, who gave everything and asked for little in return, and he prayed to the Lord that she should live, both for her own sake and for his sake, because a plan had begun to take root in Roland Thomas's mind. A plan to preserve all that he held dear. A plan which he intended putting to Emma as soon as she was fully recovered. And she *must* recover, she must, for everything depended on it.

Now, both he and Nelly anxiously awaited the doctor's verdict. When it came, there was a sigh of relief, for what Dr Shaw told them was this: 'She's mending . . . at long last Emma has turned the corner.' He went on to warn them of her poorly state all the same. 'She isn't fully recovered by a long chalk, and she'll sleep twenty out of twenty-four hours . . . sleep that she badly needs.' He stressed that, even though Emma's condition had shown significant improvement, 'The blow on her head very nearly fractured her skull. There'll be times when she appears lucid . . . and times when she'll be delirious. You, Nelly, must tend her as constantly and carefully as you have been doing. See that she takes the broth, and keep her comfortable.' With that, and the curt issuing of a few more instructions, he was gone.

'See to her, child,' Mr Thomas urged the anxious Nelly. He had accompanied Dr Shaw to the top of the stairs and now he had come into the bedroom where Emma lay; the very same bed from which he and his wife had been viciously dragged so few nights ago, but what now seemed the span of a lifetime. Nelly had already taken up position in the cane rocking-chair which was pulled up close to the bed. Her brown eyes, that normally were alive with mischief, were sore and red from the tears she had shed for Emma, her one and only real friend in the whole wide world. Many were the times these past years when Nelly had thanked God for Emma's stalwart love and friendship, and she never tired of telling Emma how, if she could choose a sister, it would be no one else but Emma. These last few days had been a nightmare, because every minute that passed, night and day, it seemed that Emma would breathe her last and be taken from them. The thought was so terrible to poor Nelly that she had gone without food or sleep, and she had found herself praying to the very same God who, for so long, she had cursed for her ill fortune. The strain of it all showed on Nelly's homely face, in her unkempt brown hair and in the way she rarely took her anxious gaze from Emma's pale, still features. It showed in the manner of her constant fidgeting, and it betrayed itself in the small bony fingers which were, even now, wrapped about Emma's seemingly lifeless hand as it lay frail and unmoving on the chequered quilt cover. 'Oh, Mr Thomas, sir,' she murmured now, raising her sorry eyes to look on his face, 'I know the doctor said she was mending but . . . well, she looks so ill and she ain't opened her eyes, not once.'

Nelly's brown eyes followed Roland Thomas as he strode further into the room. When he came to rest just an arm's reach from Emma, he stood with one hand across the back of Nelly's chair, his large coarse fingers tightly clasping the top. He gave no answer to Nelly, nor did he betray the slightest inclination of his thoughts as, for what seemed an age, he stared down on Emma's prostrate figure. His serious gaze roved over the finely structured lines of her lovely face and, every now and then, a small shuddering sigh formed deep within his chest, before softly escaping through partly opened lips. Then, with his head bowed and a dark, grim expression on his face such as Nelly had not seen before, he turned away. At the door he stopped, and in soft, halting tones, he told the watching Nelly, 'I'll never forget how Emma put her own life at risk to help me and mine. *Never!* Nor *your* part in it, child.' His heartfelt words caused Nelly to look away. Not for the first time, she was plagued with a sense of guilt. Should she tell him that, on the night his wife died and the culprits were making good their getaway, there were *three*

44

figures fleeing across the yard? She had kept quiet about it until now because, when she went to the window to shout for help, the moon had gone behind the clouds and there were dark moving shadows. But, in that fleeting moment before the three scoundrels scurried away, Nelly thought she recognised the third man. She wasn't sure and she would never swear to it. That was why she had kept it to herself when the officers questioned her. Besides which, how could she say in Mr Thomas's hearing, and with the body of his poor wife not yet cold, that the man she saw running away was to her mind Foster Thomas, his own son! It was a terrible thing, and one which Nelly wanted no part in. It had been a shock and she hoped with all her heart that she was wrong. Not least of all because, in spite of Emma's warning, or maybe because of it, she had fallen hopelessly in love with Mr Thomas's handsome, wayward son, and somehow, Nelly knew that Emma was right in all she said . . . Foster Thomas was a bad lot. He was capable of all manner of grief. But then hearts are unpredictable things, and love even more so.

*   *   *

At five o'clock, Rita Hughes helped Mr Thomas to close up the store, then, after preparing a tray for Nelly and some broth for Emma, she bade him good day and made her way down the road to the blacksmith's house. Hers was a figure which was easily recognised, being stiffly upright, reed-thin and always dressed in a long dark skirt and cloak, with a small-brimmed bonnet of black, tied beneath the chin with an unusually extravagant bow. Should even one wisp of black hair stray from beneath, it was quickly wedged back into place by small square fingers encased in fine white gloves. She was an odd, almost eccentric figure as she trod the well-worn path from Thomas's store to the blacksmith's house, occasionally deigning to smile woodenly at anyone she passed. More often than not, they would see her coming and find some reason to look the other way, for no one was quite sure how to treat the blacksmith's daughter who, those less Christian of folk claimed, was 'a little bit strange'. There was nothing to substantiate such an observation because Rita Hughes was of a responsible age . . . twenty-nine years. She was most polite to one and all, she was hard-working and helpful and she went to church regularly. She was adored by her parents, being an only child, and there was no more good or dutiful daughter than she. However, though her tight and plain features were easy to look upon, there was one physical characteristic in particular which might account for people's discomfort whenever she paid them close attention. Her eyes, while being of a most fetching hazel colour, were somewhat unnerving to the onlooker, because the right one had within its rich brown colouring a deep marbling of vivid blue, which appeared like a splash across it. This, in turn, created the impression that she was half-blind, which of course she was not.

But there was one who was glad to see Rita Hughes approaching. Quickly, as she swung her way into the front yard through the small gate, Foster Thomas briefly stepped from the shadows of the forge, before she might turn away towards the house without seeing him. When his movement caught her eye, the whole of her face was transformed by a smile which, although it could never be described as beautiful, was close to being pretty. 'Foster!' Seeing the anxious look on his face, she quickly glanced about to ensure that there was no one watching, then, in a hurry, she was inside the darkened forge and being pressed against the wall. 'What are you doing . . . hiding in here like a criminal?' she wanted to know.

'Never mind that, girlie,' he said gruffly. 'Tell me . . . is it right that my mother's been killed . . . shot? And that Emma might die?' He appeared frantic as he waited for her answer. His hair was dishevelled, his face unshaven and his dark jacket and trousers besmirched with dust, as if he had been living rough, or ridden horseback for some considerable distance. Or both.

Quickly, Rita Hughes explained all that had happened. She told how his father had sent people out to look for him and yes, his mother was to be buried the next day, and Emma was only just pulling back from the brink of death. But she was past the worst . . . the doctor had said so.

'Thank God,' he muttered. But then, on seeing her puzzled expression, he quickly added, 'Oh, but my mother! Who could do such a terrible thing? And what of my father . . . how is he taking it . . . badly, I expect?' When she confirmed that it was so, and that his own absence had made it all the more painful for his father, Foster Thomas's reaction was immediate and seemingly sincere. 'I must go to him. But first I'll need to clean up.' He explained how he had been on a business trip of sorts and he hadn't expected to be away so long.

Rita Hughes knew better. She suspected that he

had been on a drinking binge, and that he didn't want to evoke his father's anger by turning up in such a disgusting state. What he really wanted though was a good woman to bring him to heel and to show him the Christian way. She saw *herself* as that woman, and one day quite soon, she would convince him of it also.

'Stay here,' she told him. 'Give me a while and I'll bring what you need.' Then she smiled warmly at him, gently moving away a blond lock of hair that had fallen over his forehead. 'You can always rely on me, Foster.' For a moment it seemed as though he might kiss her. But then he pushed her from him. 'Be as quick as you can,' he said, trying not to show how unpleasant it was to be looked at in such a way by those odd and penetrating eyes.

*   *   *

It was half-past ten, some three hours and more since Nelly had heard the raised voices from the back store-room below, and she was relieved that Foster had returned. Even now, she refused to let herself dwell on, or believe, what played on her mind. It hadn't been Foster. He might visit the grog-shops with such men, but he would never be a party to robbing his own parents, she was sure of it. But no, she wasn't sure of it! Yet she would put it out of her mind, for nothing good would come of dwelling on such a thing.

'You go and stretch your legs, child. I'll sit with Emma awhile.' Mr Thomas had come into the room, and Nelly hadn't even heard him, she was that tired. But she declined his suggestion, for she had no intention of moving one step away from

Emma's bed until there was some sign of what the doctor had promised. 'No, Mr Thomas, sir,' she said, wedging her narrow frame deeper into the chair as though afraid he might pluck her from it, 'I ain't going nowhere . . . not till I know Emma's all right.'

As he turned away, a weary little smile appeared across Roland Thomas's features. 'All right . . . all right. Nobody's going to make you leave her if you don't want to,' he assured Nelly. 'Foster's taken my make-shift bed in the stores . . . there's no sleep in me at all this night. I've too much on my mind for sleep.' Here he paused and it was obvious that he was dwelling on the sorry fact that the following day his wife would be laid to rest. 'We've a hard day tomorrow, I'm thinking, child,' he murmured, adding as he left the room, 'should you need me, I'll be in the sitting-room next door.'

Nelly thanked him and nodded her appreciation, then she dropped her thoughtful gaze to the floor as he closed the door behind him. Neither Roland Thomas nor Nelly saw how Emma gently stirred, how her grey eyes flickered open for the briefest moment before closing again to seem as they were before. Yet behind Emma's quiet and still expression, a host of gyrating shadows was beginning to emerge and a confusion of hazy images which were too distant for her to recognise. For the moment all was dark and silent, save for the twisting spirals that moved this way, then that, gradually floating closer and closer until the shadows became people, and the people became faces . . . faces she thought she knew, plus those of strangers whose touch she feared. Now, they merged to become one, and again they split

49

asunder to become a multitude. She was afraid yet she was desperate to know who they were. But no! Don't come nearer: she cried out . . . 'Don't touch me!'

Emma had to fight them, or they would kill her, she knew! But listen. There was a voice, a familiar Cockney voice, kind and loving, which made her feel warm and unafraid. 'Ssh, darling,' it said, 'there ain't nobody gonna touch yer while *I'm* aside o' yer.' For a while her heart stopped its fearful trembling. But then she saw him. Her husband, Gregory Denton, with his body in a grotesque and twisted heap at the foot of the stairs. He was dead! And there above them was his aged mother. 'Murderer!' she screamed, her face alive with hatred. 'Emma Grady . . . you're a murderer!' Hands reached out to take Emma, to punish her. Oh, but where was Marlow? Would he not come to help her in her hour of need? Dear God above, would *no one* come to help her, and oh . . . her baby, her baby! 'Don't take my baby!' She was on her knees, pleading with them, but they wouldn't listen. 'Marlow, where are you? They mean to take our baby. No, No . . . please. DON'T TAKE MY BABY! Dear God, DON'T LET THEM TAKE MY BABY!' Frantically, she shook her head from side to side and, thrashing the air with her arms, she fought them off. Yet still they advanced, on their faces were looks of revenge as their outstretched hands threatened to grasp the tiny girl-child from her breast. 'Marlow, help me!' she cried as the child was torn from her and flung into the gutter. Her desperate cries echoed in the blackness, but there was no one to hear them.

In her terrible anguish, Emma was forced to

50

relive the horrors which had plagued her since the loss of her adored father, Thadius Grady; the awful events which led to her being accused of murder now rose into her subconscious with such stark realism that they struck terror into her very soul. As she fought and struggled against those who would separate her forever from the man she loved and from their newborn, Emma was unaware that her cries were just as painful to another who loved her dearly.

As Nelly fled to the sitting-room to fetch Mr Thomas, she could hardly talk for the sobs which racked her. 'Oh, Mr Thomas . . . come quick! It's Emma.' Then, unable to stand still even one moment longer, she ran back to the bedroom, with Mr Thomas hard on her heels.

'She's delirious.' Roland Thomas took one look at Emma's face, and when he saw the horror stamped upon it, his heart turned over. 'Quick, child,' he told the frantic Nelly, 'get the doctor!' The minute Nelly had gone to do his bidding, he set about preparing a bowl of water and collecting together a flannel, towel, and then placing them on the bedside cupboard. Next, he rolled up his sleeves and pulled the chair as close to Emma as possible. Quickly, he plunged the flannel into the water and squeezed it gently, before applying it to Emma's forehead. 'Easy does it, girlie,' he murmured, 'the doctor's on his way.' Until the doctor arrived, he tenderly wiped away the rivers of perspiration from Emma's face and upper body, all the while murmuring encouragement and soft assurances. 'You'll be all right, Emma . . . I reckon you'll pull through, just like the doc said.' He hoped so, yes indeed, he certainly hoped so, for

51

they had things to discuss, he and Emma. Important things which would affect *both* their futures.

When Dr Shaw arrived, he sent them all from Emma's bedside but they went no further than the doorway. Here Nelly and Roland Thomas stood, silently watching the doctor's every move as he carefully soothed and eventually sedated Emma. When, on stealthy footsteps, Foster Thomas came up behind them, it was to say in a strangely subdued voice, 'She'll be fine, I reckon. Emma's made of strong stuff . . . she won't buckle under so easily. She'll be fine, I'm telling you.'

His words were echoed by the doctor, who assured them, 'She's out of the crisis now . . . you'll see her grow stronger by the day.' His report to the authorities would read the same, he said, for there was no doubt that Emma would be up and about within the week, 'But, of course, I shall recommend that she be given leave from her duties for at least as long again.' A decision which was heartily endorsed by Roland Thomas, who was in no hurry to see Emma back at her work.

But there was something else bothering him, something that he should have seen long ago perhaps. It was the look in his son's eyes when he had come to see how ill Emma was, within the very first few minutes of his return. Even before he had asked after his own mother, he had gone to the bedroom where Rita Hughes had told him Emma lay. He had not made his presence known to Nelly. Instead, he had remained by the door, and from there had gazed towards the bed, his mouth set taut and his knuckles white as he clenched and unclenched his fist against the doorpost. He had not spoken a word, but remained there for a few moments before descending the stairs to discuss with his father all that had happened. Not once had he made any mention of Emma. But Roland Thomas had become curious about his son's obvious affection for her, and he wondered whether he might have misjudged him after all, for any man who could feel genuine affection towards a woman like Emma could surely not be all bad?

Yet he was not convinced, because in his own heart, he suspected that the son he and Violet had produced had more badness than goodness in him. It was a terrible thing for him to contemplate, but his every instinct warned him that it was, sadly, the truth. It was because of his instincts, therefore, that he decided to press on with the proposition he intended putting to Emma when she was well enough. Indeed, he believed there might now be more urgency to finalise his plan than he had at first realised, because, although there had been many times when he had wished his son would wed and settle down, it horrified him to think he could have designs on Emma. Women of Emma's admirable calibre were few and far between. She would be sorely wasted on the likes of his son, for it seemed that everything that one touched, he managed to drag down to his own level. So, if he had his way, Roland Thomas would persuade Emma towards greater things. She had it in her to make her mark on this land, he knew, and the thought excited him. All the same though, he did feel a small pang of guilt and there was just the slightest doubt in his mind as to whether he was judging his son too harshly. Time would tell, he thought, time will always tell.

Roland Thomas was right. Time did tell; but the tale it told was both grim and shameful.

*   *   *

'I'll stay by Emma awhile, child. You go and lay your head down in a proper bed.' It was midnight and Roland Thomas intended to turn in for the night. Foster had made himself scarce—probably gambling or supping grog with the ruffians who wandered hereabouts, he thought. Now that Emma appeared to be resting easier, the tiredness had crept up on him. In a few hours, there was a most unpleasant and heartbreaking duty to perform. He would need his strength for that.

'No, thank you, Mr Thomas, sir. I feel better when I'm near Emma.' Nelly could hear the weariness in his voice as he bade her goodnight, and it was there in the slump of his shoulders as he left the room. 'He'll sleep well tonight,' she told Emma, 'and he'll need all the sleep he can get, 'cause the ordeal ain't over fer the poor old sod yet.'

For the next half-hour Nelly continued to chatter, even though she knew well enough that Emma was in a deep sleep and heard nothing of her snippets of gossip. All the same, she told how folks had come to the store with their best wishes for Emma. She revealed how Rita Hughes had helped Mr Thomas in the store and 'been a real blessing in disguise'. Then she went on in great detail about how Foster Thomas had come home after four days, 'full o' cock-eyed excuses as to where he'd been all that time', and what was more, she had been excused from the routine of daily reporting to the authorities . . . ' 'cause the buggers know I won't be far from where my Emma is!' she laughed. After a while, a great weariness fell over Nelly. Her tongue grew heavy and her eyelids felt like lead weights against her eyeballs until every limb in her body ached for sleep. Then, unable to fight it any longer, she glanced at Emma's still and quiet form. With a sigh, she lay back her head and let the wave of welcome sleep wash over her. In a matter of minutes, she was out to the world and gently snoring.

When Foster Thomas came softly up the stairs he had but one thought in his mind, and that was Emma. The big round clock above the landing window struck one in the morning as he felt his way along the bannister in the pitch black. He dared not carry a lamp for fear he might be seen and, as he'd put away a jar or two of best grog in the company of those who were considered to be undesirable in the best social circles, he might be shown the way back down the stairs—worse still, his old father might take it into his head to show him all the way to the front door! Here he gave a small laugh, lost his balance and clung to the bannister as though his very life depended on it. Why was it, he asked himself, that Emma insisted on fending him off, when all the while she was as hot for him as he was for her? The little baggage . . . teasing him like that, when she knew full well that they were meant for each other.

Quietly now, he eased the door open just wide enough to admit his long lean body into the room. The room was in darkness, save for the shaft of moonlight coming in through the window where the curtains were not quite pulled together. In this soft yellow light, which showed the burned-down candle and which fell on Emma's pale and lovely features, he was guided towards the bed where she lay. All the while, the sound of Nelly's gentle snoring pulsated through the room, raising in him the comforting knowledge that, at long last, he and Emma were alone. And oh, he had such a longing in his loins for her . . . such a desperate need for her that he couldn't stop himself from trembling. Emma was *his*! Fight it she might, but there was no escaping the outcome. She was his, and though he could have taken her by force if he cared to, he had not, for there were any amount of women he could have in that way, but they meant nothing to him. Emma was special, and he would never rest until she came to his bed of her own accord. Oh, but in spite of her little games, she would! Yes indeed she would.

When, in a moment, he touched his fingertips to her temple, Emma made no movement at all. When he stroked the silkiness of her rich chestnut hair, she gently stirred. Afraid that she might cry out, he took away his hand from her forehead and, for a while, he stood very still, his arms loose by his sides and his blue eyes, made all the more murky by the drink he'd consumed, raked her face until they knew every finely chiselled line and curve. How greedily he devoured that creamy forehead with its heart-shaped hairline and high, perfectly shaped dark brows; even now, though they were tightly closed, Foster Thomas could imagine Emma's startlingly beautiful steel-grey eyes at their most magnificent . . . this being, to his warped mind, when she looked on him with the utmost contempt. Oh, but he wasn't disturbed by it for he

56

had convinced himself that it was all a show, a ploy to drive him crazy with desire. And it had worked! By God, it had worked because, as he gazed on her now, savouring her beauty to the full, there came over him an insatiable and feverish desire to draw back the bedcovers and to gaze upon the sleeping Emma in all her naked loveliness. The more he thought of it, the more urgent became the yearning, until the breath quickened in his throat and his pulse raced with excitement. He had never seen Emma unclothed. Not once had he feasted his eyes on her nakedness. Now the urge was too strong to resist; he *must* see her, for nothing else would satisfy him this night. And, if he were to slide in beside her, who was there to stop him? Certainly not his father, who was sleeping the sleep of the dead, downstairs; nor Nelly, who was also deeply exhausted. As for Emma . . . even if she had a mind to, she was in no position to object.

By now, every sense and nerve-ending in Foster Thomas's body was tingling at the prospect of taking Emma's nakedness to himself. There was a torment within him which pulled him two ways: he had vowed never to take Emma without her full and eager cooperation, but, having her lying before him now, so warm and vulnerable, and with the raw passion racing through his body when the need in him was as proud and obvious as ever it could be in a man, his resolve not to invade Emma's beauty without her wanting it as much as he himself did was weakening—already he had lost control.

As he reached out, with trepidation, to pluck the bedclothes from her, the palms of his hands were sweating and his every limb trembled uncontrollably. Gently now, and all the while holding his breath for fear of being discovered, he slid back the clothes which hid Emma from him. He had suspected that she might not be wearing a nightgown; not when the heat of the day was such that men were forced to cease their labours or fry in the merciless sun. In the dead of night that same heat was so oppressive and suffocating that even when lying still in bed, a body was bathed in sweat.

Emma was *not* wearing a nightgown, having come through a feverish crisis when it would have clung to her like a second skin. The doctor had given instructions that Emma be covered up to the chin by the bedclothes, and occasionally flannelled down with fresh water to reduce her soaring temperature. Nelly had allowed no one else close to Emma and not once had she failed in her duty to carry out the doctor's instructions. So, when Foster Thomas drew back the bedclothes, the sight of Emma's slender body caused him to gasp out loud. If he had thought her face the most beautiful he had ever seen, then how much more magnificent was her body!

Riveted to the spot and almost afraid of what his astonished eyes beheld, Foster Thomas scored every detail into his lecherous mind. His eyes narrowed and his desire for Emma was greatly intensified as he let his gaze wander over her nakedness. Even when she softly stirred and turned her head deeper into the pillow, he was so mesmerised that he could not drag his gaze away, nor could he move, although his instincts warned him that Nelly could wake at any minute. Greedily, his eyes took in all that he could of Emma, this adorable creature whom he had vowed to have for his own. He gazed at the long, thick hair which was fanned out over the pillow, its vibrant autumn hues a stark contrast against the starched white pillowcase. He stared long at that lovely face, with its large wonderful eyes and those high aristocratic cheekbones, the perfect full mouth and that chin which, though completing the exquisite oval shape of Emma's face, was strong and determined, as was her character. Oh, what sensual delights invaded him as he roved his narrow opaque blue eyes over Emma's youthful, thrusting breasts, so small and perfect with proud inviting nipples standing warm and dark against the creamy whiteness of her breasts. He thought her waist was small but not tiny and the curves of her thighs deliciously inviting, and how impatient he was to tangle himself between those exquisite legs. *Too* impatient, he chided himself, because already he was aching with such excitement and anticipation that in a minute it would be too late! Quickly he stripped off his clothes to stand naked and desperate for a taste of Emma's loveliness.

When with great care, or he would surely give the game away, he inched himself on to the bed, Emma was trembling from being uncovered for so long. She stirred, raising her arm above her head, and softly moaned. In a minute he was on her, covering her nakedness with his own and murmuring tender words against the warmth of her neck. With one arm stroking her hair and the weight taken by his elbow, he reached his other arm down to ease open her legs. When, this time, Emma became agitated, twisting her body this way then that and calling out the name 'Marlow', he stayed still, not daring to move for fear she had alerted the others. For what seemed a lifetime, he remained frozen against her, tormented by the touch of his body on hers, but terrified that he might be discovered. But no, Nelly was still deep in the sleep of exhaustion, her rhythmic snores breathing into the darkness like the beating of his own heart. As he waited a moment longer, listening for any sound from the stores below or perhaps a footstep on the stairs, he wondered who was this 'Marlow' whom Emma had called out to. How soft and loving her voice had been, almost a caress of his name. He would not forget the name either: as Foster Thomas emblazoned Marlow's name on to his memory, a terrible hatred crept into his black heart.

The tender feelings which had smothered him were now tempered with a fury that, even in her subconscious, Emma should cry out some other man's name! But this 'Marlow' wasn't here, coveting Emma's nakedness, while *he* was! For the moment, at least, he was pacified, and in that moment when his whole being flooded with his need for Emma's heart and soul, he placed his mouth over hers, and gently probed himself towards her. Then with such a tide of ecstasy rushing through him that he thought his heart would burst, he thrust his way deep into Emma, his great excitement causing him to cry out.

Emma cried out also, but it was a strangled and terrified cry of the kind made by a nightmare which caused her to thrash out at those who would hurt her. In her ill and confused mind, she knew only that she must escape; she must flee from the pain and horror which hounded her, and which had already pushed her over the line between nightmare and reality. When it seemed that in her anguish Emma might betray him, she was cruelly silenced by her assailant's clenched fist. Being so intent on satisfying the cravings of his own body, Foster Thomas cared not for his *un*conscious victim's helplessness for, in the throes of his madness, he was frantic to gratify only the base primitive instincts which drove him. Gripping Emma into him again and again, he smothered her with his vile body and kissed her nakedness, all the while telling her how she was *his* now . . . and could never belong to any other.

Of a sudden, there came another scream as Nelly woke to the horror of what was happening. Almost at once, there was a rush of footsteps into the room and the darkness was penetrated by the light which Roland Thomas carried high before him. With a cry of 'You filthy bastard!' he sprang forward, dropping the lantern to the floor and clawing at his son's bare flesh, his nails digging so deep into it that the blood spurted out like a crimson shower to fall in spattered drops along his back and shoulders. With the might of a demon, he yanked him from the bed and from Emma, who was as still and white as death.

'Oh God! Emma, will yer forgive me, will yer ever forgive me, darlin'?' Nelly had recovered the lamp which, in his rage, Roland Thomas had dropped to the floor and she had placed it on the bedside cupboard. Having drawn up the bedclothes over Emma's violated body, she was cradling her dear friend's head to her bosom and sobbing as though her heart would break. 'Will yer ever forgive me, darlin' Emma,' she cried over and over, 'for I'll never be able ter forgive meself!'

It was a night that no one there would ever

61

forget. For although he was an older and slower man, Roland Thomas's fury and disgust knew no bounds as he thrashed his son unmercifully. First throwing him down the stairs, he took a bull-whip from the stores and, without heed of his cowardly son's cries for mercy, he brought it down again and again across his bare back and shoulders, the tip of it lashing over his face and neck and cutting so deep that he would carry the scars for the rest of his miserable life. Afterwards Roland Thomas flung Foster out on to the porch, with his clothes and belongings in a heap beside him. 'You're a no-good bastard!' he told his son in a voice that still trembled with rage. 'Your own mother's to be buried this day, and you bring nothing but shame on our heads. Let the devil take you, Foster Thomas, because I want nothing more to do with you! *Never* set foot near me again . . . stay out of my sight. You're no son of mine. From this day on, I have no son!' He watched the crumpled figure begin to stir on the porch, and he knew that his words had been heard. It was enough.

In the darkness, Roland Thomas's terrible words had also been heard by many of the startled neighbours, who had been roused from their beds by the worst upheaval they had ever been witness to. No one knew what dreadful reason could have provoked such an amiable and mild-mannered man as Roland Thomas, the well-liked and respected trader, to cast his own son from his house, and to issue such strong and awful words that made them tremble. Yes, it was true that Foster Thomas was not the man his father was . . . nor the man his father might have wished him to be, for he was both weak and wasteful. It was also true that the confrontation between them had been a long time brewing. But, so terrible and final, and on the very day in which poor Mrs Thomas was to be laid to her rest? It didn't bear thinking about. All the same, they were intrigued to know what awful thing had triggered off Roland Thomas's fury. But, as the trader stormed back into his store, and the son spat in the dust behind him with a look of deep hatred on his bleeding face, something told them that they might never know the truth of what had happened that night, for the old one was too proud to disclose it, and the other too cowardly.

Chapter Three

It was a wonderful balmy day, with the sun playing hide-and-seek amongst the clouds, and the gentle breezes blowing in off the sea to cool the land and bring with them the promise of rain.

Four whole weeks had passed and January had given way to February since the awful night when father had disowned his only son, and that son had fled the area without trace, almost as though he had disappeared from the face of the earth. At first light after the violation of Emma, when Roland Thomas had come down to the porch, there had been no sign of the perpetrator. When the funeral procession had taken Mrs Thomas along the High Street to the churchyard, there had been no sign of her son: not during the service, nor at the graveside afterwards. There was much talk of it for many days following, with people curious to know what had taken place. They declared their sympathies to the grieving husband and he, in turn, quietly thanked them. They expressed their horror and regret at what had transpired between him and his only son, and he nodded gratefully, but made no comment. They fidgeted nervously with their black neck-ties and meticulously adjusted their prim little bonnets; then, feeling somewhat perplexed and frustrated, they went on their way. Roland Thomas was a private man, they knew, and they respected him for it. All the same, that son of his must have committed an evil deed for such a man as the trader to be so unforgiving! But now, with his wife gone, his son gone, and two female convicts residing on the premises, the circumstances at the Thomas store left much to be desired. There was talk that he intended taking on a young lad to help him in the store, and what with the upright and prim Rita Hughes having taken on the role as housekeeper there, they supposed it was respectable enough. What was more, Roland Thomas, a strong, fine figure of a man at fifty-nine years old, was not past taking himself a new wife, no indeed! Who could be more suitable than the blacksmith's daughter, they wondered.

*   *   *

Emma could hardly believe her ears. '*Marry* you!' she exclaimed, an expression of incredulity on her face as she looked at Roland Thomas through astonished grey eyes. 'Do you know what you're saying, Mr Thomas?' Surely she had misheard, Emma thought. Only ten minutes before, she had been busily attending to her duties in the store,

64

feeling grateful to be back at her work, and exchanging pleasantries with the customers. Now, here she was, summoned to the upstairs sitting-room and seated on the stiff horsehair couch opposite Mr Thomas, who was perched somewhat precariously on the edge of a tall ladder-back chair, his homely face wreathed with anxiety as he waited for her answer. But he dared not wait, for he saw the answer written plainly all over Emma's countenance, so, taking his courage into his hands, he leaned forward in the chair to fix her all the more with his dark, troubled gaze. 'Think on it, Emma,' he urged, 'don't reject me out of hand . . . not until I've been through the advantages of such a union between the two of us.'

He then went on to explain how he had thought long and hard about the proposition, and how after each painstaking deliberation he had come to the very same conclusion. 'It can only benefit both of us, Emma . . . for my part, there are two main considerations. The first is that, when my time comes and I'm called to take place alongside my Violet, that no-good son o' mine won't be able to get his hands on this 'ere business! The second gives me even greater pleasure: not only will the business come into *your* capable and deserving hands, Emma—the good Lord knows how hard you've worked to make it flourish these past seven years—but I reckon with your energy and clever business head, you'll take the Thomas name far higher than I ever could! You've got youth on your side, girlie . . . and that special inner drive to succeed. Oh, and there's so much more opportunity now, to expand and prosper in all directions; you must see that . . . Why, you yourself pointed out the openings in the pearl-shell trade, and we've got the profits to prove it! And look how you've badgered me about the benefits to be got from coastal trade. You can do it, Emma . . . with me alongside you, and our name over that doorway . . . we can branch out in whatever direction you like!'

As he talked, his dark eyes alive with enthusiasm, Emma was caught up in his mood of excitement. He was right. All he was saying made a good deal of sense, her every instinct told her so. With overland transport difficulties and more settlers arriving all the time, there was a fortune to be made from taking the goods by sea, investing in good, sturdy seagoing vessels and building up a thriving trade along the coast. The openings were there, and the benefits would be most handsome, she knew. What a challenge that would be! What an exciting and demanding challenge! But on her own it would prove to be a very difficult, if not impossible, task, because of the stigma of being a convict and because she was a woman, women being denied a place in the man's world of business. Yet Emma knew that she *could* do it, given the opportunity. Mr Thomas was right. She'd work her fingers to the bone and raise the Thomas Trading Business to such a height that its reputation and importance would be carried from one end of Australia to the other and, in time, across the oceans to England and the rest of the world! There was no doubt in Emma's mind that one day this vast land of Australia would be a great and important country, when it would play an even more important part in international trading. Indeed, it was already beginning to happen, and all

66

the signs were there that Australia was coming into its own. The convict ships had stopped coming some two years ago; there was now partial self-government, and only recently a privately-owned telegraph link with Perth had been installed. Already plans were underway to construct a network of overland telegraph lines which would link not only major cities and ports, but countries far and wide. Railways were also being constructed. It was an exciting time, Emma realised, a time of innovation, growth and expansion of a kind unparalleled before. Oh! What she would give to be a real part of it!

But could she betray herself by agreeing to marry a man old enough to be her father? Could she live such a lie, when there would never be any other man in her heart but Marlow Tanner? No, she thought not.

Once more, Emma prepared to give Roland Thomas his answer. And once again, sensing that she was about to turn him down, he bade her wait a moment longer. 'Hear me out, Emma,' he pleaded. And she did, waiting most attentively, while he outlined how, on the very day of their marriage, he would sign an official contract stating that, from that day forwards, Emma was his full partner, and that, on the day of his demise *everything* he owned, lock, stock and barrel, would become her property, and hers alone, to do with as she wished, because he knew in his heart that he could not leave his affairs in better hands than hers.

Emma could have pointed out that he had a son, and that son must surely be included in any such agreement. But she said nothing, for she knew that, as far as Roland Thomas was concerned, he had no son, and that even to mention his name would infuriate and antagonise her employer. Besides which, the very name of that creature on her lips would taste so foul that she would feel tainted ever after! Only now, after weeks of agonising, had she made herself put that terrible night behind her, when he had invaded her body while she lay ill and helpless.

For a long time afterwards, she was unsure as to where the boundaries of her nightmares ended, and where they had become stark, horrifying reality. When Nelly revealed the awful truth, in as gentle a manner as possible, Emma had felt physically sick, but more than that, she had felt dirty and degraded. There had been murder in her heart, such bitterness that coloured her every sleeping and waking thought, until she could see no pleasure in anything. All those things she loved were as nothing to her. The delightful things of nature and God's creation . . . the turquoise ocean, the brightly coloured birds and even the daily tasks of the work she pleasured in, meant nothing. She had grown morose and withdrawn for a time, and was not moved by Nelly's pleas, nor by her love and stalwart friendship, so vile and unclean did she feel.

After a while though, some deeper instincts within her persuaded Emma that it was not she who was vile and unclean, it was the monster who had forced himself on her. So, with Nelly's unswerving determination to show Emma her own worth, each day had grown a little easier to accept. Also, the fact that only she, Mr Thomas and Nelly knew of the deed Foster had committed against her that night lessened Emma's shame.

68

In spite of Emma's Christian upbringing she could not find it in her heart ever to forgive Roland Thomas's son. So now when the older man spoke of his revulsion for the 'dog he had sired', and explained how he would never know a moment's peace if everything he had worked for should come to a sorry end in the grasping hands of such a no-good, Emma understood. And she was glad that it was so.

'There's something else, Emma,' Mr Thomas told her now. 'If you and I were married, the authorities would declare you a *free* woman! Oh, think of it, Emma . . . you would be free, in command, and one day you'd inherit everything! You'd have freedom, money, and power! Say yes, Emma! You must say yes!' His voice was trembling and he reached out to lay his hand over Emma's small, work-worn fingers. 'You and me, Emma . . . not man and wife in the true sense, for I suspect your heart belongs to this "Marlow" you cried for when you were close to death, and . . . I would never want another woman after my Violet. No! *Partners,* Emma! Business partners, and an agreement that would be good for both of us. Say yes, Emma. *Please!*'

But Emma could not say yes so easily. Yet in the face of such a strong and sensible argument, neither could she now say no without first giving it a deal more thought.

Roland Thomas sensed her slight hesitation, and his hopes were raised. 'All right, Emma,' he conceded, 'I won't ask for your answer right away. But . . . I beg you not to keep me waiting too long for your decision.'

'I won't,' she promised. There the matter was

69

laid to rest for the time being.

'E's asked yer ter marry 'im, ain't he, gal?' Nelly and Emma had finished their long day's work and were presently making for the beach, where they might sit awhile and discuss matters close to their hearts. 'I *knew* it!' exclaimed Nelly with big, round eyes, her voice breaking into a giggle. 'I saw it comin' a bleedin' mile away, ever since he asked yer up ter the parlour the day afore yesterday.' Here she gave a little skip and playfully nudged the smiling Emma. 'G'orn!' she laughed. 'He *did*, didn't he, eh? What a dark horse you are, Emma gal!' Of a sudden, she grabbed Emma by the arm and pulled her to a halt. 'Hey, bugger me!' she said, as the full consequences struck her. 'T'ain't such a bad idea at that, is it, eh? When the old bugger pops orf . . . well, you'll come into everything, won't yer? Cor, just think of it, Emma darlin' . . . the Thomas Trading Business'll be yours, and yer won't be a convict no more either. Why! Yer could even go back ter *England*!' At this Nelly began trembling as she cast her mind back to that fateful dark morning when they were taken from the cell in an English gaol and bundled into a rickety cage atop a flat-waggon.

Emma was also remembering. 'Yes, Nelly,' she said in a strangely quiet voice, 'it could be the means of me going back to England . . . if I wanted to. And oh, yes, she *did* want to! It was that one thought above all others that had kept her going these past years. Back to England! How her head rose at the prospect! But nothing was ever as black and white as it looked. To her mind, there were two alternatives offered to her. One, she could refuse Mr Thomas's generous offer, and that would mean serving out her sentence, after which it could take many long and laborious years before she accrued enough money to take her back to England—there was always the possibility that her plans to return might never be realised, and that was too much to bear. On the other hand, if she were to accept the offer of marriage, there must surely come a day, as Mr Thomas had forecast and as Nelly had rightfully pointed out, when she would be a woman of significance hereabouts, a woman of property and prosperity, with the means to go wherever in the world she chose.

There were two desperate needs inside Emma, two deep and driving ambitions that would not let her be. She had so many ideas and plans with regard to exploiting the numerous business opportunities which beckoned those with the determination and courage to go after them. However, she was also driven by the desire to go back to her homeland, where she had many enemies to root out and scores to settle. Above all, she would never rest until she had found Marlow, for there was much to explain, and forgiveness to be sought.

'Oh, Emma . . . if yer do marry Mr Thomas, yer won't go back ter England and leave me, will yer? Don't do that ter me, Emma darlin' . . . 'cause what would I do without yer, eh?' There were tears in Nelly's voice as she looked at Emma with fearful brown eyes. 'Yer wouldn't desert yer old friend, would yer?' she asked, and Emma's heart went out to her. 'I ain't going another step till yer tell me yer won't clear off ter England and leave me!' Nelly vowed, putting on a brave front, yet betraying her nervousness by the manner in which she had drawn her long skirt up and was twisting it round and round her fingers.

'Come on,' Emma smiled at her reassuringly and, taking hold of Nelly's arm, she started walking at a smarter pace until they covered the entire length of the tunnel, which had been cut through the limestone cliffs by a whaling company, for speedier access from the landing beach to the warehouses inland.

Emerging from the relative gloom of the tunnel and coming out on to the sandy beach, Emma sat down on a small boulder and patted another alongside. 'Come and sit beside me, Nelly,' she said. When Nelly had done so, she brought her quiet grey eyes to rest on her friend's anxious face, saying, 'I haven't told you before, about Mr Thomas's offer, because I haven't yet made up my mind. When he first asked me my instinct was to say no right off. And, I'm still of the same mind. So you see, Nelly . . . you're working yourself up into a state for nothing.'

'But you'd be *daft* not to say yes, gal!' exclaimed Nelly, somewhat surprised. She would have said yes the minute he asked her!

'Maybe, Nelly. But I don't know that it would be right, to take him up on his kind offer . . . when I would be getting much more than I deserve, and taking more out of the relationship than I could ever give back. Here,' she paused a while before telling Nelly, 'there's a deal of thinking to be done, but . . . I mean to give him an answer this very night. And whatever my decision is, Nelly, I could *not* go back to England and leave you behind. What! I wouldn't have a minute's peace, wondering what trouble you were busy getting yourself into!' When she softly laughed, the smile returned to Nelly's downcast face and soon the two young women were in a better frame of mind.

It was gone eight o'clock when Nelly and Emma began their gentle stroll back along the High Street. When Emma made clear her intention of stopping awhile on King's Square, as she wanted to 'go into St John's Church and talk things over with the Almighty', Nelly's reaction was immediate. 'Yer can if yer like, Emma darlin', she retorted with a vigorous shake of her brown head, 'but I ain't comin' in! It's bad enough being made to go by the authorities . . . but I ain't bloody *volunteering*!' By now they were outside St John's Church, and Nelly found a shady spot in which to wait. 'Me an' the good Lord don't see eye ter eye at the minute, gal,' she laughed, 'on account of I keep finding meself up ter me neck in trouble . . . and he seems ter have no control over me whatsoever! I do believe he's washed his hands of me!'

'You can't blame God . . . or anybody else for that matter,' Emma was quick to tell her. 'The trouble you've landed yourself in has been your *own* doing!' Here she turned at the church doorway and added in a quieter voice, 'If only you didn't want to keep fighting with the authorities, Nelly . . . and if you could curb that wicked little streak in you, that always wants to chase after the kind of fellas who bring nothing but trouble.' Here she gave a great sigh as she let her concerned grey eyes linger a moment longer on that rebellious but homely figure that had thrown itself haphazardly at the foot of a gum tree. The sight of Nelly's defiant, upturned face sent a pang of affection

73

through Emma. 'You're incorrigible, Nelly,' she smiled, shaking her head. 'But look . . . it's been a good while since you've been in trouble, hasn't it, eh? So maybe you and the Lord *are* on speaking terms, after all?' She hoped Nelly might change her mind and step into the church with her, but no.

'Then I'd best stay where I am, and not push me luck, Emma, gal!' came the chirpy reply. After which, Nelly set up whistling her tavern song, and Emma left her to it.

Inside the church, Emma knelt at the altar, closed her eyes and offered up a prayer. She made a special mention for Nelly, and asked that her impetuous nature didn't get her into any deeper water. Then, feeling ashamed and guilty at bringing such a terrible thing into God's house, she spoke of the awful deed committed against her by Roland Thomas's estranged son. She asked for forgiveness because of the bitterness in her heart towards him and, above all else, Emma prayed for guidance on Roland Thomas's proposition. She reminded the Lord about her love for Marlow Tanner, and of her need to take revenge on Caleb Crowther, the trusted uncle who had betrayed her.

When Emma came to the subject of her lost baby, her heart was too full for prayer and the tears ran down her face as, in her mind's eye, she saw again that small, precious life which had been safe in her arms for such a desperately short time. The tiny face of her newborn daughter was as fresh in her mind now, more than seven years on, as it had been when she had given birth to it, there in an English cobbled street outside the gaol. It was deeply painful for Emma to know that her beloved daughter was no more.

Emma stayed a moment longer, neither thinking too deeply nor praying. It was enough that she had unburdened her heart, and so in these few precious moments, she just knelt in the peace and serenity. She let it flood into her heart and, as the moments passed, she felt a new kind of strength within her. She had made up her mind. Roland Thomas would have his answer that very day, and Emma would abide by it, come what may. First though, there was much to be said between them; things of the past which must be revealed.

*   *   *

'I don't want to know, Emma. You're a good woman, I can tell, or I wouldn't be asking you to be my wife.' Roland Thomas was seated on the horsehair couch and, when he spoke, Emma turned round from the window to look at him with her strong eyes and an unusually severe look on her face. 'I *mean* it, Emma,' he urged, 'you don't have to tell me anything!'

Emma's gaze lingered on his face for a moment longer, before she turned away to look out of the window once more. Her gaze was vague and distant and her voice painfully quiet as she told him, 'There can be no agreement between us . . . until you know all there is to know about me.' She waited, her back to him, shoulders taut, and an air of defiance in her countenance. When, in reluctant tones, Emma was told, 'Very well . . . if you feel that strongly,' she returned to sit on one of the four ladder-back chairs which surrounded the circular table.

Pulling herself in closer to the table, Emma

75

clenched her fists together on the green corded tablecloth and, after a moment spent composing herself for what she knew would be a painful ordeal, she began to unfold the story that had eventually brought her here in shackles. A story of deceit, betrayal and brutality. A story of love, of lost dear ones, and of heartbreak. A story that, though it seemed already to have spanned a lifetime and had its origins so many thousands of miles away across the oceans, was not yet over. Might not be over for another lifetime to come!

Quietly, and with great regard for the turmoil which he suspected was raging within Emma as she revealed the roots of her nightmare, Roland Thomas paid close attention to her every word.

Emma spared nothing. She told of her heartbreak when her darling papa had died. She explained how he had innocently appointed his brother-in-law, Caleb Crowther, to be trustee of his mills and fortune, and gave the same man complete and irrevocable guardian-ship over his beloved daughter, Emma. Yet no sooner had his bones been laid to rest, than Emma's uncle, Caleb Crowther, saw fit, first of all, to put her out to work . . . while his own spoilt and petulant daughter, Martha Crowther, was sent to a fashionable school for young ladies, her place there being bought and paid for by the money which Emma's father had left in trust for *her*. Then, when it suited his purpose, and in spite of the fact that Emma had fallen hopelessly in love with a young bargee by the name of Marlow Tanner who loved her in return, Crowther married her off to Gregory Denton, a manager at one of her father's mills. It was a disastrous match for Emma: Gregory was

76

impossibly possessive and wrongly suspicious of her every move, and his jealous old mother detested Emma so much that she confined herself to bed and from there she created enough malicious mischief to make Emma's life a misery. All this time, only Emma's old nanny kept her sane and remained a true and stalwart friend.

'If I had thought that things were so bad they couldn't possibly get worse . . . I was miserably wrong,' Emma went on. 'With the Civil War in America, the shipments of cotton to Britain were strangled to a halt. People starved in their millions, and mills all around were shutting down at an alarming rate.' Here the memories became too vivid in Emma's mind and, for a long moment, she paused to reflect until, in a gentle voice, Roland Thomas persuaded her, 'Go on, Emma.'

In faltering tones, Emma told how her husband had gone to pieces after he lost his job. She told how she had searched for him when he was most troubled, and how she had met him leaving a public house in the company of others as drunk as himself . . . she revealed how he had struck and humiliated her in front of them; then later, how she had to flee for her very life when one of those same men relentlessly pursued her. When it seemed as though she were lost, Marlow Tanner had been there to save her. 'It was the beginning of the end,' Emma murmured, feeling shamed at the memory of herself in Marlow's loving arms, yet at the same time feeling warmed by that precious recollection.

Soon after, Emma explained, she was horrified to discover that she was expecting Marlow's child. Her only friend, her nanny from childhood, Mrs

Manfred, persuaded Emma that her husband must be told the truth and, to give Emma moral support, she stayed over on the night Emma decided to make her confession. 'It was a nightmare. Gregory came home in the early hours . . . he was more drunk than I'd ever seen him.' Emma described how he had discovered her pregnancy after violently stripping off her clothes. 'He went completely crazy!' A struggle followed and Mrs Manfred came to Emma's help; during the confusion, Emma's husband lost his balance and crashed down the stairs. His neck was broken in the fall. Old Mrs Denton accused both Emma and Mrs Manfred of plotting to murder her son, and they were arrested. The outcome was that Mrs Manfred was hanged, and Emma sentenced to ten years and transported.

'And the child?' Roland Thomas had a great impulse to go and comfort Emma, who had been devastated by the cruel demise of her dear, gentle friend, Mrs Manfred. But he dared not, for fear that Emma would surely reject him. 'What became of your child, Emma?' he asked gently. Then, he was moved to a deeper compassion when Emma went on in faltering tones. She described how, in the dark, early hours of a grim morning as she was being loaded into the waggon along with other prisoners, the child would be contained no longer. 'I gave birth to Marlow's daughter right there, in the street, with only dearest Nelly for strength and comfort. The child never drew breath . . . She wasn't given the chance!' Emma was up on her feet now, the memory of it all causing her to pace the floor in agitation. 'She was snatched from my arms and left in the gutter, like so much dirt!'

'Can you be *sure* she wasn't alive?' Roland Thomas had unwittingly voiced the tiny hope which had burned in Emma's heart ever since that day. But no! How many times had she questioned Nelly over and over about it? What had Nelly seen when Emma passed out? Was there even the *slightest* chance that the newborn was still alive, as the waggon moved away? Could she be certain? Oh, the questions she had asked . . . and each one a fervent prayer. But always the answer was the same: 'No.' Nelly was adamant, 'Don't torture yerself, gal . . . the bairn were dead.' Gradually, the light of hope was dimmed in Emma's weary heart. But not extinguished. Never completely extinguished.

'The chances of the infant having survived are desperately slim . . . almost non-existent,' she replied now, 'and I have made myself accept it, or be driven crazy.'

Roland Thomas nodded. 'And Marlow . . . what became of Marlow Tanner, the man you loved?'

'The man I will *always* love,' Emma corrected. 'And it's only fair that you know it, Mr Thomas,' she told him, the edge returning to her voice. Then she saw him nod and heard his reply, 'I'm aware of it, Emma, and it matters not to any agreement we might make.' Emma answered his question and the words pulled on her heart like heavy weights. 'I sent him away. I *had* to . . . for his own good! If I hadn't, then Caleb Crowther would have made it his business to hound him, and to bring him forward on some fabricated charge that would have meant transportation . . . or even the gallows.'

'This uncle of yours . . . this "Caleb Crowther" . . . he had that kind of power?'

'He did . . . and has, as far as I know. He was a Justice of the Peace, and moved amongst the most influential and powerful people.'

'Was it he who arranged your own transportation, Emma?'

'I don't know,' replied Emma thoughtfully. But such a possibility had long troubled her. And if he were guilty of that, then what else did he have a hand in? What of Mrs Manfred's hanging? What of her own inheritance? And why had none of the Crowther family come to her aid when she had sent out messages from her cell, *begging* for their help? Yet they had not replied . . . not once, and she had no other family to turn to. Oh yes, these were matters which had sat long and uncomfortably on Emma's mind. One day she would learn the answers. She must.

'Now that you know all of my background, do you still want me to enter into a marriage agreement with you, Mr Thomas?' she asked of him now.

His answer was immediate. 'Now . . . more than ever!' he told her with an assuring smile, 'Just name the day, and I'll be a proud and fortunate man to have such a woman alongside me. After hearing your story, Emma, I reckon you're more of a victim than a criminal. All I ask of you now is to name the day . . . and your fortunes can't help but take a turn for the better.' He was on his feet, as though the occasion warranted it, and when Emma looked at his broad, craggy face, then smiled at him with gratitude shining in her warm grey eyes, he appeared unusually self-conscious. Lowering his dark gaze to the peg-rug where he seemed intent on studying the reds and browns of the ragged tufts there, he said quietly, 'I'll never ask more of you, Emma, than you already give.' He made no move to lift his gaze, lest it linger too long on hers. 'You have my word on it,' he told her.

'I know that,' Emma assured him, 'and I thank you for it.'

Of a sudden, Roland Thomas raised his eyes before stepping forward, saying with a more serious expression and in a sterner voice, 'There are *other* matters though, which do give me cause for concern. I've given you my word on a particular issue, Emma . . . now, I must ask you to do the same for me.'

'Oh?' Emma was intrigued yet, at the same time a deal of anxiety had crept into her heart for fear that she might not be able to give her word on whatever was troubling him. Emma was now deeply committed to their agreement, because it would indeed open doors for her that might otherwise stay forever closed. 'What is it, Mr Thomas?' she asked, her concerned eyes searching his large, loose features as though she might find her answer there.

'First of all I reckon you could forget the *Mr* Thomas . . . and begin calling me by my name, Roland. It doesn't seem right for a woman to be calling her intended by his surname. Most of all though, Emma . . . I want you to promise that you'll not be itching to make for England the minute you slip the shackles of a convict. Oh, I wouldn't blame you, girlie! Not after what the devils back there have put you through! What! . . . I'd do the very same myself. But y'see, Emma, the whole idea of this partnership between us is to deny that waster son of mine any access to my money or business, and for you and me to work side by side in building it up to the kind of business that I've always dreamed of, ever since first setting foot here. Oh, I know it's a grand concern now, and I'm right proud o' what I've achieved . . . but I feel in my bones that where I've stopped, Emma . . . you are only just beginning. I want to be a part in it, Emma, afore I'm put to rest alongside my Violet.' The darkness in his eyes grew almost black as he drew in a deep and trembling breath, and when he spoke again, Emma was struck by the pain and bitterness in his voice. 'Take the name of Thomas to the very top. Take it where the likes o' Foster Thomas can never get their grubby paws on it . . . and, while it grows and prospers, I hope the one I've disowned sees it happen and rues the day he set his hand against his own flesh and blood! Do that for me, Emma, and above all else . . . do it for yourself.' He now seemed to shrink before Emma's eyes, as, lifting his hand and drawing it wearily across his brow, he went over and sank into the same chair in which his wife had been cruelly tormented on that fateful night. Of a sudden, he leaned forward, dropped his head into the palms of his hands and began quietly sobbing, his broad shoulders shaking with emotion, and occasionally gently moaned the name 'Violet' with heartrending broken voice. To Emma, who was torn between going to comfort him and leaving the room, it was a sad and humbling sight.

'I let her down badly,' he said now, keeping his face buried from Emma's sight. 'I should have taken her home . . . that was her only wish, and . . . I let her down. I'll never forgive myself. Never!'

'Never is a long time,' Emma said softly, 'and

I'm sure Mrs Thomas understood your reasons for not going back to England. What you did here . . . the work you *both* put into this fine business, you did it for her, and for your son. She knew that, and I'm sure she understood well enough.' There was no answer and little response from Roland Thomas, and Emma expected none. Instead he nodded his head and kept his body bent forward in the chair.

'As for *me* wanting to seek out the answers I crave, well, I've waited a long time and I can wait a little longer. You're right . . . there's so much more to be done here, so many opportunities that mustn't be missed. Things are beginning to happen, and we have to be ready. Don't concern yourself about me turning my back on you after you've given me such a wonderful opportunity to prove myself. I won't desert you, I promise, and between us, we'll show the competitors as clean a pair of heels as they've seen in a long time. We *both* have our reasons for seeing the growth of the Thomas Trading Company. When the time is right for me to take leave and trace my path back to those who heartlessly forged it, nothing would give me greater pleasure than to go back, not as a young innocent upon whom stronger men would prey, but as an accomplished business woman . . . a woman of property and consequence, a woman who is more than capable of bringing her enemies to account!' There was a hardness in Emma's heart as she spoke, and it was betrayed in the icy edge to her voice. '*That* will be worth waiting for!'

And so it was agreed. For three years or more, Emma would dedicate herself to matters of business. After that, if she deemed the time to be right, she would take leave and sail for England, to attend to issues that were personal and close to her heart. The wedding date was set for the month of March, some eight weeks hence, in the year of our Lord, 1870.

*   *   *

'Married now, eh! Well . . . all the luck in the world ter yer, Emma darlin'!' Nelly raised her merry brown eyes to where Emma stood with her back to the cell door, and, in a voice that was somewhat subdued by her grim surroundings, said, 'Oh, I'm sorry, gal! I *know* I shouldn't have got to fighting with that Rita Hughes . . . but the bastard said some'at as put me back up.' Here she gave a small laugh. 'If yer ask me, she's bleedin' lucky somebody pulled me orf her. What! I'd have killed her fer sure!'

'Oh, yes? And got yourself hanged for it, eh?' Emma was angry and it showed, in her voice, in her countenance, and in the steel-grey of her eyes. 'Do you honestly think I don't know what Rita Hughes said that "put your back up"? Do you think I don't know that there are folks hereabouts who condemn the fact that Roland Thomas has taken a convict for his wife? *Their* opinions don't concern either me or Mr Thomas . . . so they shouldn't concern *you!*' Giving a deep sigh and shaking her head, Emma came forward to sit beside Nelly on the narrow iron bed, and gently patting the back of Nelly's hand, she said with tender feeling, 'Oh, Nelly, Nelly! Will you always insist on landing yourself in trouble on *my* account? Don't you know by now that I am capable of fighting my own battles? Do you think you're going to stop folk from gossiping between each other, by attacking them with pitch-forks?' For a minute, there was a deep and profound silence while Emma allowed her words to sink in, and Nelly appeared to be taking them to heart. But then, the silence was broken by Nelly's soft giggling. 'Cor, bugger me, Emma, gal,' she laughed, 'd'yer know, I've only just realised what a narrer escape I've had.' Then, just as Emma thought that her words were having the desired effect, she was told, between spurts of laughter, 'If I'd damaged that pitch-fork . . . I'd have been in *real* trouble with you, wouldn't I, eh?'

Try though she might, Emma couldn't keep a straight face when she turned to see Nelly's lively eyes and homely face all crumpled with laughter. 'Oh, Nelly!' she said, trying hard to suppress the merriment already spreading from her heart. 'What *will* I do with you?'

'Get me outta this bleedin' dark hole for a start!' came the reply. And, because of her new status, together with the fact that she had only just come from the Governor, where her pleas on Nelly's behalf had been accepted—with a warning that 'should it happen again, I'll probably throw away the key!'—Emma was able to secure the hapless Nelly's release.

The two women were a strange yet familiar sight as they made their way from the Convict Depot and along William Street. Emma looked exceptionally smart and respectable, dressed in black boots, bonnet and cape, with the long, flouncy, dark-blue skirt softly swishing with her every step. There was an air of elegance about her, and an absolute confidence that only social

85

standing and the promise of prosperity can bring. Nelly looked the worse for wear, having been deprived of the pretty white blouse and brown skirt that Emma had got her for the wedding, and dressed by the authorities in a plain grey frock, which hung on her narrow frame like a sack from a carcass.

'When we get back to the store, you'd best put yourself in a tub of hot water, and the rags from your back into the rubbish bin!' Emma told her. 'Make no mistake about it, Nelly . . . it's been the devil's own job talking you out of *this* one. If you don't curb that temper of yours, Lord only knows what'll become of you.' Emma was anxious that Nelly fully understand the seriousness of her short temper and complete lack of respect for authority. 'You *do* understand what I'm saying, don't you, Nelly?' she asked.

'O' course I do!' retorted Nelly. 'Stop bleedin' well nagging me. Look here, Emma darlin' . . . if I was ter promise yer that I won't be goaded into fighting again, will that do?'

'It'd be a *start* at least,' conceded Emma, 'as long as it doesn't go the way of all your other promises of a similar nature.'

'Oh, stop worrying, Emma,' Nelly chided, 'it'll be all right, you'll see. When I feel meself heading for trouble, I'll count ter ten . . . how's that, eh?' She didn't wait for an answer, but launched into a tuneful whistling of a bawdy tavern-song. Emma shook her head in exasperation. It was no use! Nelly was her own master, and wouldn't be shaped by any other hand, however loving and well meaning it was. 'Come on,' Emma hurried along, 'let's get you home before the preacher hears what tune you're whistling.'

'The divil himself can hear what tune I'm whistling,' replied Nelly, 'and it won't bother me none at all!' Whereupon she resumed the bawdy tune with even more gusto.

As it happened, 'the divil himself' was listening, in the form of Foster Thomas. It was still very early in the morning, the hour when most folks were only just beginning to stir on to the streets. An hour that Emma had chosen well for her errand, because the last thing she wanted was for Nelly to be paraded along the street and to be subjected to people's unkind stares. There had been enough talk as it was: with Nelly choosing to roll about in the dust with Rita Hughes, and to attack her with a pitch-fork, in full view of those guests who were loyal enough to Roland Thomas to attend his wedding. It was planned that it should be a quiet affair, which, in spite of the fracas later caused by the caustic remark made by the blacksmith's daughter combined with Nelly's short temper, had been carried off extremely well. It had delighted Emma to learn that both she and Mr Thomas had a number of genuine supporters.

Little had changed since Emma had been made Mrs Thomas, and subsequently, a 'free' woman. She wore a gold band on her finger; she entered into deep and far-reaching plans for business expansion with her husband; she walked to the church with him on a Sunday, arm-in-arm, and was dutiful as a wife to all intents and purposes. Yet there was no other physical contact between them. Each made no demands on the other. Emma could not bring herself to address him as any other than 'Mr Thomas', as she had done for so long. And the

87

one large bedroom had been divided in two, by means of placing a wardrobe down the middle.

Emma had taken over the duties of housekeeper from Rita Hughes, and a young lad had been taken on to help about the stores and warehouse. Already Emma had been instrumental in securing a more satisfactory warehouse along Cliff Street, and talks were underway to contract a sea-going vessel and reliable crew to run trading goods all along the coast. All in all, the arrangement between Emma and Roland Thomas was proving to be most satisfactory.

In the five weeks following the wedding ceremony, nothing had been seen of Foster Thomas, and no word of his whereabouts was ever heard. Emma hoped he might have crawled into some God-forsaken corner to rot away, but she suspected he had not, for creatures of his sort seemed always to survive, albeit by their predatory nature. She suspected also that, if any one person might know where he was, it would be Rita Hughes who, Emma knew, was besotted with the worthless fellow.

*   *   *

'Back! Get back, you fool . . . outta sight!' Foster Thomas gripped his fingers tight about the arm of his companion before, with an angry snarl, he swiftly drew her into the shadows. 'She mustn't see me,' he hissed through gritted teeth, 'not *yet* anyway . . . not until I'm good and ready!' There was no mistaking the loathing in his eyes, as he ran them over the upturned face of Rita Hughes. Slowly, his eyes narrowed to thin, cruel slits as he raised a finger and drew it along the angry red weal that ran from the corner of his mouth, then down over his neck to the tip of his shoulder blade. 'So! They think they have cheated me, do they? Well, let them think it! But I'll have what's mine. One way or another, I'll have what's mine.' When he glanced down at her, with the fury alive in his eyes, Rita Hughes was forced to ask herself whether she was doing the right thing in hiding him. When he had turned up some twenty-four hours earlier, there had been no question in her mind that she must help him because wasn't it true that they had cheated him, and that the news of his father's wedding had been a terrible shock. Now, though, she began to wonder just what manner of revenge he intended, and for the first time, she was afraid. Yet, amidst her fears she was filled with a love and longing for him so desperate that she could never refuse him anything! All the same, when he watched Emma out of sight, his eyes following her every move, she wished she could turn from him. But she could not. When he began murmuring in a strange and fearful voice, 'I mean to have *everything* . . . everything that belongs to me!' she knew she would do all she could to help him. Foster Thomas sensed his power over her; sensed it and revelled in it. Yet he was careful not to disclose the fact that, when he vowed to get back *everything* that belonged to him . . . it included Emma. It must include Emma, above all else, because no other woman would do. Emma might have taken his own father for her husband, but she was *his*. When the time was right, he would claim her. But he would need to be devious, and ruthless. That did not bother him. What bothered him was how, when it became necessary, he would discard Rita Hughes, for she was besotted, he knew. No matter, he would use her, like he would use others; when they were of no more use, he would employ whatever means he could to dispose of them. In the depths of his dark and treacherous mind, Foster Thomas had begun a particular train of thought with Rita Hughes foremost in his thinking. It ended with another image looming large. The image was that of Nelly, and with it Foster Thomas saw an easier way to Emma, and to all that had been taken from him. The plan was already forming in his mind. It gave him pleasure and, when he chuckled aloud, Rita Hughes gave a shiver. But when he grabbed her and took her in a passionate kiss, all her doubts melted away. He only had to ask, and she would do anything for him.

*   *   *

'Yer a good friend ter me, darlin' . . . and I don't deserve it.' Nelly was getting ready for bed and Emma had brought her a number of garments chosen from her own wardrobe. These she laid across the back of the cane stand-chair, while Nelly slipped into her nightgown and got into bed. 'How can I repay you, gal?' she asked.

'You just keep your nose clean, and work towards your ticket-of-leave,' Emma told Nelly, 'that's all I ask of you.' She sat down on the edge of the bed, her clear grey eyes roving over that bright, impish face which she loved dearly. 'I'll help you all I can, Nelly . . . you know that, don't you? When I go to England, I want to take you with me. We've been through so much together, Nelly . . . you and I.'

Of a sudden Emma fell into a deep silence and Nelly suspected that she was thinking of a particular night when the two of them had been bundled into a prisoners' waggon, and Emma's newborn daughter had been left behind. Now, when the tears began tumbling down Emma's sad face, Nelly was quickly beside her, her arms about her friend and the tears moist in her own eyes. 'Aw, Emma darlin' . . . let the past go, why don't yer? Please . . . let it go, or it'll tear yer apart.'

Emma was crying softly, and when she turned to look at Nelly, the pain was heavy in her anguished eyes. 'Oh Nelly, she was so beautiful . . . mine and Marlow's daughter.' A faint smile passed over her lovely face as she said, 'How like Marlow she was with that rich, black hair . . . so tiny she was, so very lovely. Oh, Nelly, *why* did she have to die? How could the Lord be so cruel as to punish an innocent babe for *my* sins?'

Emma was sobbing now, and as Nelly held her fast in her arms, she was smitten with guilt. All these years she had let Emma believe, beyond a shadow of doubt, that the child had been lifeless when it had rolled into the gutter. How could she tell Emma otherwise, when even the slightest hope that the child was alive would have made her exile even more of a nightmare!

Nelly was not certain. She could never be certain, because the lamplight had thrown strange shadows on the cobbles that night, and the darkness had been filled with all manner of sounds. But Nelly recalled that, as the waggon sped away to the ship which would take them to the other side of the world, an old tramp seemed to collect Emma's child into her shawl. The child made the crying sound of all newborns. She hadn't told Emma then, and she was afraid to tell her now, for fear Emma would never forgive her. And, anyway, it was far too late now. Far too late! Too much water had gone under the bridge, and there was no turning back. Besides which, it was more than likely that, even if Emma's child had lived on that night, she wouldn't have survived long. It was a sorry thing, but a true one nevertheless.

Part Two

England 1874

Old Hatreds

Repent not you that you shall lose your friend
And he repents not that he pays your debt;
For, if the Jew do cut but deep enough,
I'll pay it instantly with all my heart.
                    Shakespeare, *Merchant of Venice*

Chapter Four

'Stop thief!' The shrill cry of alarm rang through
Blackburn Market Place and, instantly, all eyes
were turned in one direction. What they saw was a
well-built young woman bedecked in a burgundy
outfit of ribbons and velvet, with a fur-trimmed
cape and extravagant bonnet, and beside her a boy
of some ten years old, both shocked and the one
attempting to console the other. From their dress,
their manner, and the way in which the woman
tenderly sobbed into her silken handkerchief, it
was obvious to one and all that they were gentry-
folk. 'See!' cried the woman, waving her
handkerchief in the direction of a small, dark-
haired waif who was making good her escape.
'*There* she is! Stop her, somebody . . . she stole my
purse!'

'Why! That's Molly!' one stall-holder cried. ' 'Er
as belongs ter the tramp!'

'You *know* the thief?' Martha Trent was
sufficiently recovered to confront the burly fellow,
her expression one of disbelief and outrage. 'Then
you must inform the authorities at once. The
ragamuffin must be brought before them . . . put
away until she learns her lesson! She had my purse,
I tell you!'

'That don't surprise me none,' replied the burly
stall-holder, grinning through the gaps in his
blackened teeth. 'What *do* surprise me, lady . . . is
that you knew about it. What! I've known that little
bugger steal the baccy from a gentleman's pipe
when it were still in 'is mouth!' He flashed a proud

and merry glance into the crowd of gawping onlookers and, knowing the little thief as well as he did and having seen the very event he described, began roaring with laughter. 'Aye!' rejoined another. 'There ain't a pickpocket anywhere as can show *that* scallywag a thing or two . . . why, I do believe she could dodge a'tween a unsuspecting gentleman's legs an' steal the very breeches from 'is arse!'

At this the crowd erupted into tumultuous laughter, which in turn sent Martha Trent into a fit. 'Fetch a policeman, Edward!' she instructed the dark-haired boy at her side. Then, when he hesitated, she nudged him between the shoulder-blades and sent him forward a pace or two. 'Hurry up, child!' she snapped and, lifting her arm above her head, she daintily touched her fingertips over her brow. 'Oh! . . . It's all too much!' she cried, calling the boy back. 'Get me a carriage . . . take me home, quickly!' As the boy turned back and came towards his mother, an older woman in a ragged shawl appeared on the scene. She had a peculiar hopping gait as she made her way to where the boy's mother was feigning a swooning fit. At the sight of the old woman, there were a few soft remarks and a series of little sniggers.

'What's the matter, dearie?' The woman sidled up to where Martha Trent was precariously perched on an upturned orange-box. 'Been robbed, 'ave yer? By! There's some bad rascals about an' that's a fact!' She cooed, becoming agitated when there was a series of giggles from the onlookers. 'Be off with yer!' she shouted, rounding on them and making a good show of castigating them. 'Yer should be ashamed o' yerselves . . . ' 'Ere's a fine lady robbed, and there's not one o' yer fetched a bobby!' She shook her fist. She also winked her eye. In a moment, the crowd had dispersed, everybody going in separate directions and each one quietly smiling at the old woman's antics. But though she was a scoundrel, they knew that Sal Tanner was harmless enough. Since her brother Marlow had been gone these past nine years and more, the poor soul had had a hard and hungry life. Then there was another mouth to feed! One which didn't rightly belong to Sal, but which she had found in the gutter nigh on eleven years back. Right outside the prison gates, or so it was said. Old Sal had called the girl by the name of Molly, and together they haunted the alleyways of Blackburn town, foraging a living where they could and occasionally 'relieving' the gentry of their fripperies and fineries. Oh yes, canny Sal had taught the girl well, until it was hard to tell who was the better thief! Often though, when the work was about, the girl loved to toil along the canal, helping to load and offload the goods ferried about on the barges. She had a deep, natural love of the sea, and often stowed away, or scrounged a ride along the Leeds and Liverpool Canal into the big docks at Liverpool. Old Sal though would go into a frenzy, because she was fearful that Molly would be taken by the sea . . . as she truly believed her brother Marlow had been.

'Now then, dearie . . . let's get yer a carriage, eh?' Sal made to take hold of Martha Trent's arm. 'We'll 'ave yer back 'ome safe an' sound in no time at all.' She stepped closer, and as she stretched out one arm as though to assist the shocked and outraged woman, her other arm came up in a

97

crafty move to pluck the cameo brooch from the lapel of Martha Trent's fur-trimmed cape.

'I'll see my mother home, thank you.' The boy Edward had stepped between old Sal and his mother. He had seen her intention, but made no hue or cry. Instead he smiled into her wrinkled face, met her bloodshot and boozy gaze with firm, dark green eyes, and in a decisive voice that caused her to step back a pace, he said, 'The authorities can't be too far away, for they do patrol the area. Don't worry, my mother will be fine.'

'Of *course* I'll be fine!' rejoined his mother, who, at the sight of old Sal creeping up on her, had made a remarkable recovery. 'Go away, you!' she told the old woman, at the same time holding her silken handkerchief to her nose and wearing an expression of disgust. 'Get away from me!'

'Be on your way, old woman.' Of a sudden, old Sal was confronted by an elderly gentleman dressed in a dark suit and topper, and carrying a walking-stick with a horse's head handle. When he spoke, he waved the stick in the air, 'Unless you want me to summon a policeman?' he asked with a threatening air.

'Not at all, sir!' exclaimed old Sal, being cheeky enough to pat him on the arm. 'I'll be on my way this very instant!' In a minute she was hurrying away. As she went, her ears caught the gentleman's remark to the lady. 'It's Mrs Trent, isn't it . . . daughter of Caleb Crowther? You remember I was introduced to you when I visited Breckleton House last December, for business discussions with your father. Your husband was away at sea, and you were staying with your parents.'

On hearing this, old Sal was stopped in her

tracks. 'Caleb Crowther,' she muttered, turning about to look again. 'Caleb Crowther . . . hated Justice o' the Peace, eh?' And this hoity-toity lady, with her fine clothes and plump bodice . . . this was his spoiled brat of a daughter, Martha! Old Sal had no liking for the Caleb Crowthers of this world, not when they took delight at throwing her in prison so reg'lar! Oh, yes, Justice Crowther was a bad one, and no matter how many times old Sal warned little Molly against him, it could never be enough, because it was well known how he had vowed to clear the alleys and streets of 'these undesirable vagrants'.

'Yer bugger! Yer'll 'ave ter catch us first!' she chuckled now, quickly hobbling away. After turning a few more corners and making her way down an alley or two, old Sal stopped, leaning against the side of a house and taking time to catch her breath. 'Let's see what we fished from the old gent's pocket,' she murmured as, with a deep-throated chuckle, she pulled a long, thick chain of silver from the depths of her shawl. Attached to the end of the chain was a strikingly handsome silver watch, which she quickly bit against her two remaining teeth. 'Solid!' she remarked to the sky. 'That'll fetch a bob or two, an' no mistake.' Of a sudden, she gave a joyful little skip and began wending her way along the cobbles, hurrying as best she could. Her gait was markedly lopsided on account of the limp, which had been the legacy of a broken leg got from a warehouse fire some years before.

As she went on her way, old Sal Tanner could be heard muttering in that familiar manner for which she was known, ' 'E were a nice enough feller . . .

but if 'e will go about tellin' poor old folks like meself ter "Be off! Else 'e'll fetch a bobby", well . . . the bugger *deserves* 'is pocket-watch spirited away. She teks 'er chances where she finds 'em, do old Sal, an' she don't give a tinker's cuss whether it's a hoity-toity lady, a fine and dandy gentleman . . . or a dark-'aired little feller wi' a cheeky smile, an' eyes that green as they coulda' been med by the little folks.' Here she stopped and looked upwards to the cold January sky. For a moment she appeared to be turning something over in her mind. Then, having apparently reached a decision, she cocked her head to one side and laughed, 'What d'yer want ter go and give that little feller such emerald-green eyes for, eh?' Laughing louder, she shook her head from side to side and lowered her gaze to the ground. 'Gi' me a bloody shock, it did . . . 'avin' them green eyes smilin' at me . . . I thought it were the little folk come ter claim my Molly, so I did!' The merriment suddenly went from her voice and her expression grew serious as she resumed her journey once more. 'T'ain't right that folks should 'ave such green eyes! Green's the colour o' the little people . . . yer 'ave ter get their sacred permission. Oh, but 'e ain't one o' the little people. I'm sure o' that. No, 'e ain't . . . 'cause all manner o' folk 'ave green eyes. I've seen 'em, but I ain't seen none so emerald-green an 'andsome as *that* little feller's.'

In her peculiar and eccentric belief that the colour green was sacred to the 'little people' and must *never* be used or displayed without their permission, old Sal had been taken aback when young Edward Trent had smiled on her, yet, by the same token, dismissed her. She had been surprised also that, having surely seen her intention to make away with his mother's cameo brooch, he had not swiftly raised the alarm. Now there was a strange kettle o' fish, she thought . . . whoever heard of one o' the gentry having a kind heart? Well, one thing was for sure . . . that green-eyed little feller hadn't inherited his grandfather's heart! No indeed, for Caleb Crowther's black heart was unforgiving and wicked. 'To Hell wi' the bugger!' old Sal shouted out at the top of her voice. 'He'll find 'is way there one o' these fine days, an' when 'e does . . . let 'im rot, for there's nobody this side o' Hell as would lift a finger ter save 'im!' Not when he watched one of his own transported off to Australia as a convict; not when he didn't lift a finger to help the poor lass; and not when he robbed her of every last penny left to her. 'Oh, yer a bad divil, Caleb Crowther!' old Sal cried out. Afterwards she broke into her hopping gait and moved a bit swifter when she feared her voice might have carried too far.

If young Edward Trent had set old Sal to thinking deeply, so had she left a strong impression on his mind. Yet not as strong as the one left by the dark-haired waif who had robbed his mother of her purse. As the carriage took him and Martha Trent back to Breckleton House, the boy couldn't get the image of her pretty face and strikingly beautiful dark eyes out of his mind. Who was she? Why did she have to *steal?* Was the old tramp her mother . . . where did the girl live? All of these questions he might well have discussed with his mother had she been the kind of mother who was open to discussion. But she was not and though his father would have shown an interest, sadly he was away at sea. A quiet despair filled the boy's eyes as he thought more deeply of his beloved father, Silas Trent. He was away too often these days, and he missed him so. Oh, but the minute he came home, Edward intended to tell him all about the incident at the market. He didn't suppose they would go to the market again, not after today. So he might never see the girl again. Such a possibility made him sad, for he would like to talk to her, this dark-haired girl who cheekily winked at him as she fled away, clutching his mother's purse. He remembered that the big man behind the stall had called her by the name of Molly, ' 'er that belongs ter the tramp'.

For the remainder of the journey back to his grandfather Crowther's house, young Edward Trent thought of little else but the girl, Molly. A pretty girl with a pretty name who, he felt sure, he would meet again. The thought cheered him a great deal, and when his mother angrily prodded him and instructed, 'Sit up straight, Edward . . . I will *not* have you slouching when you think nobody's looking!' he stiffened his back and straightened his shoulders with a smile on his face. His mother was trying to make him feel miserable again, just like she always did when she was in a mood. But she couldn't make him feel miserable *this* time. Not when he had in mind a small, impish face with black laughing eyes and hair as dark as midnight. Molly—he would remember the name well.

*   *   *

'We did well, Molly, me little flower!' Old Sal gave a hearty chuckle and roughly grabbed the girl to her bosom where she rocked her for a moment, before thrusting her away. 'Now then . . . where we gonna hide 'em eh? Like as not, that hoity-toity lady will be spelling out both our descriptions to the bobbies at this very minute! They might come swooping down on us at any time!' Of a sudden she was frantic, rushing from one side of the miserable room to the other and flinging objects aside, then lifting up boxes and peering beneath. 'Oh gawd!' she moaned, swinging round and fixing her bloodshot eyes in a stare on to the girl's face. 'We've had it *this* time . . . I feel it in me bones, Molly darlin' . . . they'll catch us fer sure this time!'

'No, they won't,' replied the girl, taking the old one by the hand and leading her to a battered old stool, where she eased her down on to it. 'They'll not catch us, old Sal . . . 'cause we'll move house, like we've done afore!' She smiled up at the old woman with bright, wide-awake eyes and a look of mischief on her heart-shaped face and, for a fleeting moment which caught Sal Tanner unawares, Molly's dark eyes and black, unruly hair touched a memory in her old heart. A precious memory of another child who used to look up at her with the same bright smile and the very same love shining from big, black eyes. Strange, she thought now, how much this lovely child reminded her of the little lad she had had to raise when their parents had suffered a tragic death. Where was he now, her brother Marlow? Had he gone to foreign parts and made his fortune as he said he would? And had he forgotten the sister he'd left behind? Sal would never believe such a terrible thing, not of Marlow, who had always been as straight and loving as a day was long. No! He hadn't forgotten her at all. 'Twas the sea. The sea had claimed him, that was the truth of it! Why couldn't he have listened to her? How many times had she warned him not to lose his foolish heart to one o' the gentry? Time and time again she had told him that his fancy for Emma Grady would be the ruin of him! Then when Emma wed Gregory Denton and it seemed like the best thing to Sal, Marlow had nigh wasted away, pining for what could never be his. Oh, the fool . . . the bloody fool. Aye, 'twas his love for Emma Grady that had driven Marlow Tanner to travel the seas and, though the poor lass met a worse fortune at the hands of her own guardian, Caleb Crowther . . . old Sal couldn't help but hold Emma Grady partly to blame for the loss of her fine brother.

'Allus wanderin' . . . wanderin' about like lost souls we are, Molly darlin', but we'll outwit the buggers, an' that's all as matters, eh?' She was laughing now, having shaken the past away from her thoughts and brought her concentration to matters at hand. 'Get yer stuff together, gal,' she said. 'Let's be off . . . afore the sods come creepin' up on us like a plague o' rats, eh?'

In no time at all, Molly had collected the few things that she and Sal could call their own . . . two chipped enamel mugs, a small oil lamp—which also served to boil a pan on—a box of candles, two best china plates purloined from a fancy store in Manchester, together with two sets of cutlery, a wooden-handled bone comb, two grey blankets and the clothes they both stood up in. After wrapping the articles in one of the baskets, Molly slung it over her narrow shoulders and presented herself before old Sal. 'That's it,' she said, 'there ain't nothing else worth carrying away.'

'Travel light, that's the best thing ter do, me darlin',' chuckled Sal, 'then yer can tek ter yer heels if needs be, eh?' She tousled the girl's short, unkempt hair. 'Mek towards the canal, up by Angela Street,' she said, shuffling towards the door. 'Happen the landlord at the Navigation might slip us a glass o' some'at strong . . . some'at ter warm the old bones.' Then, with a crafty wink, she added, 'Like as not, we'll find us a buyer there, fer the purse and watch. I'm surprised that gentry woman only had two guineas in her purse though . . . still, it'll keep us fro' starvin' fer a while, I suppose.'

Molly nodded, thinking what a good job it was that old Sal hadn't seen her slip a *third* guinea from the purse into her pocket. She didn't like deceiving Sal in that way, but past experience had taught her that Sal's fondness for 'a jar o' the best' often left them penniless and hungry. Slipping a few coins away now and then, when they had hit lucky, was Molly's way of taking care of old Sal. The one thing that frightened the girl more than hunger or not having a roof over their heads was that the authorities might put her away. And if Justice Crowther had *his* way, she'd be rooted out for sure! Who would look after Sal then? Not the drinking cronies who cadged every last farthing from her to whet their own boozy appetites, that was for sure. And not the folks who laughed at her antics, nor them along the canal who might willingly offer a lift to Liverpool on their barges, but who would not be so willing to offer a bed and board to the likes of Sal, when they knew she could be a real handful while under the influence.

105

The girl, Molly, had known no other family than the woman they called old Sal, and she loved her with a fierce protectiveness. But, though the old woman would always hold that special place in her affections, many had been the time when Molly had craved to know who her *real* family was. During these times she had asked countless questions, to which Sal would always reply, 'Yer ain't got no family but me, child. I've telled yer afore how the little people sent yer to me . . . found yer in the gutter I did . . . wi' that very watch as yer wear round yer neck. Oh, an' yer must *never* sell that pretty trinket, Molly gal . . . not even if yer close ter starvation! It belongs ter the little folk, d'yer see? Just like *you* do!'

Molly didn't share old Sal's eccentric belief in 'the little people', mainly because she had seen no evidence of them, and perhaps because she knew instinctively that old Sal was different from most folks, in that she often lived in a strange little world of her own. The watch though, which Sal had entrusted to her, was solid and real to Molly, a link with her past and a pointer to her future, she knew. But whenever she looked at it in secret, she felt afraid. It had always remained a mystery to her. *Who* had treasured it before her? Could it possibly be her own mother, or father; or did it in fact not belong to her at all? Was it instead something that had been dropped by a stranger and come across by Sal, at the same time as Sal had come across the tiny bundle of rags that was Molly?

There were things written on that watch, things that would tell Molly of its background, if only she could understand them. But they might as well be written in Latin for all the sense they made to her, because she had never learned to read. Sal couldn't teach her, for *she* couldn't read either. Molly was desperately afraid to show the tiny, delicate watch to anyone else, lest they steal it away forever. No, she must keep it safely hidden inside her vest, touching her skin. At least until she could find a way to master the art of learning words.

'Come on, young 'un!' Old Sal had hobbled down the steps that led from the dilapidated house, and now she was standing in the backyard, making frantic efforts to put a lighted match to the baccy in her clay pipe, and loudly cursing when the cutting January breeze snuffed it out. After a while she gave up trying and rammed both matches and pipe into the pocket of her long, grubby skirt. 'Come on, come on!' she called as the girl came to the steps. 'If we don't find somewhere ter lay us heads fer the night, we'll freeze for sure!'

'You go on . . . I'll catch up in a minute, Sal,' Molly told her, turning on the top step to secure the door. 'When it's quietened down in a few days,' she called after Sal, who was already shuffling her way out into the cobbled alley, 'we might be able to come back and get the stool and a few other things.'

'Aw, bugger 'em!' yelled Sal. 'There's none o' that rubbish worth coming back fer.'

Molly didn't agree. There was the stool, a little cupboard she'd made herself out of an orange-box, and that picture of a sailing ship that she'd found aside somebody's midden. Then there was that old brass clock which had been in this derelict house when they first came here some two months ago.

107

Two months! That was the longest they'd managed to stay in one place and, even though Sal had always told her *never* to look on any place as permanent, Molly had a special feeling for this house; although it wouldn't be long now before they pulled the street down. The folks had all been moved out long since, and there was talk of a mill being built here.

As Molly closed the door and turned away to follow Sal, she made herself a promise that when it was safe she *would* come back for those things she couldn't carry now. Oh, but first they had to find somewhere to live and that wouldn't be easy.

'Where's your little people *now,* Sal?' Molly called out as she ran after the bent and ragged figure. If you're so pally with 'em . . . ask 'em to find us a place to live!' She lapsed into a fit of giggles when back came the answer, 'Don't be so cheeky, yer young bugger! Ye've got more tongue than what the cat licks its arse with!'

When the girl caught up with old Sal, she hitched up the cumbersome bundle to a more comfortable position across her shoulders and slipped her small hand into that of the woman. 'I wish we could have stayed here for a while longer,' she said wistfully, 'I liked it here.'

'Aw, bless yer 'eart, luv,' replied old Sal fondly, squeezing tight the small fingers clutched to hers. 'We'll find us a place, you'll see.' When she glanced down, it was to see a more contented look on the girl's face. What would she do without the lass, Sal thought as they trudged along towards Angela Street and the canal. The young 'un had been such a companion to her, such a comfort, and she loved the bonny lass, even if at times she were a right little sod! All the same, never a night passed that Sal didn't thank the little people for bringing her such a treasure. In the same prayer when she gave thanks, old Sal whispered a more fervent one, asking that young Molly should never be parted from her because the very thought of such a thing sent her straight for the gin bottle!

Chapter Five

At half-past four on a sultry July afternoon, Molly straightened up from her labours, wiped the sweat from her eyes with coal-smudged fingers, and leaned the shovel against the black, shiny mound of newly delivered coal. 'I think my back's broken,' she laughed.

'I'm not surprised, young 'un,' chuckled the thin, wiry fellow who had been working alongside. 'By! You've done the work o' *ten* your size, an' that's the truth on it. Call it a day . . . here.' He propped his shovel against the gas-lamp nearby, then he dipped his fingers into the pocket of a grubby cord coat which was lying beside it. 'Tek your wages and get off home,' he said, counting out a number of coins from the pocket, and placing them in Molly's outstretched hand. 'Wash that coal dust off your face an' all . . . I'm blowed if yer don't look like one o' them dark wandering minstrels.' His face creased into a grin as he regarded her more closely. She's a grand little worker, he thought, a feeling of hopelessness surging through him. He might have offered the poor little bugger a home on his barge. But she'd only grow up to be a woman. And he couldn't abide women, not at any cost! Give him a dog every time . . . they were less trouble.

Molly was more than glad to call it a day because there wasn't an inch of her body that didn't hurt. The sight of those four shilling pieces resting in the palm of her hand made her feel good inside. They were worth all the coal shovelling, and wouldn't Sal be pleased, she thought. 'Thank you kindly, Mr Entwistle,' she said, her mucky features breaking into a happy smile, and her small even teeth appearing brilliant white against the dark background.

'Bugger me, if you ain't flashing like one o' them there beacons!' chuckled the little fellow. 'You'd give anybody a real fright if they wuz to meet you down a dark alley, an' that's a fact!' He was still chuckling as Molly put away her shovel on the barge and went on her way, whistling a merry tune.

*　　　*　　　*

' 'Ow much did 'e pay yer, gal?' Sal wanted to know. 'An' don't expect any tea, 'cause I ain't got no money!' she grumbled, before Molly could answer her question.

'We shall both have us tea,' Molly retorted good-humouredly, 'because Mr Entwistle paid me *four whole shillings.*'

'*Four* . . . Well, the mean old sod!' Sal had been sitting on the bank with her cumbersome skirt drawn up to her knees and her legs dangling towards the canal water some three feet further down. In a minute she was scrambling up to confront Molly with a look of disgust on her face.

'Ye mean ter tell me as the bugger had yer working all day . . . an' only paid yer *four* shillings?' She shook her fist in the air and took Molly by the shoulder. 'You come wi' me, lass,' she exclaimed, beginning to propel the girl at a smart pace towards the ramshackle wooden hut which they had commandeered as a home. 'Get thi' face washed an mek yerself look respectable, 'cause we're gonna have a few words with your Mr Entwistle!' She gave a loud hiccup and excused herself most profoundly. 'I ain't been drinking, neither!' she bluntly informed the amused Molly. 'So don't think I *have!*' Whereupon she promptly lost her footing and grabbed at Molly for support.

'Oh, Sal . . . as if I would,' said Molly with mock seriousness. 'O' course you haven't been drinking. You told me yourself that we can't have anything to eat, because there's no money. And, if there's no money for food, then there's no money for booze . . . ain't that right?' With Sal's fingers clutching her shoulder tightly, and having to pick her way carefully over the rubble and boulders strewn hereabouts, Molly couldn't afford to glance up at Sal's face, but she felt Sal's round violet eyes turned on her. 'I think Mr Entwistle paid me a good day's wage,' she said. 'He's a nice fella . . . and he always has a good word to say about *you.*' At once, she was brought to a halt.

'About *me?*' Sal demanded, a little smile teasing the corners of her mouth. 'What does he know about me, eh? I don't know the bloke . . . do I?' Her deep, ruddy forehead was creased into a multitude of wrinkles as she struggled to place the name in her mind. 'How come this Mr Entwistle knows me, eh?' She was puzzled. 'An' where might

111

I have made the fella's acquaintance, I wonder?'

'I don't know, but he mentioned summat about a public house,' lied Molly, manufacturing a suitable expression of bewilderment. 'I *think* it was the Sun.'

'Naw, I don't fancy that place too often these days . . . not since the landlord said I were blind drunk and fit fer nowt but causing trouble.' Sal gave a little chuckle, before resuming a serious face. 'Well . . . I might a' been just a *bit* tipsy . . . but there were no call fer the bugger ter set his dog on me!' She fixed her round, marble eyes on Molly's upturned face and, even though they were shot through with tiny pink blood vessels and appeared vague from drinking, Molly thought what a pretty violet colour they were. 'The Swan!' Sal exclaimed, seeming pleased with herself. 'I bet it were the *Swan* 'e were talking about. What do he look like, this fella?' When Molly gave a deliberately inaccurate description, for fear that Sal might still track him down and cause a rumpus, she jubilantly slapped Molly on her back, and grinned broadly, saying, 'There! I've a feeling I know the bloke . . . played cards with him, I expect. And, who knows, it's likely we've supped many a pint together!' She put her hands on her hips and surveyed Molly in the closest manner. 'Yer an ungrateful child!' she scolded in her most serious voice, broken by a series of loud hiccups. 'Four shillings is a very *generous* wage! An' I'll thank you not to call a drinking pal o' mine a "mean old sod". I'm surprised at you, Molly gal. C'mon . . . get orf home an' clean yerself up. Then we'll away ter the Navigation fer a pie and a pint. We'll mek a little hole in Mr Entwistle's four shillings, eh?' She laughed, swaying until Molly was sure she'd fall over.

As they wended their way along the canal bank towards the hut, Molly kept tight hold of old Sal's hand, because the way the old one was swaying and stumbling, it was likely that she'd lose her balance at any minute. When she did, and the two of them ended up fighting to stay upright, Sal erupted in a fit of cackling and shouting. 'Did yer see that, young 'un?' she laughed, setting her booted foot forward again. 'Yer nearly went arse over tip an' dragged ol' Sal with yer! I reckon you've been at the gin bottle, yer little sod!'

Molly felt herself coming out in a cold sweat when she thought how Sal had been sitting over the canal bank, with her legs dangling down. It was painfully obvious that she'd been drinking, after she'd promised *not* to! What will I do with her, agonised Molly as she took a tighter hold of Sal's meandering figure. Get her back to the hut, and get her to sleep it off, that's what! Oh, and what a good job she'd had wit enough to mislead her about poor Mr Entwistle, for Molly was well pleased with her wage and she knew it to be fair. Besides which, if Sal had gone back and caused trouble, he might not have given her any more work, and that would have been a bad thing because honest work was getting harder and harder to come by.

The hut which was now home to Sal and Molly was situated at the widest area of grassy bank, and was half hidden in the undergrowth. There was a tall stone wall immediately behind, and directly behind that, the vicarage. This fact had given old Sal a great deal of pleasure as she told one and all:

113

'What more could a body want, eh? . . . I've got the ale house down one end, and the vicar at the other. If I'm tekken bad after a jolly night out, I have only ter whistle and the vicar'll come a'runnin' with his Bible. He'll get me ter the gates o' Heaven right enough. Drunk or sober, the good Lord won't turn me away, I'm thinking!'

When they had first come across the dilapidated workmen's hut, there were chinks between the weathered boarding 'wide enough ter drive a horse and cart through', as Sal had complained. Now, however, the chinks were stuffed with moss which Molly had painstakingly gathered, and the wind couldn't force its way in so easily. On a hot day like today, though, the air inside the cramped hut was stifling. 'Bloody hell, lass . . . prop that door open with some'at!' instructed Sal as she fell on to the narrow bed, this being a scrounged mattress set on four orange-boxes, the whole length of which swayed and creaked beneath Sal's sudden weight.

In no time at all, Molly had filled the pan from the wooden rain-bucket by the door, and brought it slowly to the boil on the oil-lamp. She might have brought some wood and lit the rusty old stove, but it was such a lengthy palaver and, anyway, it was too hot a day. When the water had boiled, Molly tipped a spoonful of tea-leaves into each of the two cups, put three spoons of sugar into both and topped them up with the boiling water. She threw out the milk, which had gone sour. 'Come on, Sal,' she said, fetching one of the cups to where Sal was lying flat on her back, 'you'll feel better when you've had a sup of hot tea.'

'Is there milk in it?' came a muffled voice from beneath a tangled shawl.

114

'No. It was sour, so I threw it out.'

'Then I ain't having none!' came the surly reply. Molly knew there was no point in trying to persuade her.

'I'll go to Angela Street and get a gill from the shop,' she promised, returning the cup of hot tea to the floor beside the oil-lamp.

'Go on then, and be sharp about it,' Sal muttered, 'me tongue's hanging out.'

Quickly, Molly took up the pan and went running along the canal. It took only a few minutes to arrive at the shop in Angela Street. It was a quaint little place, filled with shelves of all manner and description, and these in turn were filled with jars, tins and other miscellaneous items. Above the wooden counter hung small hams and strings of onions; on the counter were placed huge cheeses and fresh baked loaves of bread; behind the counter stood a short sturdy woman with a broad, welcoming smile and a white floppy mob-cap on her rolled-up grey hair. She wore a severe black dress with starched white collar and cuffs, and the bodice pulled in so tight at the waist that the poor woman had a permanent red face.

'Well!' she exclaimed, on seeing Molly's black face and generally unkempt appearance. 'You look like you've been up the chimney and no mistake!' She kept smiling all the same and took the pan which Molly offered. 'Milk, is it?' she asked. Molly politely requested her to pour in a gill, 'if you wouldn't mind, please . . . and a loaf of bread, with a pat of best butter.' It was done in a minute; the pennies were paid and Molly hurried back to the hut. Sal was fast asleep and snoring loudly, and Molly left her to it. 'The best thing you can do is sleep it off, Sal,' she told her fondly, at the same time perching on the stool which she'd rescued from their previous home, gratefully sipping her tea.

Some time later, Molly went down to the canal and refilled her pan. The month of July had been a dry one and she didn't want to waste good rain-water on washing. When the water had boiled, she mixed it with a pan of cold water in a tin bowl; she stripped off her dress and undergarments, washed herself first and after dipped the clothes. Next, she laid them over the stool and put the stool outside in the sun. Then, very carefully, so as not to wake her, she climbed in beside old Sal. When a long scrawny arm reached out to enfold her, Molly snuggled into it. She was aching all over, and she was suddenly tired. That coal shovelling was hard work, but it wouldn't stop her from turning up tomorrow. Mr Entwistle would probably be laid up till Monday, but there might be other work to be found. If not, tomorrow was Sunday, and that was the day when most of the gentry took to strolling about in Corporation Park up on the hill. If there was no work to be had along the wharf, it was likely there might be a fat wallet or two just waiting to be separated from its owner. At one time, Molly had told Sal how she thought it was wrong to steal on a Sunday because when, out of curiosity she had taken a peep inside the church, there were 'all these grim-faced folk sitting there, and a preacher in a long black frock with beads round his waist, talking to the folk in a terrible frightening voice!'

Molly had never forgotten how he had warned that Sunday was the Lord's Day and a day when all sinners should repent or go to Hell. It had been a

116

glorious summer's day one minute and the next, in the very moment when he bellowed out in that fearful voice, the sky went black and there was a terrible clap of thunder. 'The devil's coming for me, Sal,' Molly had run home to tell her with big shocked eyes, 'the preacher's sent him!'

'Is that right, Molly lass?' Sal had asked with a laugh and a twinkle in her eye. 'Well, the bugger'll have ter get past me afore he gets ter you! An' he won't be the *first* divil I've sent packin' . . . nor will he be the last!' But, seeing that young Molly was not convinced, she went on in great detail about how 'the preacher were warning the folk in the church . . . them with their fancy frocks an' pretty bonnets . . . 'cause its folks wi' money as do the most sinning. An' don't you worry none about the divil chasin' yer, Molly lass . . . 'cause the Lord looks after them as looks after themselves. 'That's what *we* do, lass, you an' me . . . we look after us selves. Ain't that right?' Molly couldn't deny it, so she told the Lord that very night, 'I hope them rich folk stop their sinnin' Lord. Me and Sal, we'll go on looking after ourselves, and thank you kindly.' Sal thoroughly approved. 'That's the way, darlin',' she cackled, 'y'see . . . we're doin' these rich folks a favour when all's said an' done. The more money we can relieve 'em of . . . the less likely they are to be sinnin' with it!' And Molly's admiration of old Sal was increased tenfold.

*   *   *

Saturday night saw most hard-working folk hereabouts heading in the direction of the nearest ale house, the Navigation. It was across from the canal bank at the top of Angela Street and it was from there that the jolliest and loudest accordion music emanated, telling its tale up and down the canal and bringing the bargees from their cabins.

'D'yer hear *that,* me darlin'?' chuckled Sal, a deep grin lighting up her wrinkled face, and her feet giving a little joyful skip as she swung from the mattress. 'You stay an' get yer sleep,' she told Molly with a crafty look. 'That coal shovellin' fair wore you out, I know.'

In a minute, Molly had got from the bed and collected her dry clothes from outside. 'I'm coming with you,' she informed Sal, and Sal knew from that determined look on Molly's small face that it was no use arguing.

'All right then, young 'un.' She fetched her flat neb-cap from its nail behind the door and rammed it over her grey wispy hair. 'But I want none of yer naggin', like last time! We've a few bob in us purse, an' I mean ter have a pleasant pint . . . an' happen a game o' cards.' She hurried out of the hut, leaving Molly to close the door and secure it. 'Follow me if yer must. But yer ain't telling *me* what I should an' shouldn't do!'

Molly stayed a small distance behind as Sal's bent and untidy figure scurried away in her odd, dipping gait. Every now and then she would pull the long shawl about her and make sure her flat cap was secure on her head; all of her sharp jerky actions betrayed her frustration that Molly was on her heels and, before the evening was out, would no doubt remind her that playing cards was a fool's game. Had Sal forgotten how she lost her lovely barge through playing cards? Forgotten! Sal hated being reminded of it. How could she forget? *How*

118

would she ever forget losing the barge that had been a treasured home to her and Marlow all those years? She *couldn't* forget, and she had no intention of doing so. But, she did intend winning it back, an' *that* was a fact! It was only a matter of time, that was all. A matter of time.

Molly had grown wise to Sal's moods and tantrums, so she intended to tackle the subject from a new angle, although she hoped it would still get the message across. The opportunity presented itself when a big chestnut cob went by on the towpath, pulling behind it a brightly painted barge, with a swarthy-looking fellow at the tiller, whistling a jolly tune. 'Evenin' to yer,' he called when he saw the two figures hurrying in the direction of the Navigation. 'Lookin' ter cool yerself down and wet yer whistle at the same time, eh?' he laughed.

'T'ain't no business o' yourn if we are!' Sal retorted, jerking her shawl over her shoulders and beginning to mutter to herself. The man took no offence, for he knew of old Sal and her misfortunes. 'Take care o' yerself, Sal,' he called out, 'an' mind out for the young 'un.'

At the last minute before he disappeared away round the curve in the canal, Sal thought better of her surly mood and came to the water's edge to shout after him: 'Thank you very much, bless yer. An' you mind how yer go, me darlin'!' Whereupon, seeing him wave an acknowledgement, Sal caught Molly into her shawl, saying with a little laugh, 'See that, Molly? . . . We've still got a few friends, you an' me, eh?'

Molly saw her chance. 'What's it like, living on a barge, Sal?' she asked, looking up with round innocent eyes. She was secretly pleased when Sal

119

took the bait.

'What's it like? Oh, it's *grand*, Molly lass . . . right grand! There's no better life in this 'ere world than rovin' the waterways in yer own barge . . . wi' yer own pots an' pans an' the treasures about yer.' Of a sudden, her eyes grew sad and a look of nostalgia came into her weathered old face. 'The good Lord shoulda struck me dead fer losin' that grand old barge,' she murmured. Molly was hopeful that Sal would not be tempted to go gambling tonight.

Having arrived at the Navigation on Mill Hill, Molly took her place on the flagstones beneath the window of the snug. 'Shall I look after some of yer money?' she asked of Sal. 'There might be pickpockets and ruffians about tonight.'

'Don't you worry yer little head about *my* purse, Molly lass,' protested Sal, with an impatient wag of her finger. 'Yer talkin' to the best pickpocket an' ruffian in the whole o' Lancashire!' With that, she disappeared inside. A few moments later, the window of the snug was slid up and out came two hands, with a small jug of sarsaparilla and a pork pie. 'Get that down yer, lass,' Sal's ruddy face appeared, 'an' if yer little arse goes ter sleep on them cold flagstones, get yersel' off home. I can find my own way later.'

'Oh aye!' came a man's cheery voice from inside. 'An' 'appen thi' can . . . straight into the bloody cut!' There erupted a roar of appreciative laughter, as Sal promptly told Molly, 'P'raps ye'd best wait fer me after all. When I go ter Paradise, it'll be downing a bucket o' best ale, not a belly full o' canal water!'

''Course I'll wait.' Molly had no intention of

going back to the hut without Sal.

'Yer a good 'un,' Sal told her, as she handed over the stone jug and the pork pie. There came another wave of laughter as she added with a chuckle, 'Enjoy yer meal, Molly lass. An' don't forget to thank the gentry fer it!'

Molly settled down as the window was slid shut above her. She wondered what kind of meal the same 'gentry' might be settling down to this very evening. 'Best roast, all steaming and crackly,' she said softly to herself. 'And the finest port in fancy glasses.' All manner of images conjured themselves up in her imaginative mind: one was of a long, polished table and little servants in smart, black frocks with white collars and cuffs, starched so stiff they dare hardly move for fear of cutting themselves. She'd heard folks talking about the gentry, and Molly didn't care much for what she heard. As she bit into the hot, succulent pork pie with its fine flaky pastry, she wondered whether, if one of them should turn up now and offer to change places, she might be tempted. The answer was no! She and Sal hadn't got much, it was true. But they'd got each other, and they didn't go in for lying and cheating, the way folks claimed the gentry did. It was said that the gentry would even rob their own kind if there was a profit to be made. Well, that wasn't the way with proper folk! If one of the gentry was to show his face here and now, Molly would tell it to be off, and no mistake!

There was one, though, that she might exchange a few kindly words with, and that was the boy in the market yesterday. The boy with dark hair and friendly green eyes, whose mammy she had robbed. Molly felt no remorse about taking the

121

woman's purse, because she had seen how that woman had harshly treated the boy when he had accidentally stepped on her expensive boots. Molly's attention had been drawn by the awful fuss Martha Trent made and, feeling upset for the poor boy, had given his mammy the chance to make a fuss for a different reason by stealing her purse. Molly was not sorry about that at all. But she was worried that she wasn't able to get to know the boy. He looked so nice, so friendly, and when he saw her cheeky wink, Molly was sure that he had tried not to laugh. She liked him, but she didn't suppose she would ever see him again. Even if she *did,* it would be safer for her and Sal to keep well out of sight—especially since Sal had told her that the boy's grandfather was Justice Caleb Crowther. *That* fellow wanted her put away, and though Molly wasn't afraid of much else, other than her darling Sal falling into the canal on a dark night, she was afraid of this Justice Crowther, for it was well known that he was a bad and cruel man, with a particular hatred for bargees, poor folk, and for what he scornfully called 'alley urchins'.

Molly took pleasure from her memory of the boy, yet she felt awfully sorry that he had been cursed with such a man for his grandfather, while she had been blessed with someone like Sal to look after her. But then Molly giggled as she dwelled on that a bit longer, because she wasn't rightly sure whether Sal looked after *her* . . . or whether she looked after *Sal.* 'It's a bit o' both,' she decided at length, taking a healthy bite out of the pie and afterwards enjoying a great nose-tickling gulp of sarsaparilla. 'We look after each other, so we do!'

'Hello, Sal, I ain't seen you in a long time. How's the world treating you, eh?' Sal had turned from the bar with her gill of frothed-up ale, and had almost collided with a thick-set fellow with big, bushy brows and a 'tache which drooped from either side of his top lip to the bottom of his chin, where the ends met to form a closed circle. Sal recognised him as a pal of Marlow's who had deserted these parts for a merry widow, some ten years before. 'Where's Marlow, then?' continued the fellow, stretching his neck and looking about, then, seeing no sign of Sal's brother, he brought his soft, brown eyes to look down quizzically at her. 'The widder got fed up, and threw me out of the door,' he said casually. 'It seems my charm wore off. I got back last night . . . staying in lodgings till I get work and a place of my own. Where is he then, eh? . . . Where's that brother of yourn? If I remember rightly, I owe the bugger a drink.' Here, he threw back his head and laughed aloud. 'He warned me the widder would chuck me out afore she'd wed me. And he were right. I shoulda' listened to him. He always were a sensible bloke.'

Sal appeared upset by the fellow's remarks; his reference to Marlow being 'a sensible bloke' had cut deep. It was true. Of the two of them, *she* had always been the one to get them in trouble, and Marlow the one to get them out of it. Whatever would he have thought about her gambling their barge away? God forbid that he should ever find out; although it wouldn't matter so much if she was to win it back. Oh, but he was gone for good! Marlow wasn't coming back, or she would have had a sign of it before now. The sea had taken him, she felt it in her bones. Emma Grady had driven him to sail the seven seas, and he was lost. Gone forever, and Sal's heart broken because of it.

To hear this fellow talk so fondly of the darling brother she'd lost put Sal in a bitter frame of mind. When she answered him now, it was with a sharp and dismissive tongue. 'Get outta my way,' she told him, clutching her gill of ale and nudging her way past him by the use of her elbows. 'Marlow's gone. 'E's *gone*, d'yer hear? An' he ain't *never* comin' back!' She then sat in the corner sulking, but by the time she'd supped the last dregs of ale from the jug, she was softly crying and muttering aloud, 'Damn and rot every gentry there ever was! Where the bloody hell are yer, Marlow Tanner? An' where's that gormless dog o' yourn, that yer left be'ind ter look after me?' Sal had searched far and wide for Marlow's bull mastiff. But she had never found it after it ran off some three years back. 'I expect it's gone the same way as Marlow,' she cried into her glass, 'an' I shall never see *either* of 'em agin!'

'Cheer up, old un, things are never as bad as they seem.' There was a fine-looking fellow with a spotted scarf about his neck, seated at a table nearby, and he had watched Sal for some time, feeling downright sorry for anybody who could be so miserable about supping a jug of best ale. He had mentioned to another fellow the surprising fact of a woman being admitted into the bar. Straightaway he had been told that Sal Tanner was always the exception, 'being one o' the lads, so to speak'. He was also enlightened as to Sal's misfortunes, in first having her brother leave to

124

make his fortune in foreign parts, and so it now seemed, to have lost his life in the process. 'Marlow Tanner would never have deserted his sister on purpose, you can rely on it!' Then, as if that wasn't enough, Sal had taken very strongly to gambling, and just as folks predicted, she had come up against a better player than herself and lost all her possessions. 'That barge had been in the Tanner family for *generations*. Oh, I can tell you, if Marlow's ghost ever did come back to these parts, it would haunt old Sal to her grave . . . and rightly so, if you ask me!' The fellow was most unsympathetic to Sal Tanner's plight, 'seeing as she brought it on herself. Then, to top it all, she comes back from a hanging with a newborn child that somebody left by the wayside . . . Some whore dropped it there to be rid on it, I expect.' Here he chuckled quietly, after looking to make sure that Sal wasn't listening because he knew well enough that she had a vicious temper when put out. 'Sal reckons the infant was put there by "the little people" . . . for her to raise . . . as a punishment and a burden for her sins.'

The fellow with the spotted scarf took a more sympathetic view of Sal Tanner's troubles, having always had his own fair share. 'Let me get you another gill,' he offered, leaning over to pat her fondly on the arm and to smile at her with bright blue eyes.

'Yer what?' It was a long time since any stranger had shown a kindness to Sal, and though it made her suspicious, it also cheered her no end. 'Offerin' me a drink, is it, eh?' she asked, her head cocked to one side and her violet eyes twinkling. Of a sudden she was roaring with laughter, then she became

125

quiet and intimate in her manner. ' 'Ere . . . d'yer have a fancy for me?' she said in a low, excited voice. 'Got an urge ter tek me ter bed, have yer?' It was ages since any man had laid her down, and the thought of a tumble had her all excited. 'It'll cost yer a bit *more* than one gill though, me darlin',' she finished with a chuckle and a suggestive wink.

'Don't be so bloody daft, woman!' The poor fellow was shocked. 'I'm offering you a drink out of the goodness of my heart! Whatever gave you the idea that I'd want to take an old soak like you to bed?'

Sal was on her feet in a minute, sleeves rolled up and looking for a fight. *'Old?'* she demanded. *'Old!'* . . . You listen ter me, matey! I'm never old . . . Ask anybody in this bar. They'll tell yer as I'm not much above forty . . . an' I'll warrant you yourself is already long past *that*, yer cheeky sod!

'Oh well, pardon me,' replied the fellow with a crafty wink at one and all, 'but you look nearer *eighty!'* At this, everybody there roared their approval . . . with the exception of Sal; however, she did see the funny side to it. What an old fool she was, to think any man could take a fancy to her. Them days were long gone, she was sad to say. 'Ere then!' She banged her empty jug on the table in front of him. 'Fill it up. If yer don't want ter *tickle* me whistle . . . yer can *wet* the bugger instead!' There then followed a great wave of laughter, and various shouts of 'Good ol' Sal!'

' 'Ave a gill on *me,* an' all, luv.'

Sal took up the offers, and soon she was in high spirits, doing a jig on the bar and showing one and all that she had 'a good pair o' legs on me yet'!

Outside in the growing dusk, young Molly was

excited by the feverish hand-clapping and the merry music, and she wished she was old enough to go in and join them. 'It sounds like Sal won't be able to put one foot afore the other when they chuck her out,' she murmured, tapping her feet to the jollity and watching with interest as an old man shuffled by. He had a partly bald head with isolated tufts of grey hair, a long, unkempt beard, and a gaudy, green waistcoat some two sizes too small for his podgy chest. His jacket and trousers were an odd match; the trouser legs stopped short of his ankles and the hem of the jacket came down to his knees. In the light emanating from the pub windows, Molly recognised him as old Gabe Drury, a long-time and loyal friend of Sal's. 'Hello, Mr Drury,' she called out as he was about to disappear into the pub doorway, his legs being the worse for drink and his eyesight somewhat blurred. He reached out both arms to steady himself against the door pillars while he focused on the source of the greeting.

'Well, if it ain't young Molly . . . Sal Tanner's little 'un. Inside, is she?' he asked. When Molly replied that yes, she was inside, he laughed aloud, saying, 'I shoulda' known. The music's allus loudest when Sal Tanner's around.' After a concentrated effort, he manoeuvred himself inside and was gone from Molly's sight. In a moment though, her interest was taken up by the arrival of a two-horse carriage, which drew up some small distance away. In the growing darkness, Molly could see very little of its occupants, although there looked to be two of them, and one appeared to be wearing a top hat. It was a grand sort of carriage, thought Molly, her interest aroused. The kind only used by toffs and the like. She was about to get to her feet and maybe sneak a closer look, when the carriage door was flung open, and out climbed . . . not a toff, but an ordinary-looking fellow with a flat cap on his head and a look of slyness about him. When he came so close to her that she could have reached out and touched him, Molly was taken aback because, in spite of his common clothes and the way he pretended to swagger as if he'd had a drink or two, Molly was convinced that he was neither drunk nor ordinary.

Puzzled by such strange antics, Molly watched him go into the pub, then craned her neck to see whether the carriage might now pull away. But it didn't. Instead, the gent with the top hat seemed to slink deeper into his seat and all was deathly quiet from that quarter.

Molly was so intrigued now that, first of all, she got to her tiptoes and took a peep through the window of the bar. There in the farthest corner was the strange man, his eyes staring at a group of men some three tables away, one being Gabe Drury, who appeared to be holding a few boozy regulars entranced by the story he was telling. Then, even as Molly was taking stock of the man, he got up from his seat and moved to within an arm's reach of Gabe Drury, afterwards conversing with him and showing great interest in every word the old man said.

Turning her attention back to the carriage, Molly had the feeling that even while *she* was watching the fellow in the pub, the other fellow in the carriage . . . the toff, was watching *her*. It was all a strange to-do, and Molly became even more curious. Pretending to look away, she made as

128

though to saunter along in the opposite direction; when she was hidden in shadows, she quickly doubled back and crept along by the canal wall, coming up on the carriage without being seen. But if Molly thought she might get a better look at the gentry inside, she was mistaken, because his face was deep within the dark recesses of the carriage, and he turned his head neither one way or another, so intent was he on keeping his gaze fixed on the pub doorway.

Molly had no intention of giving up though, and, in a minute, she was boldly tapping on the carriage window. 'Hello, mister,' she called out, even beginning to move the handle which would open the door, 'got a shilling, have you?'

At once the driver had swung down from his seat. 'Clear off,' he warned Molly, 'else I'll take my horse-whip to your backside!' However he wasn't quick enough to stop Molly from flinging wide the carriage-door. At the same instant, an arm reached out from inside with the intention of quickly closing the door again, just as the driver was bearing down on Molly. At once, before the flesh might be flayed from her legs, she sprinted away. And with her she took a vivid and disturbing picture of the toff inside the carriage: a big man, whose face and neck were smothered in iron-grey hair, and who had the most vicious, piercing eyes she had ever seen, which stared down on her with a look of pure hatred!

From a safe distance, Molly kept watch on the carriage; she wished that Sal would hurry up and come out, so they could go home to the relative safety of their hut. It wasn't too long before the odd one or two revellers began emerging from the ale house, so Molly kept her eyes peeled for Sal's familiar figure.

But it wasn't Sal's familiar figure that came out. It was Gabe Drury's, together with the fellow who had arrived in the carriage. There they were, arm in arm, the older man swaying and staggering, occasionally bursting into song, and now and then laughing out loud at some genial comment made by the other fellow.

With Molly still watching from the shadows, Gabe Drury was led towards the carriage, and unceremoniously bundled inside it, with the other fellow standing watch outside and talking quietly to the driver. Molly crept nearer, until she was crouched below the door, with her ear pressed close against it. She could hear old Gabe Drury protesting most strongly at being 'brought away from me drinkin' pals!' Whereupon the toff showed great interest in 'the story you've been telling . . . regarding a certain man by the name of Thadius Grady . . . and the murder of a bargee by the name of Bill Royston?'

'What's it to *you*, then, eh?' Molly thought Gabe Drury's voice seemed more sober and suspicious, especially when the toff offered him 'two guineas to repeat the story to me. But, leaving nothing out, mind . . . nothing at all!'

'Two guineas!' Molly couldn't help but gasp softly at the price this gent was willing to pay, just to hear a story! Why! *She'd* tell him a better tale than old Gabe Drury, at half the price. Then she recalled the gent's words—'the *murder* of a bargee by the name of Bill Royston'—and something inside her froze. The name was familiar to her, because hadn't Sal once revealed that her *own* name had been Royston, but was changed to Tanner when she was a child. Beyond that, Sal would say no more. But Molly had been left with the feeling that there had been a terrible tragedy of sorts, because of the sadness in Sal's face when, on that one occasion only, she had talked of her background, and of her parents, Eve and Bill Royston. Was it the same 'Bill Royston', Molly wondered now. Had Sal's father been murdered? And, if he had, then why was this gent so interested, and what did Gabe Drury know of anything?

Molly was tempted to steal away, lest she should hear something which was best not heard. But she was more tempted to *stay.*

'Let me out. I don't want ter talk to no bloody toffs!' Gabe Drury's voice was trembling with fear, not booze. 'Let me out, I tell yer. I don't know nothing about any "murder" . . . an' I've never even heard of a fellow called Thadius Grady!'

'You're a liar! You've been spreading gossip about the town . . . malicious and dangerous gossip that could have you put away . . . or likely hanged! In fact, I think I'll tell the driver to take us straight to the constabulary this very minute.'

'No, I don't want no truck with the bobbies,' came Gabe Drury's fearful cry, 'I've done nothing wrong, I'm tellin' yer.' When the gent appeared to brush aside the old fellow's fears and to lean out of the window ready to instruct the driver to move off, the old man began blubbering and pleading, 'All right . . . I'll tell you all I know.'

'And I shall see you get your two guineas,' promised the gent in velvet tones.

Molly listened most intently, while Gabe Drury

131

hurriedly spilled out his story, his nervousness evident in the way he halted and stumbled on every other word. He described how, on the day Bill Royston was shot to death, he saw a man fleeing from the place . . . a gent . . . 'much like yourself, sir', but not he, no, not he! 'Blood all over him, and a look on his face as guilty as any I'd ever seen!' The memory of it all was too much, as Gabe Drury pleaded, 'That's all I know. Now, let me be . . . let me out of here!'

'In a minute. Tell me first, and think hard, man, because your life might depend on it. You say you saw Thadius Grady running from the place where Bill Royston lay dead? . . . Did you see anything else, man? Any other person, anyone *else* you could recognise? Speak up, man, speak up or I'll have you hanged, I tell you! There should be enough to bring a charge against you!'

'No . . . I weren't there, sir!' protested Gabe Drury. 'I were in the grass some fair distance from the canal . . . sleeping off a night o' revelry. Oh no, sir . . . I weren't *there*. Not at all. What's more, I never saw nobody else . . . only that gent, Thadius Grady . . . just like I said. An' he's dead an' gone himself now . . . so it don't matter.'

'You're sure? He was the only one you saw?' When Gabe Drury reassured him, there was yet another question to answer before he was allowed to go. 'Just now . . . before you entered the public house, you addressed a scruffy urchin?'

'Scruffy urchin?' Gabe Drury's mind was still shot with fear at his experience here this night, and what with the booze, he was having trouble thinking straight. 'Oh aye! Yer must mean young Molly . . . Sal Tanner's lass.' He was relieved to have remembered, but puzzled as to why a posh gent might be interested in the likes of Sal Tanner's little 'un.

'Sal Tanner, eh?' The gent raised his hand and thoughtfully scratched at the mass of hair about his face. Then, leaning forward and looking the old fellow hard in the eyes, he repeated, 'Sal *Tanner,* you say?' He waited for an affirmative, if nervous, nod. 'Hmm . . . the same one who ran her barge from Liverpool and carried coal and cotton to the Wharf Mill?' Again, he waited for the nod. Then, when it was cautiously given he went on, 'The same one who had a brother . . . I believe his name was Marlow?'

'That's right, sir . . . Marlow, a fine young fellow. Went off to seek his fortune and ain't never come back since.' By this time, Gabe Drury was glad that the subject had come away from the night of Bill Royston's murder. Funny though, how two things in particular stood out in the old fellow's mind, in the wake of the gent's questions. First, it was speculated at the time that a *woman's* body had been found alongside Bill Royston's. And, if rumour had it right, it was said that the woman was not one of the usual run, but a well-bred lady of the gentry, no less. But it had been carefully hushed up. Then as if that wasn't enough, here was a fellow of the same class . . . asking about none other than Sal Tanner. Sal Tanner! Whose father was the same Bill Royston that got himself murdered!

'This scruffy urchin . . . you say she's Sal Tanner's daughter?'

'Well . . . not *exactly* her daughter. Sal never had any children of her own. Folks don't rightly know where Sal got the young 'un from.' Of a sudden, the gent was leaning forward again and, when Gabe Drury saw the cunning look in those piercing eyes, some deep instinct warned him to keep his mouth shut. So when he was asked, 'What *more* do you know of Sal Tanner . . . the brother, or the urchin?' he shook his head. 'I don't know nothing else, sir, an' that's the truth. I ain't been round these parts fer a long time, an' I ain't got that many friends ter speak of.' He winced beneath the other fellow's close scrutiny of him. But he was determined that, two guineas or no two guineas, wild horses wouldn't get him to admit that he'd known Sal and Marlow since they were no bigger than a blade o' grass . . . an' he knew their parents, Eve and Bill Royston, a good many years afore that. It wasn't widely known that when their daddy was shot to death and their mammy hanged for it, the two Royston children were whisked away to safety by the barge-folk, and their name changed to that of Tanner. Somehow, Gabe Drury suspected that even this gent 'ere wasn't aware of the connection. But if that was the case, why was he asking after Bill Royston and Sal Tanner in the *same* breath? There was something strange going on here, thought Gabe Drury, although he was convinced that the gent was not aware of the blood ties between Sal and the murdered man. But he felt he might have said far too much, and stopped short of revealing how Sal Tanner had come across young Molly after a hanging . . . found the little wretch right outside the prison gates, or so it was said . . . when it was still wet and warm from its mother's womb.

'You've told me all you know?' The voice had a

sinister ring to it, as it came out of the dark shadows in the carriage. 'You're certain that the man you saw was Thadius Grady? You saw no *other*?'

'None at all. Like I said, I don't know nothing else, as God's my judge,' and he hoped God might forgive him for lying.

'Then here's your two guineas.' There was a chink of coins and a grateful 'Thank you, sir' before the carriage door was opened and Gabe Drury set his foot on the pavement. As he hobbled off into the darkness, a song on his lips and thankful that he was at last on his way, the gent himself stepped down out of the carriage and muttered into the ear of the other man, who had kept watch outside. This one now nodded his understanding of the instructions just issued. In a minute he went stealthily after the homely figure of Gabe Drury, the both of them being swiftly engulfed in the darkness.

Having quickly scurried back to her hiding place when she knew the conversation was over, Molly watched everything. She felt afraid, yet didn't know why. But having been taught well by Sal, and not being one to miss an opportunity, she sidled up to the carriage; before the gent could climb back inside, she had slipped her fingers into his coat pocket and stolen away what felt to be an unusually thick wallet. Molly smiled craftily as she crept back into the shadows. Sal will be pleased, she thought, as the carriage moved away. It wasn't too often that the gentry presented themselves so easily for the picking! But how would she explain it to Sal? How could she tell her about the carriage an' all . . . yet *not* tell her about that fearful

135

conversation? Molly thought better of telling Sal about that, because there was something awful about it. From what Molly could understand, old Gabe had seen the fellow who had murdered Sal's daddy . . . and his name was Thadius Grady. There would be no sense in raking all of that up when it would upset Sal, especially since this Grady fellow was 'dead and gone'. And especially since Gabe had seen fit to keep quiet about it up till tonight. Molly supposed Gabe hadn't wanted to upset Sal over it then, any more than she did now. She expected Gabe had been afraid to go to the constabulary before, and Molly could understand that. You didn't go looking for trouble, and the constabulary was trouble, for the likes of folk such as Gabe.

Molly's stomach had turned somersaults when that gent began asking after her and Sal. That in itself was enough to make her keep the whole thing from Sal, because she did like to get to the bottom of things, did Sal. Molly sensed that it could only bring trouble down on their heads. No. The best thing was to forget all about it, and tell Sal that she'd found the fat wallet lying there on the pavement. The thought made her chuckle. Wouldn't Sal be surprised, she thought, taking up her place at the door of the public house, just as the revellers began pouring and stumbling out of it. She kept her eyes peeled for Sal's shawled figure, and she returned a cheery 'G'night' to one and all as they went away down Angela Street, singing and laughing at the tops of their voices— one or two starting a fight, afterwards rolling about in the gutter with a crowd of cheering drunks egging them on. Bedroom windows were flung

136

open, and out came angry instructions to 'Piss off, yer drunken sods!' and 'Bugger orf out of it . . . else I'll set the dog on yer!' Molly grinned from ear to ear. She'd seen it all before. And many was the time when it was Sal who might be fighting and rolling about in the gutter, especially when she'd had a few too many and lost at cards into the bargain.

*   *   *

As the carriage sped away into the night, leaving behind the alleys and cobbled streets of the old quarter, the gent inside smiled to himself. He had done well, he thought, and covered up his tracks most cleverly. It always paid to keep an informer amongst the riff-raff, because who could sniff out a rat better than another rat? When the news was brought to him that a certain old fellow was spreading a story that could so easily have pointed the finger in *his* direction, there was no other course but to track the fellow down. He had to find out just how much the fool did know of the canal murders which took place all those years ago.

The smile which had crept over the gent's face deepened into a cruel and smug grin. He had satisfied himself that the fellow had no knowledge of any person fleeing the scene, other than the hapless Thadius Grady, who was always a weak and unfortunate fool. Now, had the old man Drury stayed a moment longer on that particular day, and looked in the opposite direction, he might well have seen the very gent who was seated in this carriage now. In fact, if he hadn't been so intent on fleeing from Thadius Grady, he might well have seen a real murderer. And, if he had, thought the man, if he had, then he might not have lived until this night!

Though he was pleased with his night's work, there was something else that played on his mind and set him wondering. It was to do with Marlow Tanner and Emma Grady who, thankfully, everyone believed was no more than a ward to him, left in his care by his wife's brother, Thadius. The image of the small, dark-eyed urchin insisted on troubling him also, and it made him furious inside, firing his avowed determination to rid the streets of these vagrants and thieves!

As his thoughts continued to mull over Marlow Tanner, Emma Grady and the dark-eyed urchin, a distasteful thought began to grow in his mind and to haunt him. Until he murmured out loud, 'No matter! She'll go the way of all her kind . . . to meet a sorry end.' Yet he had not forgotten that Emma Grady was with child when she was convicted and that, according to the report he had received, soon after its untimely birth, the dead infant was abandoned to the gutter and afterwards disappeared. He had believed, as had the authorities, that some marauding dog or hungry rats had carried it off and made a meal of it. He had hoped that such was the case. He was *still* of the same mind. Nevertheless, he suddenly felt uncomfortable.

How much more 'uncomfortable' might Caleb Crowther feel if he were ever to learn that the 'scruffy urchin' was indeed Emma's child and his own grand-daughter.

*   *   *

'Oh, I can't believe it, child!' Sal had staggered home, moaning and wailing, and giving thanks to the girl on whose small shoulder she leaned her considerable weight.

'Don't upset yourself, Sal darlin',' coaxed Molly, easing the drunken burden from her shoulders and taking it gently to the bed, where she laid it down. 'I'll make us a brew, shall I?' she asked.

'No, no, lass.' Sal had dragged herself into a sitting position, although she appeared a twisted and bedraggled sight. 'Stay aside o' me . . . I don't want ter to be left on me own,' she pleaded, at the same time taking Molly's hand and tugging the girl to sit beside her. 'Oh, I'm that upset, lass,' she cried, rubbing at her eyes until they were puffy and sore-looking, 'an' I were in such a good mood when we come outta the ale 'ouse.'

Molly could vouch for that. It was ages before Sal had come out, and she was in such high spirits that Molly couldn't help but forgive her. It seemed that she'd won half-a-guinea, made a new friend, and had a wonderful night into the bargain.

It was when they were some short way along the canal bank and heading for the hut that the hue and cry went up. The outcome of it all was that Gabe Drury's body had been found floating at the water's edge. He had drowned, they said, and had a deep cut on his temple, 'no doubt where he hit the kerbing as he lost his footing and accidentally tumbled in', it was agreed. And Sal Tanner was the very first to curse the old fool for 'wanderin' so close ter the water when he's drunk as a bloody lord!' Afterwards, she shed genuine, heartfelt tears.

139

Molly however was not so satisfied that Gabe Drury had 'accidentally tumbled in', though she was wise enough not to say so. All the same, she couldn't help but wonder about the gent in the carriage—whose face she had not seen—and the conversation between him and the old fellow. Nor had she forgotten how the gent gave instructions to the other one, who then followed Gabe Drury into the darkness. She didn't care for the way things had shaped up, and that was a fact. But she wouldn't dwell on it too much if she could help it, because Molly had that same fearful sensation inside: one that told her to stay well away from that sort of trouble, and to look after herself and old Sal. *That* was all that mattered to her, and nothing else. Still and all, Molly felt sorry about the old fellow, even though she didn't know him as well as Sal did. But having heard a few unsavoury truths tonight, she wondered how much of it old Gabe had brought on himself?

Of a sudden, Molly remembered something, and it brought a smile to her face. 'Look here, Sal,' she cried, fishing the fat wallet from inside her tatty dress, 'see what I found!' She was sure it would do Sal a world of good.

At once Sal was attentive, stretching her scrawny neck and struggling to see what it was that Molly clutched so triumphantly. 'What yer been up to, yer little sod?' she demanded to know, as Molly laughingly thrust the article into Sal's grubby fist. ' 'Ere, fetch that candle a bit nearer,' she instructed Molly, 'I ain't a bloody bat, y'know . . . I can't see in the dark!' Gabe Drury's fate was quickly forgotten. 'Feels fat, does this!' she chuckled, turning the wallet over and over, and excitedly hoisting herself

140

up to a sitting position. 'Let's see what we got, eh?'

When Molly brought the candle and held it close, Sal tore open the wallet, and out spilled a fistful of notes, together with a carefully folded letter and a number of calling cards. 'Bugger me, lass . . . if we ain't hit the jackpot!' cried Sal jubilantly. 'Where'd yer get it, eh?'

'Found it.'

'*Found* it? . . . Well, I'm blowed!' Of a sudden, Sal was rolling her small eyes heavenward, saying in a reverent voice, 'There y'are . . . I *knew* it! It's the little people, tellin' me I'm fetchin' yer up right!' Molly didn't think so, but she wouldn't dream of spoiling Sal's astonishing recovery from the sad news concerning Gabe Drury.

'What's *that* say?' Sal pushed one of the small cards under Molly's nose. 'I can't mek head nor bloody tail o' these words.' She squinted her eyes and looked down the length of her nose at the card.

'Oh, Sal . . . you know I can't read the words either,' protested Molly, making no effort to take the card from Sal.

'Hang on a minute, lass!' Sal pointed a dirty fingernail at the bold, black capitals printed there. 'I've seen them words afore.' Of a sudden, she had thrown the card down on the chequered quilt and was scrambling from the bed, her eyes wide with fear and her finger still pointing to the card. 'I *know* where I've seen them there words! It were when me an' a few drinkin' pals were fetched afront o' the Justice. It was Justice Caleb Crowther as had the lot on us flung in the cells.' She had backed away from the bed and was standing by the door, her stocky figure held stiff and upright as she told the astonished Molly, *'Caleb Crowther!* That were it. It were them words as were fixed on a board for all to see. Cissie Bent learned to read when she were in service at the big house down Lytham Way . . . it were Cissie as told me what them words on the boards were sayin'. *Caleb Crowther* . . . same as them words on that card!' The next minute, she shot forward and caught hold of Molly by the shoulders. 'Where'd yer get it, lass? *Found* it, yer say? Tell me the truth now . . . I'll not have yer tellin' me lies!' She proceeded to shake the girl but instead was violently shaken herself when Molly instinctively braced herself. 'Has Justice Crowther been round these 'ere parts? Is he looking fer us? Oh dear God . . . dear God! When will the evil fella leave us in peace!' She was beside herself, and her face had turned bright crimson from the futile efforts she was making to loosen the girl enough to shake her hard. Of a sudden, she gave up the effort and ran round the room gathering up her bits and pieces. 'We shall have ter gerrout o' this place, an' that's a fact.'

'Calm down, Sal,' Molly told her, collecting the few sorry articles from Sal's hands, and replacing them, 'we're safe enough here. Justice Crowther ain't been nowhere near this place.'

'Then where did yer get that there wallet from, eh?' Sal demanded.

'I told you . . . I *found* it!' lied Molly, feeling satisfied in the face of poor Sal's fit of panic that she had done the right thing in keeping secret that meeting between Gabe Drury and the gent. Sal was afraid. *Really* afraid, like Molly had never seen her before. 'So you needn't worry,' she assured her.

Sal needed more convincing and, looking deep

142

into the girl's big, black eyes, she asked, 'Are yer *sure*, lass? Yer not lying? Yer really *did* find that there wallet?' When Molly nodded, saying, 'It was like I told you,' Sal visibly relaxed. Then in the next minute, she became anxious again, 'Where? . . . *Where* did yer find it?'

Molly had to think quickly, because she daren't frighten Sal by telling her that the Justice was in a carriage right outside the ale house, or Sal would *never* be convinced that he hadn't come to cart every last one of them off to jail: ' . . . so I wandered about a bit, and found myself nearer town. That's where I found it . . . down Ainsworth Street.'

'Oh aye? Well, *that's* where yer gonna return it!' declared Sal, going to the bed and folding everything back into the wallet.

'Return it!' Molly could hardly believe her ears. 'What? Now?'

'That's what I said, lass! You're gonna *return* it . . . right away. My God! The minute that fella finds his wallet gone, he'll not rest till he's found it. What! . . . The bugger'll turn Lancashire upside down if needs be!'

'But if we throw the papers and the wallet away . . . and just keep the money, he'll never know it was us that had it,' argued Molly, who was loath to let go of her prize.

But Sal would have none of it. 'Oh, he'll know right enough, my gal!' she retorted, shaking her grey head from side to side. 'He'll *know* well enough . . . 'cause he's got spies *everywhere*! He's a bad 'un, child,' she said, thrusting the wallet into Molly's hand, then frantically wiping her hands down on the fringe of her shawl, as though the very touch of Caleb Crowther's wallet might have left its mark. 'You don't know that fella like I do! Long afore the little people sent you ter me, that Justice Crowther had a grudge agin the Tanners. Why! . . . He even took a horsewhip to my Marlow, when the lad were doing nothing more offensive than talking ter Justice Crowther's ward, a nice enough lass, by the name of Emma Grady. Stripped the skin clear off his shoulders. An' he hounded Marlow ever after . . . sacked him from running goods to his mills . . . not carin' whether we *starved* because of it! Oh aye, he's a wicked, spiteful bugger, is that one.' She opened the door of the hut and pushed Molly towards it. 'That ward of his . . . lass by the name of Emma Grady . . . she were accused o' murderin' the bloke as Crowther wed her off to. An' d'yer know, child . . . that lass were innocent, an' there's plenty o' folk who'd vouch fer it, I'm sure. She were heavy wi' child an' all, when they took her. An' it were said that she begged an' pleaded fer him ter come an' help her. But the bugger never lifted a finger . . . an' he could have done! Oh, aye, he could a saved the lass, I've no doubt at all.' Here, she bent forward to whisper in Molly's ear. 'So y'see, Molly darlin' . . . y'see how dangerous such a fella can be? If yer don't shiver in yer shoes at the very sound of his name . . . then yer bloody well should.'

Molly felt herself being firmly propelled through the door and out into the blackness of the night. With Sal's instructions to 'tek it right back where yer found it, mind!' she took off at running speed in the direction of Angela Street. She had learned a very important lesson, and one which she wasn't likely to forget in a hurry. This fella, this Justice

144

Crowther, was someone to be avoided if at all possible because, if he frightened Sal in that way, then he must be fearsome. 'Blimey!' Molly muttered aloud as she ran along the bank. 'What a good job I didn't tell Sal that he were asking after her. Or she would have gone mad.' She was struck by a sudden thought, every bit as unpleasant. He was asking after *her* as well. Of a sudden, Molly's reluctance to return the wallet didn't seem as strong. In fact, the more she thought of it, the faster her thin little legs ran, because now she couldn't get it back to the spot fast enough.

By the time Molly turned out of the canal banking and made towards the spot where the carriage had stopped, everything was quiet. She supposed that the sorry Gabe Drury had been taken away in a waggon by now, and folks had gone home to their beds. She wondered again about that strange meeting between the Justice and the old fella, but her young mind couldn't make head nor tail of it except to be even more certain that she'd done right in keeping her mouth shut. 'After all,' she whispered aloud, quickly laying the wallet on the flagstones, and looking round furtively before making her way back, 'look what happened to old Gabe Drury!'

No sooner had Molly disappeared into the darkness than a carriage drew up in Stephen Street, some short way from the Navigation. Out of it stepped Caleb Crowther, who moved softly, first to instruct the driver to 'stay quiet', then hurriedly to where he suspected his wallet might have fallen when he had climbed out of the carriage earlier. Coming to the top of Angela Street, he stayed close to the wall of the Navigation. Then, peeping

145

round to satisfy himself that all was quiet, he quickly crossed the cobbled road and began searching the flagstones on the opposite side. It took a moment or two, as there was only one gas lamp lighting the corner, but after a determined and frantic search, he gave a small, jubilant cry and snatched up the wallet.

In a few moments he had made his way back to where the carriage waited in an unlit part of Stephen Street. 'Quickly man . . . get away from here!' he told the bowler-hatted driver in an urgent whisper.

As he settled back into the seat, before going through the wallet to satisfy himself of its contents, Caleb Crowther gave a sigh of relief. On discovering earlier that his wallet was missing, he had half-persuaded himself that the urchin might somehow have picked his pocket, though he could not see how she would have had the opportunity. But one thing was certain, if the little wretch had been guilty of stealing his wallet, it would have been the worst act of thieving she had ever committed. It would have been her *last*! He had been fearful that the wallet might have been ransacked before he could recover it, and with his name on those cards for anybody's eyes to see, he had spent more than a few frantic moments being anxious of the consequences, for they did not bear thinking about.

*　　　*　　　*

Agnes Crowther watched from her bedroom window, a tall and solitary figure with a regal head and unbending neck, her two hands joined

146

together in that posture of prayer which was her particular trait. With staring, unfriendly eyes, she followed the carriage as it turned into the drive. Instinctively, she knew that it would not come right up to the house, but would halt some distance away, in order for her husband to disembark and make a quiet return from his nightly exploits. The pattern was always the same: on the days when he was not travelling the circuit as Justice, he would go to the Wharf Mill, for the purpose of satisfying himself that the recently appointed manager was carrying out his instructions to the very letter. Afterwards, he would make his way into Manchester for a long and detailed discussion with his accountant.

Then, usually between the hours of five and six in the evening, he would return to Breckleton House and sit throughout dinner with a surly face and make no conversation. The moment he had swallowed his last gulp of wine he would fold his napkin in a most meticulous fashion (which had become infuriating to the watching Agnes), and with a curt nod of his balding head and a moment to run his fingers through the profusion of hair on his face, he would stand up and take a last lingering look at his empty plate, before going quickly from the room, leaving his long-suffering wife feeling desperately frustrated at the lack of civilised exchange of a few words. In the time it took to spruce himself up and don his outdoor garments, he was gone from the house, and it was always the early hours before he returned.

As the carriage was taken round the back and she heard her husband's footsteps coming up the path, Agnes Crowther stepped back from the window, fearful that he might see her. Always when she enacted this particular scene, it gave her a strange sensation of excitement. This was a cat-and-mouse game, when she had both the patience and the cunning to wait for the right moment to pounce. 'I'll have you in my clutches yet, Caleb Crowther,' she muttered, climbing into her bed. It was a long, lonely time before she could get to sleep, because the thoughts racing through her mind would not let her rest. Agnes Crowther had only recently suspected her husband of bedding other women and the suspicion had festered inside her, until she could think of nothing else. Four weeks ago he had moved his things out of her bedroom on the pretext that, 'I don't want to disturb you on the occasions when I must be late home.' Agnes Crowther was acutely aware of the unkind speculation that was rife amongst the servants, and it was a hateful experience. She had become a more spiteful and bitter person because of it. Yet she found every excuse not to believe what she suspected because, in spite of his hostile nature of late and his lack of affection towards her, she still loved him. It was that sorry fact, and her stiff pride, which prevented her from taking the steps which her instincts urged. The very idea of a private investigator was most distasteful.

If Agnes Crowther had spent a restless night, it did not show when she breezed into the dining-room the following morning.

'Good morning, Caleb,' she said in as amiable a voice as she could muster, smiling sweetly as she poured out her tea and met her husband's eyes across the table.

'Good morning, my dear,' he replied, at once

looking away to fix his eyes on the folded newspaper before him. He obviously had no intention of addressing her further. But then he raised his eyes and looked at his wife with a quizzical expression, which both surprised her and caused her to ask, 'Yes? What is it?'

Without laying down his knife and fork which he held like a threat over the liver and bacon on his plate, and without even straightening his neck which was bent forward ready to devour the contents of his plate, he said in a quiet and thoughtful voice, 'We know Emma Grady was pregnant, and that the child was born . . . presumably dead, or so we were informed?'

Agnes Crowther was astonished. It was her husband himself who had forbidden the mention of Emma Grady's name in this house. There had been times when her own conscience had made her think deeply about the girl. Times when she thought her brother Thadius might haunt them for their callous treatment of Emma. Yet now she was intrigued. 'Yes,' she agreed, 'Emma was pregnant . . . and the child still-born, as you say.' At this she quickly looked away with guilt written in her downcast eyes. 'It was a great pity that the child did not receive a Christian burial . . . being abandoned in such a way.' She would have gone on at great length about how the officer responsible should have been severely reprimanded, but she knew from past experience that her words would fall on deaf ears.

'The child.' Caleb Crowther was speaking again, but still he had not moved another muscle. 'Is it likely, do you think, that her husband, Gregory Denton, was not the father?'

149

Agnes Crowther was shocked. *'Not* the father?' She picked up her napkin from the table, dabbed it furtively at her mouth, then put it down again. She could not face another mouthful. 'Heaven forbid that a niece of mine should go outside her marriage in that way.' She was quite overcome. 'And if her husband were not the father, then who was?' Of a sudden, she could almost read his mind as he kept his eyes fixed on her. *'Marlow Tanner!'* The name sprang to her lips, and as though it had burned her, she put her hand across her mouth, and stared at her husband with unbelieving eyes. 'You think *he* was the father of Emma's child?' she asked through her fingers.

For a moment, Caleb Crowther gave no answer, and seemed to grow more cautious in what he might be suggesting. Lowering his knife and fork, he sliced into the liver, pierced it with his fork and poked it deep into the mass of iron-grey hair around his mouth. When he spoke again, minute segments of the chewed liver shot out in a fine spray across the table. 'It was just a thought,' he grunted, 'We never did find out what caused the terrible row that led to her husband's death, and if you remember, Marlow Tanner had left the area shortly before. It was just a thought, that's all.' He was anxious to assure her, 'Just a thought. Don't worry your head about it.'

But Agnes Crowther did worry her head. Of course it was possible that Marlow Tanner pursued Emma even after her marriage, because it was no secret that he loved her. And Emma would never have married Gregory Denton if it hadn't been for Caleb threatening to have Marlow Tanner transported. Emma loved him so much that she

150

sacrificed herself to save him from her guardian's animosity. That was what it all amounted to. Now, as she was reminded of such distasteful events, Agnes Crowther faced her husband with steely eyes, saying, 'As Emma is a world away and her child no more, I can't see that any of it matters now. Even if Emma were to come back to England, you have been clever enough to secure the mill in your own name . . . so she represents no threat.' She watched him nod his bowed head. But he did not raise it, being so intent on wolfing down his breakfast. Again she spoke, in a quieter, more intimate voice. This time, he raised his head and met her gaze with stiff, angry eyes when she told him, 'I saw you arriving home in the early hours. What manner of . . . business . . . kept you out so late?'

'Whatever manner of "business" . . . it is certainly none of yours.' His knife and fork clattered to the plate while he stretched his neck towards her and spat out the words in a furious voice, 'If you're wise, my dear . . . you'll refrain from questioning my activities. I shall depart this house . . . *my* house . . . whenever I please. And I intend to return at whatever hour I choose. What I do not intend to do is be accountable to you, or to anybody else. Is that perfectly understood?'

'Perfectly.' Agnes Crowther forced herself to smile sweetly, being more convinced than ever that it was not only the likes of Emma Grady who had gone outside of marriage. It was her own husband also. The guilt was plainly stamped on his face, and she loathed him for it.

Caleb Crowther thrust his chair back from the table and rounded on the little maid Amy, who, at that moment, had entered the room and was checking the big silver tureens on the sideboard. 'You!' As she turned round, he shook a fist at her. 'Inform the cook that if she serves such pig-swill up again, she'll find herself finished in this house . . . without references!' When she hurriedly made a slight, nervous curtsy and scurried from the room, Caleb Crowther looked down scathingly on his wife, who deliberately kept her eyes averted. 'Be careful not to question me or my movements again,' he warned, 'or it won't just be the cook who finds herself out of the door.' Then he left the room, slamming the door shut behind him.

'Hmh,' snorted Agnes Crowther, 'you think so, do you?' She laughed softly. 'Well . . . be careful yourself, because I may not be quite the fool you take me for.'

*   *   *

'He said *what*?' Cook's big round face went a painful crimson colour, and Amy feared it might explode. Why should she always be the one made to deliver such messages, she thought with alarm. She would have explained to Cook how the master was already in a terrible bad mood and perhaps didn't really mean it, but Cook didn't give her a chance. *'Pigswill!* . . . I've never heard the like in all my born days.' The shock was so much that Amy had to fetch her a drop of port wine from the pantry.

'I'm sure it wasn't your breakfast that upset him,' Amy assured Cook. 'I'm sure it was the mistress. They'd been having an awful row . . . some'at about the mistress shouldn't ever question him again.' Oh dear, Amy never did like upsets. There were enough of them when poor Miss Emma was here, and there were always upsets when Miss Martha came to stay. That Justice Crowther seemed to be at the root of any upset. He was a misery. A real misery.

Before Cook had sipped the last of her port, she received another shock, which caught her unawares yet left her in a better mood. It was the sight of Agnes Crowther sweeping down into the kitchen, coming to tell the tearful woman, 'Mr Crowther spoke too hastily, and you are not to take it to heart. As usual, your cooking was exemplary.' After the mistress had gone, Amy declared how good it was of her 'to come downstairs like that'. She also made mention of how the mistress had changed over the years 'since poor Miss Emma were sent to Australia, for murderin' her husband'.

Cook wasn't having that. 'Emma Grady did no such thing!' she retorted, her own dilemma paling by comparison. 'That lass didn't have it in her to "murder" anybody.'

'No . . . *she* didn't actually murder him, did she? It were that Mrs Manfred.' Amy's brown eyes swelled as she suddenly remembered. 'Ooh! Just think, Cook . . . she were livin' right under this roof as housekeeper. Ooh! . . . We might'a been murdered in our beds.' The thought was so frightful that she clapped both her outstretched hands up to either side of her face, her wide-open mouth and eyes giving her the look of a fish out of water.

'They were neither of them murderers!' exclaimed Cook, losing her patience. 'Get away

153

and clear the dining-room, you little fool,' she told her. Amy knew Cook's unpredictable moods well enough to make a hurried exit.

*   *   *

That night, in the safety and privacy of her own quarters, Cook took an envelope from its hiding place, this being the silk lining in the lid of her portmanteau. 'Murderers indeed!' she muttered, carefully opening the envelope and unfolding the letter from inside. She had read its contents many times before and she knew them word for word. Yet even now it struck her heart cold to read the letter again. It had been delivered by hand only minutes after Mrs Manfred was hanged. It was in her handwriting, though unusually sprawling and hurried. Cook had tried to appreciate how terrified the poor woman must have been with the gallows waiting. But it was beyond her comprehension, and she prayed it always would be. The letter read:

Dear Friend,
There isn't much time left before I meet my maker. I don't know if I am guilty of pushing Emma's husband down the stairs, but I do know I am guilty of having the intention in my heart. My poor darling Emma is innocent of all, except for loving a man other than her husband, and being foolish enough to bear his child.

If there is a victim in all of this nightmare, it is Emma alone, and my heart goes out to her.

You may wonder why I am writing to you,

154

instead of to my only relative. The reasons are these. Firstly, my sister has chosen to believe that I am guilty and has disowned me. Secondly, and for Emma's sake, I feel I must confide in you on very delicate matters regarding Caleb Crowther. Please understand that nothing of what I am about to tell you can be substantiated, or would hold up in a court of law. But I must rid myself of the awful burden which I carry, and I trust that sometime in the future when, God willing, Emma is a free woman, what I am about to reveal might put into her hands an opportunity to question Caleb Crowther, and somehow, to expose the truth which would incriminate him.

I have reason to believe that Caleb Crowther is a murderer!

As I say, I cannot prove anything, and for that reason I have kept silent. Also, God forgive me, I have been cowardly enough to consider my own fate, were I to openly accuse him. I would do it now. But I believe my accusations would not only be received with ridicule by those in authority, but would warn Caleb Crowther enough to cover up his tracks.

When I first came to look after Emma, which was very soon after her mama's killing, I was greatly alarmed by snippets of gossip in the area which suggested that Emma's mama had been indiscreet with her affections, and had been unfaithful to Thadius Grady on more than one occasion. Mr Grady himself confided this to me, in a moment of deep despair. Also, I came across the burned remains of clothing in a secluded corner of the garden. It was only later that it occurred to me that the dark iron-like stains on the garments, which I disposed of, might have been *blood* stains. Of course, I instantly dismissed what, I convinced myself, were foolish and dangerous notions. But the discovery of such a fire, and in such a secluded part of the garden so soon after the brutal murder of Mary Grady, left me with many disturbing suspicions. These same suspicions were stirred up by the furtive comings and goings of Caleb Crowther to the house. Also, these visits, when he and Mr Grady would retire to the drawing-room in deep and whispered conversation, always left Emma's papa in a most distressed state of mind.

I have no doubt that, if the two of them were involved in some dreadful secret, then it was brought about more by Caleb Crowther's hand, than by the gentle Mr Grady's. My only concern at the time was for little Emma.

There is something else also. On the day when Thadius Grady died, I was in the linen cupboard. I heard the bedroom door being locked and, on looking out, I saw the ashen, still face of Emma's papa with all life gone from it. And I saw Caleb Crowther, with as guilty a countenance as I have ever witnessed, hurriedly replacing the pillow beneath poor Mr Grady's head. I was surprised and filled with doubt when the doctor saw nothing untoward.

I pray to the Lord that I am wrong in the terrible notions that have haunted me since. And, if I am *not* wrong, then I pray to the Lord for his forgiveness, in being too cowardly to speak up. Yet always in my heart is Emma, and the fear of what such knowledge might do to her. As you know, she idolised her papa, and still deeply grieves for him. So I ask you to be very careful with this information; none of which can be proved, I think.

Yet, if you ever find an opportunity to use it in order to protect Emma from her appointed guardian, do not hesitate. I have a feeling that Caleb Crowther will try to rob Emma of everything her papa left to her. I pray you do all you can to prevent that.

A kindly warden has promised to deliver this letter to you. I trust you will get it. Goodbye and God bless,

Your friend,
Mrs Manfred.

*   *   *

The moment her eyes had read the last word and it was etched into her mind, Cook meticulously folded the letter, put it back into the envelope and carefully replaced the awful but precious thing into the silk lining of her portmanteau. On her round, shocked face there crept a look of cunning, as she raised her small pink eyes to look in the direction of her master's quarters. 'Them's terrible words in

157

that there letter!' she murmured, as though addressing someone in person. 'Words as say that *you* . . . a fine upstanding Justice . . . are a thief and a murderer.' Her mouth closed tight and the flabby jowls began working until they actually trembled. Then, lowering her head but keeping her accusing gaze fixed to the ceiling, she said in a grim voice, 'Aye! *Terrible* words. But told by a poor woman who faces the gallows. An' terrible they may be, Caleb Crowther . . . but I believe every last one to be the truth.'

Returning to her work, Cook began muttering to herself. 'I shall guard that letter with me life. It's me insurance against a sorry old age. But you'd best watch your step, else I might be tempted to use the letter afore I intended, Mr fine an' mighty bloody Crowther!' As she whisked the eggs around in the mixing bowl, she chuckled to herself, knowing that she had in her possession the means by which the wind might be taken out of the devil's sails.

Chapter Six

The long harsh winter of 1873 had come and gone. The summer which followed was glorious and, on a day in September 1874, Caleb Crowther received his son-in-law, Silas Trent, into the library. His mood was brighter than usual, believing that this pre-arranged meeting would prove beneficial to himself and improve his finances considerably. The thought appealed to him, and when both he and his son-in-law were seated, he bestowed a rare smile upon his visitor. 'Your business, then?' he asked in a genial voice, and settled back in his chair while his son-in-law, somewhat encouraged by Caleb Crowther's friendly disposition, eagerly outlined the reason for his visit.

Before he had even finished however, Caleb Crowther had sprung to his feet and gone to the fireplace, where he stood with his legs wide apart and his fists clenched by his side. The smile had gone from his face and in its place was a look like thunder. 'You want me to throw good money after bad!' he roared, afterwards storming towards the library door and flinging it wide open. 'I'm surprised that you even had the gall to put such a proposition to me! Good-day to you, sir!' He tapped his foot impatiently as he waited for Silas Trent to rise from the leather armchair, then, when the tall, well-built man with brown hair and military moustache approached him, he added sneeringly, 'Your father left you a thriving shipping line, Mr Trent . . . and in only a few years you have seen fine ships slip through your incompetent fingers, until there is just one vessel left. One, Mr Trent . . . and the *bank* half-owner of it! I trust you have more sense than to let your marriage go the same way, because, to be quite frank . . . I am wearying of supporting your family while you travel the seven seas. If you're not man enough to keep a shipping line successful, then your father should have had more sense than to leave it to you in the first place.'

Silas Trent stood only the smallest distance away from his father-in-law, so close in fact that he could see the delicate criss-cross pattern of purple veins which marbled the whites of the other man's eyes. For a long moment he met Caleb Crowther's vicious stare with steady, unswerving brown eyes, and it ran through his mind what a fool he had been to let Martha persuade him into approaching her father. He felt humiliated and, in the wake of Caleb Crowther's cruel, unjust accusations, he felt a tide of dark anger rising in him. Yes, it was true that he had been left a fleet of proud ships, and that, sadly, that same fleet was now reduced to the *Stirling,* which he himself captained. But what the arrogant Caleb Crowther refused to acknowledge was the colossal cost of running and maintaining a large fleet of ships. While the contracts were plentiful, and there was money enough to take on the crews, there were no problems. But in recent years it was proving more and more difficult to secure good lucrative contracts. There were too many shipping lines chasing too few cargoes which, since the closure of many cotton mills and the stopping of convict transportation, had become more scarce. Indeed, if anything, Silas Trent was proud of the fact that he still ran the *Stirling* at a profit when so many other shipping merchants had lost everything. Then there was the growing threat from faster, iron-built steamers. Recently though, he had heard that a firm in Australia had invited tenders for the shipping of sandalwood to Singapore. There were also opportunities to get in on the expanding wool trade out there. In fact, Australia had become increasingly important for merchant trade, and Silas Trent regretted the fact that he had concentrated on other markets and routes these many years, since losing the government contracts to carry convicts. He had made his one big mistake there, and he was the first to admit it. However, the opportunity to make amends had presented itself. He *knew* he could make the most favourable tender for the sandalwood route from Australia to Singapore, and with careful planning secure the shipments of wool and other cargoes which would bring him back to England and his family. But he needed capital to get him started. He had been to the banks and other lenders without success. Caleb Crowther had been his last hope. Silas had stressed that he would win the contracts to carry goods to and from Australia, if only he could get the financial backing.

He had voiced these convictions to his father-in-law, who had rejected them out of hand. Now, he replied in a firm but cutting voice, 'As for my marriage, don't let it concern you, Mr Crowther, sir. Your daughter and I may have our difficulties like any other couple, but they are not insurmountable. Then, being fully aware of the frostiness between Caleb Crowther and his own wife, Agnes, he quietly added, 'When we have a problem, sir, we discuss it. I fully recommend that course of action: you will find that it works wonders.' Before Caleb Crowther could recover from such insolence, Silas Trent gave a courteous nod, bade him good-day, and in a moment had departed from the room, left the house and climbed into the waiting carriage, which went sedately down the drive and out on to the street.

Seated in the ornately furnished drawing-room busy with her tapestry, Agnes Crowther had heard the conversation which had taken place between her son-in-law and her husband. The outcome had been exactly as she had warned her daughter

Martha. Yet that foolish woman had insisted on harbouring false hopes and sending Silas on a fool's errand. Silas Trent was a good man and had been a good husband to Martha. He was a wonderful father to the boy, Edward, and if there was a way by which he might recover from his present financial predicament, Agnes Crowther felt confident that he would do it. He must do it, for the sake of Martha and the boy, because it was a certainty that, should the worst happen and Silas Trent lose everything, neither he nor his family would be made welcome in this house. Martha's father had made that very clear on several occasions, when he had stated, 'I believe a man should be responsible for his own family. Martha has passed from my care into that of her husband's, and she must stand or fall with him!' The boy, Edward, however was a different matter: Caleb Crowther saw him as the son he had never had.

Sighing wearily, Agnes Crowther sank her needle into the tapestry and gave it her full attention. But not before murmuring, 'You will find a way, Silas . . . I know you will.' Just as *she* would, she thought. In the past she had done much to be ashamed of, and she had come to dislike her own husband because of it. Yet even now, if the opportunity came when she might make amends, she wondered whether she would be capable of doing so.

*   *   *

'Sell the *Stirling*! There are other ways to earn a living!' Martha Trent was in a fury when she

162

realized that her husband had borrowed money on their home in order to finance his journey to Australia, where he intended to secure his future prospects. 'You'll see us without a roof over our heads,' she accused him now. 'Is that what you want? . . . To see us wandering the streets like beggars?'

'Don't be foolish, Martha. It will never come to that, and you know it . . . even if I have to buy a barge and fight for a cargo up and down the Leeds and Liverpool Canal!' Silas shook his head and came to where his wife was petulantly beating the top of the piano with one hand, and dabbing a delicate handkerchief to her eyes with the other. Taking her by the shoulders, he would have held her close, but she tore away from him, crying, 'Go on then! . . . Go to your precious ship, and sail to the ends of the earth for all I care! You don't want me and you don't want the boy . . . or you would not be so heartless as to put up our home for security! You'll never be the successful man of business that my *father* is, and you could do no better than to listen to his advice. Isn't it enough to know that he will not invest in you?'

'You know why he won't invest in me, Martha,' protested Silas, growing impatient at Martha's hostile attitude. Like father like daughter, he thought. 'Caleb Crowther won't back me, because he has already backed one of my competitors. If I'd known at the time that he was hand in glove with Lassater Shipping I would never have been persuaded to approach him in the first place. I've also recently learned that not only do Lassater Shipping hold long-term contracts to carry cotton from your father's mill and that he is a large shareholder in that shipping-line, but he has passed on confidential information which I confided to him during our conversation. The result being that Lassater Shipping is now a major contender for the sandalwood cargoes from Australia to Singapore. He betrayed us. Do you hear what I'm saying, Martha? . . . Your father who, in your eyes, can do no wrong . . . *betrayed* us!'

'Liar!' In a swift and unexpected movement, Martha Trent swung round, taking the silver candlestick from the piano top and, with a scream of 'Get out!' sent the object flying. Silas Trent was caught unawares, saw the heavy candlestick at the last minute and ducked quickly sideways, but not in time to avoid a glancing blow to the side of his head. When he put his hand up to touch his temple, the blood ran through his fingers and a small pool of crimson dripped on to his jacket.

Martha showed no sign of regret. Instead, she stood stiff and unyielding with bright angry eyes which continued to stare at her husband unflinchingly. He also showed no remorse for the heated argument which had raged between them, nor did he make any move towards her.

In the hallway outside the room the boy, Edward, sat on the stairs, quietly crying as his parents ranted and raged at each other. Now he got to his feet as his father came from the drawing-room, a look of utter desolation on his face when he saw the boy there. 'Oh, Edward! Edward!' he moaned, quickly covering the boy's head with his two hands and pulling him tight into his body. 'What must you think of us?' he asked in a voice which betrayed his shame. When he received no answer, he went down on his knees and looked into his son's face, seeing the terrible anguish in those dark green eyes, knowing that he had caused it. 'I'm sorry, son,' he said with a sad apologetic smile. 'I'd rather you had not heard all that. But she's wrong, you know . . . your mother. I won't let you down, I promise.' Still there came no acknowledgement from the boy, who had lowered his gaze and seemed unwilling or unable to raise it to Silas Trent's concerned face. After a while Silas released the boy and got to his feet. For a moment longer he looked down at his son's bowed head, then, ruffling the dark hair with the tips of his fingers, he said with a small laugh, 'I'm off to turn our fortunes round.' When there was still no response, he said in a quieter voice, 'Take care of your mother.' In another moment he was gone. Still the boy did not move, his dark head bent to the rich, floral-patterned carpet with the tears falling down his face.

When he sensed a movement close by, Edward lifted his eyes to see his mother standing in the door of the drawing-room. Her face was smudged with tears and there was a look of bitterness in her brown speckly eyes, as she told him through gritted teeth, 'Get upstairs to your room, and don't come down until I send for you!' With a heavy heart he did as he was told. Behind him Martha Trent angrily issued instructions to their one and only servant, a young woman of stocky build whose blue eyes showed no surprise. 'Master Trent and I will be leaving for Breckleton House straightaway. I dare say we shall be away for several weeks,' adding in a tone too low for the servant to hear, 'and probably for good!'

The maid gave a hurried little curtsy. 'Yes,

165

ma'am,' she acknowledged, thinking as she went about the business of packing how she wouldn't mind being left alone in the house for weeks on end; indeed, if anything, taking into account her mistress's dreadful disposition, she much preferred it. But her heart went out to that poor little lad, dragged from pillar to post and never a friend to call his own. And that tutor who came in of an afternoon to teach him his lessons, well, he were a miserable old bugger an' all. On top of which, the lad were expected to work twice as hard when he got back from these frequent trips to Breckleton House. It were no wonder the poor little blighter looked like he'd got the weight of the world on his shoulders. Still, the lad seemed to have a right fondness for his grandad, Caleb Crowther, and by all accounts that surly-faced fellow had an unusually soft spot for his only grandson, so that was one blessing, thank the Lord.

*   *   *

All was still and pitch black outside Breckleton House when the small figure clothed in night attire rose from his bed. Cautiously opening his bedroom door, Edward Trent listened intently and was pleased to hear no sound other than the slumbering tick of the wall clock on the landing. He knew that his grandfather had gone away on his legal duties, and his grandmother had long ago retired to her bed. Softly now, he crept to his mother's room, peeped inside and satisfied himself that she was sound asleep. Afterwards, he went back to his own room, put on his breeches, with a clean white shirt and green corduroy waistcoat, pulled on his knee-length socks and lace-up ankle boots, which he loosely fastened. Then, grabbing his cap and fixing it securely on his head, he took the handful of coins from his cash-box, and went softly down the stairs and out of the back door.

As he stumbled across the fields, then through the narrow cobbled alleys of Mill Hill, fearful of the strange shadows and of where the dark alleys might lead him, yet even more fearful of his father never coming back, the boy began to sob. He had never seen them fight as fiercely as that before, and it made him unhappy. He didn't want to stay in the house without his father, and even though he liked his grandfather, he also frightened him a little.

He was going to find his way back to Liverpool, to the docks where all the big ships came in. He would find his father's ship, and steal on board. The thought cheered him and he hoped he was going in the right direction, because he did not intend to be left behind again. He hoped that the Stirling had not already sailed for Australia. That awful possibility spurred him into a little run when, time and time again, he stumbled on the sharp, jutting cobbles. In the pitch black of the early hours, when he was imagining some kind of monster in every dark, terrible corner, his courage began to desert him. Faster and faster he ran, convinced that he could hear the soft thudding footsteps of his pursuers. When a large shadowy cat crossed his path suddenly, he actually screamed out loud in terror.

The boy's scream echoed against the high, smoke-coated buildings which rose up about him like the walls of a prison. The disturbance created more disturbance as alarmed cats, rats and other creatures of the night fled to safety.

Yet if it alerted some night marauders to run away, it alerted others to stay and watch, in the happy event that it might be turned to their own advantage. Such a pair were engaged in the unlawful entry of a darkened warehouse in this isolated area, but, on hearing the scream close by, promptly abandoned their efforts in the hope of better pickings. Careful not to utter a single word to each other, and using a well-developed system of sign language, they crept from the back-yard and out into the alley. At once they heard the frightened figure of Edward Trent running towards them, his boots playing out a tune on the cobbles, and the coins in his pocket chinking frantically against his leg.

Quickly, the two shadowy figures slithered back into the recess of the wall, waiting for the very second when the approaching figure would be so close that they could leap on it from behind.

Edward Trent never even knew what stopped him in his headlong flight. One minute he had been determined to reach the end of the dark, terrifying alley, so that he might come into a more open and less threatening area. In the next minute, the ruffians had pounced on his back and wrenched him sideways; his head smacked hard against the brick wall, and he crumpled to the ground, a pool of blood trickling from the back of his head to the cobbles, where it congealed to form a dark, sticky stain.

'Bloody 'ell, yer fool!' cried the smaller and younger one of the two in a forced whisper, as he touched his fingers to the stain, promptly snatching them away when the liquid clung to his fingertips. 'Ye've *killed* 'im, dah.'

Quickly now, the older fellow struck a match and held it over Edward Trent's face, which, in the eerie glow of matchlight, looked a sickly shade of parchment. 'It's a brat,' he remarked with surprise. 'Can't be above a couple o' years younger than you, what . . . ten or eleven.' Here he gave a gasp of astonishment as his eyes roved over the prostrate figure, which had not moved even an inch nor shown any flicker of life. ' 'T'ain't no *ordinary* brat neither! Look at the cut of 'is togs . . . this ain't no street urchin. This is a bloody gentry, I'm telling yer.' He was all for making good his getaway the minute he had emptied the victim's pockets. But his companion had other ideas.

' 'Elp me strip 'is togs off!' The younger one began tearing at the blood-stained waistcoat. 'These buggers'll fit me. Me an' this feller are about the same size . . . just shows yer, don't it, eh? I bet I'm a good three years older, but no bloody bigger . . . 'cause 'e lives on the best, an' folks such as us . . . *we* live on the soddin' dregs.' There was a deal of hatred in his voice as with the help of the older fellow he viciously stripped off every last garment from the boy, and afterwards, without compassion—but with every intention of fooling whoever came across the lifeless body, and also of diverting suspicion—dressed it up in his own filthy flea-infested clothes. When he prepared to exchange boots though, he realized Edward Trent's were far smaller than his own, so he thought better of it.

'Now, let's get the 'ell outta 'ere,' instructed the older one. In a minute they had fled without a

169

second thought as to whether the boy might be dead, or still alive. It mattered not anyway, because folks hardly ever came this way, and if he wasn't a gonner now, he would be by the time he was found. The younger ruffian was all for rolling the body in the canal because 'it's nobbut a stride away'. But he was dissuaded. 'We ain't got time. An' somebody might come along. The feller's 'ad it anyway.'

So they fled, with only each other and the night as witness to their awful deed.

Chapter Seven

'Well I'm buggered, Molly lass,' cackled Sal Tanner as she watched the girl strip-wash over the bucket of canal water, 'yer nobbut comin' up twelve year old . . . an' already ye've got pointed little tets!' When Molly looked at her in disgust, with a deep uncomfortable blush spreading over her lovely face, Sal rocked with laughter. 'Don't be embarrassed, gal,' she told her, 'at lest, not 'till yer get ter my age, an yer tets 'ang down ter yer knees like withered balloons!' She roared again, when Molly hurriedly finished her wash, quickly replacing her panties and misshapen grey dress, which came down to the top of her boots in a ragged, uneven hem. The boots she pulled on had also seen better days, the laces being too short to do up the top eyelets, and the toe of one boot having come slightly apart.

Taking her wooden bone-toothed comb, Molly raked it through her short black hair until it shone blue as a raven's wing. 'I ain't taking no notice of you, Sal Tanner,' she said with a toss of her head, 'you're just trying to rile me, and it won't work!'

Sal had been making a determined effort to chew the small slice of apple which she had just pared with her penknife. Fast losing patience at her inability to enjoy the juicy apple, because it was difficult to chew with your gums when all your teeth had fallen out, she spat it out through the hut window and threw the remainder of the apple after it. 'Sod an' bugger it!' she yelled. 'As fer you, Molly lass . . . yer gerring too bloody big fer yer boots. Aye! Too cheeky, an' too 'igh an' mighty by 'arf'.'

Molly paid no heed. She knew that Sal had to take her frustrations out on somebody, and as she was the only other one here, then it might as well be her. 'I shan't wash in the hut anymore,' she told Sal Tanner, at the same time picking up the handle of the bucket and lifting its considerable weight off the floor. 'If you're gonna make fun of me, I'll wash by the canal.'

'Oh aye? That'll be a grand idea, won't it, eh? Gi' the passin' barges a right old treat . . . show *them* yer little pointed tets, why don't yer?' Her humour having returned in the face of Molly's innocent remarks, Sal Tanner threw her two arms up in the air and began rocking back and forth in a fit of helpless laughter, her toothless mouth wide open and her legs the same. Molly patiently shook her head, gave out a little laugh at the merry sight, then went down to the canal and emptied the bucket into it.

When she returned to the hut, she found Sal in a worse state, filled with panic and trying desperately to cough up a chunk of apple which appeared to

171

have lodged itself in her gullet. It took a few frantic minutes of pushing, pulling, thumping and shaking, but eventually the offending piece of apple was dislodged and thrown out of the window to follow the rest. 'Have a little sleep, Sal,' encouraged Molly, who had suffered quite a fright at the sight of Sal choking.

'Only if yer promise ter wake me up at midday, when I'm off ter the Navigation fer a tipple,' replied Sal, carefully sipping the water which Molly held up to her. After a couple of sips she thrust it from her, 'Bloody 'orrible stuff!' she moaned, pulling a wry face. 'Did yer save it from yer washin'-up water?'

When Molly assured her that she had done no such thing, Sal gave a little chuckle and winked a cheeky violet eye at the girl. 'Course yer didn't!' she told her. 'But yer *will* wake me up at midday, won't yer, eh? 'Cause I've a feller ter see!' She winked again, 'A proper gentleman friend, an' I'm fotchin' the bugger back 'ere . . . fer a little . . . quiet session, just the two on us. So mind yer gives us an hour or two on us own, won't yer lass?' She insisted, 'Ye'll do that fer yer ol' Sal, won't yer?'

Molly didn't mind, because she'd promised herself to go fishing down the quiet end of the canal. She had even collected a few juicy worms and got her willow stick all ready, with a good strong twine and a bent nail. All the times she'd been trying, and never once had she caught a fish. Today was going to be different, Molly felt sure. Today, she *would* catch a fish. It must be a lucky day, because at long last Sal had a boyfriend.

Sal's face crinkled into a multitude of crevices as she smiled into those big, wonderful black eyes.

172

'Yer reckon yer gonna catch us a fish, d'yer?' she said. 'Wi that bent nail an' balin' twine? Well now . . . won't that be a celebration, eh? Fresh caught fish fer us tea!' She didn't laugh at the idea, but kept on smiling.

'You'll see!' returned Molly. 'You'll see!' Then off she went to get everything ready for the big event, quietly closing the door behind her while Sal swung her legs up on to the mattress and settled into the bolster for what she considered to be a well-earned nap. 'Gotter be bright an' fresh fer me new feller,' she chuckled, pulling the shawl about her and folding her arms over her breast. Soon the little hut was filled with the echo of her contented snores. In the heat of a lovely September day, the tiny enclosed hut was also filled with the rancid aroma which rose up from Sal's unwashed body and dirt-laden clothes. But deep in her amorous dreams, Sal was blissfully unaware of such trivialities, because at last she had a fellow to call her very own. Her last thought was of him as she murmured, 'Thank the Lord he ain't one of them particular kind.'

*   *   *

At four minutes past midday, Molly duly shook Sal awake, made her a brew of tea and persuaded her to polish off just one jam butty. But try as she might, Molly could not persuade Sal to dip her hands and face into a bowl of hot, soapy water. 'Gerraway wi' yer!' Sal was horrified: 'Time enough fer soap an' water, when I'm laid out an' ready fer the knacker's yard. I expect the buggers'll throw a bucket o' the wet stuff o'er me then . . .

173

when I ain't in no position ter argue, eh? Till then, I'll thank yer kindly ter keep the disgustin' tack away fro' me!' However, she did allow Molly to comb her wispy grey tufts of hair, saying with a mischievous wink, 'Yer never know, Molly lass . . . me feller might just want ter run 'is fingers through me lovely locks.' Then she rolled about laughing, and couldn't resist adding, 'There's about as much chance o' that . . . as you catchin' fish!'

'Have a good time, Sal,' Molly called after her as she hobbled off towards the Navigation.

'Aye, I will!' returned Sal with a naughty and suggestive wiggle of her bum. 'I've caught my bloody fish. So now, you gerrof an' catch *yourn*!' She was singing merrily when she rounded the corner and went out of sight, and Molly's heart swelled with love. 'Sal Tanner, you're as bad as they come,' she said, shaking her head, her dark eyes smiling contentedly, 'but I wouldn't swap you for all the world.' Then with her willow fishing-stick and a can filled up with fat, wriggling worms, she set off towards the far end of the canal. She had no intention of coming away until she had caught a big, swashy gudgeon to show to Sal!

*   *   *

Molly settled herself in the shade of an old silver birch tree, whose spreading branches gave welcome shade from the hot sun. '*This* is where the gudgeon are hiding,' she murmured with a rush of pleasure. 'They'll be looking for a cool spot, just the same as me.' In no time at all she had wedged her fishing-stick into the bank and kept a close watch as the baling twine sank deeper and deeper into the water, with the fat worm wriggling on the end of it. Many was the time Molly had tackled Sal and other fishermen about how afraid she was the worms might be terrified when lowered into the water as bait. Her fears had been allayed when she had received the very same answer from one and all: 'Don't be so bloody daft, lass . . . 'tis a well-known fact that worms ain't got no nerves, so they can't *feel* owt.' Molly had been obliged to accept this, but it still made her cringe when the worm went out of sight, because she couldn't help wondering how she would feel if she were in its place. Molly had decided that she wouldn't like it at all, no, not at all.

After a while, when she seemed to have been scanning the water for hours, until her eyeballs ached, and the warm, sultry afternoon made her feel tired, Molly wrapped her legs round the fishing-stick and wound the baling twine about her toe, so that if a fish were caught up on the other end she would know about it. She lay back in the grass, feeling wonderfully contented with life, thinking how quiet and peaceful it was here. On top of which, Sal had a feller and he just might be the one to look after them both; although somehow Molly doubted it. There had been other fellers, some long time back, but they never came to anything worthwhile either. She wondered how the two of them were getting along, and she felt sure they must be gone from the hut by now, in search of a card game perhaps? Unless of course they had brought a supply of booze with them, but Molly doubted that as well, because Sal never had any money, and neither did the fellers she picked up. Molly gave a small laugh. 'It's a good job I've still got a few bob tucked away, Sal darling,' she giggled, 'so we'll not go short of a loaf yet.'

Of a sudden, Molly sat bolt upright as the twine tightened about her toe. 'Ssh now, gal,' she told herself, moving with the utmost care as she slid her toe from the loop and put her two hands around the willow-stick, which began bending towards the canal, as the twine was pulled tighter and tighter. In a minute it was all-out war! If Molly hadn't whipped the stick from the ground and taken charge, the entire lot would have gone flying into the water. Unable now to contain her excitement, Molly began whooping and hollering, giving the line its head, then drawing it back again. Inch by inch she shortened the line and wound it round the stick, bringing her struggling quarry nearer and nearer until she could see the fish-tail thrashing furiously in the water. 'It's no good you arguing, you old bugger!' she yelled. 'I've got you, and I ain't letting you get away!' At the right moment, she flicked the stick in the air, bringing both line and fish out of the water. With a soft thud the exhausted fish fell to the grass. 'You little beauty!' cried Molly, reverently collecting it up in her hands and gently easing the small bent nail out of its mouth. 'Oh, you're a *real* beauty!' She gazed in wonder at its small sleek body, its silver colour speckled with gold, and the sheen in its tail and fins almost translucent in the light of the sun. 'Oh . . . you really *are* lovely!' gasped Molly, and she knew in her heart that she could never take its life. She was held fascinated for a moment longer, then, when its mouth gasped frantically and its eyes began popping, she knelt down by the water's edge and lowered it back in. When it moved away, slowly at first, then in a rush of excitement, Molly was not sorry. She had caught a fish, and her only thought was to tell the world.

'I *caught* him!' She stood up and yelled at the top of her voice, 'Sal . . . *I caught a fish*!' Without stopping to collect her precious fishing tackle, she sped along the bank like the wind. 'Sal . . . Sal, I did it!' There was a fever in her, and the greatest need to tell the only person who mattered in her young life.

When Molly saw the hut in sight, she was spurred on, her whole being alive with excitement. 'Sal! . . . Sal!' she was calling as she flung open the door. Then she was cruelly silenced by the scene which greeted her. Sal was there, and so was her fellow. But they were both stark naked, the small wiry man bending over the bed where Sal was lying, and Sal lying so still that Molly's heart shrank inside her. At once the man swung round, his eyes large and terrified as they stared at Molly. ' 'T'ain't my fault,' he said in a trembling voice, 'we were having a good time . . . a good time, I tell you! Then she couldn't breathe. *Look* at her, oh God in Heaven . . . 'tweren't my fault!' He began shivering limb from limb as Molly came further into the room, a look of confusion and horror on her face. All the while he was scrambling into his clothes the man kept repeating in a tearful voice. ' 'Tain't my fault! We were having a good time, I swear.' When he was fully dressed, he came to where Molly was stooping over her beloved Sal, and touching her gently on the shoulder he promised, 'I'll fetch help, I swear . . . I'll fetch proper help.' Then he was gone in a great hurry.

'Let 'im go, Molly lass.' Sal made no move other

than to raise her eyes to Molly's face. There was the twinkling of a smile in them, but only a twinkling, and to Molly it seemed as though somewhere deep inside those bright merry eyes a light had been switched off. 'Oh, Sal . . . what shall I do?' Molly felt torn two ways, because part of her wanted to rush out and find help, but a deeper instinct kept her there.

'Don't do nowt, lass,' murmured Sal, as Molly reverently drew up the blanket to cover Sal's nakedness. 'Yon feller'll get 'elp. But it won't do no good, dar-lin' . . . 'cause old Sal's gone past being 'elped. 'She made an effort to laugh, but it seemed to cause her pain, as she brought both her arms up and clutched them across her chest; then she smiled a toothless smile, softly chuckling as she went on with difficulty, 'The bugger were right, y'know. We *were* 'aving a "good time". Best good time I've 'ad in bloody years! Only . . . me old ticker let me down, sod an' bugger it.'

Every word was an effort. 'Oh, but it were *grand* ter feel a feller's weight atop o' me after all these years, lass. Pity it's fer the last time, eh?'

Molly didn't think it was such a 'grand' thing. And she wanted Sal to stop talking that way, because it frightened her.

'You're going to be fine and dandy,' Molly said in a choking voice, 'you *are* Sal . . . you are!' The thought of losing Sal was more than she could bear. As hard as she tried to hold back the tears, they would not be held, and as they flowed down her sorry young face, Sal reached up a grubby hand to wipe them away. 'No, Molly lass . . . don't do that on my account.' Her fingers touched the tiny delicate watch that Molly always wore about her

178

neck. 'An' don't yer *dare* to sell that there trinket! It don't belong ter you, y'see . . . it belongs ter the little people. You promise me now, lass . . . *promise* ye'll never sell it!' Molly promised, but with Sal's next words, she wished she hadn't. 'Let the buggers put me in a pauper's grave,' she told Molly, 'it meks no difference ter me, 'cause I'll be past carin'.' Again she would have chuckled, but was gripped with such a fierce pain that it took her breath away.

'Lie still, Sal . . . please.' Molly was also racked with pain, but it was a different kind of pain . . . a sort of terror. 'I'm going to get help for you, Sal,' she said now, beginning to move away.

'No! *Don't leave me.* I want yer next ter me when I go . . . I'm a coward, yer see,' she finished with a tight little smile. 'You stay aside o' me, Molly lass.' Her smile faded into a look of sorrow as she softly added, 'You an' Marlow . . . yer all I've got. An' *that* bugger's gone afore me, I'm thinking . . . 'cause if 'e ain't, then 'e's deserted me . . . an' I'll *never* believe that of 'im. Never!' She had Molly's small hand secure in her own, and she had no intention of letting go.

'Sal, *please* . . . let me get help,' pleaded Molly. But then something happened which riveted her to the spot, because Sal uttered three words to her that she had never said before, 'I love you,' she whispered. Then she closed her eyes, and her hand fell back on the bedclothes. She never heard Molly's terrible cry of anguish as the distraught girl threw herself into Sal's lifeless arms.

When the man came back, just as he had promised, together with an old gypsy-fellow who was renowned for his knowledge of medicine, they

179

saw the child still cradling the woman who had been the only mammy she had ever known. They heard her crying softly as she murmured a prayer, and they knew there was nothing left to do but notify the authorities to fetch old Sal away to her last resting-place. As for the young 'un, well, she'd have to fend for herself, because times were hard and folks had enough mouths to feed.

*   *   *

Word spread quickly that very day about how poor Sal Tanner had gone. 'In the arms of a feller,' said one, 'enjoying herself right up to the very end,' and everybody agreed whole-heartedly that, if Sal had to go, 'the old bugger wouldn't have wanted it any other way'. All the same, it was a pity about the young lass, they said, and an even bigger pity that old Sal led the girl to believe she'd never had no parents and was 'left by the little people' because where were 'the little people' now, eh? Well, nowhere else but in Sal's twisted, merry mind, that's where! But then where were the lass's proper parents? For all anybody knew, they might just as well be the little characters dreamt up by old Sal. The top and bottom of it all was that young Molly had nobody. She was on her own, and it was hard enough to survive in this world even when you were a grown-up fellow and had a companion to watch out for you. When you were a lass though, not yet twelve years old, *and* all alone in the world, surviving could turn out to be a nightmare. But everyone had more than their fair share of troubles, and had to work through them the best they could.

'You *cheated* me! And you cheated Sal!' Molly's tear-stained face was raised to the sky and her small fist was clenched and held up as though to threaten some unseen thing. 'I hate you! D'you hear me . . . I *hate* you!' She continued to look upwards, as if waiting for a reply, and when the sky remained unchanged, she crumpled to the ground, sobbing as though her heart would break. 'Give her back to me. Oh, please . . . give me back my old Sal.'

For a long while Molly stayed still on the grass, her heart so filled with grief that she didn't care whether she herself went the same way as her darling Sal. In fact, she would have preferred it to being left all on her own.

'Aw, it ain't so terrible, Molly,' said a kindly voice immediately above her, and when she looked up, blinking her dark unhappy eyes against the bright sunlight, Molly saw that it was one of Sal's drinking cronies, a small, shrew-like creature with pointed features and a narrow body almost completely shrouded in a long, dark cotton shawl. In a minute she was seated on the grass beside Molly, her tiny pea-like eyes swallowed up in the great rolls of puffy flesh which surrounded them. 'None of us can live for ever, y'know . . . 'specially not the likes o' me and Sal, who don't gi' a cuss for nothing and nobody.' She went on, 'Anybody as enjoys their tipple, like me an' Sal, well . . . they're on their way out a sight quicker than most folks, ain't they, eh?' She inclined her head to one side and took a while regarding Molly's slim, taut, little figure, with the promise of great beauty emerging; she looked into the dark oval eyes and saw something unusual and lovely there, and a look of

181

cunning came over her face. 'No, you forget Sal Tanner,' she said, edging a little closer, 'she's laid out in that cold place now, waiting her turn to be put in the ground. Poor old sod . . . *she* won't be knocking back any more jugs of ale . . . no, nor bedding any more fellers neither, unless o'course it's a free-for-all up *there.'* She kept her prying eyes on Molly's unhappy face, while she jerked a thumb heavenwards.

'I'd be obliged if you'd please leave me be,' Molly told her. She didn't care much for the woman, she never had done, and she didn't like the things that were being said now. On top of which there was an awful ache in her heart, and she wanted to be left on her own.

'Oho . . . want rid of me, do you? Well, I expect you're not too keen on company just now . . . and it's only to be understood, in the circumstances, what with poor Sal not proper cold and all.'

The woman watched while Molly went to sit by the water's edge, where she absent-mindedly began to skim small clods of soil into the canal. 'They wouldn't let me go in where they took Sal,' murmured Molly in a forlorn voice, the tears still tumbling softly down her face. 'I wanted to stay with her.' She brought her two small fists up and scraped the tears away. 'But they wouldn't let me.'

'Well, o' course they wouldn't let you!' The woman was astonished that anybody should want to stay in a parish mortuary, unless of course they were stretched out and had no option. 'You don't want to go upsetting yourself any more than you need,' she told Molly, who made no response other than to lean forward, fold her arms across her bent knees and drop her dark head into the cradle

182

there. She felt utterly lost, and she knew in her aching heart that nothing would ever be the same again.

The woman sidled closer, all the while regarding the trim attractive figure: all manner of unsavoury thoughts ran through her mind. She was well aware that there was a ready market for young virgin girls, because hadn't she already fattened her purse from it time and time again?

'It comes to us *all*,' she went on, attempting now to move the subject away from Sal, when there might be an opportunity to lead on to other, more profitable matters. But first she had to deal with the girl's hostile attitude towards her. 'Don't take it too much to heart,' she said, 'Sal had a fair old innings. Why! . . . Look at the poor little bugger who got crushed unrecognisably under a coach and four in the early hours of this very morning . . . and not a spit too far from this very spot neither! Came dashing out of an alley they did, two o' 'em . . . the bigger one scarpered when a bobby blew his whistle, but the young 'un, well . . . after the wheels and hooves had gone over him, there wasn't much left, so they say. Funny thing, though . . . y'see, the undertaker is a cousin of the Navigation landlord . . . an' the word is that the little feller as was mangled, well . . . he were a *gentry*! What d'you think of that then? And if that don't top it all, it seems that he was Justice Crowther's own grandson! Well! . . . It don't bear thinking about, does it, eh? What would a young gentry like that be doing out at all hours . . . tell me that, eh? If you ask me, they're no better than *any* of us.'

She dug deep into her shawl, drew out a clay pipe and proceeded to light it, puffing away until her face grew an uncomfortable shade of pink. When it was firing nicely, she peeped at Molly, who up to now was too steeped in her own thoughts to pay any heed to the old woman's mutterings. 'Well, as I was saying . . . Justice Crowther's grandson no less! They do say as how he went wild when he was told . . . and the mother, she just passed right out in a faint. The boy's father's away on the high seas, and can't be contacted. I expect it'll break his heart, because the lad were an only child . . . happen he ran away or some'at, it's hard to say, ain't it? Got some fine and dandy togs on, by all accounts, except for his boots . . . which looked like they'd trudged for miles, according to the undertaker. And it was said how the lad had big coarse feet for a young gentry. Still . . . they don't wear boots in Heaven, I don't suppose, eh?' She gave a little laugh, before nudging Molly and saying slyly, 'What have you done with Sal's boots? I'll give you a pretty penny for 'em . . . her shawl too, if you've a mind?'

'They're not for sale. They're Sal's . . . and she's keeping them!' Molly had paid little heed to most of the woman's rantings, but the mention of Sal and her clothes had caught her attention.

'All right,' the woman was keen to pacify the agitated girl, 'let her be buried in 'em . . . though it seems a terrible shame to let good boots go to rot in a pauper's grave. And what about you, eh? You come and stay with me . . . you'll have plenty of friends, I promise . . . and a chance to turn a pretty penny.' Her pea-like eyes glistened, 'What d'you say?'

Molly was past listening, ever since the woman had said 'pauper's grave'. Now she was on her feet, her black eyes blazing. 'Sal ain't going in no *pauper's* grave!' she yelled, beginning to run in the direction of the hut and calling behind her. 'If that's what you think, you're *wrong*. I won't *let* her go in no pauper's grave!'

'Huh!' Takes hard brass to pay for a proper funeral, you little fool,' returned the woman. 'If you come with me, I'll see you earn it. Then you can pay for a proper funeral . . . I'll even be so good as to *lend* you the money, and take it back out of your earnings. What d'you say?'

Molly said nothing as she sped away into Blackburn town to make sure the parish officials didn't put Sal in a pauper's plot.

The fat bearded man was not altogether unsympathetic. The small dingy office fronted the parish yard where in one small corner stood a red-brick building with long narrow windows and a big black painted door. It was in there that they kept all the 'vagrants' and 'vagabonds' who had departed this world.

'No, I've told you before, you're not allowed in there. Tomorrow though, it won't matter anyway . . . because she'll be in the communal plot behind the churchyard. You'll be able to go and see her there.' He felt sorry for the pretty dark-haired girl, but rules were rules, and it was more than his job was worth to let her in. 'Go on, off you go,' he told her.

Molly stood her ground, her dark eyes beseeching as they looked up over the desk, her fingers clutched tight to its edge. 'Sal *ain't* going in no pauper's grave!' she declared, with such firmness that the fat bearded man put down his pen, and reached forward to look at Molly more

185

closely. 'I want Sal to have a proper burial,' she told him, her gaze unflinching beneath his intense and curious stare.

'Oh I see, young lady,' he said with a patronising smile, 'and how do you propose to *pay* for this "proper burial"? Got plenty of money, have you? . . . Come into a tidy sum?'

Only then did Molly realise the enormity of the task she had set herself. Fleetingly her small fingers toyed with the tiny watch secreted beneath her dress. But the thought of Sal, and the recollection of a promise she had only recently made caused her to feel ashamed. Yet somehow she would see that Sal was not thrown into the ground like some dead dog. She and Sal had come across such a pauper's burial once, and Molly had never forgotten it. She was determined it would not happen to her beloved Sal.

Molly told all of this to the man with the friendly eyes, and though he argued that she was looking to do the impossible, he did agree to delay Sal's departure from the yard until Monday next. 'Today being Wednesday, that gives you a good four days. After that, she'll have to be put down with the rest of them . . . or stink to high heaven, and nobody will want to touch her. And we can't have that, can we?'

Molly thought it unnecessary to say such a cruel thing, but she went away with a lighter heart. All the same, she was desperate as to how she might find the money. 'Two guineas, he said,' she muttered as she made her way back towards the canal, 'and Sal would get a proper church burial.' She hoped that the shrew-like woman was still there on the canal bank because, much as she didn't like the idea of going to live with that one and doing whatever work she was offering, Molly felt she had no choice. Not if she was to get two whole guineas in such a short time. It was true that Molly could pick a few pockets at Blackburn market on Saturday, but there weren't always gentry about, and it would be a miracle if she made *two guineas*. No, she daren't risk it. The woman's offer was her best bet. Once she'd repaid the two guineas, she would be free to go her own way again. But without her Sal. What a frightening thought. Yet her grief was eased by the intention of doing the very best she could for her darling Sal.

*   *   *

There was no sign of the shrew-like creature. So, armed with a vague notion that the woman lived somewhere down George Street, Molly set off again, thinking to look in the window of the Navigation on the way in case she had gone there. She was desperate to find her and she was prepared to do anything to see that Sal wasn't given a pauper's farewell.

Molly was just on the point of stepping from the canal bank and over the short wall—beyond which was the road and the Navigation—when the merest flicker of movement caught her eye and made her turn her head. In that split second she saw a boy on the bank, moving slowly at first, then staggering clumsily until, even as Molly looked, he lost his footing altogether. With a pitiful, weak cry he fell sideways and down, slithering into the water and disappeared out of sight, his small white hand grasping at the air in an effort to save himself. By the time Molly had sprinted the few yards to where he had vanished into the water, there was no sign of him at all, save for an odd bubble here and there, and the scuff mark along the bank where he had fallen in.

In a minute Molly had slipped out of her frock and was launching herself into the air, towards the spot where she had seen the boy go down. Surprisingly the water struck cold as she sliced into it, but the deeper she went, the warmer it seemed. Molly was a strong swimmer, having learned the skill as naturally as she had learned to walk, and often she had scoured the canal bottom in search of the odd coin which might have rolled from a drunk's pocket. Yet in the murky depths a coin might sparkle and catch the daylight from above, whereas there was nothing Molly thought as she swam this way and that, that might sparkle on a drowning boy. Except perhaps the terror in his eyes.

Molly would not give up though. She would go on searching until her lungs came near to bursting. Straining her eyes, she noticed a patch of unusually thick reeds where the fish had been disturbed. Quickly, she kicked her strong legs and swam the short distance, and in a minute she had caught sight of the boy. Thank God, she thought, his lungs were not yet swamped, seeing a thin spasmodic trail of bubbles escaping from within the tangle of reeds. Quickly she had him freed and in her grasp, a rush of relief flooding her heart. At the same time, Molly was aware of the desperate urgency to get him to the surface.

On the bank, Molly pummelled and squeezed him, until he began coughing and spluttering.

'Good!' she told the wet and bedraggled boy, yanking him to a sitting position, before pulling on her frock, and hoisting him to his feet. 'Now, lean on me, because we've a fair way to go afore we come to the hut.'

Later, when his clothes were dried and he was full of Molly's hot tea and jam butties, the boy sat by the rusty stove which Molly had lit to thaw his bones. 'You're a silly bugger!' she chided him. 'What were you doing . . . wandering along the bank like that? Don't you know better?' She had little patience with such foolishness.

The boy gave no answer. He just kept his eyes fixed on the stove and began shivering again. He wasn't sure how to react. In fact, he had no idea *how* he came to be 'wandering along the bank'. He didn't even know his own name. All he knew was that he had found himself in an alley, then he had walked and walked until he came to the canal. It was all a nightmare to him, and he knew above all else that if it had not been for this scruffy girl with the big black eyes and sharp temper he would surely have drowned. But he did not want to speak to her, because he hurt all over, and he was afraid.

'Oh, I see . . . cat got your tongue, has it?' teased Molly. Then, as he bent his head away from her, she saw the deep gash and the hair still matted round it. 'When did *that* happen?' she asked, reaching forward on her stool to take a closer look. 'That's bad!' In a minute, she had gone to fill the pan and, while it boiled, she searched about for a clean piece of cloth with which to bathe the wound. Tearing a strip from the pillowslip, she tested the water in the pan. Finding it warm enough, she drew the pan away and stood it on the stool. 'Keep still now. I don't want you struggling,' she instructed the boy. He did not move though, and nor did he protest because he felt lost and confused, but he had no intention of betraying his fears to a girl.

'Me and Sal . . . we never light this old stove, because it smokes like the billows and burns up more wood than we can find.' Molly kept up a banter of talk as she swabbed the gash on his head. She wished he would talk back, but she respected the way he must feel. He had suffered a nasty shock, she knew. But what puzzled her most was that the boy couldn't swim. Most children in these parts could swim before their legs were properly grown. That was another thing: Molly didn't think the boy came from here, or she would have remembered him. Yet she hadn't seen his face, not properly, because he kept avoiding her, turning his head away so she wouldn't get a good look at him. She supposed he must feel embarrassed at being rescued by a girl. Boys were like that, she knew. Strange though, how he couldn't swim. And he wasn't the usual sort of scruff because, although his clothes were tatty and probably smelt to high heaven before they got a ducking in the canal, his *hair* was properly cut, and his nails were *clean.* Strangest of all though, were his hands: so small and lily-white, it was plain he had never done any coal shovelling or hard work of any kind!

'Where do you come from?' she asked him now. 'And why were you stumbling along the bank, with such a terrible gash on your head?' A thought suddenly came to her. 'Did somebody *knock* you on the head?' That would account for why he was staggering like he was drunk. 'Is *that* it? Were you

190

set on by somebody?' She was sure of it now. 'You ain't from these parts, are you?' Molly leaned forward as she spoke, hoping she might get a look at his face again, because she was growing more curious by the minute. But he deliberately turned his face from her. The things she was saying made him think, and the things that began creeping into his mind were too unpleasant to dwell on.

'All right then. You lie on the bed and rest awhile. When you're feeling stronger, just let yourself out and shut the door behind you. I've got to go and see about Sal's funeral.' She opened the door and threw out the remainder of the water from the pan. 'You don't have to tell me nothing,' she called to him. When she came back into the hut, the boy was lying on his side, with his back to her. 'You're a strange one,' she murmured, her gaze resting on his tousled dark hair, 'and no mistake!' For a long poignant moment, Molly kept her gaze fixed on him, thinking how she had found Sal in that very bed, not so long ago. Sal, who had always been there, drunk or sober, Molly's best friend. Now she was gone, and the more Molly thought about it, the more desolate she felt. Without her being conscious of it, the tears began filling her eyes, then spilling over to run down her face.

It was then that the boy turned to look at Molly. When he saw her crying, she quickly looked away and pretended to busy herself clearing away the pan and other things. Of a sudden, she was aware that he was taking an interest in the tiny watch that hung forward from her neck as she stooped. 'I'll be on my way in a minute,' she said in a matter-of-fact voice. 'When I come back, I'll expect you to be gone.' When she straightened up to glance at him, he was still looking at her, his dark green eyes resting on her face, and Molly was riveted with shock. She *knew* him! How could she forget those emerald-green eyes and that particular way he had looked at her in the market place that day? Sal too had remarked on the boy's eyes. ' 'E put me in mind o' the little people . . . gave me a real nasty turn,' she had told Molly afterwards. She had told Molly something else as well: the boy was none other than Justice Crowther's *grandson*!

Molly was mesmerised as her own dark puzzled gaze bore into the boy's face. How could it be Justice Crowther's grandson? Molly began vaguely to recall snippets of what the shrew-like woman had told her only this very day. 'Justice Crowther's own grandson . . . after the wheels and hooves had gone over him, there wasn't much left, so they say.' How could it be then? How was it possible that the boy she had saved from drowning could also be the same boy? The answer was that he could *not*. Molly looked at his quiet face; she saw how clean and decent it was; she saw those eyes and that rich dark hair, cut in the way of a gentry; she remembered how clean his nails were, then how soft and white his hands. And she knew! Knew without a doubt that somehow there had been a trick played on Justice Crowther. She couldn't quite fathom it out, but she was certain of it. *This* boy was Justice Crowther's grandson, not the boy in the fancy togs who was run over by a coach and four. Something else was triggered off in Molly's mind. Something the shrew-like woman had said, to do with the undertaker remarking how the boy who was mangled 'had big coarse feet for a young

192

gentry'. Of course he did, thought Molly now. Of course he did, because he wasn't a gentry, that was why!

'How did you come to be wandering along the canal bank?' she asked him now, coming closer to the bed. 'Did you run away? Who knocked you on the head? Somebody did, I'm thinking . . . because there ain't nothing in the water that could have done it.'

'I don't know . . . anything,' Edward Trent replied, meeting Molly's gaze and feeling certain he had seen her before. Of a sudden, he recalled disjointed images of himself sneaking out from a big house, and of running from the devil in a dark alley. But the more he tried to think, the more he became confused. 'I know you though . . . I'm sure of it. I've seen you somewhere . . . somewhere.' The pain in his eyes deepened as he struggled to remember.

'It's all right,' Molly assured him, becoming convinced of his identity by the refined tone of his voice and the fact that he had seen her somewhere before . . . in the market place, no doubt. 'You'll be fine . . . after you've rested. You've had a nasty knock on the head . . . and you nearly drowned. It's not surprising that you can't properly recall what happened. Don't you worry. Get some sleep, and you'll be fine, I promise.' A plan was forming in her mind. A daring plan that might be the way to pay for Sal's burial. But she'd have to be quick, or it might be too late.

'What's your name?' the boy asked, settling himself into the bed as weariness came over him.

'Molly. I'm Sal Tanner's lass.' Molly felt a deal of pride as she told him that. But it was mingled

193

with a deep and painful sense of loss, which betrayed itself in her dark eyes. The boy was quick to notice, and to recall that Molly had earlier remarked that she had to go and 'see about Sal's funeral'. His instincts told him not to talk of 'Sal', or outstay his welcome. 'I want to thank you for what you've done for me,' he said, 'if I can just rest awhile, I'll be gone and I won't be a burden, I promise.'

'That's right,' encouraged Molly, 'you rest, while I go about my business. But you don't need to hurry away.' If her plan was to work, the boy must be kept here. 'Old Sal used to give me a herbal drink when I was feeling under the weather and couldn't sleep. I'll get you a drop,' she told him. After a frantic search, she discovered Sal's gin bottle hidden inside the orange-box. Quickly mixing a measure of it with a drop of water and a sprinkle of sugar, she held it to the boy's lips. 'Here we are. Drink this and you'll sleep like a hedgehog in winter.'

When Molly was satisfied that he was in a deep contented slumber, she covered him over, took one of the shoes which had shrunk to his feet after the canal soaking, then went swiftly from the hut, shutting the door tight behind her. Glancing up to ensure that the window was left open for ventilation, she tucked the expensive shoe into the pocket of her frock and went at top speed along the bank.

Molly was not too proud of what she intended to do now, because she liked the boy. She thought him to be a cut above the other gentry she had come across, but she made herself recall an old saying of Sal's—one which she often used to

194

excuse her more unsavoury activities: when needs must, the devil pays, was what Sal would claim in her own defence. It was what Molly told herself now, as she sped through Mill Hill and on towards the outlying fields. She had a rough idea that she was heading in the right direction. Anyway, Breckleton House shouldn't be too difficult to find.

*   *   *

'Get away from here, yer little ruffian!' Cook had been summoned to the kitchen door by Molly's insistent knocking, and she was not too pleased at the sight of a filthy little urchin standing there. 'There's misery enough in this house today . . . wi'out us being bothered by beggars!' She would have slammed the door in Molly's face, but when she was told, 'Justice Crowther's grandson *ain't* dead. *I've* got him!' Cook hesitated, just long enough for Molly to blurt out, 'He's got dark eyes the colour of emeralds . . . and he can't swim.'

'How do yer know *that?*' Cook demanded, inching the door open, yet not coming back out. 'An' when did a filthy little baggage the likes o' *you* see the colour of 'is eyes, eh?' There was no doubt she was intrigued, because it was true that the young master had never learned to swim. There had been arguments about it between his mother, who saw it as being unnecessary, and his father, who claimed that every boy should be given the opportunity to learn to swim, especially when he might follow in his father's footsteps and be a sailor. Martha Trent's reply had been a caustic one, 'I shall *never* let him be a sailor!' From there,

195

the argument had raged on.

'How d'yer know all this?' insisted Cook, keeping her sizeable frame secure behind the door.

'I know . . . because he fell in the canal and I saved him from drowning,' replied Molly, beginning to take the shoe from her pocket. '*He* wasn't the one who was run over and killed. I reckon as it was another fellow altogether. I don't know if it were a rogue or a gentry, but it weren't Edward Trent, I'm telling you, missus. Because *I've* got Justice Crowther's grandson, hidden away and safe enough.' She brought the shoe with the shiny buckle from her pocket, and when Cook saw it, she nearly fainted. 'Oh, upon my word . . . it's the young master's boot!' she cried, flinging the door open and making a grab for it.

'Oh, no you don't!' warned Molly, immediately dodging backwards and remaining at a safe distance. 'I ain't giving this shoe to *nobody* . . . anyway, not till you fetch the lady of the house. Don't fetch the Justice, because I'll not tell *him* nothing! I'll only do business with the lady of the house.' Molly had never forgotten Sal's warning concerning Justice Crowther, and the very idea of being confronted by the fellow himself made her shiver in her boots.

'As it happens, yer little dirty baggage . . . there's only the mistress and the boy's mother here. The Justice is at the undertakers, making final arrangements.' She rolled her eyes upwards and made the sign of the cross on herself.

'In that case, he's making final arrangements for somebody else,' Molly reminded her, 'because I've got his grandson safe, I'm telling you. Now . . . if you'd be so kind as to fetch her ladyship?'

'You cheeky little madam!' snorted Cook. For two pins she would have brought Thomas to see the little wretch off down the road, but there was too much in what the girl said. Cook felt it was more than her life was worth to ignore the evidence of the shoe and all. 'Wait here. I'll see if the mistress is interested in what you have to say . . . but let me warn you: if you're here to cause mischief, you'll be given every opportunity to explain it to the authorities!'

When the door swung to, leaving Molly staring at the grotesque brass gargoyle which served as a knocker, she put out her tongue at it. She went to the window, where she pulled herself up by the wall and sat on the deep stone window-ledge, swinging her skinny legs back and forth, and waited somewhat nervously for the lady of the house to emerge.

Molly did not have to wait long: no sooner had she settled herself than there came a flurry of activity at the kitchen door. 'Where is she?' came a woman's agitated voice. Then, as Agnes Crowther swept out on to the flag stones, one hand plucking the folds of her long taffeta skirt and the other waving loosely in the air, she caught sight of Molly, who quickly jumped down from the window-ledge. Molly's stomach turned nervous somersaults at the sight of this fancy lady, whose husband had the power to have her flayed alive. As Agnes Crowther approached, Molly backed away. 'Don't you come no nearer, missus,' she warned, 'if you try to grab me, I'll make a run for it and you won't see your lad again.'

'No!' Agnes Crowther stopped some short distance away, lifting her hand from her skirt and putting both palms up to Molly. 'It's all right . . . I won't come any nearer.' She gestured for Cook and the maid, Amy, to go back, saying, 'Make sure that my daughter is not disturbed. Let her sleep.' When the two women were out of sight Agnes Crowther turned her attention to Molly. 'Tell me all you know of my grandson . . . please.' Then, in a harsher tone, 'But be careful you tell me no lies, or you will live to regret it, I promise!' She then recovered her composure, stiffened her back and raised her two hands together in a posture of prayer, holding them close to her breast as she asked, 'What *do* you know? Cook tells me you don't believe it was Master Edward who was killed. What makes you say such a thing? The truth, girl. Out with it!'

Her courage returning, and with Sal's predicament paramount in her mind, Molly described how she had seen the boy stumble and fall into the canal. 'He would have drowned, missus . . . he *would*, if I hadn't saved him,' she assured Agnes Crowther, who merely nodded impatiently and bade her go on. Molly then explained how, in spite of the boy's clothes, she suspected that he was not an urchin off the streets. 'His nails were too clean, and his hands were too soft and white,' she said. After which she went into great detail regarding his appearance, how dark was his hair, and how deep-green his eyes. She told of the way he had spoken to her. 'Too *posh* by half! . . . And look here'—she snatched the shoe from the depths of her ragged frock—'this is the boy's shoe!'

All the while Molly had been talking, Agnes Crowther had paid the closest attention, and the

198

more she heard, the paler she became. When the shoe was brandished before her, she cried out and swayed as though she might faint, her posture of prayer broken as she put out an arm to grasp the wall for support. 'It is Edward's shoe!' she gasped, her eyes fixed on the black ankle boot which had a small decorative buckle to the side. 'Oh . . . I had my suspicions all along that it was *not* my grandson lying there in the mortuary . . . but no one would listen. They were all quick to grieve. Too blinded by what they saw before them, and too easily led by what they were told.' Of a sudden she was moving forward, her face a study in compassion, and her arm outstretched as though to take the shoe from Molly's grasp. 'Where is he . . . this boy? You must take me to him at once!' she urged.

But Molly was no fool. She had not forgotten the purpose which had brought her here, nor had she forgotten what a fearfully powerful family she was dealing with. 'Not so fast, your ladyship,' she told her, teasing the shoe away and taking a step backward. 'I *will* take you to where your grandson is, but it will cost you a pretty penny.'

'You scoundrel!' retorted Agnes Crowther. 'I shouldn't be at all surprised if you and your kind hadn't arranged this whole dreadful affair!' The fire had returned to Agnes Crowther's eyes, and for a brief moment Molly's courage began to waver. But it took only a thought of where Sal was and where she might end up to restore her flagging spirit. 'No, I didn't!' she retorted indignantly. 'I might be a thief when things get desperate . . . but I ain't no crook!'

'What is it you want then?' demanded Agnes Crowther. 'If this boy really is my grandson . . . and there is no real proof of that . . . you may depend that Justice Crowther will reward you handsomely.'

'I won't do no dealings with *him*!' Molly told her. 'I need two guineas . . . it ain't for me, neither.'

'So! . . . There is somebody else. Somebody who has put you up to coming here and telling lies.'

'There's nobody else, missus. The two guineas is to pay for a proper burial for . . . well, that don't matter none. You just pay me now, and I'll fetch the boy from where he's hidden.'

'No. I must come with you, or how can I trust you?'

When Molly saw that Agnes Crowther was adamant, she reluctantly agreed to a compromise. 'You take a carriage to the warehouse at the end of Stephen Street in Mill Hill . . . and I'll fetch the boy to you, within the hour. Mind you . . . if I so much as catch sight of anybody but just yourself, I swear you'll not get him back! And I want paying now.'

'Half now, and the remainder when I see that the boy really *is* my grandson.'

So it was agreed. With one guinea safe in the palm of her hand, in exchange for the shoe, Molly set off at a run to rouse the boy from his slumber. Still not fully convinced but filled with hope and excitement, Agnes Crowther hurried indoors to don her cloak and bonnet, emerging some ten minutes later to climb into the carriage, with Cook's words ringing in her ears: 'Yer don't want to get yer hopes too high on the word of a street urchin, m'lady. Set the authorities on the little baggage . . . they'll soon find out what she's up to!'

Agnes Crowther's reply was to remind her of her place. 'Make sure you leave my daughter resting. And, if the master returns in my absence, you are to say nothing of my errand. If it turns out to be a trick I myself will inform Justice Crowther to root the girl out; but . . . if by some miracle my grandson really is safe . . . bringing the boy home will speak for itself.'

*   *   *

Some time later, after Molly had successfully roused Edward Trent enough to walk him along the towpath and down Angela Street towards Stephen Street, Agnes Crowther was alerted by her driver Thomas. 'This looks like them now, milady,' he said, leaning down from his lofty seat and pointing a finger towards the two children approaching. Being a woman not easily given to Christian values, Agnes Crowther had never set great store by prayer and rarely indulged in it with much heart. But when she reached her head out of the carriage window, the sight of those two small and bedraggled figures coming towards her brought tears to her eyes. When she stepped down from the carriage and waited, as Molly had insisted, she actually uttered a heartfelt prayer. Then, as they came ever closer, and she kept her anxious eyes on the boy, the familiar shape began to grow, the manner of his walk, his hair, she began to recognise him as her own grandson. Forgetting that she had promised to stay by the carriage, Agnes Crowther began walking towards them, completely oblivious of the one or two people who hurried by to go about their business.

When Molly saw that Agnes Crowther had gone back on her word, she was unsure as to what to do. The boy was leaning so heavily on her shoulder

201

that, were she to let him go, he would slump to the floor. Besides which, she *must* collect the other guinea. So she stood still and waited. When Agnes Crowther saw this, she hurried her steps until she was almost running. When in a moment she was on them and the boy looked up at her through hazy eyes, she threw out her arms and wrapped them about him. 'Edward . . . oh, thank God!' For Molly, who had never witnessed such humanity in the gentry, it was a humbling scene. 'I *told* you he was safe, didn't I?' she said. 'He would have drowned if it weren't for me.' She mustn't let them forget that, she thought, *nor* that she was still owed a guinea!

When Thomas had gently lifted the boy into the carriage, Agnes Crowther kept her promise to Molly. 'I don't know whether you've played a guilty or an innocent part in this business,' she said sternly, at the same time handing over the guinea, 'but you kept your word to me . . . and I shall keep mine to you.' Then, before Molly turned and took to her heels, she was given a warning: 'Stay out of Justice Crowther's way. I have no doubt that he would insist on knowing more than you have told me.'

*   *   *

'Goodbye, my Sal.' Molly was on her knees in the churchyard, her small grubby hands lovingly arranging the flowers over the mound of earth. 'I'll miss you . . . and I'll never forget you, not as long as I live.' Her face ran wet with tears, and her sad dark eyes betrayed the pain which racked her heart.

When, reluctantly, she left the churchyard,

Molly was glad at least that she had been able to keep her promise to Sal, because how could she rest, knowing that Sal, her one and only friend in this world, was not lying in properly consecrated ground? Now the priest had said the right words over Sal, there had even been a hymn sung in church for her, and Molly's heart was once more at peace as she wended her way home on that wind-blown Tuesday evening.

As she rounded the canal bank and made towards the hut, Molly thought briefly about the boy, Edward Trent. There was talk on the wharf of how some ruffians had kidnapped him, then held him to ransom, only setting him free when a great sum of money was paid. It was also rumoured that Justice Crowther had vowed to hunt down the 'villains responsible', to bring them to justice and to punish them with the severest penalty that the law would allow. According to the gossips there was a bad rift between the Justice and his wife, Agnes, because of the whole sordid business; the boy himself, though greatly improved, was still under medical supervision and therefore protected from being more closely questioned on the matter. As for his mother, Martha Trent, she was as determined that the 'kidnappers' be apprehended and made to pay, as was her father. Silas Trent, Martha's husband, was away on the high seas, and knew nothing yet of the narrow escape his son had had. As for the lad in the fancy togs, nobody ever found out who he was or where he belonged, because never a soul came forward to claim him, and it wasn't surprising, they said, in view of all the fuss he'd caused, as well as the puzzling fact that he had been found wearing togs that were the property of none other than Justice Crowther's grandson.

Molly had heard all of these rumours, but had paid them little heed. It was a known fact that folks did love to exaggerate.

By the time Molly had brewed herself a pot of tea and finished off the last crust of bread, together with a wedge of cheese, it was already twilight. Later, when she had strip-washed at the bowl and pulled on the well-worn cream-coloured shift which Sal had brought home one day as a surprise, Molly slipped the bolt on the door and knelt by the makeshift bed, her hands together, eyes closed tight and her young heart flooded with memories of Sal. 'Take care of her, please, Lord,' she murmured. 'I know she did bad things sometimes, but she weren't really bad, and she always took good care of me. Sal always said I shouldn't ask for too much in my prayers, Lord . . . but I'd be very grateful if you could please help me to find my own mam and dad. I don't know where to start, because all I've got is this little timepiece.' Here she withdrew the tiny watch from round her neck and gazed at it fondly. 'I don't know what the words say, and I don't know where it came from, but I must have a mammy somewhere, Lord,' she went on, 'and I would dearly love to find her.'

It suddenly struck Molly that even if she did have a mammy somewhere and the Lord only knew how it would gladden Molly's heart to see her, there was always the chance that her mammy didn't want her, because hadn't Sal described how she had found the bundle in the street. 'An' it were you . . . left by the little people.' If she *had* been left in the street, Molly knew it wasn't by no 'little people', but by somebody else. And if that somebody else was her own mammy, then it followed that she didn't want her own child, and, if she didn't want it *then*, when it was a tiny helpless newborn, then it was certain that she wouldn't want it now.

The more Molly thought about it, the more desolate she became until, feeling suddenly exhausted and more lonely than ever, she climbed into bed. Life was a funny old thing, she told herself, deliberately shutting out the world and drifting thankfully into sleep. Until this very minute, Molly had not realised just how tired she was. 'Tomorrow,' she promised herself, 'I'll go down to the wharf and see if I can get a regular job.' The thought cheered her no end.

*   *   *

When Molly awoke, it was amidst a barrage of noise and confusion. She knew at once that it wasn't yet morning, because the inside of the hut was dark, except for an arrow of moonlight coming in through the tiny window. 'Who's that?' she shouted, her heart pounding as she swung her legs out of bed and began frantically searching for her boots. There was somebody out there. She could hear all manner of noises, like rats scrabbling to get in, or maybe it was ruffians who knew she was here on her own! In a minute, she had found her boots, and was hurriedly pulling the first one on. 'I've got a shot gun!' she yelled, hoping that might send them scurrying away. 'If you come near me, I'll blow your bloody head off!' Oh, how she wished Sal were here.

Suddenly, two things happened, and Molly was lost. The hut was filled with light directed in through the window and, before Molly could think what to do, the door burst open and in rushed several large figures, at least two of them carrying huge lamps whose halo of light swung eerily from wall to wall. 'Get out of here!' yelled Molly, her hand raised threateningly, and the boot she held aimed at the figure who stealthily approached her, while the others remained both still and silent. She could not see his face, but the tall and grotesque silhouette he made struck fear into her heart. He lifted his arm and made a sign with his hand, a beckoning gesture to call the others on. In a minute, Molly was surrounded, the lights all seeking out her face, and the silhouette taking on the shape of a man, a man who was unusually large, with a profusion of iron-grey hair covering the lower half of his features, and blue eyes that were both piercing and hateful. When Molly looked up, she instantly recognised the man, and she was in mortal terror. It was the same man who had talked with Gabe Drury before that poor soul was found floating in the canal; the same man whose wallet she had stolen, and was made to return when Sal discovered its awful identity. Molly would never forget how fearful Sal had been on that night: 'Justice Crowther would search far and wide to find you,' Sal had warned her and, instinctively, Molly also had been fearful of him.

Boots or no boots, Molly decided the only thing to do now was to make a run for it. With a cry of 'You ain't taking me!' she flung her boot at one of the lamps, and made a frantic dash towards the door. Her swift reflex appeared to have caught the intruders off guard. 'Stop her, you fools!' yelled Caleb Crowther, himself swinging out an arm to catch her as she ducked and dived out of his reach.

Being thin and wiry, Molly was also quick on her feet and she might have made it to freedom, were it not for the constable outside. As she rushed out of the door, he blocked her path and caught her by the shoulders, afterwards holding her aloft by the scruff of her neck with her feet kicking furiously in the air. 'Let me be!' she screeched, lashing out at him with her two fists; 'I ain't done nothing wrong! . . . I *ain't,* I tell you!' She was cruelly silenced by a spiteful blow to the side of her head, as her pursuer stepped from the hut.

'Know when to keep your mouth shut, urchin.' Caleb Crowther took a lamp from the constable nearby, and holding it up high, he looked deep and long into Molly's tearful face. 'Robbery, violence . . . abducting my grandson? . . . You call this "nothing"?' His voice was soft and smooth as velvet, but at the same time intense and terrifying. 'Rogues have *hanged* for less,' he told her, 'but we've got you and, no doubt, we'll soon have your accomplices.'

'I didn't do *any* of those things,' Molly protested, angry that she should be accused. 'He would have drowned if it weren't for me. I found him in time . . . and he already had a gash on his head. Whoever it was that attacked him . . . it weren't *me!*' She was lashing out with her legs and arms. 'I only fetched him back 'cause I needed Sal's burial money. If I hadn't fetched him back, he would have run away . . . he told me! But I can't blame him . . . wanting to run away from *you.* I should have let the poor little bugger go!' Of a sudden,

Molly realised she had gone too far and let her tongue run away with her. Sal was right when she always used to warn that 'yer too quick-tempered by 'arf! That tongue o' yourn'll get yer in trouble one o' these fine days, my gal!' She gave up her efforts at struggling, and hung in the constable's fists like a rag-doll. 'I did save him from drowning,' she finished lamely.

'Bind her well,' instructed Caleb Crowther, his face a study in rage. 'Let her escape, man . . . and you won't see daylight for years.'

While the constables set about securing Molly's flailing figure, Caleb Crowther went back inside the hut, his mind working feverishly and his determination to be rid of that dark-eyed urchin made stronger by what he had just seen. His earlier suspicions had been undeniably confirmed, and he was deeply bothered by it. Just now, when he had lifted the lamp, its light had picked out a glistening object on the urchin's neck; he was convinced that the object was the very same watch that had belonged to Emma Grady's mother, Mary. Mary, whom he had loved beyond the grave, whom he still craved for in his sleeping hours, and who had suffered the ultimate penalty for deceiving him with another man.

He recalled having seen that same urchin before, on the very night he had talked to Gabe Drury and, even more disturbing, he now suspected that she might have seen his face; although of course he had kept well hidden, and there was no proof whatsoever of his having seen Gabe Drury. Who would listen to a street urchin, already implicated in all manner of the worst possible crimes? No, he was safe enough, he was sure. But that wasn't all, because he strongly suspected that this girl, who bore the same dark features as the bargee, Marlow Tanner, was the child of that man . . . and borne by the woman whom everyone believed to be his niece, Emma Grady! The sight of that watch, which had been Emma's mother's and was still in Emma's possession at the time of her arrest, left him with only one conclusion. The brat was Emma's off-spring, and as such represented a threat in the long-term. A threat which was every bit as irritating as Emma Grady herself, and one which he did not intend to tolerate under any circumstances. Here he smiled to himself, as he drew out a small tin of matches from his waistcoat pocket. Fortune was sometimes a wonderful ally, especially when it offered the perfect opportunities to be rid of one's enemies, he mused.

Striking the match alive, Caleb Crowther waited awhile, until the bright yellow flame was rearing and spitting. Then, with the smile deepening his features, he dropped the lighted match on to the mattress, afterwards going to the door and watching while the mattress gave up a fierce and rosy glow.

Before they dragged her round the corner and away from her beloved canal bank, Molly glanced back, towards the hut which had been her and Sal's home. When she saw the flames and smoke reaching to the night sky, she was filled with shock and horror. In that moment, she saw the look of satisfaction on Caleb Crowther's face, and for the first time in her young life, she felt real hatred in her heart. When, in a moment, they were bundling her into the waiting waggon and her sobbing was pitiful to hear, Molly knew that she would never forget this night. Nor would she ever forget, or forgive, the man they called the Justice.

Caleb Crowther kept a close eye as Molly was ushered into the jail-cart along with other miscreants who had been dragged from their beds this night. He had not forgotten the delicate watch around her neck, or his intention to take it discreetly from her at the first opportunity. But he must not be seen in the act of securing it from her, or that might well arouse too much interest.

'What did the buggers get *you* for, eh?' Molly felt herself being nudged by the person thrust in next to her, and when she turned to see who it was that was so interested in her, she was pleasantly surprised to be faced with a pair of smiling eyes and as handsome a fellow as she'd ever seen. Besides which, he appeared to be not much older than Molly himself, about fourteen she reckoned.

'They've accused me of robbery, and of abducting Justice Crowther's grandson,' she replied, always being one to tell the truth when it mattered. Though, if Molly thought the fellow might be shocked at the charges against her, she was not wrong.

'*What*? Robbery and abduction . . . and the grandson of the Justice, no less!' Of a sudden, he was rocking with laughter, and so were the other two captives in the waggon. 'Yer having me on, ain't yer?' he chuckled. 'Why! There ain't two-pennorth of yer, and that's a fact!'

Molly would have been amused too, if it weren't for the fact that it was she who was in this terrible predicament, and not him. 'It's all right you laughing,' she said, 'but I don't think it's so funny!'

'Aw . . . it ain't so bad, you'll see.' He had lowered his voice, so the two accompanying constables might not hear. 'In a few minutes we'll be crossing Mill Hill bridge at the top of Parkinson Street. The horses don't like it, on account of it being narrow and having a sharpish turn. They'll slow right down, you mark my words . . . *that's* when we'll make a run fer it.'

'Stop that whispering!' thundered the constable seated at the front, and for a moment everything was quiet.

'Are yer game?' insisted the fellow, nudging Molly again and whispering close to her ear.

It only took Molly a second to give her reply. because, truth be told, this handsome likeable fellow might be her only chance to get away. What was more, she had taken a real liking to him. 'What d'you want me to do?' she asked, then sat rigid and silent when the constable leaned forward to see who was being so insolent as to go on whispering in the face of his instruction.

When, in order to distract the constable's attention, Molly developed a seizure of coughing, the fellow beside her murmured quietly, 'Just be ready, that's all!'

Molly knew the Mill Hill bridge well, and she kept her eyes glued to the open slats in the wooden cage, constantly looking ahead for when they would pass the bottom of Stephen Street, on the approach to the hump-backed bridge. The journey seemed painstakingly slow as the cart wheels picked their way over the small uneven cobbles. Molly's heart was thumping fearfully, because she knew that if the escape bid were unsuccessful, both she *and* the handsome fellow would be made to

211

regret the effort. Yet, in spite of the instincts which warned her always to be on her guard, Molly trusted the lad sitting next to her, and she had unusual confidence in him. Wasn't it strange, she thought, how sometimes a body warmed to a stranger without ever knowing why.

As the waggon approached the bridge, the horses instinctively slowed down.

'What's the delay?' called Caleb Crowther, leaning out of the carriage window behind. He sounded highly impatient.

'It's the bridge, sir,' replied the constable in the rear of the waggon as he climbed out to monitor the situation more closely. 'The horses . . . they don't like it, being so narrow and sharp, like.'

In a minute, Caleb Crowther was out of the carriage and striding towards the waggon, which at this point was stationary, the horses having come to a standstill. 'Drive them on, man!' he roared. 'Don't let them have their head!' At the front of the waggon, the driver could be heard cracking his whip and threatening the terrified animals with all kinds of terrible fates.

'Quick gal . . . get ready!' The young fellow took hold of Molly's bound hands, gripping them tightly as he urged in a frantic whisper, 'Wait till the Justice has his back to us . . . then *jump*! Run for all you're worth and don't let go of me.' No sooner had he spoken the last word than Caleb Crowther engaged the constable in a row, turning his back to the waggon and demanding the fellow's explanation as to why he had come this way at all, instead of going straight down Parkinson Street and out by way of Havelock. Not being as familiar with the Mill Hill area as was the constable, he was unaware that the dark narrow viaduct at the bottom of Parkinson Street would have sent the horses into even more of a blind panic.

'Now!' the fellow cried, and Molly felt herself yanked from her seat and propelled forward at a furious pace. Before she knew quite what was happening, the two of them were launched from the waggon and sailing through the air. 'Run, me darling!' the fellow yelled, as their feet crunched to the ground. Suddenly, all hell was let loose. The constable shouted, 'The prisoners are escaping!' The horses bolted in fright, and the constable still in the waggon, together with the remaining hapless prisoners, was flung from side to side as the waggon went careering over the bridge, with the first constable taking up chase.

Molly scrambled to her feet, with her hands still securely held by her companion. She laughed out loud at all the commotion and thought the whole escapade to be a real treat, until, with a cry of rage, Caleb Crowther darted forward to grab her, viciously, by the neck, at which point she felt herself being tugged in separate directions as the fellow and the Justice pulled with equal determination. It only took a few seconds, but to Molly it seemed like a lifetime before the fellow gave an extra tug and she was yanked free. Unfortunately, she felt the precious timepiece ripped from about her neck as she sprang forward close on the fellow's heels. But there was no going back. The uppermost thought in her mind at that moment was that she must run like the wind, until safe out of harm's way. Behind them they could hear the constables' whistles piercing the night air.

When at last the fellow brought himself and

Molly to a standstill at the bottom of Myrtle Street, they were both coughing and wheezing, gasping for air and dangerously unsteady on their legs. Molly truly believed that she would never walk again.

It was a long and painful few minutes before either of them could get enough breath to speak. It was Molly who recovered first. 'He took it . . . that awful Justice broke the chain and took my timepiece.' She felt desolate.

'Timepiece? What . . . yer mean a pocket watch?' The fellow seemed surprised that a scruffy girl should keep something as useless as a 'timepiece'. 'Aw, it don't matter none, gal. Who cares about it, eh? I'll get yer another.' He discarded the binding which had secured Molly's wrist and watched with curiosity while Molly gathered together the bits of broken chain which had tangled about her neck. 'Steal it, did yer? Why didn't yer sell it, then? It ain't no use round yer neck, is it?'

'I *didn't* steal it!' Molly retorted. 'It belonged to *me* . . . ever since I was born.' Now she would never find her real mam and dad. 'There were *words* on it,' she told him in a tearful voice.

'Words? . . . What did they say?'

'I don't know,' replied Molly, 'but I would have found out one day.'

'Yer mean yer can't *read*?' He was suddenly proud of himself. 'I learned ter read when they put me and me mam in the workhouse . . . after the old fella ran away. The beadle made all us children say our prayers and learn ter read. Then he threw me out on the street when my mam died.' He seemed momentarily lost in thought. 'Was it worth a bob or two . . . that watch o' yours?'

214

But Molly didn't want to discuss it. It was too painful. 'What's your name?' she asked instead.

'Jack . . . Jack-the-lad they calls me; what's yours?'

'Molly . . . Tanner,' came the hesitant reply, because Molly had never used the name 'Tanner' before. She had only ever been known as 'Molly . . . Sal's lass'.

At once the fellow's face broke into a wide and attractive grin, and, in the light from the street gas-lamp, Molly saw that his eyes were a warm shade of brown, and his teeth were surprisingly white and even. 'I like your name . . . Molly,' he said, chucking her under the chin and making a cheeky suggestive wink, and I like *you* . . . I reckon yer a real good-looker, with that coal-black hair and them big midnight eyes. You'll do for me,' he said boldly.

'Hmph! You've got a bloody nerve,' Molly told him sternly, thinking he was one of them certain 'charmers' that Sal was always warning her against.

'I have! You're right, Molly gal. I have got a bloody nerve, and I'll tell yer some'at else . . . I'm gonna *marry* yer just as soon as ever I can!' Then, before Molly could get her breath, he took her by the hand, pulled her towards him and planted a loud hearty kiss on her mouth. 'Yep,' he said, shaking his head and drawing his lips together, 'you'll do fer me, Molly gal! First though . . . we've to steal yer some togs, 'cause I ain't having my future missus wandering the streets in her nightshift.'

Molly bit back the caustic retort which rose to her lips. With his warm, strong hand clasped over hers, and the feel of his kiss still burning on her

215

mouth, it did seem peevish to be so ungrateful. Besides which, she had a warm, contented feeling inside that even the thought of losing Sal, or being hunted down by the Justice . . . or even losing her precious timepiece . . . couldn't spoil. Molly liked him. She *really* liked him, this 'Jack-the-lad'. 'Where we going?' she asked as they trudged along.

'Never you mind, darling,' came the reply, with a comforting squeeze of his hand. 'We'll make a good few miles before daybreak . . . leave Blackburn town behind and go where the buggers'll never find us.' He stopped and turned to look at her. 'That's a fault o' mine,' he said, with surprising shyness; 'me mam allus said I were a bossy bugger. What I want ter know, Molly gal, is . . . them plans o' mine, how do they sound ter you? Do they suit you?'

Molly returned his warm, quiet smile, and when she spoke it was with a song in her heart. 'Whatever you say, Jack,' she told him. For a while, he simply looked at her, his smiling brown eyes reaching into her trembling young heart. 'Oh yes, Molly gal,' he said at length, 'you'll do fer me!'

As she followed him, not knowing where and not really caring, Molly felt comfortable in his presence. Oh, but her precious timepiece. She opened the palm of her hand and glanced down at the dainty mangled chain with its pretty petal fastener. 'Don't you fret, Molly lass,' came Jack's voice in her ear, ' 'cause I'll mend that for yer. And I shall keep me eyes open for a new watch along the way.' Molly thanked him. But her heart was sore at the tragic loss of that watch. How will I ever find my mam now, she wondered with a stab of regret. If you're listening up there, Sal . . . have a word with your 'little people'. Happen they'll know what to do. She laughed in warm memory of Sal's antics. Then, with softly spoken words, she murmured, 'You shouldn't have left me, Sal . . . you shouldn't have left me.'

Part Three

Australia 1876

Always Searching

The times I have dreamed,
The dreams I have known,
Will stay within my heart.
I will cherish them
And cherish you,
Loathing the miles
That keep us apart.

J.C.

Chapter Eight

'Where are you bound for, mate?' The handsome dark-haired sailor swung his knapsack to the ground, glad to be relieved of its cumbersome weight, even though the August day was one of the coolest he had known. The breeze blowing inland held the threat of rain. 'Captain Trent, isn't it?' he asked of the sturdy looking figure with quiet brown eyes and military moustache who was making his way down the gangplank towards him.

'That's right . . . Silas Trent's the name.' He fixed the sailor in his sight, noting at once how able-bodied and pleasant the fellow seemed. He also sensed something very sad, or lonely, in his countenance. When he dropped to a level footing with him, he took the hand which was outstretched and, closing it in his own strong fingers, he shook it warmly. 'This is my ship, the *Stirling,*' he said, inclining his head sideways. Then, with a laugh he added, 'My wife, Martha . . . she accuses me of being in love with the old hulk.'

'She's no hulk,' remarked the sailor, envyingly roving his dark eyes over the ship's lines and noting that she was as good a barque as he'd seen in a long time. 'She's a fine vessel. You're a lucky fellow, Captain . . . and owner, I take it?'

'That right. And yes . . . she *is* a "fine vessel". The last of a grand sailing fleet built up with sweat and blood by my own father, and left to me when he passed on. Unfortunately I've come on harder times than he ever witnessed . . . fiercer competition, and capital finance being that much

221

harder to acquire. It's the larger lines who call the tune now . . . They're the ones who get first crack at the best cargoes. On top of which, all the experienced crews are lured away by better wages.' He shook his head and thoughtfully stroked his 'tache, before saying in a quieter tone, 'It's been two years since I've seen my wife and son . . . Edward's going on sixteen years old now, away at school he is. I'm glad to say he's a better bookworm than I'll ever be. It would have been grand though, if he had the sea in his blood, like me, and his grandfather before him. But he's not interested . . . wants to be a doctor, he says. Well, each to his own, I expect. My lad had a nasty experience a while back . . . set on by some ruffians and very nearly drowned in the process. It left its mark on his mind, I dare say. All the same, I intend to build my father's fleet up again . . . it's a promise I've made myself.'

The dark-eyed sailor smiled, a dashing, gypsy-like smile, when all the sadness went from his face and only the eyes betrayed an inner conflict. 'We all make ourselves promises, Cap'n,' he said; 'only some of us don't have wives and children to go home to. I do have a sister, though . . . and I've promised myself that I won't go back to her empty-handed. I'll make my fortune, I'm sure of it.' He laughed out loud. 'The only thing is . . . it's taking a bit longer than I thought! Yet, if I went home now . . . I wouldn't be going altogether empty-handed.'

'Looking to sign on, are you?'

'I am. I've just come in on the *Augustus* . . . see there?' He pointed to the three-masted barque berthed alongside. 'I've finished a three-year stint

222

with her . . . Calcutta out of Melbourne mostly . . . wool and sandalwood. The skipper landed a good contract from one of the big traders.'

Silas Trent knew of the ship. It belonged to the Firth Line and was one of four. 'I know that well enough,' he said, wincing. 'That was the very contract I was chasing when I came out here. Why aren't you staying with her?' He was curious to know.

'She's making ready for England. I'm not about to go back yet.'

'Then you won't want to come aboard here either, because Liverpool is where I'm bound. Liverpool and good old England . . . first tide in the morning; we're already battened down and the last of the crew are due back any minute.' When he saw the disappointment on the sailor's face, he pointed to a clipper which was lying off shore. 'You might try the *Linesman* out there. I believe she's headed for Swedish waters.'

The sailor shook his head and swung up the knapsack to his shoulder, saying, 'No luck there, I'm afraid. She already has a full crew . . . I made enquiries about that one soon as ever I came off the *Augustus*.'

'What are your plans then?'

'A jug of ale and a good night's sleep at the tavern. Like as not I'll get me a ship on the morrow. Good day to you, Cap'n.'

Silas Trent nodded his head and touched the neb of his cap as he watched the sailor walk along the jetty and round the corner towards the inn, thinking that the fellow was not the usual coarse type of sailor he'd come across. When, out of the corner of his eye, he caught sight of his first officer

223

returning with the authorised papers, he gave him his full attention. 'Everything in order?' he asked.

The officer nodded before making a gesture after the sailor whom he had seen leaving. 'Taking him on, are we?'

'Unfortunately no . . . we're one man short and could have done with that fellow. But he won't be bound for England.'

'Aye, and you couldn't have done better than him if you'd searched from one end of Australia to the other. He's a good man.'

'You know the fellow, then?'

'Did a year's stint on the *Eleanor* with him about four years back. He goes by the name of Tanner . . . Marlow Tanner. Pity he won't sail for England with us, but he's intent on making his fortune.' He laughed softly, but not with malice. 'Fine bloody chance o' that, I'm thinking. If he ain't made his fortune these past fifteen years, there's not much chance of him making it at all!'

'Marlow Tanner, you say?' Silas Trent was racking his brain. He knew the name, but where? . . . When?

It was some time later when Silas Trent recalled the name of Marlow Tanner, and where he had come across it before. Wasn't *that* the fellow who, according to Martha, had been 'Emma Grady's downfall'. Of course! By all accounts, Emma was in love with Marlow Tanner, even after she was married off to Gregory Denton, and he was crazy in love with her, so much that he had left England on the news of her marriage. A terrible and riveting thought crossed his mind as he continued on his way. How unpredictable the hand of Fate was, to bring Marlow Tanner to the very place where Emma lived, and neither of them aware of it.

He felt himself to be in a great predicament for, even on this very evening, he was heading for the house on Phillimore Street where Emma lived with her husband, Roland Thomas. Since her marriage to him some six years back, Emma had expanded the firm of Thomas Trading Company beyond the boundaries of Australia, with shipments of wool, sandalwood and other cargoes being commissioned to the likes of him. She had worked hard, he knew. Who didn't know of her admirable progress in the trading world? The results of her determination and the incessant ambition which drove her to succeed were most evident in the house on Phillimore Street, a grand, white-painted place, with impressive well-kept gardens and massive pillars fronting the main verandah. But for all that, Emma was neither happy nor contented. She had made a comfort-able home for her husband, who, following a bad fall from the loft in his old shop, was unfortunately confined to a bath chair. He was a good man, but, like Emma, he kept quiet in his sorrow. He had never really come to terms with the loss of his beloved first wife, or his guilt arising from it. Added to that was the fact of his crippled legs which cruelly robbed him of his freedom and dignity. Then there was the tragedy of his son, Foster Thomas. His only son, who, because of his rakish and deceitful nature, had forced his father to throw him out of the house on the very eve of his mother's funeral. To this day, Roland Thomas had never forgiven him.

Emma's discontent stemmed from three things:

the fact that her husband's state of health prevented her from returning to England, where she had long planned to confront her old enemies and seek out those who had loved her; the pain of always remembering how she had lost her one and only child; and lastly the futile love she carried in her heart for the child's father, Marlow Tanner.

Here, Silas Trent paused in his thoughts. Should he tell Emma that the man she craved was no further away from her than the inn at the docks? Or would it be a cruel and spiteful thing for her to know? Silas Trent decided against telling her. He would not be the one to cause her unnecessary heartbreak, because even though his heart still belonged to his wife Martha he was more than a little in love with Emma himself.

As usual, Emma was delighted to see him, but as she swept across the marquetry floor of the spacious entrance hall, looking slim and attractive in a bustled dress of burgundy, her rich auburn hair swept back with two mother-of-pearl combs, it struck him how pale she looked and how subdued her strong grey eyes.

'Oh, Silas, I'm glad you came. I thought you might stay on the ship this evening. I know you intend sailing on the first tide.' Emma's lonely heart was always gladdened at the sight of him. In this last year she had found a friend in Silas Trent, and whenever they were together, she would ask him of England and the way it was when he had left. And always, he would avoid talking of his wife, and of his father-in-law, Caleb Crowther, because he knew of their callous treatment of Emma, and he felt ashamed. Emma, too, avoided the subject, in order to spare him embarrassment. But she revelled in news of his son, Edward, and had been horrified to hear of the unfortunate incident which had befallen him, the news of which was relayed to Silas in some distant port. Silas had not been home since, and Emma knew how very much he was looking forward to it. 'Just think,' she told him now, leading him towards the library, where she regularly spent many long hours at work, 'if you're not laid over too long at Singapore, you'll be home well in time for Christmas.' She added softly, 'Oh, how I envy you!'

Silas had not missed her gentle utterance, nor the longing behind it, and his heart went out to her. 'How is Roland, Emma?'

'He's fine,' she said, gesturing for him to help himself to a tot of rum from a tray on the sturdy oak dresser. When he had poured himself a drink he extended the sherry decanter towards her. Emma nodded and then gratefully took the half-filled glass which he handed to her.

When they were both seated in brown leather armchairs situated either side of a large, rather ornate dark-oak desk, Emma told him, 'Roland is no worse . . . and he's no better. But there are times when he has these unpredictable moods of deep depression and, to be honest, I don't know how to handle him.' Emma deplored her husband's awful predicament and was determined to do all she could to make life comfortable for him. But it was not easy. It was never easy.

'You'll cope, Emma,' she was told now. 'but you're driving yourself too hard . . . you know that, don't you?'

Emma knew it. She knew also that, without her work, she would grow slowly crazy. 'My work keeps me sane,' she said, sipping the sherry but hating the taste of it. 'Talking of which, I have a proposition to put to you. I've thought on it long and hard. Roland and I have discussed it, and as usual he's left the decision to me.'

'A proposition, Emma?' Silas Trent was intrigued. 'What kind of proposition?'

'One that will benefit us all.' Emma put her sherry glass on the desk before getting to her feet, where she walked slowly and deep in thought around to the back of her chair. Here, she put her two hands on the chair and leaned forward to look at Silas with a direct and friendly gaze. 'As you know, the Thomas Trading Company handles increasingly vast quantities of goods . . . all manner of goods pass through our hands every working day. In these past two years alone, we've doubled the business. Eighteen months ago we invested heavily in the running of pearl, wool and sandalwood . . . prize cargoes for which we commissioned ships such as yours, to carry far and wide . . . we're expanding all the time, you know that.'

'Everybody who's involved in shipping or merchandise knows it.' Silas Trent was already following Emma's thinking, but he dared not let himself believe it. 'What exactly are you getting at, Emma . . . how does all of this involve *me*? Apart from being fortunate enough to secure a cargo from you wherever possible, and being well paid for it too,' he gently laughed, 'though I do believe I'm honest and reliable enough to deserve it!'

'You have certainly proved that, Silas . . . in fact, if that *wasn't* the case, I wouldn't be talking to you now, and I would not be about to offer you a stake in a new venture. Perhaps even a partnership later

228

on, if all goes well.' Her steel-grey eyes never left his face.

'*Partnership*!' Of a sudden he was on his feet.

There came the sound of a voice from the doorway. 'That's right, Trent, a partnership . . . of sorts and all in good time.'

Seeing that it was her husband being pushed in his bath chair by the nurse hired to care for him, Emma went quickly to his side. 'Mr Thomas!' she gently reproached him. As always Silas Trent was amused to hear Emma address her husband as 'Mr Thomas'. Not once, since discovering that Emma Grady as was, was now Mrs Thomas, had he heard her call him by the name of Roland. It was an odd thing, but apparently accepted by them both. 'I thought you were sleeping.' Emma had given strict instructions that he was not to be disturbed.

'Couldn't sleep,' returned Roland Thomas, affectionately patting Emma's hand which rested on his shoulder. It always seemed to Emma to be a very cruel thing when she saw how helpless he had become. Her husband was still a striking figure, tall with large bones and a strong-featured face which was shaped harder by a coarse beard around his mouth and chin. Yet, if a person looked closely enough, it was not difficult to perceive the futility in his deep-set eyes, nor to see the weary stoop of his once broad and powerful shoulders. To Emma, and to those who knew him well enough, Roland Thomas was not a happy man. Yet Emma kept alive his interest in the business by actively involving him in day to day routine affairs, while ensuring he was involved with the greater issues— of which the proposition to Silas Trent was one example. In such a way, and by promising that she would stay by his side for as long as he needed her, Emma had successfully rekindled his passion to see the Thomas name 'up there above the rest'. She was well on the way to fulfilling his long-held ambition, an ambition which had been interrupted by the fateful accident he had suffered. The same accident that had cost Roland Thomas the use of his legs. By the same token, it had also cost Emma very dearly.

Because of it, all of Emma's carefully laid plans were now postponed, for how could she leave him and return to England? It was his greatest fear, and only when Emma had fervently given her word that she would not desert him had he acquired peace of mind. But if he had gained peace of mind, Emma had not. Often, in the solitude of her room, she would think about the man who was her husband, the man in the specially-adapted room downstairs, and she was torn a multitude of ways. Without him, she would likely never have had the opportunity to see a company grow and prosper, and to be an integral force in the excitement of it all. She would not be on the way to becoming wealthy, nor would she be in such a respectable and envied position. Emma knew all of this, and was thankful for the unique opportunity which the kindly Roland Thomas had put her way. On the other hand though, Emma sometimes wondered whether the price she was asked to pay was too high. There was no love in her life, only the ever-painful memory of Marlow. She had been blessed in her life with only one child, and that child had been snatched away for ever. She had no real friends, with the exception of Nelly, who, in spite of the frustrating habit she had of landing herself in trouble, was always a delight and great comfort to Emma. In all truth, she longed for freedom of spirit, and she longed for home.

Yet, there were times when Emma was forced to ask herself just where her home was. Here, she had risen above the pit into which her enemies had thrown her, and she had forged a life of some consequence. She had Nelly, and Roland, and she had her work. Why then did she crave for England? Was it only because there were things to settle there and questions to be answered? Was it for revenge, which in all truth, had long been her driving force? Was it in hope of a long desired reunion with a lover she could never forget? Or was it simply because England was her home, her roots, the land of her birth, from which her body had been torn, but in which her mind, heart and spirit would ever dwell? All of these considerations caused Emma a great deal of agonising . . . until she had decided that her deep longing to return to the homeland was a combination of all these things.

The one truth that grew ever stronger in her heart was that on a day in the future, she knew not when, she *would* return. When she did, all the questions which had tormented her would be answered. Until that day, she must remain patient and stay true to her ideals, for if she did not, then she would be as much a prisoner now as on the day she was brought here in exile.

Dismissing the nurse by asking that she arrange for refreshments to be sent in, Emma wheeled Roland to the desk. She and Silas Trent also took up their places there. 'Perhaps you would explain to Mr Trent what we have in mind?' Emma asked of her husband. She knew how such a suggestion would please him.

'I'll do that . . . of course I will, Emma,' he replied, afterwards turning his serious gaze on the man seated before him. 'Let me make it plain, Mr Trent . . . when Emma first made the suggestion I was dead set against it, but as always, she made me see the advantages of her plan.' He smiled warmly at Emma, before returning his attention to Silas Trent. 'I won't beat about the bush, Trent,' he said. 'Since you've been running cargo for us, you've proved yourself to be a reliable, honest fellow with an appetite for hard work. Now then . . . Emma has it in mind that we're missing out, by commissioning the odd ship at a time. She sees the big shipping companies regularly snatching valuable cargoes right from under our noses . . . because they don't have to commission the odd barque or clipper. They have the advantage of sailing their *own fleet*, so they're not subject to the same limitations and frustrations as we are. The consequence being that, whilst the Thomas Trading Company is rapidly expanding overland, we haven't made as much headway on the shipping of goods. It's not an area that we've ever had that much experience in, you see.' Here, he winked at Emma, saying, 'But Emma intends to change all that. Y'see, she's a woman who don't like to be beat, and I reckon she's just itching for a fight with the big boys . . . ain't that right, Emma?' He appeared to grow excited at the prospect.

'You know it is,' she laughed. Then, as there came a light tap on the door, heralding the entrance of a short, sturdily built maid carrying a tray of food and drink, she got to her feet and cleared a place at the desk. 'Thank you, Judy,' she said, watching while the young woman gingerly put down the tray before quietly leaving the room. It was when Emma had poured the tea and prepared to hand a cup to her husband that she noticed how pale he had suddenly become and how his face seemed pinched as though in pain. 'Are you all right, Mr Thomas?' she asked, putting down the cup and saucer and hurrying to his side. She had seen these attacks before and recalled the doctor's warning: 'The paralysis isn't the only problem, Mrs Thomas,' he had told her soon after the accident. 'There will always be pain, I'm afraid, and the risk of spinal deterioration. That in turn will bring its own more dangerous complications. There's very little we can do and, in the circumstances, your husband is not likely to survive beyond five years.' That was almost three years ago, when Emma had decided to devote herself to making her husband's life as easy as was humanly possible. He himself had insisted on being told the truth and, knowing it, he had come to lean on Emma all the more.

'Don't fuss!' he told her now, putting his fingers to the stiff collar of his shirt and frantically loosening it. He was acutely aware that Silas Trent was also on his feet, looking concerned. He cursed the paralysis which seemed at times to creep into every corner of his being, squeezing and torturing him until he felt like screaming out in the rage which it wrought within him. He fought it with every ounce of the strength he had left, but it was not enough; it was never enough.

Over the years, Emma had come to recognise the signs, and now, seeing him writhing in the chair with a look almost of hatred on his face, she sensed the onset of a deep depression, and her heart went out to him. 'Mr Trent,' she said, in a deliberately calm voice, 'would you be so kind as to summon the nurse? . . . You'll find her in the room adjacent to that of Mr Thomas.'

'Right away,' Silas agreed, going at once from the room and hurrying down the corridor which led from the hallway to the east side of the house. He knew the direction, because he had visited Mr Thomas in his room on previous occasions, when that unfortunate fellow had been confined to his bed.

By the time the nurse was alerted and both she and Silas Trent hurried back to the study, Emma was already on her way, pushing the heavy weight of her husband and the cumbersome bath chair before her. In a matter of minutes the protesting Mr Thomas had been whisked off to his room and one of the servants sent to fetch the doctor.

Some short time later Emma was seeing the doctor from the house, thanking him, and quietly nodding her head as he explained, 'He'll be fine now, Mrs Thomas. It's just as I told you . . . he will become more subject to these attacks as the illness takes its hold. At present they only last for a very short time, but they will worsen, I'm afraid.' He smiled reassuringly. 'No man could be cared for better than you care for your husband. Good day, Mrs Thomas.'

*   *   *

Silas Trent patiently waited in the study. He had watched the incident, been a part of it even, and he was filled with admiration for Emma. How unlike his own wife she was, he thought, for as much as he loved the petulant Martha, he could never imagine her making the sacrifices for him that Emma had made for her husband. It was made more remarkable by the fact that she did not love him, nor, he suspected, did her husband feel for Emma what a man should feel for his wife. Silas recognised the marriage for what it so obviously was . . . Purely a business arrangement, because there was no doubt that it was Emma who was the brains and force behind the business which Thomas Trading Company had become; Emma had initiated the big deals that had propelled the company ever upwards. But it was also plain to see that, without the finance and opportunity supplied by her husband, Emma would have been very hard put to have achieved her astonishing business coups, and to have become so well regarded in what was essentially a man's world.

Knowing how heavy Emma's burden was, Silas Trent's heart urged him to tell Emma of Marlow Tanner's presence here. But his head warned him against it.

'He's sleeping peacefully now.' Emma returned, full of apologies and eager to continue the discussion. Silas Trent noted for a moment how the light had gone from her lovely grey eyes. Then, when she began to outline her plans, the excitement was there again, in her voice and in the whole of her manner. 'I don't pretend to know the first thing about shipping, ships . . . or the moods of the ocean with which you have to contend. But I *do* know about merchandise and the market value of it. I know how to acquire your cargoes, even if I don't know one end of a hold from the other. If Thomas Trading Company had its own fleet . . . by God! I'd give the big boys a real run for their money.'

'A fleet of your own!' Silas Trent was astonished at the ambitiousness of Emma's plans. But he was also enthused by it, sitting forward on the edge of his seat, his brown eyes alive as they looked at Emma with awe. 'Do you have any *idea* how much you're talking about?' he asked her. 'Why, it would cost a fortune! Every penny you have.'

'Every penny we have, maybe. A fortune . . . perhaps not.'

'How then? . . . At any rate, Emma, it sounds too much like a gamble to me.'

'It *will* be a gamble,' Emma conceded, 'but that's how fortunes are made, Silas . . . nobody ever grew rich by hiding their capital under the floorboards. I know we'll have to start off with the very basics . . . ships that are seaworthy without being too fancy or expensive. Ships tailormade to our immediate needs . . . then, as we prosper in that direction, we can begin to plan for better ships, and more of them. Do you see what I'm getting at?' Emma's enthusiasm was so contagious that Silas Trent, being greatly moved by it, jumped to his feet and immediately began pacing up and down, all the while ramming one fist into the other, appearing deep in thought.

'You're right, Emma . . . of course you're right!' He came to a halt and swung round to face her. 'The big companies do sell off their vessels occasionally . . . but no, they ask too much money for them. But the single owners like me . . . who captain their own ships, *there* lies our chance, Emma!' He was no more than three feet away from

236

her now, and when Emma saw the corresponding excitement in his face she knew that she had chosen the right man. 'I know of at least two who have run into trouble and are hanging on by the skin of their teeth. A good offer for their vessels would make the decision for them: Oh, they're not ships of great beauty, because they've seen better days. But they *are* seaworthy, and still have a few sailing years left in them.'

'I'm all set to move into coastal shipping in a big way, Silas . . . already I've paid for vessels to carry many thousands of pounds of cargo. But the cost of commissioning vessels to carry it is crippling my profits. Oh, I'm well aware that running and maintaining my own fleet will draw heavy on the purse-strings . . . but I calculate that such expense will be offset by the fact that, not only will I be in a position to take a greater slice of the trade, but that the decisions as to when and how often the cargoes go, and how big a cargo it will be, will not be dictated by the vessel's captain but by me . . . and you, Silas. Roland and I want you in on this venture . . . the three of us . . . each with an equal share.'

'But I have no money.'

'I know that. But you do have a ship, and if I'm right, you do have it mortgaged?'

'Unfortunately, yes.'

'How heavily?'

'The bank owns a fifty per cent share. I own the remainder.'

Here Emma gestured for him to be seated opposite her. 'What I propose then is this . . . presuming of course that you're interested?'

'I certainly am!' He was no fool. This could turn

237

out to be the chance of a lifetime, the break in his fortunes that he had prayed for!

*   *   *

It was an hour later when Emma walked Silas Trent to the door, and already it was coming twilight outside. 'You're satisfied with our arrangements then?' Emma asked. 'I can go ahead and have it drawn up, ready for you to sign on your return?'

'The sooner the better,' he agreed, wondering how he could ever thank her, for words alone seemed so inadequate. 'Meanwhile, I'll try and make contact with the two owners concerned . . . and I'll explain the entire deal to the bank. I'm sure they'll be delighted . . . as I am.'

'You don't mind relinquishing full ownership of the *Stirling?*' Emma asked.

'To become a full and active part of the Thomas Shipping Line? It's more than a fair exchange, Emma . . . and I really don't know how to thank you for your trust and confidence in me.'

'You have *earned* it, Silas. And the decision was based on the fact that, while Thomas Trading has a wealth of experience in merchandise . . . you have the experience in seafaring. To be honest, we couldn't really do it without you. It's only the beginning though, I do promise you. Today, your barque and one other, together with the large clipper ship you mean to acquire for us. Tomorrow, who knows . . . we could grow to be bigger even than Lassater Shipping.' She laughed, but Silas Trent had every confidence in Emma's prediction. She had created for him also a unique

238

opportunity. Instead of being half-owner of one vessel, he could go home with the wonderful news that he was about to become a part-owner of a newly formed shipping line. His great joy was momentarily clouded by the fact that, at some later date, it might be necessary for him to be based here in Western Australia, and, whilst he himself was enthused by the possibility, he knew how strongly attached his wife Martha was to England and to her parents. However, he would cross that bridge when he came to it.

'God speed,' said Emma, smiling up at him with encouraging eyes. For a moment, Silas Trent was sorely tempted to lean down and kiss that warm, perfectly shaped mouth. But his respect and admiration for her would not let him take such a liberty. Instead, he gently lifted her hand in his, and gazing deep into those sad grey eyes that so touched his heart, there was an even greater temptation growing inside him. A temptation which, God help him, he could not resist, for he believed that Emma had earned the right, by the sacrifices she had made, to grasp every opportunity for happiness.

'Is there something troubling you, Silas?' Emma had sensed the struggle within him.

'Yes, Emma . . . it's you . . . *You* are troubling me.'

'Oh.' Emma felt the need for caution, but she was not sure why. Stepping away from him, she opened the front door, saying with a smile as she returned her attention to him, 'Now, why should you be troubling yourself about me?'

For a moment he gave no reply, but came to where she waited with the door open and her hand resting lightly on the glass knob. 'Emma, please forgive me if it seems I've taken too much on myself in thinking that you are not happy.' She put up her hand with the intention of interrupting him, but he shook his head, saying more firmly, 'I have more respect for you, Emma, than I have *ever* had for any other woman. You're not only spirited and ambitious, but you are loyal, kind and, when the occasion demands it, always prepared to put others before yourself.' She softly smiled and lowered her head, as he continued in a gentler voice, 'I know how you grieve for your lost child and . . . I know about Marlow Tanner.'

Emma jerked her head up, her eyes wide and surprised as she stared at him. 'Marlow Tanner!' She was afraid that somehow he had discovered that her late husband was not the father of her child. The shame she felt in that moment was all-engulfing. '*What* do you know of Marlow Tanner?' she demanded, instinctively casting her eyes towards the room that was her husband's. 'Mr Trent . . . the agreement between us does *not* give you the right to discuss my private life!' Emma opened the door wider. 'I think you had better go, and we'll just forget this conversation.' She was astonished, though, when he made no move.

'You do love him, don't you, Emma?' he said softly. 'You love him still . . . after all these years.' He watched her small, stiffened shoulders relax. He waited whilst she slowly closed the front door, and he remained perfectly still and patient as she kept her back to him. He had triggered something very deep and precious in her, he knew. He wished he had not done so. When she turned to look at him, with imploring eyes that were softened by the

240

touch of tears, he fervently trusted that he was doing the right thing. 'I will *always* love Marlow,' she told him simply, 'and I have never kept that truth from my husband.'

'Forgive me, Emma, but I don't talk of these things merely to pry, but because . . .' He was unsure as to how he might reveal that the fellow was here, without shocking her too much. ' . . . I wasn't going to tell you, Emma, but I must! I couldn't leave with an easy conscience unless I had told you that I met Marlow Tanner very recently.'

'You . . . *met* him?' Emma's heart soared as the image of the man she loved rose in her mind. Oh, how very clearly she could see him, with his tall powerful figure and those black laughing eyes. It had been so long, so very long, and her heart ached for the sight of them. '*Where* did you meet him? How long ago? Was he well?' The torrent of questions poured from her. There was so much that she needed to know. And, seeing the joy light up her eyes, Silas Trent was convinced that he had done the right thing. 'Oh, Silas . . . where did you see him, and when?' Emma asked breathlessly.

'He is well, Emma, I promise you. At least he seemed well enough some hours ago, when I saw him on the jetty.'

Emma was visibly shocked by his words. 'Some *hours* ago? . . . You saw him then? Here, in Fremantle?' She could hardly breathe for the pounding which stifled her throat.

'He had just arrived . . . wanted a return ship. When I told him I was bound for England, he said he might well spend the night at the inn and seek a ship on the morrow.'

In a moment, Emma was hurrying away in the

direction of the nurse's room, after saying to Silas, 'Please wait. I'd be obliged if you would walk me as far as the jetty.' Silas began warning her that she should not walk the streets at night. But Emma had already gone. In another moment, she returned with her bonnet and cape on. 'You're sure it was Marlow? How could you tell? I wasn't aware that you and he were acquainted,' Still she could not believe it.

All the way to the jetty, Silas was made to answer the detailed and persistent questions which Emma directed at him. Now, as they stood at the foot of the Stirling's gangplank, her courage began to desert her, and once again she insisted on going over the incident when he had met Marlow, while Silas Trent unsuccessfully made every effort to dissuade her from going to the inn alone.

*   *   *

Marlow felt the need for sleep coming on him. He had intended enjoying a tankard of ale before retiring, but suddenly he had no appetite for it. Then, at the very moment when he was about to get to his feet and make for the attic room which was his for the night, an old Darwin fellow sat alongside him and engaged him in conversation. 'Looking for a ship, I hear,' he said. 'Anywhere but England, is it?'

'News travels fast round here,' returned Marlow in a friendly voice. 'But yes . . . I *am* looking to sign on, for Singapore if I can find a ship that's bound that way.'

'Well now, mate . . . I reckon you've struck lucky, because there's a clipper due on the morrer . . . the

242

Statesman . . . belongs to the Lassater Line. I'm looking to sign on myself.'

'Oh aye?' came the caustic comment from a nearby table. 'Well, you'd best be quick about it, the pair of you! There's a rumour going about that Mrs Thomas has set her sights on putting Lassater's outta business.' He laughed out loud, and straightaway there were others, making similar observations and enjoying the whole thing, seemingly at the expense of Lassater Shipping. 'Well, for my money,' said one, 'I'll back Mrs Thomas. If past experience is anything to go by . . . the poor buggers don't stand a chance.'

'I reckon there's a lot of truth in what they say, mate,' the Darwin fellow told Marlow. 'There have been rumours right enough, and if it's right that Mrs Thomas intends moving into the shipping business . . . the big boys had best keep their wits about 'em. She's a sharp one, that.'

Marlow had heard of Thomas Trading, because they were rapidly making an enviable name for themselves wherever goods were bought and sold. But now he was intrigued to know more about this 'Mrs Thomas' who, according to the talk here, was a formidable force.

'She's well respected round these parts,' obliged the Darwin fellow. 'Never been known to cheat nobody . . . gives a fair price and always deals above board. Oh, there was a Thomas Trading Company long before *she* came on the scene. Roland Thomas had built a nice little business up for himself, but that's how it would have stayed . . . a "nice little business", if he hadn't married again.' Pausing, he took a swig from his jug of grog and made a noisy celebration of licking it from his lips,

243

before wiping the back of his hand across his mouth and continuing. He described to Marlow how poor Mr Thomas had suffered one thing after another. First having his wife killed by robbers, then being forced to throw his only son out on to the streets. 'Rotten to the core, that one,' he said, with disgust. Then he outlined the events which followed, of how Roland Thomas's son, Foster, had gone from these parts to roam the outback. 'There was even talk that he'd taken to robbing and the like . . . though of course nobody ever really knew.' All they did know was that some six months ago, he came sauntering into Fremantle, boasting about having made a wad of money and that he wouldn't rest till he'd put his father outta business and claimed what was rightfully his. 'Some folks reckon he doesn't *only* mean the Thomas Trading Company, which is signed over completely to Mrs Thomas should anything happen to her husband, but that he's got his eye on another prize! He's a bad bugger . . . a real bad bugger. Furious he was, when old Roland up and wed the girlie who worked in his stores . . . but, if you ask me, that was the best thing Roland Thomas ever did! He's a good man, and it was a crying shame when he took a bad fall which crippled him. Still . . . that wife of his, she treats him like a lord . . . always the best for her husband, and that's a fact.'

'Mrs Thomas . . . she runs the company, does she?' Marlow had never heard of any woman actually running such a company, and he was intrigued by the fascinating story he was being told.

'*Runs* it?' The Darwin fellow gave a small chuckle. 'Why, she made it what it is today! And

244

I'll tell you summat else, bucko. I reckon she'll not stop there, oh no. Not if she's a mind to go into shipping!' He took another swig of his ale. 'And that ain't bad, is it mate? . . . Not for an ex-convict who was shipped out here at the tender age of seventeen.'

'An ex-convict?' Marlow was astonished. 'She's English?'

'Through and through. Emma she's called . . . Emma Grady as was . . . convicted of having a part in killing her husband, Gregory Denton. Oh, it's well known . . . but it's hard to believe that girlie killing anybody.' The Darwin fellow turned to see if Marlow was still listening and to exaggerate the point he was making that Emma was incapable of 'killing anybody'. But his companion was long gone, having been struck with shock by what he had heard, and consequently being desperate to escape outside, where he might breathe the fresh air and compose himself enough to reflect more sensibly on the news of Emma, news that had devastated him.

Once outside, Marlow just walked, with no particular destination in mind. He was like a man in a trance, possessed of a nightmare which seemed to be choking the very life from him. Emma! His darling Emma! Transported as a convict! The things he had been told by the Darwin fellow raced through his mind and churned his stomach, until he felt physically sick. 'Oh, Emma!' he murmured with a voice that was both savage and tortured. 'How could I know? Oh God . . . I should never have gone away . . . never have left you, my darling.' His thoughts careered back over the years, to the night when he and Emma

245

had found such perfect and wonderful love, when he had taken her to himself and she had given both heart and soul to him. He thought of how desperately he had pleaded with her to leave her husband and come away with him. What he had suggested was morally wrong, he knew that at the time, and he knew it now. He remembered the anguish he had put Emma through, by asking such a thing of her, and oh, he had loved her all the more because of her loyalty. But now he was forced to ask himself whether his selfish act might have triggered off a life for Emma that eventually proved to be unbearable.

Marlow tormented himself with all of these things, but in his deepest heart, he could never believe that Emma had taken a hand in killing her husband, Gregory Denton. She had a temper. Yes, he knew that well enough, and she was frustratingly stubborn. But she was also kind and loving, with the greatest loyalty and compassion, these were the very virtues in her that he so adored. In his travels he had known other women, fought with them, and slept with them. But he had never loved them. How could he, when his heart would always belong to Emma? Emma, who was *here*. And *married*! It was all too much at once, far too much for him to come to terms with.

As he walked, Marlow felt as though he were in a frenzy. What should he do? Should he go and see her? Back came the answer. No! He must not do that, because she had been through enough. And she had been through it alone, because he had not been there when she needed him most. How could he ever forgive himself! Also, Emma was married, and heading a thriving business. He was not surprised that she could build up such a concern, for she was always known for her tenacity and ability in that way. But *married*! Did that mean that she had forgotten him, that the glorious love they had shared, and which was still so alive in him, had meant less to her? He had no way of knowing, but the longer and deeper he dwelt on it, the more despondent he became.

Instinctively, as always when he was deeply disturbed, Marlow headed for the sea. There was something in watching the waves roll over, and listening to the peculiar sound they made, that had the greatest soothing effect on him. He had no intention of going back to the tavern just yet. He had a need to be alone, and there was no sleep in him now. He wondered whether he might ever again feel the need for sleep.

The daylight was being slowly covered by the darkness as, his thoughts in a turmoil, Marlow headed towards the far end of South Bay, where he hoped to find a quiet, isolated spot where he could sit awhile and think over the events which, even now, he could hardly believe. But it was *true*. It must be true.

*   *   *

As Marlow walked with a determined stride, yet not in a hurry, towards South Bay, Emma—who was in a great hurry—rounded the corner from the direction of Arthur Head. She saw the figure some way along South Bay. In that split second her heart leaped, and her every instinct urged her to turn back before it was too late. Yet she could not. She could turn back now no more than she could deliberately stop breathing.

All the same, the sight of that figure brought Emma to a standstill, and a tremendous surge of panic went through her. It was *him.* It was Marlow. But he was changed. Older. Yet he was *not* changed. The long years rolled away. Into her mind's eye came the image of how he had been. The way his strong, lithe figure had moved, that rich black hair, and the way he had had of holding his head erect and looking straight ahead as he walked: all of these characteristics were long etched on her heart and as familiar to her as the act of putting one foot before the other. It was also true that she had come to love her husband over the years. But in a very different way, a tender, compassionate way. Not at all in the all-consuming, passionate way in which she loved Marlow.

She watched him now, and her heart was paralysed. Time had frayed his youth, and there were lighter shades in his hair, and a slower purpose to his step. But the essence that was Marlow remained strong. She wondered at the manner in which he had arrived here. But then, she knew he had gone away to seek his fortune all those years before. Australia was an exciting place to be now. It was only natural he would find his way here. In her heart she gave thanks for it.

After agonising over what to do, how to approach him, and what she might say when he looked at her with those intense dark eyes that had always seemed to reach into her very soul, Emma was plagued with doubts. Would he even want to see her? Did he still love her in the way that she loved him? Or had he forgotten her? After all, it was some fourteen years since that wonderful, unforgettable night when she had conceived his child, and, when she refused to leave with him, he had gone away wretched. It was even possible that he might still be bitter and would never want to see her again.

For another moment, Emma's courage began to desert her. But never being one to accept defeat or to turn away from life's cruelties, she began walking, this time with more urgency, towards the curve of the beach round which Marlow had by now disappeared.

It was the most beautiful evening. The air was warm, yet cooled by the incoming breeze, and the sea lay still and glistening like a stretch of sky littered with sparkling stars. Here and there the soaring seagulls were beginning to seek a haven for the night, and their cries were strangely subdued, making a weird haunting sound which softly echoed in the twilight. The sky was the deepest blue, streaked with ribbons of white and black, and on the horizon where the sun was already going down, the myriad of colours shot the sky purple and red.

It was a most awe-inspiring and magnificent sight, which lifted Emma's spirits as she drew nearer to the figure hunched on the small rise of cliffs beside the beach. He looked a lost and forlorn soul, and Emma's heart went out to him as, softly, she came ever nearer. She wondered how much of a shock it would be for him to discover that she was here, in this place, and it crossed her mind how uncanny was the hand of fate, which had torn them apart so long ago, only to bring them together on the other side of the world. Life was a strange and unpredictable thing, she thought. It also occurred to Emma that Marlow may well have returned to England at some time or another during his travels, and maybe he did know something of her fate. It was *possible*, because she remembered how sensational her trial had been and the great interest it had aroused, because of her relationship to Justice Caleb Crowther.

When Emma came close enough to see the strong profile of the man she loved, and even sense the utter despair which was so evident in his manner, all the determination and courage she had mustered drained away. She must not go any further, for she loved him too much. She was married, committed to a life which had been shaped for her here, so how could she bring herself to cause this man any more pain, which, if he *still* loved her, she would certainly do. In all of her life, Emma had been called upon to make many painful sacrifices, but none of them . . . *none* of them was ever so painful as the one she must make now, as slowly and reluctantly she turned away. She had seen him, almost touched him. It was another poignant memory to carry her through the years. And yet . . . and yet.

Lost in thoughts of Emma, and agonising over their cruel destinies, Marlow felt the deepest despair. But then, of a sudden and for no reason that he could ever recall later, every instinct within urged him to turn his head to look over his shoulder in the direction of the small narrow beach path which over the years many footsteps had trod. What he saw there was the very image which had flooded his mind this past hour, which had brought him both joy and torment, and which was now hurrying away. After all this time, he couldn't really be sure, but something in his heart told him that it was Emma! Not a girl any more. Not young. But his lovely Emma all the same.

In the same moment when Emma heard the soft, rushing footsteps coming up behind her, she heard also the sound of her name, soft and caressing like the breeze, and filled with such longing that it made her heart turn over. 'Emma.' It was Marlow's voice, and it struck at her like the blade of a knife, bringing shock, surprise and a sense of something awful. Yet at the same time, it was something else entirely, rippling through her being with delicious urgency and making her want to cry.

When she stopped and the hand touched her shoulder, she shivered, afraid to turn round, yet compelled to do so. Lowering her head and keeping her gaze to the ground, she moved her body until it was facing his. She saw the long, black-clad legs, and the boots on his feet all spattered with sand; she felt the warmth and presence of his body, and her heart reeled beneath the gentle touch of his hand on her shoulder. Yet she kept her gaze to the ground, because, however much she longed to look up and see again that strong, handsome face that she knew so well, she dared not, for though she was exhilarated, she was also afraid, and that fear betrayed itself in the trembling of her hands which now Marlow took tenderly in his own. 'Look at me, Emma,' he softly urged, and the voice that she had remembered was just the same. It touched her heart so deeply that, without her even being aware of it, the tears ran from her eyes and spilled down her face. Still she dared not lift her gaze to his.

Now he moved her hand until the long, lean fingers of his own were wrapped about both of her small fists; then, lifting his free hand to her face, he tenderly wiped away the tears, afterwards cupping his fingers beneath her chin and slowly raising her head.

When, in a moment, her heart pounding fearfully inside her, Emma's gaze was brought to mingle with Marlow's, she thought that never again in the whole of her life would she experience anything so beautiful, so astonishing. It was as though, in that precious moment when they gazed on each other, the whole world stood still. It was she and Marlow, just as they had been fifteen years ago. They were both older, perhaps wiser, and the flush of youth was long past. But now, in this moment of time, none of that mattered. What really mattered was the youth and joy in their hearts. Their love had not changed with the passing of time. It had only grown stronger. Emma thought that if ever it were possible to choose the moment when she might depart this earth, it would be in this split second when she and Marlow were united, not only in the flesh, but in their very souls, each being the essence of the other.

When, with a broken cry, Marlow caught her to him, and buried his head in the curve of her neck, Emma felt the warm, sticky wetness of his tears against her skin, and she knew beyond all doubt that he loved her with all his heart, as she did him. Lost in each other's arms, they found such contentment as neither had known in many a long, long year. The moment was too deep, too precious for words, so, keeping one arm about each other,

252

they walked together to the small cliff where Marlow had been sitting. There, in a deep recess which gave them privacy, they rekindled a love that had been forbidden when they were very young, that had driven them both to despair and forced them apart. A love that had conceived a child, now lost to them, and that had spanned longer than fifteen years, not suppressed by those years, nor by the great distance between them . . . only growing stronger, and more dangerous.

Emma was not afraid, nor would she sacrifice this precious time with Marlow. When eagerly, yet with the softest touch, Marlow unclothed her, and took her into his own magnificent nakedness, Emma was ready. When she felt the warmth of his skin mingling with her own and saw how his dark eyes burned as they roved over her body, she was proud. When she heard him murmur in the most tender of voices, 'I love you, Emma . . . adore you,' she knew the feelings that were stirring within him, because those same feelings stirred within herself. When his warm eager mouth covered hers and he slid on top of her, oh, she wanted him so desperately that everything which had governed her life until then was as nothing. She clung to him and coveted him. She caressed him, kissed him with a passion that frightened her and when, with a fierceness to match her own, he entered her, Emma experienced a tide of exquisite pleasure that forced her to cry out. It was like a dam had burst open inside her, a huge rolling wave surged through her emotions, taking with it all the loneliness, the heartache and the pain she had ever known. She arched herself into Marlow's demanding nakedness and she gave of herself

253

without reservation, but she took also, drawing both strength and passion from her man. There was a rhythm between them, like pulsating music which enveloped them both and pushed their pleasure senses to the limit.

As the waves of sensation washed over Emma time and time again, she thought she couldn't bear it, because in the pleasure and the fulfilment, there was also pain. Yet, it wasn't a physical pain, but a suffering that came from deep within herself. It was the pain of the heart, and which was both destroyed and created by love itself. Because of it, she clung all the more tightly to her lover, being fiercely loath to let him go.

Later, when the urgent passion had subsided, and all that remained was the different passion of a deep, abiding love, Emma was content to lie in Marlow's reassuring arms, and together they talked of all the things that were in their hearts. Emma explained the tragic events which had brought her to Australia. She told him everything, how Gregory had died and not by her hand. She outlined the reasons for her marriage to Roland Thomas, and told him of the unfortunate Nelly, who had been a staunch friend, and whom she considered to be just as much her responsibility as was her crippled husband. She assured him of the great love she would always feel for him. All the things which had befallen her she told him; all but one, and that being the one which still haunted her dreams. She did not reveal that he had been a father, or that the child was lost, because she knew that he would suffer the same guilt and anguish which she had suffered ever since. At least she could spare him that. And so she did. Neither did

254

she tell him of her suspicions regarding Caleb Crowther, for that would serve no purpose. Besides which, she herself must deal with that, when the time came.

'You've been through so much, Emma. If only I'd known . . . if only I had stayed.' Marlow saw the guilt and failing in himself, and was angered by it.

'You couldn't have changed anything,' she told him. 'Please believe that.'

'All the same, I should never have deserted you.'

'I sent you away,' she reminded him, and he could not deny it.

Of a sudden, he sat up straight, and taking Emma by the shoulders, he swept her to her feet, standing before her and looking with sudden determination into those strikingly beautiful grey eyes. 'I must go back,' he said with a surge of enthusiasm, 'back to England. To my sister, Sal . . . because, even though I left to seek my fortune and make a better life for her, it seems to me that I deserted her also!'

'No.' Emma could see that he was unjustly punishing himself. 'You never deserted *anybody*, my darling. You're not capable of that. Everything you did was with others in mind.'

'All the same, Emma . . . I must go home, and seek another kind of "fortune" there. It's strange, I think, how you come to realise what good fortune really is. It isn't gold or material things . . . it's having a family who needs you . . . it's enjoying good health and contentment. And it's having the hands and strength to toil for a living.' Here he paused and his gaze lingered on her face awhile, seeming to search for something there, yet knowing he could not find it. 'Most of all, my

255

darling,' he went on, 'good fortune is loving someone until your heart sings . . . and having your love returned. I know you love me, Emma . . . I've always known that, and if I never hold you in my arms again, you've given me the greatest joy a man could ever know.'

'Don't, Marlow . . . please.' Emma was close to tears.

Now, he gazed at her long and hard, stroking the palm of his hand down her tumbled auburn hair; then, as he looked on that fine and lovely face and those grey eyes that smiled at him so, he thought how fresh and youthful she was, how still like the girl of fifteen he had first met by the canal. The years in between had taken nothing from her beauty, only enhanced it.

'I can't bear to let you go again, Emma,' he told her, gripping her shoulders more tightly, 'yet I can't stay here knowing you're married, loving you as I do.'

'I know,' she said, the sadness rising in her eyes. She was aware of the impossibility of it all and, as she looked at this man who had matured and grown even more handsome with the years, she was sorely tempted. But it could not be. There were too many entanglements, too many people to be hurt, and how could she live with her conscience if she chose the way he would have her go? She began to explain, but he put his hand to her mouth and afterwards pulled her to him, leaning forward and tenderly kissing the top of her head. 'Forgive me, Emma . . . but I want to take you here and now, from this place. I'm afraid that if I don't, I'll never see you again, and I couldn't bear that. I couldn't!' He held her more tightly, for only a moment, before easing her away from him. 'I asked you once before to come away with me. I'll never regret that. But I won't ask you this time, Emma, because you know in your heart what I think and feel. Whatever you decide to do, I must wait for that decision and I promise you, my love . . . I will abide by it. I don't want to cause you pain, or to put you in an impossible situation.' He put his two hands one either side of her face and tilted it up towards him. 'You do know that, don't you, Emma?' When she gave no reply, instead turning her sorry eyes away, he told her, 'The *Stirling* leaves for England on the morrow. If the cap'n will sign me on, I'll be aboard and headed home. Unless, Emma . . . unless you ask me to do otherwise. I'll look for you, my love . . . before she sets sail and, if you're not there, I'll understand.'

When Emma brought her gaze back to look on his face, and he saw the tears in her eyes, Marlow's heart turned somersaults inside him. Dear God above, how he loved this woman! How he needed her!

As Marlow reached down to kiss her, Emma was filled with sadness at their predicament, and she knew there could be only one ending to their glorious reunion this night. She raised her lips to his, she put her arms about his neck and clung to him as though she would never let him go. When, after a long and exquisitely painful moment, he released her, she put her hand up to stroke his face tenderly, that strong and familiar face that, even if she were to die a very old woman, she would never forget.

No more words were spoken between them then, before Emma tore her gaze from the dark pained eyes that never left her face for even a second. Then, with scalding tears running down her face, she turned away and left him standing there. The interlude was over, the dream was short-lived, and the future just as uncertain as it was before.

Marlow watched her go and his heart went with her, but he made no move to stop her. Instead, he waited until she was out of sight, before turning to trudge along the beach to the other side, where he knew the *Stirling* to be berthed. He felt certain that Captain Trent would sign him on, and yet he prayed that he would not sail for England with her on the morrow. He *would* return home, yes, but he hoped above all else that when he did, it would be because Emma had made him a happier man. Yet even as he dwelt on the possibility, he realised how impossible it was. All the same, he would keep watch before the tide carried him out to sea. He could never give up even the slimmest hope.

*   *   *

As the *Stirling* got underway, Marlow kept his eyes peeled towards the shore for signs of Emma. But she never came, and he was a man lost. He could not have known how, in the hour when she knew that he would be gone from these shores and from her life, perhaps for ever, Emma sat in her study with the door locked against the outside world, quietly sobbing.

After a while, she got to her feet, wiped her eyes and composed herself. Then, with her small, straight shoulders set in a stiff, upright stance, and wearing the expression of a woman with a purpose, she threw open the curtains, telling herself in a firm voice, 'Come on, my girl! There's a business to be run!' She had learned the art of making the head rule the heart. She had learned it well.

Chapter Nine

Emma suspected that she was pregnant! These past two months and more, since she and Marlow had made love, had proved to be one of the most difficult times in her life. Not only was she plagued by the physical consequences, such as nausea and a general feeling of being unwell, but she was haunted also. Here she was, a woman past the age of thirty, and carrying a child that was not her husband's. She would not be able to hide that fact for very much longer, because once the outward signs of her pregnancy became evident, it would also betray the truth, that she had been unfaithful to Roland Thomas, because how could a man who was paralysed from the waist down father a child? There would be questions, Emma knew, and gossip of a spiteful nature; yet for all that, Emma was filled with a great happiness and every day had taken on a new meaning. It struck her how curious and condemning it was, that she should have been married to two different men, yet the children she had conceived were not fathered by either of them. It did seem as though, in spite of the many obstacles put in their way, her and Marlow's paths were meant to cross. Emma nurtured and cherished the tiny life that was forming inside her, and she wanted to believe with all her heart, that it

259

was the Lord's way of compensating for the child she had so cruelly lost. But then, she reminded herself, what she and Marlow had done was wrong. No amount of soul searching could change that. Emma knew that she should be tormented with guilt and a sense of shame, but she was not. What had happened was the culmination of a wonderful love, which she could never deny, whatever the consequences.

At seven o'clock on a balmy October evening, Emma stood by the jetty, with the keen warm breeze blowing about her skirts and lifting the hem of her dress into a gentle arc which whipped the air and revealed the layers of her cream-coloured petticoats. She had slipped off her bonnet, leaving it fastened about her neck and resting on her shoulders, and, as the breeze teased both the long strands of her rich auburn hair and the flowing blue ribbons of her bonnet, she made a strikingly lovely figure, with the evening sky silhouetting her still slim and shapely form.

The torment that countered Emma's joy showed in her eyes, those strong grey eyes that so vividly reflected her every mood. Now there was a sadness in them, as she gazed out across the sea towards the horizon, her thoughts dwelling on Marlow, and the way in which their love had been beset by insurmountable problems all these years. How wonderful it would be, she thought, if things were different and Marlow could share the miracle of this little life already beating within her. Why is it, she asked herself, that bearing his children must be painful and forbidden? Emma did not know the answer, only that it was so.

For a long time Emma kept her eyes fixed to the

horizon, wondering where Marlow might be at this very minute. There was a strange calmness in her heart as she thought more deeply about this man whom fate seemed determined to keep from her, and Emma marvelled at the peace she felt. It was as though some quiet instinct told her that, when Marlow had instilled in her that most precious seed of life, there had also been created a hope for their future. Even though Emma could see no possible way in which she and Marlow might be together always, the murmurings of optimism would not be denied.

Chiding herself for being foolish enough ever to believe that her future lay with Marlow, Emma turned from the ocean which had taken him from her, and sighing deeply, began her way towards Cliff Street and the warehouse. Marsh Williams was back with the waggon train which did the regular run into the outback and she must have his report firsthand. Besides which, there was news of a pearl-lugger having been lost, taking with it a deal of shell which was destined for the Thomas Trading Company, and some twenty-five men were reported to have lost their lives. The cargo was extremely valuable, but it was to the unfortunate men and their loved ones that Emma's heart went out.

As always, Emma's arrival at the warehouse was greeted with mixed feelings. Most of the men respected her for being the fair-minded and clever business-woman she was. But there were those who bitterly resented having to take orders from *any* woman, yet were shrewd enough to make an effort at disguising their feelings; after all, the Thomas Trading Company now had the edge on

261

most of the competition, and the wages were the best around. There wasn't a man among them who could honestly deny that it was Emma herself who had achieved this.

When Emma first acquired a large warehouse on Cliff Street it was a single unit. Now the company owned almost a third of all the property down the left-hand side of Cliff Street, and every inch of space was used to its full. By the time Emma arrived, the whole place was a hive of activity. Already the two largest waggons were hitched to and loaded with all manner of tools, such as shovels, galvanised buckets, oil, candles and other basic necessities. The last items—twelve sacks of flour—were being carried out one by one aloft a burly labourer's shoulders who, on sighting Mrs Thomas, gave a wide grin and an awkward nod of the head. 'G'day,' he called, and Emma returned the greeting. Afterwards, hurrying through the noise and organised chaos within the busy stores, where there was a deal of counting, checking, stacking and carrying going on, Emma found Marsh Williams out in the rear yard where the big geldings were stabled. He was a large and fearsome-looking man, with unusually wild red hair, yet he had the gentlest manner and a considerate nature, which belied his formidable appearance. He was so deep in conversation with the warehouse manager—a tall, thin and authoritative man with a surly face called Oliver Barker—that neither of them saw Emma approaching. It was only when Emma said, 'Good morning, gentlemen,' that they turned in surprise.

'Mrs Thomas . . . I might have known you'd be out bright an' early to catch me before I'm off again,' remarked Marsh Williams. Mr Barker suggested they should 'seek a quieter place to talk', whereupon the three of them made their way to the office at the far end of the warehouse. Here Emma was informed that all had gone well on the previous trip. 'But I'm telling you, Mrs Thomas,' said Marsh Williams with some excitement, 'I reckon if we'd taken twice the merchandise we could'a sold it.' He thrust the signed dockets into her hand, then, as she thoughtfully perused them, he went on, 'There's more and more prospectors setting up an' looking fer a fortune . . . an' *settlers* too.' He thrust another paper on to the pile of dockets in her hand. 'See that? . . . That's a list of goods we hadn't got room for. Orders . . . mostly from the women folk . . . cloth, an' fancy things like pictures and china stuff. There's even a request for a tablecloth, would you believe? . . . And a tapestry frame.'

Emma's sharp business instincts told her that here was something of real interest. Her trading post already dealt in stock of the items mentioned. But up till now there had been no call for such things actually to be carried to the customer. This was a market created not by the frantic search for gold, or by farmers who looked to scratch a more down-to-earth living from the land, but a demand from the women who had bravely uprooted themselves in search of a better life. What was more natural than that they should want to retain a degree of civilisation, even though they might be in a raw and primitive land where, often, the code of culture and behaviour was lost in the struggle to survive?

'We must supply this demand,' Emma told her

263

manager now. 'Get these women their cloth, and their china plates! If we can't cater to them, there are others who will.'

'And what should we leave behind in order to make the space?' asked Mr Barker, with a touch of sarcasm in his voice. 'The flour and sugar? . . . Or perhaps the tools which they so desperately need? You're wrong, Mrs Thomas, there isn't a trading outfit in the whole of Western Australia who would supply these women's fripperies. There's little profit in it, and there are other, more important priorities.'

Emma saw it differently. She knew how a woman might influence her husband to her way of thinking. She felt also that any woman who had courage enough to brave the adverse elements of this demanding land had a mind of her own and would not rest until she had those things about her which, however much they might be seen by some as 'fripperies', made life tolerable to her. Emma was quick to realise also that, because other traders might not agree with her, there was a unique opportunity here to get in first, and to build this particular market up, before the others became aware of its potential. Oh, it was true that, once they saw it opening out, they would make every effort to secure a large slice for themselves. But Emma knew from experience that if a trader got in first and gave full satisfaction, the customer tended not to change to another supplier. It was an opportunity not to be missed. Yet, there was a difference of opinion here, between the warehouse manager and herself. Such a situation, though it at times caused little difficulty, was of paramount importance in this instance, because if she were to make strides into this promising market, she must have his full backing. Most of all, it was important that he viewed the project with enthusiasm.

Giving nothing of her own opinion away, Emma asked him now: 'So you think it's of little consequence?' Mr Barker had only been with Thomas Trading for a very short time and he came with good references. But he had a surly disposition and he had yet to prove himself fully to Emma. 'I reckon it's just women's fancies . . . won't come to nothing. Anyway, we're short of waggons as it is . . . *and* the men to drive them. Good men are always hard to find.' With the heat of the morning already beginning to tell, and the small office being somewhat stifling, the door had been left open. Outside, two of the workers heard Mr Barker's comments and one observed to the other, 'It ain't surprising the bugger can't keep a good man, when he treats 'em like dingo shit!' The other nodded in agreement, spat out his chewing tobacco through his teeth, and the pair of them went about their work.

'You leave me in no doubt about *your* feelings in this,' Emma told Mr Barker, purposely keeping her own opinion to herself. Then, turning to Marsh Williams, she asked, 'And you, Mr Williams . . . are you of the same mind as my manager, bearing in mind that he has had some long experience in the trading business,' she warned him deliberately.

'Well . . . I reckon it don't matter too much what I think.' Marsh Williams knew he might be treading on delicate ground here, but he was an honest man, and must give an honest answer. 'In my opinion, most women know what they want, and more often than not they get their own way. I

265

think that if we were to ignore that fact . . . we could end up by losing out. The women in the outback ain't got fancy money, and they ain't got easy ways of getting to town. But it won't always be like that.'

'So, you're saying that we should go all out to satisfy their modest demands?' When he nodded without hesitation, she went on, 'And if we did, how do you imagine we could provide enough waggons and good men to drive them . . . a problem which Mr Barker so rightly pointed out. It's one thing catering for the town's women who come to the store . . . but we'll need extra waggons, horses and these "good men" to take the goods to the customer.'

'I don't see it as a problem, begging your pardon, Mrs Thomas. Waggons are easily secured and the horses we can find well enough. I don't deny that the men might not be so easy to locate, but I think it's worth a hell of a try!'

'And so do I, Mr Williams!' Emma took the two men unawares by her bold admission. 'In my experience, small, seemingly unimportant markets have a canny knack of growing into a lucrative business . . .' Here she turned her sharp grey eyes on Mr Barker, telling him in a firm angry voice,' . . . but only for those who have the guts to get in there first!'

When Emma left Cliff Street two hours later, she had gone through the books thoroughly, and given Mr Barker the opportunity of taking on Marsh William's job as lead driver; when, infuriated he had refused, Emma put him under notice and appointed Marsh Williams as the new manager. His first task was to secure the services of

266

top drivers, who were not afraid of giving a hard day's work for a good pay-packet. On her way out through the warehouse, Emma was stopped by several men, who had overheard her instructions. From what they told her, it was plain to Emma that not only had she made the right decision—which some ventured to say was long overdue—but that there should be no difficulty in recruiting the kind of men required, once they knew that Barker had been shown the door. Her next stop was the trading post, to see how Rita Hughes and Nelly were coping. Emma always looked forward to spending a few hours in their company, in the comforting knowledge that the Thomas Trading post was in better hands than hers.

*　　　*　　　*

'Pregnant!' Nelly's brown eyes popped out of her head as she stared at Emma. 'Cor, bloody hell, gal. I *knew* it! The minute yer told me about that meeting with Marlow Tanner . . . I just *knew* it!' She was so agitated that she swept herself up and out of the cane chair in the little room that she once shared with Emma and which was her own abode now. 'What yer gonna do, Emma? . . . How in God's name d'yer think yer can keep a thing like *that* to yerself? What! . . . You'll be as big as a ship in a few months, and how are yer going to hide yer belly then, eh? Oh, yer silly bugger . . . yer silly little bugger!' She turned to look at Emma, who was astonished to see that Nelly's friendly gaze was wet with the threat of tears. 'Oh, Emma . . . you've got yerself in a right pickle, and no mistake,' she wailed.

267

Emma had not been prepared for the fact that Nelly might feel fearful for her, only that Nelly would give her a proper telling-off. Now, however, she found herself in the position where it was she having to comfort Nelly. 'Come and sit down, Nelly,' she said, going to put her arm round Nelly's shoulders and drawing her back towards the chair, where she persuaded her to sit down. After they were both seated, facing each other, Emma told her how she intended to 'talk to Roland about the whole business, when he's in a better state of health. I realise he will have to be told the truth,' she said quietly. 'But he knows about Marlow . . . and I'm sure he will understand.' She prayed that he would.

'He bleeding well won't, y'know!' exclaimed Nelly. 'Not if my experience of men serves me right. And, even if he does . . . there are others in this town of Fremantle who'll be only too glad to point the finger at you. Oh, I'm telling you, me darling . . . yer don't know what you've let yerself in for!' Nelly was full of woe, but Emma would not be depressed. She clung to the belief that all would come right in the end, because she had no intention of ever being separated from the child she was carrying. Not by hell or high water.

Feeling that her problem was one that only she and she alone could contend with, Emma deliberately directed her attention to other matters, of how pleased she was that Nelly and Rita Hughes got on so well, and how well the store was doing. 'But are you sure that you wouldn't prefer to come and stay at the house with me, Nelly? There's plenty for you to do there, and it would be nice to have you close by.'

'Naw . . . it ain't that I'm not grateful, Emma gal,' Nelly replied, pulling a face, 'but I'd be lost in that grand place, and what's more, I like working the store and meeting people. Besides . . . you ain't so far away, and I do see you every day, don't I, eh?' Nelly could not be persuaded so, as on previous occasions when Emma had raised the matter, she pressed it no further. All the same, Nelly's reluctance to come and live in the house was surprising. But then, when they had both returned to the store, Nelly to her tasks and Emma to her business discussion with Rita Hughes, something happened which gave Emma grave reason to fear for Nelly. It explained also Nelly's reasons for not wanting to leave the store, in favour of lighter work at the house.

'Morning, Mrs Thomas . . . beats me how you always manage to look cool in this blistering heat,' called a portly little fellow who was at the counter, busily heaping a wad of 'baccy from the jar and into his pipe. He had a ruddy face with a blue neb cap perched on his bald head in a jaunty manner, and Emma recognised him as a nearby settler who insisted on buying his 'baccy only by the pipeful, having developed a raking cough and rationed his 'smoke' because of it. When Emma warmly returned his greeting, he paid for the 'baccy and left, whistling a merry tune.

The store was busy, with customers constantly milling in and out, when Emma murmured her intention of perusing the ledgers to Rita Hughes, and afterwards went into the office. She made copious notes about various things which she would need to discuss with Rita, but on the whole, she was delighted to see that everything was in

269

good order and the business running smoothly. Emma congratulated herself on seeing the potential in Rita Hughes, and following her own judgement in offering her a responsible position here. Rita had not let her down.

It was about an hour later, just coming up to midday, when custom had slacked off enough for Emma and Rita Hughes to retire to the small office together in order to discuss the points which Emma had noted. 'You'll be all right on your own, Nelly?' asked Emma. 'We shouldn't be above an hour. Then you can get straight off for your break.'

'You two bugger off from under me feet,' instructed the incorrigible Nelly, ' 'course I'll be all right!'

Rita Hughes and Emma looked at each other with amusement, but they were not surprised by Nelly's familiar light-hearted abuse. They had grown used to it, and saw no offence in her attitude, for there was none intended.

'I gave up on her years ago!' laughed Emma, shaking her head.

'She's a good worker and harmless enough,' rejoined Rita Hughes, as she followed Emma to the back office, 'though I do have to keep my eye on her with the likes of Marjorie Hunter and her snooty cronies. Given the opportunity, they would report Nelly to the authorities and have her reassigned to cleaning out the prison pigsties.'

Emma knew this Marjorie Hunter well. She was a social climber who had nosed her way on to every committee that was formed, and Emma made a mental note to have a word with Nelly before she left. That woman, and others like her, could prove to be Nelly's downfall if she weren't very careful,

270

and it would be tragic if that were to happen, because lately Nelly had made every effort to mend her ways. In fact, Nelly had earned her ticket-of-leave, gone out of her way to appear more disciplined and it had been *months* since she'd been in any kind of trouble. Emma was full of praise for her friend, but there was something which bothered her. This was Nelly's unusually quiet manner on the occasions when Emma began talking of her future, and of how one day she would take Nelly home to England and 'find you a handsome husband there'. At one time, Nelly's jubilant reaction would have been to prance about her little room, with a mischievous look about her, and the comment, 'What 'andsome feller could resist a little beauty like meself, eh? Oh . . . I'll show the bugger a thing or two and no mistake!' Lately however, Nelly seemed to have other things on her mind, so that when Emma talked of England and their future, Nelly's quiet indifference was both astonishing and disturbing to Emma.

The reason for Nelly's curious behaviour was made painfully evident to Emma, when both she and Rita Hughes emerged from the office in less time than Emma had anticipated, having concluded the business discussions with satisfaction and efficiency. It was Emma who saw them first, and she couldn't believe her eyes! The store entrance was closed up and the shutter pulled down. There, with her back against the door was Nelly, her arms stretched round the bent form of a man, and the two of them locked in a kiss which was so obviously passionate that Emma felt her own cheeks flaming.

Rita Hughes had been walking alongside Emma, paying careful attention to Emma's suggestions for display, her own eyes looking downwards to a sketch in her hands which Emma had made to emphasise her point. When, of a sudden, Emma came to a halt, Rita Hughes looked up at her briefly, before following Emma's startled gaze to where the two figures were so rapt in their enjoyment of each other that neither had heard the two women approach.

'Nelly! What in God's name do you think you're doing?' Emma demanded, lifting the cumbersome folds of her skirt with both hands as she swept forward in anger. As she did so, the man, whose back had been to her, now swung round and Emma was so shocked to see who it was that she came to an abrupt halt, exclaiming in a voice that was filled with horror. 'You! . . . Foster Thomas!' At that point, Rita Hughes made a loud gasp, afterwards coming forward on hesitant steps to face him. 'No! . . . I won't believe it. You and . . .' Here she inclined her head towards Nelly, who had stepped up to half-hide herself beside Foster Thomas. ' . . . and *Nelly*!' So terrible was her voice that Emma quickly glanced at her. She was riveted by the awful look on Rita Hughes's face, which was drained white, her odd-coloured eyes stark with panic. Emma knew then, without any doubt, that Rita Hughes adored this man, this fiend who had it in him to force himself on a woman who was ill and helpless, and who was as low as any man could get.

'Look here, girlie,' Foster Thomas appeared unperturbed by the intrusion as he half-turned his murky blue eyes to Nelly, with a sly smile moving

272

over his lean handsome face, which was marred only by the thin low scar made by the lick of his father's whip, 'I reckon we've been caught in the act.' He laughed, a quiet sinister sound which chilled Emma's heart. She had not forgotten how Roland had disowned this man, and how it was common knowledge that he sought to avenge himself on Emma who had been made full heir to all that was 'Thomas Trading'.

'Get out!' she told him now, going in a rage towards the door and flinging it open. 'Get out . . . and *stay* out!' she told him, her grey eyes ablaze.

'It ain't all his fault, Emma!' Nelly protested, running forward in his defence and touching Emma on the arm. She was amazed when Emma shrugged her off, never once taking her stony glare from the man she had every reason to loathe. 'I'll only tell you *once!*' she warned him in a dangerously quiet voice.

'All right, Emma my beauty. There's no reason for me to stay now, is there?' He smiled down on her, his blue eyes boring into her face, 'Not when you've spoiled my fun.' He turned to look at Rita Hughes, who was softly crying and for whom he had always felt a certain repugnance. 'Sorry, girlie,' he said without feeling, 'but y'see . . . Nelly's a better bet.' He now glanced at Nelly who was beside him. 'Ain't that right? Through you . . . I'll definitely achieve so much more.' Nelly giggled foolishly, taking his words to mean that he loved her as she loved him, heart and soul.

But Emma was under no such illusion. She recognised his words for what they really were, a threat against herself and against his father, her husband. She knew in her heart that he would stop

273

at nothing to get to her in any way he possibly could. Nelly was such a way, a poor gullible creature with a heart of gold, and it was filled with love for him. He knew well enough that Emma adored her friend Nelly. That she had watched out for her all these years, and that it would bring her the greatest joy to see Nelly free and settled with a good man who could give her the love and care she so much deserved. To see her entangled with a monster like Foster Thomas was devastating. He was cruel to the point of being sadistic, and Emma knew that he would use Nelly, break her spirit in the process, then fling her aside as though she were nothing.

Emma was tempted to accuse him loudly of these things in front of Nelly, to show him up for what he was and to goad him into revealing his real character. But she gritted her teeth and said nothing, because she suspected that to belittle him in front of Nelly would only fire that foolish young woman to leap to his defence. Instead, she opened the door wider and stepped back for him to pass. As he did so, he leaned down to murmur in her ear, 'It's too late, Emma. *I have her*! I'd rather have you . . . but one thing's for sure, I'll make you suffer. All of you!' Then, as he blatantly bent to kiss Nelly full on the mouth and she, with adoring eyes, followed his long lean figure as it went down the steps, Emma was frantic. When he turned round to tell Nelly with an intimate wink, 'I'll be back for you, girlie,' Emma's worst fears were realised.

'I won't listen to you!' Nelly pressed her hands over her ears, before running to the far end of the room to which Emma had brought her. Emma deplored the havoc Foster Thomas had already wreaked here: Nelly growing more agitated by the minute, and Rita Hughes quietly serving the customers, with a look of abject sorrow on her face, the light gone from her eyes. Foster Thomas had a great deal to answer for, and if Emma had her way, both these foolish women would see him for what he was. Yet Nelly was besotted beyond the point of reason, and Rita Hughes would not even discuss the matter. Whatever Rita's thoughts, she obviously intended to keep them to herself.

'The man's no good for you, Nelly!' Emma argued now. 'Can't you see that he's *using* you? Using you to hurt me. Oh, Nelly . . . be sensible. He'll only break your heart.'

'He *won't*!' yelled Nelly, taking her hands down and flinging herself into the cane chair. 'Foster Thomas loves me. And I love him!' Then, in her anger, she said something that cut Emma's heart to the quick. 'You're jealous, that's all! Don't think *you're* the only one who can have a husband, Miss High and Mighty . . . with your fancy house and all your money!' At once, a look of horror spread over her face, and when she saw how deeply wounded Emma had been by her cruel words, it seemed for a moment as though she might go to her and make amends. But when Emma murmured in a tearful voice, 'Oh, Nelly . . . Nelly,' her back stiffened, and the resolve returned to her face. 'You've got it all, Emma Thomas,' she said in accusing voice, 'and you're carrying your lover's child to prove it!' She turned her eyes from Emma's face because she could not bear to see the pain she had caused. Yet Nelly was convinced that Foster Thomas *did* love her. She was certain also that Emma would stop

275

her from seeing him if she could. Well! In these past months she had earned her ticket-of-leave, and she had the right to choose her own employer. For the first time in her life, Nelly was head over heels in love, and being convinced that her man truly returned her love, she was adamant that *nothing* would come between them, not Emma, not anybody. Oh, she loved Emma like she was her own sister, but what she felt for Foster Thomas had seeped into her every nerve-ending, every bone of her body, and it had given her life new meaning, and a fresh purpose. How could she let it be spoiled? Emma hated him, she knew. And, truth be told, there was every reason, for wasn't she herself a witness to how he had taken Emma when she was desperately ill and lying unconscious? But he was drunk at the time! She had questioned him on this very issue, and he had told her how he was filled with remorse that he should have done such a dreadful thing. Oh, he was no angel, Nelly knew that. But then, neither was *she*.

'I'm leaving. I'll report to the authorities and find new work in Fremantle.' Nelly's voice was cold and unfriendly, but still she could not lift her eyes to Emma. 'I'd be obliged if you'd piss off . . . go on! Leave me be, and let me live me own bloody life!'

Emma stared down at Nelly's familiar brown unruly hair, and she could hardly see for the tears which swam in her sorry eyes. In a moment, she had taken a step forward, her hand outstretched as though she might stroke Nelly's bent head. When Nelly sensed Emma's intention, she looked up to meet Emma's unhappy gaze. For a while, she said nothing, a great and terrible struggle going on

276

inside her. Then, when Emma asked, 'You don't mean that, do you, Nelly?' she got to her feet, quickly rummaged about in the room to collect a few belongings, then brushed past Emma, turning at the door to tell her in an angry voice, 'You ain't gonna piss off . . . so *I* will. Don't come after me, and don't contact me . . . 'cause I've washed me hands of yer. Yer turned yer back on my feller . . . so, you've turned yer back on what I want most in life. That tells me that yer ain't the friend I took yer for. Don't you ever interfere in my life again!' She flounced out of the room, and slammed the door, leaving the only person in the world who genuinely loved her totally devastated by her parting words, 'Don't contact me and don't ever interfere in my life again.'

*   *   *

That night, when Emma lay in her bed looking back on that most dreadful scene, she felt a deluge of sorrow within her that she had not experienced in a long, long time. She knew that she had no right to go against Nelly's furious insistence that Emma should not contact her, and if truth be told, Emma was convinced that she could never change Nelly's obsessive love for Foster Thomas . . . in the same way that Nelly would not change Emma's own loathing for him. She had hurt Nelly badly, she had threatened what her friend saw as her only chance of happiness, and Emma wished that it could have been different. She feared for Nelly. But there was nothing to be done, except to pray that no real harm would come to her, before the truth of Foster Thomas's character was revealed. Love was a cruel master. Who should know that better than Emma herself!

Even while Emma cried herself to sleep, Nelly was settling down in the attic of a nearby inn where she had found work. She too was desperately unhappy because of the terrible things she had said to Emma. Yet she would stand by her decision now. She wouldn't contact Emma and she wouldn't retract any of those things which had been said, because she loved Foster Thomas too much to risk losing him. In fact, when she had found him to tell him how she had been so cruel in saying those things to Emma, he had been quick to defend her and to reassure her of his love. What was more, Emma had been wrong in saying that he was only 'using' her. Because this very day, he had asked her to marry him! The authorities were duly informed and soon Nelly would be Mrs Foster Thomas . . . a *free* woman. So much for Emma's warning, she thought bitterly.

Nelly was convinced that she would never come to regret the path she had chosen. But if it had been within her power to see where that path might lead, she would never even have taken the first step!

Chapter Ten

'It's no use you keep worrying over Nelly . . . you're only making yourself ill!' Roland Thomas reached his arms up to the wooden bar which Emma had arranged to be fitted to his bedhead, and with a determined effort he pulled himself up to a more

278

comfortable sitting position. 'She's married . . . made her own choice. and I reckon she'll have to live with it.' He pursed his lips as he looked from Emma to gaze thoughtfully at the chequered eiderdown, and all the while he was cursing whatever ill-fortune it was that had brought him a son like Foster Thomas.

'If only she would answer my notes, Mr Thomas . . . if only she would show willing to make amends between us, that's all I ask.' Emma was standing by the window, looking out on to the verandah and occasionally lifting her eyes to scour the distance beyond the road which led down to the sea. Always, when she let her thoughts wander over the horizon, the image of Marlow would flood her heart and, like now, she turned away. It was no use craving for what could never be. She had come to realise that much, and to be thankful for whatever blessings the Lord saw fit to bring her.

With her naturally slim figure, and being sensible enough to choose dresses that were not nipped in too tight at the waist, Emma's condition was not easily evident. But she knew that in another few weeks, when she came into the fourth month of her pregnancy, there would be no hiding it. Already Mr Thomas had remarked how pinched and pale her face was. He had put it down to one thing only. The very same issue which he was raising now. 'Come and sit beside me, Emma,' he suggested in a kindly voice.

Emma turned from the window, momentarily surveying the bedroom, which was Roland Thomas's own little world. Following the accident that had crippled him and which dictated the need for a downstairs room, Emma had chosen this one, because of its spaciousness and because it was always flooded with light. It was a lovely east-facing room, having large windows with a triple aspect, and from his bed Mr Thomas had a wonderful view of Queen Square. Emma had employed a man to work on creating a garden which was riotous in colour and, on a summer evening, when the windows were flung wide open, the scent from the shrubs and flowers would permeate the room. It was the most delightful room in the whole house, made even more pleasant by the chintz fabric and articles of light-coloured wood furniture which Emma had imported from England. Indeed, the decor of this room, and the drawing-room where Emma received her visitors, had made such an impression on certain people of social standing that Emma had built up a strong line of sales in various furnishings which she brought in from the homeland.

'Listen to me, Emma.' Roland Thomas reached out his hand to where Emma was now seated in the wicker armchair by his bed and, gently touching her shoulder, he went on, 'Nelly went into that marriage with her eyes wide open. Oh, I know she's prone to do silly things, and she often jumps in with both feet without looking where she's going . . . but, she's a grown woman! You can't watch out for her forever, girlie.'

'I know,' Emma conceded, 'but there have been rumours ever since she and Foster took on that small store in Perth. Word has filtered back that things are not well between them . . . and *that* doesn't surprise me!' Emma added bitterly, 'But *why* won't Nelly answer my letters? Every time the mail coach comes back, I feel positive that this time there'll be a reply . . . but there never is.' Of a sudden, Emma sat bolt upright in the chair, then she was leaning forward, her grey eyes alight with enthusiasm. 'I'm of a mind to go there, Mr Thomas,' she declared. 'I'm certain she'll talk to me . . . if we're face to face.'

'No, girlie.' Roland Thomas closed his homely brown eyes as though in pain, and shaking his head, he told her, 'You're only hurting yourself in thinking that. You've known Nelly a good deal longer than I have . . . and, by God, you've been through some terrible times together. But I'll tell you this. In the years that I have known her, Nelly has shown herself to be foolhardy and stubborn. *I'm* fond of her too, you know that, Emma . . . but you can't deny that if she sets her mind against some'at, well . . . she's hard put to change it. And I know it's painful for you, Emma . . . but the truth is that Nelly's set her mind against you! You'll drive yourself into the asylum if you don't accept it. And you know as well as I do, *that's exactly* what that no-good son of mine planned right from the start.'

'But he's using her, Mr Thomas.' Emma felt so utterly helpless and wretched. 'He has no feelings for Nelly! He'll make her life a misery. And I must do something . . . I can't just watch it happen and do nothing!'

'There isn't a thing in this world you can do, Emma. You've written to Nelly and you've offered both friendship and support. If she chooses to throw it all back in your face, then I'm afraid . . . you must respect her wishes.' He saw how distraught Emma was, and he despised his son all the more for it. 'Y'do see that, don't you, Emma?'

281

Emma reluctantly nodded, for she knew that he was right in what he said. She got up from the chair and, assuring him that she would try to put it all from her mind, she went to the door and was on the point of closing it behind her when Roland Thomas said in a strong convincing voice, 'Mark my words, Emma, Nelly will seek you out, I'm sure of it. One of these days, she'll come to realise what a good friend she has in you, and she'll turn up on the doorstep. She will. You see if I'm not telling the truth.'

Emma smiled, nodded to him, and softly closed the door. If only that were true, she thought sadly, realising how Foster Thomas was so cruelly right when he promised to make her suffer because, since that day when she and Nelly had parted on such awful terms, there had been no real peace in her life. Oh, if only Nelly *would* seek her out, Emma thought, as she composed herself to brace the long business meeting which even now awaited her in the study, in the form of her accountant and a representative from the Jackson Chandlers Company, a modest but promising little concern situated in Fremantle. Emma had challenged the Lassater Shipping Line in making a bid for Jackson Chandlers, which she saw as a natural addition to the newly formed Thomas Shipping Company. However she must be very cautious, because only yesterday she had received the news that Silas Trent had met up with the two shipowners whom he and Emma had discussed and it seemed that, for the right price, they were willing to sell. That would greatly deplete her financial resources and, though a Chandler's business would be a great asset, she had to gauge the price right, without losing the chance of acquiring it altogether.

As Emma bade the two smiling gentlemen good morning, her thoughts inevitably lingered on what her husband had told her. If only it could be true, she thought, if only Nelly would 'turn up on the doorstep'. What a joyous day that would be.

*   *   *

Three days later, on Saturday, the twenty-fourth of October in the year of our Lord, 1876, the promise which Roland Thomas had made to Emma came true, but instead of being the joyous occasion which Emma had hoped, the unexpected arrival of Nelly heralded a series of tragic consequences.

The day had been particularly harrowing for Emma, because as yet she had been unable to replace Nelly satisfactorily in the store. Since Nelly's departure, there had been one new employee after the other, a young girl from Bunbury, a lad who had served some time on a whaling ship, and a middle-aged woman from the prison. Each and every one of them had proved to be a disaster in one way or another. The girl had shown herself to be bone idle, the lad to be accident-prone, and the woman to have a weakness for thievery and argument. The last straw for Emma was when, that very morning, Rita Hughes was made to fend off a vicious attack from the prisoner, who had every intention of splitting Rita's head open with a pickaxe. Apparently, Rita had quite rightly made the comment that the floorboards needed a fresh sprinkling of sawdust. The employee saw this as the very excuse she had waited for in order to pick an argument. She replied that she had other jobs to do, and if Rita Hughes wanted more sawdust down, then she'd better 'do it yer bloody self.' A raging row erupted and Rita Hughes was seen to flee into the street, to escape serious injury. Emma was given no choice. The woman had to go, and she herself was obliged to take her place. That didn't worry Emma though, because she was never one to be afraid of work.

What *did* worry Emma was the way Rita Hughes appeared to be letting herself go in these past weeks. As a rule, she was meticulously dressed, her collar and cuffs always starched and sparkling, and her entire appearance of such trim smartness that was beyond reproach. Her hair, which was now more marbled with grey, would be neatly secured into a roll and fastened tightly in the nape of her neck. Her small dark boots were highly polished and she was most particular never to be seen with a hair out of place at any time during her long working day. The same pride and joy which she took in her tidy appearance was always extended to include the execution of every task she did, however demanding or menial. People used to admire her for it, and make regular comment on it. Now, however, their admiration had turned to curiosity and their comments had turned to whispering in little gossiping groups, about how sloppy Rita Hughes was becoming and how little she seemed to care for her appearance of late. 'Why, you'll never believe it,' declared the butcher's round-eyed wife, 'but a pin actually fell from her hair and into the salt-bin only the other day. And did she take the trouble to retrieve it and to secure her hair from her face? No, my dears . . . she did not!' There was much speculation and on two occasions at least, the customers had seen fit to complain quietly to Emma. 'Whatever's the matter with the poor woman?' asked the kindly seamstress. 'Is she ill?' Emma promised that she would certainly have a discreet word with Rita, and so she did; after which Rita Hughes appeared to make a great effort to improve, or to be seen to improve. But Emma was not fooled. She knew well enough that Rita had been devastated by Foster Thomas's preference for Nelly, though if she had her own suspicions as to his motive, she kept her thoughts to herself.

'Are you all right, Rita? You do look very tired.' Emma was seated on the tall stool which was pulled up to the bureau in the back office; she was about to close the ledger after making the stock entries, when she glanced through the glass partition to see Rita Hughes gazing out of the window. 'Rita . . . it's been a very long day, I know—' Emma was by her side now '—you go on home. I'll lock up.' Normally they would have closed the store some hours before, but this was the last Saturday in the month and the stock-taking must be done.

'It's getting dark,' came the reply. Of a sudden, Rita Hughes had swung round to face Emma and it was plain to see that she had been crying. Now though, she displayed a half-smile and told Emma in a brisk voice, 'I wouldn't dream of leaving you to finish up on your own. There's still the stock to be brought through from the back, and the displays to be set up ready for Monday morning.' She donned a serious expression on her face as she swept past Emma, saying, 'Better get on with it then . . . the two of us will make light work of it and be done in

285

no time at all.' She fetched two lamps from beneath the counter, lighting them both, then placing one on top of the counter and hanging one from the hook in the beam situated over the bureau. It was only then that Emma realised how rapidly the daylight was fading. No wonder she had a throbbing headache, when she had been poring over the ledgers in half-light.

An hour and a half later, at a quarter to ten, everything was done, and the two women prepared to leave. 'I don't think I've ever felt so tired in my whole life!' Emma declared with a warm smile to Rita Hughes, who was fussing about the way her cape just would not sit right on her shoulders. 'My head aches . . . my feet are on fire, and I could fall asleep on the spot!' She put out the lamp in the office, before coming through to the store. 'I expect you feel exactly the same, Rita.' She looked at the other woman, who seemed painfully preoccupied, and Emma felt a rush of compassion for her. 'Thank you for the hard work you've put in,' she told her warmly, 'I'll see you're suitably rewarded, you know that.'

'Of course. Thank *you*, Mrs Thomas. An extra guinea or two is always very welcome. It's a shame that we've found no one to take Nelly's place . . . I know you have more than enough to do, without having to take up responsibility here.'

'Well, I can't deny that there are never enough hours in a day, Rita. Still . . . I am seeing that young man from Perth next week. He seems to be very keen on coming here to work, and he has sent exceptionally good references. Let's just hope he's a distinct improvement on the other three, eh?' She smiled, and was surprised when Rita Hughes actually laughed out loud, saying, 'Make sure he doesn't have a weakness for chasing women with a pickaxe!'

The two women were still softly chuckling as they made their way towards the door, with Rita Hughes carrying the lamp and Emma beginning to sort out the right key from the bunch in her hand.

When the door suddenly burst open, both women were taken completely by surprise. In the few seconds of confusion which followed, Rita Hughes screamed out and dropped the lamp to the floor and Emma's first thoughts were that the intruders were robbers, who obviously knew that she had the day's takings on her person. When the dark shadowy figure lunged at her, and Rita Hughes continued screaming, Emma began fighting it off, aware all the while of the flames which had erupted from the broken lamp; fortunately the oil had not been spilt. But then Emma heard a familiar voice calling her name, 'Emma . . . oh Emma!' At once she knew the voice. It was Nelly, Nelly, who had burst in through the door and who had fallen against her, Nelly, now slumped in her arms and sobbing her name as if it were her salvation.

Quickly, and without panic, Emma took stock of the situation. The flames must be put out before anything else, or the whole place would go up. Easing the figure from her, she yelled to Rita Hughes to 'put the flames out! Use your cape . . . anything!' She had already whipped off her own cape and was frantically smothering the fire, which thankfully had not got a proper hold, but was a fearsome thing all the same. When she saw Rita being quick to follow her example, Emma ran to the back wall where the water buckets hung, and in quick succession she used all six of them, dousing the flames and afterwards satisfying herself that enough water had been poured through the cracks between the floorboards. She had seen other disasters from fires that were thought to be put out, but which smouldered under the building until finally flaring up again when least expected.

'Rita, do you think you could find your way to the office, and fetch the lamp from there? There are matches in the top drawer of the bureau.' While she spoke, Emma could see the outline of Nelly in the faint light from the street lamp outside, and when the figure didn't move from the floor where it had fallen, Emma's fearful heart turned somersaults. Stooping down to look more closely, Emma slid her two arms beneath her dear friend's arms and, with all the strength she had left, she raised Nelly to a sitting position. By that time Rita Hughes had come back with the halo of light from the lamp going before her. 'It's *Nelly*, isn't it?' she asked in a trembling voice. 'What's wrong with her, Mrs Thomas?' She raised the lamp and as she did so, the light fell on Nelly's face. 'Oh, my God!' she cried out, the lamp trembling in her hand. '*Look at her face!*'

Emma had seen, and was both shocked and sickened by the sight of Nelly's bruised and battered body. One of her eyes was so swollen as to be virtually unrecognisable; there was a deep, vicious indentation on her forehead that might have been imprinted there by the shape of a ring, so sharp were the edges; and the gash along her cheekbone was all the more misshapen by the blood which had dried on it. From her right temple to a cut on her lip there was a long, meandering red trail, which was not so much a deep cut as a mark made by a blunt instrument being drawn along it.

Emma saw that Nelly was not unconscious, but sapped of all strength, in pain, and obviously filled with terror. Emma now tried to help her to her feet, saying in a gentle, soothing voice, 'It's all right, Nelly . . . it's all right. Don't be afraid, I'll take care of you.' Nelly began shaking violently and the tears rolled down her sorry face as, lifting her brown eyes that were normally so merry and were now terribly scarred by her ordeal, she kept saying over and over again in a small trembling voice, 'It ain't the first time, Emma darling . . . it ain't the first time he's got drunk and thrashed me.'

'Ssh!' Emma clung to her friend, yet she could hardly see for the scalding tears which blurred her eyes. 'Ssh now, Nelly. He won't "thrash" you again. You have my word on that!' In that moment, if she could have placed her bare hands on the worthless creature who had done this, she wouldn't have been responsible for her own actions.

'Oh, Mrs Thomas,' Rita Hughes had gone a deathly shade of white, and for one awful moment, Emma thought the poor thing was about to faint. 'She won't *die*, will she? Oh, she can't mean that *Foster* did this to her . . . she can't!' She peered closely at Nelly, who was leaning all her body weight on Emma's slim form. With her tiny eyes stretched open in horror and her voice filled with awe, she said again more softly, 'She won't die, will she?'

'She might,' Emma told her in a firm voice

289

designed to jolt her senses, 'if you don't give me a hand to get her up to the house!' At once, Rita Hughes came forward to take some of Nelly's weight from Emma; then, with Nelly's bedraggled and sorry figure supported between them, they went at a careful if hurried pace towards the High Street and the Thomases' residence. Emma hoped they would not disturb her husband, who had suffered a great deal of pain and discomfort these past few days, and was at the end of his patience.

* * *

'If you have any idea who did this, then it's your duty to inform the authorities!' The doctor's expression was severe as he spoke to both Emma and Rita Hughes; the latter found it difficult to tear her eyes from Nelly's scarred face even though she had helped to wash and clean the wounds which so offended her.

'I ain't sure who did it, doctor!' Nelly called out from her bed. 'And it ain't no use you asking them two neither . . . 'cause they don't know who it was no more than I do!' Nelly sensed from the look on Emma's face that she had every intention of telling the doctor that it was Foster Thomas who had battered her friend, and so great was Nelly's fear of that man, so deeply had he instilled in her a riveting terror of him, that she would have crawled from the bed on her bended knees to prevent sending the authorities after him. Nelly believed that if she allowed that to happen, she would be signing her own death warrant. 'That's right, ain't it, Emma . . . ain't it Rita? . . . You ain't got no idea who attacked me, have you, eh? No idea at all. You make sure the good doctor knows that!' She didn't recognise her own voice as it sailed through the room from her bruised and swollen lips. In her anxiety to keep secret the name of Foster Thomas, she pulled herself up from the bolster, crying in pain as she did so.

'You lie still!' instructed the doctor. 'I'm afraid you have a broken rib or two. Lie still, or suffer the consequences.' He watched while Nelly fell back on to the pillow, her face contorted with pain and misshapen by the beating it had taken. Yet she kept her frightened brown eyes on Emma, willing her not to betray her.

'Now then, Mrs Thomas . . . do you have any idea who did this? She knows, I'm sure,' he cast a concerned glance at Nelly, 'but, for some reason, she won't confide in me.'

Emma was suffering a bitter conflict. She *should* tell. With every bone in her body she wanted to see that fiend pay for what he had done to Nelly. But now, as she looked towards her friend and saw the desperate pleading in her tearful eyes, she was torn a thousand ways. 'She has told me very little,' she replied, convincing herself that Foster Thomas would be made to pay, if not tonight, then tomorrow, when she would persuade Nelly that the authorities must be told. Nelly was back, and she was safe, thank God. Tomorrow, she might be ready to see things in a different light. She saw the great rush of relief and gratitude in Nelly's face as she buried it in the pillow and began quietly sobbing. 'Thank you so much, doctor,' Emma said now, showing him to the door, 'I'll talk to Nelly when she's rested.'

Emma waited while the doctor attended to her

husband. He had unfortunately been woken by all the comings and goings, and demanded to know what had happened. Emma told him the truth, that Nelly had taken a terrible beating, but she deliberately kept his son's name out of it. 'You can't hide the facts from *me*, girlie!' he had told her scathingly. 'It's him that's beaten her, that's right isn't it? That no-good son of mine who's never done anything worthwhile in his life. But he can take up his bloody fists to a helpless woman! By God! There'll come a day when he'll drive me too far!' At this point he had thumped his clenched-up fists time and time again into his lifeless legs. 'Curse these useless things! If it weren't for these, I'd show him a beating all right. Man to man . . . not man over his helpless wife.' He had worked himself up into such a pitch that Emma had to ask that the doctor see *him* as well as Nelly.

'He's sleeping now, Mrs Thomas.' The doctor's face was grave however. 'I'm afraid his pain will soon be beyond medication.' He watched the light go from Emma's wise eyes, and he was filled with admiration for her courageous spirit. She was a fine woman, a woman who never stinted in her friendship or loyalty, and she was rightfully well respected hereabouts. 'I've done all I can. Your friend won't scar . . . although she'll be some long time mending, I'm afraid. But as for your husband, Emma'—he had never addressed her by her Christian name before and the point was not lost on Emma—'he won't mend at all.'

When the doctor's carriage had gone from sight, Emma glanced down at herself and was strangely surprised by the fact that her dress was blackened by the smoke from when she had beaten out the flames from the lamp. Strands of her hair hung loosely about her neck, and the hem of her skirt was still damp from the water which she had flung on to the flames. Strange, she thought, how none of it seemed to matter now. And oh, she felt so very, very tired, her whole body was stretched with a weariness she had never experienced before. She supposed it was because of the child she carried inside her. Of a sudden, she remembered Rita Hughes, and it struck her how late in the evening it was.

Going to her husband's room, Emma made certain that he was sleeping. She was satisfied also to see that the nurse had made herself comfortable in the wicker chair and was keeping watch. 'Call me if you need anything,' Emma whispered to her; when the chubby-faced nurse gratefully nodded, Emma went softly up the stairs to where Nelly was in a deep, healing sleep.

'I'll get Taylor to walk you home,' Emma informed Rita Hughes. 'Your family will be frantic, wondering why you're so late.' She collected a long fringed shawl from the chair back and wrapped it loosely about her shoulders.

'Thank you, yes, I would like to go home and clean up. My parents won't be worrying though because they're away visiting an aged uncle in Perth. They're not due home until tomorrow.'

'Oh, I see. Well . . . if you'll just watch Nelly a while, I'll go and rouse Taylor to accompany you along the streets. There's no safe place in the dark for a woman on her own.' She left the room and began her way down the wide dogleg staircase, her path lit by the four oil-lamps, strategically placed

293

atop of each of the four thick oak posts which supported the stairs. In the flickering light, Emma wondered what a dishevelled sight she must look. There hadn't been even a moment since Nelly had arrived to wash and spruce herself up. No matter, she told herself, lifting one hand in an effort to tuck her straying auburn hair into a more disciplined appearance, there'll be time enough when Rita is safely on her way. The thought of a hot tub followed by a good night's sleep sent her feet hurrying down the thickly carpeted stairway, as she began to wonder whether Taylor, the handyman, might still be awake and pottering about his room above the outbuildings. She would collect a lamp from the kitchen on the way out, because the area directly behind the house was exceptionally dark.

Two steps from the bottom of the stairway, Emma halted, inclining her head to one side and listening hard. What was that slight sound that had disturbed her? Emma stood still a moment longer, not daring to move, her fearful heart pounding. She turned her anxious eyes towards the gloomy hallway below, as she held her breath and waited to hear the sound again. But the air was silent and brooding. I must have imagined it, Emma told herself, yet she was not fully convinced and, if it hadn't been for the fact that she was anxious to see Rita Hughes safely on her way, so that she herself might be bathed and asleep that much quicker, Emma might have been tempted to go back up the stairs and ask that good woman to accompany her on her errand. But no, Rita had done quite enough for one day, and did not deserve to be put on any further, Emma decided. Besides which, there would be no one to keep an eye on Nelly in the next few moments. Emma had already made up her mind that she would spend the night in the chair in Nelly's room, in case she needed her.

Emma resumed her descent into the hallway, chiding herself for letting her imagination run riot. Now she convinced herself that there had been no noise, except perhaps for the rustling of her own silk skirt as it swept against the stair-treads. She even smiled to herself, saying in a small whisper, 'You should be ashamed, Emma. Fancy! A woman of your thirty-two years being afraid of the dark.' Emma would not have been so 'ashamed' had she known that someone was hiding below, listening to her words, and smiling.

What happened next was done so swiftly that Emma was not even able to cry out. As she stepped into the hallway, the figure sprang from the shadows, clamping one hand over her mouth and gripping her two arms behind her back with the other. As the intruder forced her along by the wall which skirted the drawing-room, Emma kicked and struggled, but she was held so fast that her attempts were futile. She was being dragged round the corner and into the narrow passage, where the door to the left led to the room that was Roland Thomas's and the door to the right went into the drawing-room. Whoever it was who had her in a grip of iron was both immensely strong and obsessively determined that she be given no opportunity to raise the alarm. The hand which smelled of stale tobacco and which had her silenced was stretched from her nostrils to her chin, holding her lips tightly together and preventing her from getting even a pinch of skin between her teeth to bite through and shock her attacker into releasing her.

Emma realised that, if she were to summon any help at all, she must use her feet, even though her legs were swept from the floor. There was no other way. When her assailant pushed her beyond Roland Thomas's door, Emma's frightened eyes saw that the door was half-open. She knew also that, situated on a small table outside the drawing-room, was a large pot plant. If only she could kick out and upset the table so that the plant fell to the floor, surely to God *someone* would come running.

When Emma's chance came, she was ready. But it was unfortunate that the drawing-room door was also partly open, because if the intruder had been made to relax his hold on Emma's arms in order to open the door, nothing on this earth could have held her. As it was, she was pinned fast. But in that split second when he used Emma's body to push open the drawing-room door Emma took her bearings. Praying that she would not miss, she lashed out with her foot in the direction of the pot plant. Her heart soared when she felt that she had made contact and she waited for the crash which must surely follow. But, except for a scraping noise where the pot plant moved along the table only a few inches, there was no loud crashing sound that could summon help to her side. She knew at once that her captor was enraged by her attempt, when he cruelly pushed his hand tighter into her face and gave her arms a spiteful twist. She felt herself being dragged into the room, and her terrified heart sank within her when she realised that the door was softly closed behind them, and that she was alone with her assailant in a room that was pitch black. All Emma could do was to offer up a silent prayer and believe that somehow her ordeal would be over quickly. Her heart bled for the tiny life which beat inside her, and she had to trust in the Lord that he would not be so cruel as to let her lose *this* child.

Emma struggled as her hands were bound so tightly together that her wrists felt as though they were being sliced in two. When a rag was thrust into her mouth and secured there by the broad hessian binding, Emma was totally helpless. Her terror was heightened when she felt herself being pushed to the floor, and her arms tied to the table leg. In a minute, she was left alone while the creature who had brought her here busied himself opening wide the long tapestry curtains which had shut out the moonlight. When, after an instant, he returned and knelt before Emma, he smiled to see her startled grey eyes as they stared at his face in the revealing light of the moon.

'Surely you ain't *surprised*, are you, my beauty? You should have known I'd come back for you!'

Emma found herself looking into the worst evil she could imagine. It was Foster Thomas, handsome as ever, but in that wicked, smiling face with its deep blue eyes, there was a depth of ugliness of the kind that came from within, a hideousness which clung to him like a mantle. His eyes bore deep into Emma's, and she shivered as they touched her soul. Quickly Emma looked away, wondering what dreadful tortures this madman had put Nelly through, and what awful intentions he had towards her this God-forsaken night.

Of a sudden, he began giggling, and it was plain

to Emma that he was either drunk out of his senses, or he had completely lost his mind. Either way, she was riveted with the most awful and compelling belief that neither she nor her unborn child would ever see the morrow.

The thought made her frantic, and she desperately searched her mind for ways in which she might escape, or alert others in the house. It wouldn't be too long before Rita Hughes went looking for her, she told herself; have faith, Emma, trust in the Lord! But if Foster Thomas intended killing her, Emma knew that he could do it easily, in a moment, before the door could be opened. She knew it and was terrified.

'Don't turn away from me, Emma.' She felt his rough fingers beneath her chin as her head was yanked back. She felt his booze-laden breath fanning her face, but still she kept her gaze lowered from him. She would have thumped her boot heels against the carpet, but he was crouched on her legs, his weight keeping them secured. He was devious. But then, madmen usually were. 'So Nelly came running to you, did she?' he asked in a whisper, still smiling. 'I knew she would. I planned it that way, y'see.' The smile went from his face and, to Emma's horror, he began slowly undoing the buttons of her dress. When she struggled and squirmed, he fetched his hand up and slapped it hard across her temple. 'No, Emma . . . you're not to struggle against me. You're mine, y'see . . . you've *always* been mine, I've told you that so many times and still you fight against it!' His eyes were wild as they stared at her, yet they were vacant also. In that moment Emma knew that he was completely and utterly mad.

'That Nelly . . . she knows too much for her own good.' He was talking in a whisper as he leaned close towards her, all the while undoing her buttons. 'She saw me, y'know . . . the night my mother was shot. I set the whole thing up, but it went wrong.' He laughed very softly as he slid his hand into Emma's dress and began caressing the warm firmness of her breast. Emma felt physically sick, but she knew that if she were to save herself and her child, she must not goad him, for he was quite capable of sliding his hand to her throat and squeezing the life from it. 'If things had gone well that night . . . then I would have Thomas Trading . . . and all this.' He waved a hand to encompass the whole room. 'But there's still hope. Oh, Emma . . . you and me, we can do anything we set our minds to!' He looked into her face as though searching for some sign of encouragement. When he saw only hatred and fear in Emma's accusing eyes, he made a curious expression, like an animal in pain, Emma thought; then without warning he placed his two fists one either side of Emma's dress and, with a low growl sounding deep in his throat, he ripped the bodice apart, exposing her bare breasts, now scarred red by his fingernails.

In that same instant, the door crashed open. Foster Thomas scrambled to his feet, his wild eyes picking out the figure of his own father, who was lying twisted on the floor. He was exhausted by the immense and determined effort it had taken for him to get from his bed—without waking the nurse—take his hand gun from the drawer, then to crawl along the passageway, hampered by the dead weight of his legs, and finally to reach up and open the door. The terrible ordeal he had gone through showed on his face, which was contorted with pain. But when he stared up at this man, this terrible coward who was his own son, Roland Thomas's heart was filled with a strange guilt. Somehow, he imagined, the blame must lie with him. He had spawned this worthless creature, and only he could make amends. He raised the gun and pointed it at his son's heart.

'No!' Emma's terrified scream stayed trapped in her head. But there came another sound, a loud ear-splitting sound, when the room was pierced with fire. Foster Thomas stood perfectly still for a split second, then, with his startled eyes staring into his father's distraught face, he crumpled silently to the ground, his eyes fixed in a round, surprised expression.

The silence which followed was eerie, but then there came the sound of anxious voices and running feet in the distance. Emma saw the nurse first, as holding a lamp before her, she came to a halt by the twisted, sprawling figure of Roland Thomas. Her unbelieving eyes went from her patient to the body lying nearby—its vacant stare seeming to fix itself upon her—then, her mouth falling open as though in slow motion, she rested her shocked gaze on Emma's bound and gagged figure, with the dress almost torn from it. She saw the devastation in Emma's terrified eyes and was paralysed by it. Emma's paramount thoughts were of her husband, who had been made to commit a terrible crime, murdering his own son!

It was as though Emma's heart had stopped beating when, her eyes drawn once more to the face of Roland Thomas, she saw that he was softly crying. It was with a rush of horror that she realised the dark intent in his expression, yet she was powerless to stop him. The frantic protest which was cruelly stifled in her throat found an outlet in her eyes, as they pleaded with the nurse to lower her gaze and see what dreadful thing her patient was about to do. But the nurse was already giving urgent instructions to the servants and to Rita Hughes, who had also heard the shot and had come to investigate.

In those few vital moments when the frantic expression in Emma's grey eyes conveyed itself to her husband, it was already too late. He looked at her, smiled gently and moved his lips in a silent whisper. Emma read those two words as easily as if they had been shouted from the rooftops: 'Forgive me,' her husband asked. Then he turned away.

When remembering it over the years to follow, Emma thought it strange how very quickly the whole thing had happened—in the space of mere minutes—but how tortuous and endless it had seemed.

She relived that awful night many times before she could finally rid herself of the look in her husband's tragic eyes when he had mouthed his pitiful words; of the sound which his bath chair made as Taylor hurriedly trundled it down the passageway towards the nurse; and of how, even as Taylor and the nurse prepared to arrange it in order to lift Roland Thomas more easily into it, a second shot rang out. Emma was haunted by the vision of the nurse's starched white dress all spattered with crimson, and that poor woman's scream rang in Emma's dreams for some long time afterwards.

Later, when the authorities had completed their

investigations, and she sought solace in Nelly's room, Emma fell like a child into her arms, clinging to the one person who knew her almost as well as she knew herself. 'Oh, Nelly . . . *why*?' she sobbed. 'Roland was such a good man.'

Nelly held her tight, nuzzling her own bruised and battered face against Emma's hair. Like Emma, she had witnessed things that would long torment her. 'Who knows why, Emma darling,' she murmured. 'When the good in us is faced by terrible evil . . . who knows what we might do?'

Chapter Eleven

'It's a boy, Emma!' Nelly had watched the final moments from when the small dark head had first appeared. Now, as the tiny shoulders came into sight and then the baby's whole perfect little form slithered into the world, she was unable to contain her joy and excitement. 'Aw, Emma . . . you should see the little bugger! He's gorgeous!' she shouted gleefully, her brown eyes watching Widow Miller's every movement, as she collected the tiny babe into her arms. Holding the squirming bundle upside down, the plump woman gave it a number of short, sharp spanks on the buttocks, smiling broadly when its loud cries filled the room. Then, taking it to the dresser, she quickly washed it, wrapped it in a shawl and came back to the bed, where she placed it in Emma's arms. 'Nelly's right,' she said with a kindly smile, 'you have a beautiful son.' She then set about washing Emma and making her comfortable.

When the tiny bundle was put into Emma's out-stretched arms, she was so full of emotion that she could only nod her gratitude. When she took the child to her breast and lowered her gaze to see its tiny face, her vision was blurred by the tears of joy which sprang from her heart. There were no words which could convey how Emma felt in that most precious moment. Here, in her arms, warm and real, was her son, Marlow's son, as perfect a boy as she could ever have wished for. In her heart she gave thanks to God for her baby's safe deliverance, because, in the weeks following the tragedy which had unfolded right before her eyes, there were anxious times when the doctor feared that Emma might lose her child. Yet never once did Emma lose her faith. She made herself believe that this child was meant to be, that she and Marlow were meant to be, and that if there was a merciful God, he would bring her through the ordeals which he had set her, for she had weathered them in as courageous and determined a manner as was humanly possible. Surely now he would help her to find a kind of happiness and peace of soul. In her son, he had answered her prayers.

'He don't look like you, Emma gal.' Nelly had waited for the Widow Miller's departure before sitting on the bed alongside Emma. 'He ain't got your auburn hair . . . and he ain't got your grey eyes neither!' She was fascinated.

Emma smiled up at Nelly's homely face, which was as jubilant as though the infant might be her very own, and her heart was touched by memories of Nelly's dreadful ordeal at the hands of Foster Thomas. For just a moment her joy was marred. She knew that, even were she to live to a ripe old

303

age, there could never be anyone who would be as close to her in friendship as Nelly. Impulsively, Emma held the child towards this woman whom she had loved like her own flesh and blood, for more years than she cared to remember. Together they had been through so much, yet all their ups and downs had only served to bring them even closer. 'Hold him, Nelly,' she offered now, 'feel how warm and soft he is.'

'Oh, Emma! . . . Can I? Aren't you afraid I'll drop him?' Nelly's face was a picture, as her brown eyes grew big and round and she put her hands behind her back to prevent them from grasping the child until she was good and ready. 'Ooh, look at him,' she laughed, 'I do believe the little bugger's smiling at me. No! I won't take him, Emma . . . I just know I'll drop him.' When Emma insisted, she gave a sheepish grin and brought her two hands from behind her back. Taking a few moments to prepare herself, she vigorously wiped the palms of her hands on the deep folds of the blue silk dress which Emma had bought her. Then, after a deal of nervous coughing and throat noises, she held out her arms, a look on her face that amused Emma: a mingling of bliss and sheer terror. 'Tell him not to wiggle, Emma gal,' she muttered, taking the bundle and holding it close, 'it's been a good many years since I held a young 'un, and I might have forgotten the right way to do it.'

'Isn't he beautiful, Nelly?' Emma gazed at her son, her adoring eyes following his every feature. Nelly was right. He did not have auburn hair or grey eyes, because in that tiny face there was a wonderful likeness to his father. He had hair as black and rich as Marlow's, and the eyes, though touched with sapphire blue, were dark also. Even the strong lines of his face, the shape of his nose and that straight set chin were reminiscent of Marlow, and Emma's happiness was overwhelming. Yet in her great joy, there was a tinge of sad regret when she thought of that other babe which she had borne, a little girl with the same dark colouring, and who would have been a sister to this son of hers and Marlow's. But that was over sixteen years ago now, and if the child had lived, she would be almost a woman. Emma let her thoughts dwell on that for a while, looking to find some measure of consolation in the knowledge that it was all too far in the past now, too late. But it only made her pine all the more, as she made herself think about a girl of seventeen, a dark-haired girl with the striking vivacious looks of Marlow, and perhaps having also some measure of Emma in her character. The years had not diminished Emma's loss nor her pain, but only intensified it. She would have to learn how to live with the memories and not let them cause her pain. In time, maybe, she would be able to, Emma thought. But she could never forget.

'Here, Emma . . . you'd best take the little darling back.' Nelly placed a gossamer kiss on the infant's forehead. 'I do love him, Emma. He's precious,' she said.

Emma collected him in her arms. 'Thank you, Nelly,' she said, gratefully squeezing her friend's hand, 'he is . . . very precious.' She thought that nobody in this world could ever know just how much. Now there were plans to be made, exciting plans which she had kept to herself these past months, but which were now pushing themselves to the front of her mind. 'Nelly,' she said quietly, afterwards seeming lost in thought, as she looked for the best way to broach the subject, in view of Nelly's excitable nature.

'Yes? . . . What's on yer mind, gal?' Nelly had got to her feet, but now she looked down at Emma with a puzzled frown. 'Oh look! Yer ain't worrying about the business and such, are yer?' she demanded. 'Rita Hughes is doing a *grand* job at the store . . . she's a changed woman since that . . . awful business.' Nelly's face became crestfallen as she was forced to remember. But then, in that way she had of pushing away anything which disturbed her too deeply, she went on, 'And that Silas Trent . . . well! If yer don't mind me saying, Emma . . . the bugger's work-mad! I mean it, dar-lin' . . . yer couldn't fault him. He's running that business like it were his own! What! . . . I'm telling yer . . . yer couldn't do better yourself!'

'I know that, Nelly.' Emma wondered how she could ever repay Silas Trent for giving up the sea in order to watch over her interests while she herself had been unable to.

'You'll be up and about in no time now,' Nelly reminded her, 'but o' course . . . you'll have this little 'un here to look after. What name are yer giving the lad?' she asked.

Emma had not decided on that issue yet, because she was torn between her own father's name, Thadius, and Marlow's father's name, which if she remembered right, he had told her was Bill. It would have been lovely if she could talk it over with Marlow. But as yet, Silas's enquiries as to his whereabouts had been unsuccessful. The news from Blackburn, Lancashire, was that he had left

306

the area on learning of his sister Sal's demise. It was said that he had been heartbroken. Emma did not intend to give up though, and had told Silas that Marlow must be found. He was not alone in the world any more, because here was a woman who loved him. And he had a son! What better purpose was there for a man to live?

'You ain't to worry about the business, Emma,' Nelly reminded her now, 'it's being well taken care of.'

'No, I wasn't worrying about that,' Emma assured her. 'Silas has it all in hand. I know that, from his weekly reports to me. Also, Mr Lucas from the bank has expressed his admiration for Silas Trent's business acumen. Thomas Shipping has proved to be a very profitable venture all round . . . and we're picking up inland trade all the time. No, I'm not worrying on that score, Nelly. In fact, there are only two things that concern me now. One is that Marlow hasn't yet been found.'

'And the other?'

'The other is *you*.'

'Me? Oh, Emma . . . what have I done wrong now? Look here, if that parlour maid's been telling tales about me breaking that white statue on the mantelpiece . . . she's a little liar. I know nothing at all about it!'

Emma was amused to see that Nelly's face had gone a bright shade of pink. She knew all about the statue, which Nelly *had* broken, and which the maid had reported, but Emma had dismissed the matter. 'I don't know what you're talking about,' she lied, to save Nelly's pride. 'What I have in mind has nothing at all to do with a statue.'

'What then? If she's accused me of something

307

else, I'll *do* for her . . . I bloody will! Just you tell me what she's been saying. What's on yer mind, Emma . . . come on, me shoulders is broad enough, and I'm ready fer anything?'

Emma was really enjoying herself, putting on her most serious face, she beckoned for Nelly to sit down on the bed once more. Then, when her friend was seated and looking at Emma with a bold, defiant expression, Emma asked, 'Ready for *anything*, you say?'

'That's right, me girl! You just tell me what's on yer mind! But I'm telling you right now . . . I didn't do it!'

'Would you be ready to set sail for *England*, I wonder?' Emma blurted out, watching with amusement as Nelly's whole face appeared to fall open with surprise.

'England!' Nelly was on her feet in an instant, looking down on Emma with disbelieving eyes, as she asked in a voice filled with awe, *'We're setting sail for England?'* Her voice tailed off and caught in a strange little choking sound. When she spoke again it was in a whisper, and the tears were spilling down her face. 'D'yer mean it, Emma gal? . . . We're really going home?' The sight of Nelly's tears and her obvious happiness touched Emma's heart. She swallowed the lump which had straddled her throat and when she nodded, Nelly threw herself down on her knees, her two arms stretched out to embrace both Emma and the child. 'I can't believe it!' she cried through her laughter. 'We're going home. Oh, Emma, Emma! At long last . . . we're going home!'

The torrent of emotion created by Nelly's simple delight engulfed Emma, moving her also to tears of joy. 'It's been a long time, Nelly,' she murmured, holding her son fast on one arm and stroking Nelly's bent head with her free hand, 'but yes . . . at long last, we're going home.' These two devoted friends clung to each other. They cried a little and laughed a little, and the hardships they had endured fell away.

Outside, it was growing ever dark and on this June evening there was a wintry nip in the air. But in the room where Emma's son had been born, there was warmth of a human kind, there was sunshine and hope. Soon there would be a new dawn, when long cherished dreams might be realised.

*   *   *

'You can count on me. All will be well taken care of in your absence, Emma.' Silas Trent looked around the ship's cabin, then, satisfied that Emma and her son would be comfortable on their long sea voyage, he swung the two large tapestry bags up on to the bunk. 'Nelly's beside herself with excitement,' he laughed, 'I've just left her examining every nook and cranny in her cabin . . . there isn't a dial that she hasn't twisted, or a cupboard or drawer that she hasn't investigated.'

'Leave her be . . . she'll soon tire of it and come looking to see what I've got that she hasn't!' Emma's laughter was light-hearted and, with her son in her arms, there shone from her lovely eyes a peace which Silas Trent had not seen there before. 'If the weather is kind to you, Emma, you should arrive in Liverpool on or about the 16th of September. If our information was correct and

309

Marlow receives the message I sent to the Navigation pub, he should be waiting when you disembark. God speed, Emma. And don't concern yourself about matters at this end.' He smiled broadly, saying, 'Now that you've made me a full partner . . . I wouldn't dare let you down.'

'You won't let me down, I know that,' she told him warmly, adding, 'or you would never have been made a full partner!' Emma had no qualms where Silas Trent was concerned, because she knew him to be a man of integrity and honour.

'All the same . . . that fellow at the bank has his beady eyes on my every move!' he laughed, wagging a finger at Emma.

'And so he should!' Emma chided with a smile. 'After all, where would we be without the darling man?' Of a sudden, Emma grew serious, as she asked, 'Has your wife promised to come out?'

'Not yet. Martha's ties with home are too strong for her to let go, I'm afraid.' There was disappointment in his voice, and a sorry look in his dark eyes, 'I haven't given up though. Edward has expressed the wish to come and see me before he pursues his own career . . . I'm counting on him to persuade his mother that her place is here with me.'

'And are you so sure you don't want to return to England . . . to be with her?'

'I've already made it clear to Martha that I'll *never* go back.' Here he leaned forward to kiss first the child, then Emma. 'She knows that I love her, and would welcome her here with open arms. She also knows that my mind is made up . . . Australia is the place I want to be. It's my home now, and my future is here. If Martha loves me, she'll want to

310

share my life, and that means breaking away from her parents long enough at least to give this country, and me, a chance to prove ourselves.'

'You're a good man, Silas Trent.' Emma knew no better. 'Martha is a lucky woman.'

'Martha is not made of the same stuff that you are, Emma . . . unfortunately!' There was anger in his voice as he turned and walked to the door, 'But I love her. I always have.' When he had stepped out of the doorway, he looked back at Emma. The smile had returned to his craggy, moustached features and his brown eyes were twinkling, 'Take care of young Bill. I've no doubt he's got the makings of a sailor in him.' He gave a chuckle and a wink, then was gone and Emma was left staring at the oak-panelled door.

Of a sudden, the door burst open to reveal Nelly's bright excited face. 'Cor, bugger me, gal!' she cried, rushing into the cabin and tugging at Emma's arm. 'Ain't we posh, eh? Quick, gal . . . let's get topside and wave at the folks on the jetty!' Before Emma could resist, she found herself being propelled out of the cabin, along the dark narrow gangway outside, then up the short flight of steps which took them to the upper deck. Here there were crowds of people all milling in one direction, towards the railings, from where they could see the jetty below.

In this month of August, the sun was at its winter's height and folks were well wrapped up against the cool breeze. Most of the women wore short flouncy capes over their wide skirts and boaters or peaked bonnets fastened with ribbons. Others were swathed in long fringed shawls which were pulled up right over their heads and caught

311

fast beneath the chin. The men wore tall straight top-hats or trilbies with wide curved brims; their long jackets were dark and severe, as were their trousers. Most of them sported great sprouting moustaches, or beards, or both, and all eyes were turned to the shore as, frantically, they scanned the multitude of upturned faces below, searching for the one which was most beloved and familiar. From one end of the deck to the other handkerchiefs fluttered like flags. There were murmuring voices, people tearful and laughing, and occasionally a loud cry when a loved one was spotted.

Such was Nelly's cry now, as she excitedly tapped Emma on the shoulder. 'There he is!' she called out, taking off her bonnet and waving it in the air, until the breeze caught it and whipped it away. But Nelly's enthusiasm was not dampened. 'Silas! Up here . . . look up here!' Whereupon, dozens of eyes did as she bid them, afterwards looking away when they saw a stranger, but smiling at the woman's obvious excitement and being all the more enthused by it. 'Here, Silas . . . to your left!' Nelly shouted, and when at last he caught sight of the little group, he snatched off his hat to make a wide circle in the air, his face wreathed in a smile and his eyes playing now on Emma and the child in her arms. Emma saw his mouth move, but such was the din all round that it was impossible to hear what he was saying. Securing her small son in one arm, she waved enthusiastically with the other. She kept on waving, even after the vessel began moving away, until Silas was at first a tiny speck in the distance, then he merged with the others until no one face was distinguishable.

Long after the other passengers had left the railings and gone in their different directions, and Nelly had taken Emma's son to the cabin, Emma stood alone, her knuckles stretched tight as she gripped the rail, and her thoughtful grey eyes scanning the horizon as the shoreline rapidly disappeared from her view. The sea is a solitary place, she thought, as a great feeling of loneliness suddenly took a hold of her and her gaze roved across the distance. It was a humbling and terrifying experience to be completely surrounded by deep, dark waters, stretching out from all sides like a glittering carpet that looked solid, yet was not. Emma shivered. She was not a good sailor, though she did love to see the fine ships and the colourful vessels that hustled for space in the docks. There was something uniquely fascinating about it all and now, as the seagulls soared above, calling, and following the ship for as far as they dare, Emma thought how peaceful it was. Her thoughts were back on the shore, as they wandered over the years she had been exiled in this beautiful land of Australia; it was with a shock that she realised how the years amounted to almost half her lifetime! In this land to which she had been forcibly brought, she had suffered indignities and fear; she had known terror and hopelessness, poverty and deprivation. Yet through her hard work, determination and strength of character, she had also achieved a great deal to be proud of, and she was thankful for it. Her long struggle had been an uphill one, but she had never given in.

Now, as Emma relived those years in her mind, she came to understand how, perhaps even without knowing it, she had sunk her roots deep in this

313

great new land. She had achieved almost everything her heart had desired. Yet if she were to set those achievements against being with Marlow for the rest of her life, the choice was simple: everything she had would be less of a prize than their life together, with the many children who, God willing, would surely follow.

All the same, as the ship sailed further and further away from the shores of Australia, Emma felt a pang of sadness, for she knew in her heart that she would never return. At least, not before she was a very old woman, who might wish to show her grandchildren that part of her life which came about long before even their parents were born! For now though, she was going home—sailing towards her ultimate dream and praying that when the ship came into dock in the port of Liverpool, she would see Marlow waiting there.

When the tears crept into her eyes, Emma blamed the stinging sea-air, but she knew that it was a memory which had stirred her to tears; the memory of a young boy swimming in the canal, a young handsome lad who teased her and laughed with her, and because of that, was later cruelly beaten until his back lay open. Even then, Emma's heart had been lost to him, just as hopelessly as it was now. Now that same boy had become a man, and she was a grown woman. But the deep abiding love between them was still as young and strong, indeed, had bound them together over the turbulent years which had cruelly parted them.

Emma looked up at the great expanse of sky above her. She watched the small puffy clouds scurrying in and out of the blue pockets, she saw how beautiful and serene it was. Something deep within told her that beyond the sky that she could see, some almighty force was at work. She murmured a small prayer of gratitude for having come so far, and she asked that the thought of revenge against her old enemies might not drive her too hard. Above all, she asked for Marlow to be waiting for her, and that they might be blessed with a new life ahead. Her deepest regret was that they had been robbed of seeing their first-born grow up to be a woman.

'Are you gonna stand there all day, Emma, gal?' Nelly's abrupt interruption surprised Emma from her thoughts. 'The lad's flat out exhausted for now,' she said, adding with a shake of her tousled head, 'but there'll be blue murder when he wakes up, screaming fer his tit . . . and his mam's out here star-gazing!'

'Go on with you!' Emma laughed out loud, coming towards the steps which would take them down to the cabin. 'Perhaps we'll have a minute to unpack before young Bill Tanner demands his supper!'

As Emma followed the chattering Nelly along the gangway, there was a song in her heart and a spring to her step. When the ship gave a gentle roll and Nelly, laughing, said, 'This is the life, gal! Rolling about like a drunken sailor, and not a tot o' bloody rum ter show fer it!' her heart was flooded with laughter, and she felt fortunate to have such a friend by her side.

Nelly, too, had suffered bad times, thought Emma, but, thank God, she had emerged without lasting damage. Certainly, her liking for the opposite sex was beginning to return, if her behaviour on the jetty earlier this morning was

315

anything to go by. She had taken a real fancy to what Silas had called 'a rough-looking bloke with a koala bear on his shoulder'. It was only when the fellow got carried away by Nelly's amorous attentions that he proudly drew a snake from his jacket pocket. Nelly had turned all shades of green, before making a hasty retreat behind Silas and Emma, saying in a wounded voice, 'Did y'see that bloke pestering me? . . . I've a bloody good mind ter report him to the authorities!'

Part Four
England 1877
New Hope

Joy and grief were mingled in the cup;
but there were no bitter tears:
> Charles Dickens, *Oliver Twist*

Chapter Twelve

'Your father is a fool. You are *not* going to Australia . . . I forbid it!' Caleb Crowther slammed his clenched fist on to the desk, rose from his seat and, with a look of thunder, he fixed his piercing blue eyes on his grandson's face, saying in a threatening voice, 'While you and your mother choose to live under my roof, you will do as I say. Your father deserted you both, as far as I'm concerned, and this . . .' he snatched a letter from the desk and crumpled it in his fist, '. . . *this* is what I think of him and his letter!'

'Excuse me, sir. My father did *not* desert us.' Edward Trent met his grandfather's stare with a forthright expression. 'He's worked hard over the years to build a future for me and my mother. He wants us there, with him . . . and, if anything, it is we who have deserted *him*! I've disappointed my father by choosing a career other than the sea . . . but he hides that disappointment and gives me great encouragement in my chosen profession, even though it means we remain far apart. As for my mother, he begged her on his last voyage home to return to Australia with him. She refused, and since then, my father has written many letters, pleading with her to join him, but still she refuses. No, sir . . . it is not my father who has deserted us, but the other way round in my opinion. You have seen the letter which I received only this morning, arranging for me to visit him in Australia before I embark on my studies. I owe him that much . . . and if I may say so, sir . . . I intend to go, with or

319

without your blessing.' The whole time that he was speaking, Edward Trent kept his dark green eyes intent on his grandfather's face, and even though the older man continued to test him with a challenging stare, the young man never once flinched or hesitated in his defence of the father he loved.

'The devil you say!' Caleb Crowther stormed round the desk and came to a halt only inches away from his grandson, who believed for a moment that he was about to be physically struck. Instead, he was surprised to see a devious smile uplift the other man's face as he said in a goading manner, 'So . . . you intend to go with, or without, my blessing, do you?'

'I'm sorry, sir, but yes . . . I do. My first duty is to my father.'

'Hmh!' Caleb Crowther's unpleasant expression grew even more devious. 'And do you intend to go with, or without . . . my money?'

'I have money of my own. A regular allowance sent from my father,' Edward Trent reminded him.

'Indeed you do . . . you do!' agreed his grandfather, still smiling as he stepped towards the desk, where he eased himself back on to its edge, his eyes drilling into the young man's face. 'And . . . as I understand it, your mother is trustee of this money?'

'She is, yes, sir.'

'Then you *won't* go, I'm afraid!' Caleb Crowther's smile broadened as he watched the puzzled look come on to his grandson's handsome features. 'You see, Edward . . . you might be prepared to go off to the other side of the world . . . with or without my permission, but my

320

daughter, Martha, is another matter. Like the dutiful woman I have raised her to be, she will do *nothing* without my permission.'

Edward Trent's heart sank within him. What his grandfather was saying was sadly the truth. He had his daughter exactly where he wanted her and if he instructed that Edward's money was not to be released, then nothing would persuade her to go against her father's word.

'May I go now?' Edward asked, trying not to let the disappointment show in his voice. 'It seems our conversation is at an end.'

'Oh, look here, Edward,' Caleb Crowther knew well enough that, as always, he had won the day. The boy would stay here, in Breckleton House, until the day he would leave for London and his studies. That was as it should be! But it did not please him to be at odds with his only grandson, whom he admired as a likeable and worthy young man. 'Please understand that I'm doing this for your own good. Who knows what dreadful accident could befall you on such a long and arduous journey? It really is foolhardy and selfish of your father even to suggest it! Rogues and ruffians abound everywhere . . . waiting to pounce on such innocent fellows as yourself! Have you both so easily forgotten how you were set upon and almost killed by such people?' He waited a moment before continuing, 'Well, let me tell you, Edward, my boy, that *I* will not forget so quickly! That urchin girl who had you secreted away will not elude me forever, believe me.'

'The girl did me no harm, sir. I told you that, the very moment it all started coming back to me. She was the one who found me . . . she saved me from drowning, and afterwards, she returned me safely to my grandmother.'

'Of course she returned you! Half-dead . . . and for a *price*!' Caleb Crowther could not contain his rage at the girl who had escaped him that night, when he thought he had her safely in his clutches. Like always, when he was made to think of it, his reason became impaired by his fury at being so easily outwitted by an alley urchin, and, if he suspected right, by the offspring of Marlow Tanner and his own sinfully begotten daughter, Emma Grady!

'You have it wrong, sir,' insisted Edward Trent, 'the girl is innocent of everything. Her only crime, if indeed there was one, was in asking the price of a friend's funeral . . . someone she dearly loved, and who otherwise would have been buried in a pauper's grave. I ask you, sir, how can that be a crime?'

'Don't be so gullible, boy! She's no better than the worst rogue who might roam the streets. But I have her face imprinted here.' He tapped his temple, before going on with conviction, 'She won't escape me for ever, make no mistake of that!'

'Why do you hate her so? I'm no liar, sir, yet you will not believe me when I tell you that this girl committed no crime against me. She only did all she could to help me. Have you another reason for wanting her put behind bars?'

When Caleb Crowther realised the way in which his grandson was looking at him, and even questioning his true motives for wanting the girl put out of the way, he grew more cautious. 'Leave such matters to me,' he said abruptly. 'Now you may go. Ask your mother to come and see me . . . about better investing your allowance. I was wrong to let her handle it in the first place. Put all nonsense about going to Australia out of your head. In less than a year, you'll be immersed in your studies. Until then, you can better prepare yourself, and perhaps find time to become more involved in the day-to-day running of a textile business . . . which, I might remind you, will no doubt be your own one day.'

*   *   *

It was Saturday, the second day of September, and Cook was in a bad mood. 'Don't talk nonsense,' she snapped at the scullery-maid, 'wherever did you hear such utter rubbish . . . electric lighting indeed! I'll not see the day when they put it in *my* kitchen . . . I shall be kicking up the daisies first, I tell yer!'

'Well, I know what I heard!' retorted Amy. 'When I went past the dining-room last night, the door was partly open and I heard the master's guests talking about it . . . honest I did.'

'Get away with you!' snorted Cook, brandishing her rolling-pin and causing the maid to scurry from the room into the pantry, where she made an act of cleaning the shelves. 'If your hands worked half as hard as your ears, my girl, we'd get things done a lot quicker round this place!'

'It looks like I've arrived at a bad time.' Edward Trent poked his face round the door, saying with a half-smile. 'Shall I come back later?'

'No, lad.' Cook was always pleased to see this young man, who had a likeable character and a winning way with him. 'Get yourself in here.' She inclined her head towards the noise which was coming from the pantry. 'Amy!' she called.

'Yes?'

'Away upstairs and see to the fire-grates. There's a nip in the air and the master will want the fires lit tonight, I've no doubt. Find the housekeeper . . . tell her you've done your tasks in the kitchen, and I'll not have idle hands about me.' When the little figure had gone, as quickly as her legs would allow, across the room and up the stairs, Cook turned to the young man with a hearty laugh, 'Poor Amy doesn't move so fast as she did some twenty years ago!' She shook her grey head and cleaned the flour from her hands, in order to fetch the big enamel teapot from the trestle by the fire. 'Still . . . we're none of us getting any younger, my lad . . . I'm sure it won't be long now, afore the master sends me packing through them doors.' She filled up two rose-patterned teacups and pushed one towards him. 'If there's one thing I'm really afeared of, young Edward . . . it's growing too old to be of use, and being left to rot in some dingy back room down some dark forgotten alley.' She was in a very sorry and melancholy mood, on account of the fact that her old bones were beginning to stiffen, and her eyesight wasn't what it had been.

'That won't ever happen to you.' Edward Trent thought his own troubles seemed like nothing when compared to the dreadful fate which Cook anticipated. 'I've heard my grandmother say often how marvellous you are, and how she could never find another like you in a month of Sundays.'

'Oho! . . . It ain't the mistress who I'm afeared

324

might chuck me out, lad. Oh no! It's your grandfather as worries me. Me and him have never really hit it off, y'see, we're allus . . . suspicious . . . of each other. I'm no fool, and I knew fer sure that, given the proper excuse, he'd take real pleasure in seeing me pack me bags!' She took a moment to squeeze her sizeable frame into the wooden armchair situated at the top of the table, then, taking a noisy slurp of the hot tea, she made a small grunting noise and shook her head. 'My! He's a sour-tempered man is your grandfather . . . if you'll pardon me saying so?' Yes, and a rogue of the worst kind into the bargain, she thought to herself . . . a murderer too, if that precious letter was anything to go by!

'I'll even say it *myself*,' rejoined Edward Trent. 'I know he's fond of me . . . and I have a certain respect and liking for him. But he will ride roughshod over anything he takes a dislike to . . . however much he might be upsetting others.'

'My very point exactly!' remonstrated Cook, putting her cup on the table and leaning her great chubby arms on the table ledge. 'Been at loggerheads, have you . . . you and your grandfather?'

'He insists I won't be going to Australia to stay with my father a while. He's talking to my mother at this very minute . . . forbidding her to finance the venture.'

'Oh dear!' Cook pursed her thin lips into a perfect circle of wrinkles.

'But it's *my* money . . . sent to me by my own father!'

'Makes no difference, lad. Still . . . I can't say I'm surprised he won't let you go. Not if it's true what

325

they say . . . that your father's set up in business with Emma Grady.' Of a sudden, Cook realised how she was letting her mouth run away with her. Emma was forbidden talk in this house . . . had been these many years.

But Edward Trent's interest had been aroused by the mention of Emma Grady's name, and not for the first time. His father had spoken highly of the woman who had gone into business with him. Edward himself recalled when he had shown curiosity about Emma, in a communication he had intended sending to his father. But it had been snatched from him and flung into the fire. His mother had been very agitated and had straightaway sat herself at the bureau, where a letter had been angrily written, instructing his father never to mention that woman's name again. In all the letters Edward had received since, there had never been one single reference to 'Emma'. 'Who is Emma Grady?' Edward asked now, his eyes intent on Cook's anxious face.

'Why, I'm sure it's none of my business, young Master Trent,' Cook replied in a jolly fashion. 'Now then . . . off with you, and let a poor soul get on with her baking!' When she saw how unhappy he looked, Cook's old heart was sorry at his plight. 'Aw, look here . . . talk ter yer grandmother, why don't yer? Why! Yer the very apple of her eye, and I'm sure if it were only a matter o' money that prevents yer from visiting yer father, well . . . she'll help, I'm certain of it. Y'know, the mistress don't *always* agree with what yer grandfather says, and she's allus had a special liking fer Silas Trent, 'cause he's a good man, and she knows it.' A slight noise on the stairway caused her to gasp out loud and clutch at her chest. Seeing that it was only Amy returning, she visibly sagged with relief. 'Oh my poor heart!' she cried, sinking back against the wall. Then, fixing her small worried eyes on Edward Trent, she told him, 'Go on! Do as I say, lad. But, don't you mention to anybody that you and me were discussing yer grandfather's business . . . else me life won't be worth living!'

'Why, I swear the thought never even crossed my mind.' Edward Trent laughed, and put a finger to his closed lips. Halfway up the stairs, he called back in a quiet voice, 'Thank you for your suggestion, all the same. It's the very thing, I'm sure.'

Amy had watched Edward Trent go, then, leaning her whole body across the table, she whispered something to Cook which made that woman's kindly eyes grow big and round with astonishment. '*What* was that you said?' she demanded, not being at all certain that she had heard right the first time.

'It's true!' Amy nodded, her face alive with excite-ment. 'I heard the mistress and Martha Trent. They were talking just now . . . in the drawing-room. Ooh! In a real fit that Martha was . . . and Mrs Crowther well, she was pacing up and down, not knowing what to do. After all, her and the master were partly to blame for what happened, weren't they? If they'd helped poor Emma when she begged 'em to . . . the authorities might not have transported her!' She gave a delicious little giggle, as she reminded Cook, 'Emma won't have forgotten how they turned their backs on her! No wonder the buggers are shivering in their shoes at the news, eh? Oh, and what news it is. After all these years, *Emma Grady's coming home!*'

Chapter Thirteen

Emma was coming home! Marlow must have read the letter a dozen times and more; each time his excitement grew. He could hardly believe it when the landlord of the Navigation had given him the envelope. Apparently, the good man had received it the week before, with a letter addressed to himself and requesting that the enclosed be given to Marlow Tanner at the earliest opportunity, as it was of the utmost importance. 'What you been up to, you bugger?' the landlord had laughed, and when he saw Marlow's face drain of colour on reading it, he gave him a jug of ale on the house. 'Oh, I'm sorry, mate,' he said, 'bad news, is it?' Then, when Marlow had told him how it was the best news, the very best he'd ever heard, he poured *himself* a jug of ale and drank to Marlow's good fortune.

That was two weeks ago. Now, it was the fourteenth of September and the ship bound from Australia was due to dock at Liverpool on the morrow. Tonight Marlow was seated in the corner of the Navigation, listening to revelry all around him and thoughtfully sipping his ale.

'Funny that . . . you're sitting on the very bench where your Sal used to sit, God rest her soul.' The man was of medium build, with tufts of grey hair above each ear and a large expanse of baldness between. He had warm blue eyes, a large loose

328

mouth and long square teeth, from which protruded a clumsy, curved clay pipe. 'Shame about old Sal . . . she were a good sort,' he went on, settling himself beside Marlow, who inched along the bench in order to make more room.

'The *best*!' Marlow rejoined. 'There'll never be another like her.' His handsome dark eyes clouded over.

'From what I hear, she would have been proud o' you, Marlow Tanner. I hear you've done right well for yourself since coming back from seeking your fortune. I heard tell that you had to come right back to your own front doorstep afore you made good. Started off by getting your own barge back . . . at twice what the bugger were worth! Then you worked like a dog, 'till you've now got three cargo barges . . . everyone kept busy from contracts fetching and carrying goods from the docks. Atop o' which, or so rumour has it, you've bought one o' them big houses up Park Street. Is that the truth, mate? Have I heard right?'

'You have, but don't think it came easy. Anything that's worthwhile never comes easy!'

'Don't I know it. You're a bit of a legend in these parts, Marlow Tanner, and, if I've heard a dozen things told about you, the one that's told most often is about the way you've sweated blood to make your way up. And good luck to you, that's what I say! It can't have been easy to come back home and find your only family buried in the ground . . . oh, and the fellow who knew you both since you were toddlers . . . what were his name, Gabe Drury? Aye! . . . Drowned not twenty feet from this 'ere pub!'

Marlow didn't want to hear any more. He was so

329

filled with excitement and dizzy with thoughts of Emma that talking of the bad things which happened would only spoil it all. He didn't want to be depressed. Not tonight. Not on the very eve of Emma's return. 'I'll say goodnight, then,' he told the man, at the same time getting to his feet.

'Aye, well . . . mind how you go.' He nodded and slid further along the bench, saying as Marlow negotiated his way round the table, 'That were a funny business, though . . . about the urchin, I mean. Strange, how nobody knew where she came from . . . Sal would insist as how she'd been left by the little people, but then, you know how fanciful Sal's imagination could be.'

'I expect it was some poor little foundling Sal came across,' Marlow told him, 'she always did have a heart of gold.' He too had heard all about the girl, and for a while his own curiosity had been fired. Weeks upon weeks, he'd searched for the girl and enquired after her, until all trace of her had vanished and he was forced to give up. The last he had heard was that, when the girl had somehow found the money to pay for Sal to have a proper burial, she just disappeared. There was talk of her having fired the hut where she and Sal had been living, then gone from the area. Nobody knew anything more. Marlow would have liked to have found the girl, if only to thank her and to repay her for taking care of Sal's funeral. It would have broken his heart to come home and find his sister in a pauper's grave. Marlow made mention of these things now, in view of the fellow's kindly interest. And he was alarmed to hear something he had not known before.

'By all accounts, she thought the world o' your

330

sister, and the lass did find the money to bury her proper. But, if you ask me, she went about it the wrong way because, for some reason, she set herself up badly with no other than Justice Crowther.'

'How was that?' Marlow resumed his seat. 'Where does that loathsome fellow come into it?'

'Don't rightly know, and folks tend to keep their mouths shut tight when his name's mentioned. But, not long back, I spent a term behind bars. There was an old lag there who got dragged from his bed one night, and thrown in the waggon. He saw things, he said . . . to do with that girl and Justice Crowther. The lass ran off, with another fellow who was in the same waggon. The old lag reckons as how Justice Crowther swore and vowed to track the urchin down.'

'This "old lag" . . . where can I find him?'

The man gave a strange little laugh as he told Marlow, 'Huh! In the very pauper's plot the urchin saved your sister from, I shouldn't wonder!'

'You're telling me that he's dead?'

' 'Fraid so . . . had his guts rotted by the drinking . . . or so I heard tell.'

Of a sudden, the accordian music started up, and someone called for Marlow and the fellow to join in the singing. While the fellow did so, with merry enthusiasm, Marlow chose that moment to leave, and to walk home at a steady pace while he pondered what the fellow had told him. It was a few years since his Sal had passed on and the girl had gone from the area. He supposed she must be many miles away by now, and doing well. Yet Marlow could not forget what that girl had done for Sal and he realised how much she must have loved his wayward sister. God knows, thought Marlow, Sal was no angel, and if truth be told, there's no doubt he would have given her the sharp end of his tongue for having gambled away the barge that had been their parents' and their grandparents' before them. But, as always, he would have forgiven her, because he loved her. No doubt just as the girl had done.

As he let himself into the grand front door of his Park Street house, Marlow thought how proud he would be to tell Emma of his achievements. Lady Luck had smiled on him and he was grateful. Now, he must force himself to be patient until the morrow when he would be waiting on the docks for his Emma. He wondered what Silas Trent had meant when he spoke in the letter of a 'wonderful surprise' which Emma was bringing with her. He was filled with excitement at the prospect of seeing her, of holding her, in this land where they both belonged.

Marlow tried hard to push away the thought of that girl whom Sal had raised, and to whom he owed a debt. With Emma paramount in his thoughts, it was not difficult after a while. But he could not entirely quell the curiosity within him, as he recalled what the fellow in the pub had said. 'For some reason, she set herself up badly with no other than Justice Crowther . . . the old lag saw things that night.' Marlow couldn't help but wonder what it was that the old lag had seen. If in fact he had seen anything at all, or if he had seen it all in the bottom of an ale-jug. Folks did like to talk and gossip; even more so if there was the price of a drink in the offing.

All the same, Marlow thought there were

questions left unanswered—like who were the girl's real parents? And *had* Justice Crowther a vendetta against the girl. If so, why? He hoped it was all just idle speculation, because who should know better than himself, and Emma, what it was like to be hounded by that man!

Marlow came into the hallway and lit the lamp on the small circular table. 'Wherever you are, young 'un,' he murmured in a serious voice, 'if you really *have* made an enemy of Justice Crowther, don't ever come back to this area. And may God keep you safe!'

Chapter Fourteen

'Cor, bugger me, gal! It's like a bleeding sale at the fishmarket, ain't it?' Nelly cried out when her toe was trodden on and a great surge of bodies sent her along at a faster pace towards the gangway. 'I'm blowed if these impatient folk won't send us arse-uppards into the water any minute!' She flashed an angry look at one burly woman who was so intent on pushing her way to the front, that she actually took Nelly a few paces along with her. 'Did y'see that?' Nelly demanded of Emma, who was some way behind. 'I've a bloody good mind to fetch 'er one!'

Emma was caught in a crush of her own, when her only thought was to keep safe the child in her arms, and to emerge intact from the excited throng of passengers who were, understandably, excited at the prospect of meeting their loved ones waiting on the Liverpool quayside. 'Just watch where you're going!' Emma called back to Nelly. 'If we get separated, wait for me at the bottom of the gangway.'

Within the hour, Emma and Nelly were reunited, having come to no harm and gone safely through the process which awaited all disembarking passengers. Now they had their luggage on the ground beside them, a small trunk, five portmanteaus and three large tapestry bags. They were both utterly exhausted, and the child, who up to now had been content in Emma's arms, was beginning to fret. 'The young 'un wants his tit, I expect,' Nelly told Emma in her usual forthright manner, being quite oblivious to the disapproving stares of several elderly women who happened by. 'Look!' She pointed to a sign over the far wall. 'There's a waiting-room across the way. You'll not be disturbed there. Go on with yer. I'll stay here and keep watch.' She lowered her voice and smiled at Emma in a knowing way. 'Don't worry, gal,' she said, 'you've told me enough about yer fellow fer me to pick him out in any crowd. I'll keep me eyes skinned . . . and I'll fetch yer the minute I suspect he's come a-looking fer yer.'

But Emma would not be budged. Looking down at her son, she saw that he was not upset in any way. It was true that he'd become more fidgety and was beginning to make protesting noises, but Emma believed that was more a consequence of being pushed and shoved in every direction, and being made hot and uncomfortable because of it. 'He's fine,' she told Nelly. 'As soon as Marlow finds us, we'll be on our way.' She raised her anxious grey eyes to scan the crowds, who were still milling around them. Nelly's eyes were anxious too, as they gazed on Emma and saw how determined she was to make no move until Marlow Tanner came, as Emma fervently believed he would.

'Aw, look Emma . . . don't get yerself all worked up, darling. Fellers is the same the world over. He may not come, y'know. Yer have ter be prepared fer that. I mean . . . it's been a year and more since he left Fremantle. Yer told him then that there was no chance fer the two of yer. Yer sent him off without so much as a goodbye . . . oh, and quite right it was, at the time. But that poor feller may not have got the message sent by Silas Trent. For all yer know, he might a' got wed. I'm sorry, gal, but yer have ter think o' these things when all's said and done.'

'Please, Nelly.' Emma had turned to look at her friend, and there was reproach in her eyes. Did Nelly think that all the things she was saying had not already run through Emma's mind? Of course they had, every day and every night, even before she had embarked on the homeward journey. There had been no word from Marlow, there had been no time. Yet Emma had hoped and prayed that he *had* received the message, and that he was here now, searching for her just as desperately as she was searching for him. Beyond that, Emma dared not think. 'Marlow is here, somewhere,' she said in a strong, quiet voice, 'I know it!' In a minute, she had placed the child in Nelly's arms, saying, 'I'm going to find him, Nelly.' Then, with a squeeze of Nelly's hand, she smiled. 'Don't move from this spot,' she said. 'I'll be back as quick as I can.' She wrapped the shawl more securely around the infant, and fussed awhile.

Nelly saw the tall handsome fellow with black

shoulder-length hair and intense dark eyes, even before Emma had turned her head away. He had come upon them from the rush of people and was now standing directly behind Emma, his eyes willing her to turn round, and a look of such profound love on his handsome features that Nelly's own heart was moved by it. She said nothing, yet she could not take her eyes off him, any more than he could take his eyes off Emma.

When Emma saw how transfixed Nelly's gaze was, and how she was smiling in that infuriatingly secret way she had, Emma knew. Some sixth sense from deep inside her told her that it was *Marlow* who had captured Nelly's attention. She swung round, and fell straight into his open arms. 'I *knew* you'd be here,' she cried through her laughter. 'I prayed you wouldn't let me down!'

'Oh, Emma, how could I let you down?' Marlow swept her tighter into his arms, taking off her bonnet and showering her with kisses. 'I've only lived for this day, ever since I knew you were on your way home. Wild horses couldn't keep me from claiming you.' He gripped his hands about her small shoulders to ease her away. When she was looking up at him, her lovely face wet with tears and the joy in her heart shining through, he spoke in the softest voice, telling her, 'I love you, Emma Grady . . . adored you for so long that nothing existed before you. And now, at long last, my darling, we're really together. Oh, Emma . . . I've waited for this day *all of my life!*' He held her gaze a moment longer, before bending his head to her upturned face. 'I love you so,' he murmured against her mouth, and when he drew her towards him, kissing her and holding her fast against him,

Emma knew what happiness really was.

Seeing the warmth and joy of such a reunion, Nelly also was softly crying. And when she sniffled noisily, juggling the child in her arms in order to wipe her face with the cuff of her jacket, Emma drew away from Marlow, saying to him, 'I've brought you something, Marlow . . . something very precious.' She smiled at the puzzlement on his face, as she reached over to collect the child from Nelly's arms. Then, uncovering the tiny face, she held the small squirming bundle out to him, saying softly, 'This is Bill. Take him, Marlow, for *he's your* son.' Marlow's dark eyes grew wide, going from Emma to the child and gazing at the infant for a long painful moment, then the tears started to rain down his face and a small cry escaped him as he cradled the boy to his chest.

'He's beautiful, isn't he?' Emma murmured. 'And so like you.' She reached out to touch Marlow's face, which was still bent in fascination towards that tiny being, his own son! Now as he looked up to meet Emma's loving gaze, his dark tearful eyes held wonder. 'God bless you, Emma,' he said in a voice filled with awe, 'I have all that a man could ask for.' He placed an arm around Emma and drew her close, and for a moment there was no need for words.

*   *   *

From a short distance away, a girl of some sixteen years watched the tender scene unfold; black-eyed she was, with long loose hair dark about her narrow shouiders and a pinched hungry look in her features. She was painfully thin, and clad in a calf-length threadbare dress, covered by a brown shawl. There was a sadness in her eyes as she watched, and loneliness in her voice when she clutched the fair-haired toddler in her arms. 'See that, sweetheart,' she told the child, 'happy, ain't they, eh?' She kissed the child and pointed its attention towards Emma and the little group. 'That's a *proper* family . . . not like you and me. Oh, but at least you've got a proper mammy, eh? And I love you more than life . . . so, you're better off than I am! Y'see, Sal, darlin' . . . I never had no mammy, nor daddy neither. Oh, you got a daddy sure enough, but that Jack-the-lad lived up to his name right enough, didn't he, eh? Cleared off and left the pair of us! Still, I expect he'll turn up again . . . like he's done afore.'

Molly chuckled as she swept the child on to the bony part of her hip. 'Hold on tight, lovely,' she told its pretty trusting face, ' 'cause we've a crust to earn . . . aye, and happen a bit o' fast footwork to do and all!' She was still chuckling when she passed within an arm's reach of Emma and her family. Molly had pondered on relieving the pockets of the dark-haired gent, but she decided against it, telling the little girl, who was presently twisting its mammy's thick black hair round its fingers, It'd be a shame ter spoil such a lovely reunion, wouldn't it? Besides which . . . the gent looks fit and able enough ter catch me, and we can't be having that, can we, eh?' Her dark eyes swept the milling people, passengers, workers, visitors and sea-men alike, until eventually they came to rest on a bent old gentleman in top hat and long-coat. He carried a walking stick and wore that particularly arrogant and surly expression

338

which characterised most wealthy toffs. 'I reckon we can outrun *that* old geezer.' Molly chucked little Sal under the chin, tucking her in tight and pulling the shawl taut about her. After which, and with her eyes kept fixed on the old gent, she went into the throng of people and disappeared from sight.

*　　　　*　　　　*

'Well now, ain't we the posh ones?' Nelly climbed into the carriage and turned about to collect the child from Emma's arms. 'When yer think, Emma gal . . . how, so long ago, the two on us were packed off from England as branded criminals . . . outcasts in society . . . and look at us now, eh? . . . I'm buggered if we ain't come back like a pair o' queens!' She winked at Marlow, who handed the luggage up to the carriage driver and was greatly amused by Nelly's forthright manner. He turned his dark smiling eyes to Emma, who smiled back and blushed a little, as she prepared to follow Nelly into the carriage.

Of a sudden, there was a hue and cry, with some kind of skirmish going on a little way along the quayside. 'What the bleedin' 'ell's that?' asked Nelly, leaning out of the carriage door and gawping towards the source of the noise in the distance. 'Well . . . will yer look at that! It ain't but a ragamuffin got herself in trouble!'

By this time, Emma had come to stand beside Marlow and the carriage driver, as everyone's attention was drawn by the sight of a strapping bobby with a red angry face, and a great deal to say to the girl beside him, a dark-eyed girl with an infant clinging to her. 'You've been warned

339

before,' he was saying in a breathless voice, 'but this time you've been caught red-handed, my girl. You'll soon find out that the law doesn't take kindly to pickpockets!'

Emma turned, curious, as the carriage driver gave a low chuckle. 'I fail to see anything amusing in a young girl having to resort to thievery!' she said, in a disapproving voice. 'Why the poor thing can't be above fifteen or sixteen . . . and she has a child to look after.' She turned to Marlow. 'Can't we do something to help her?' she asked, looking up at him with concern.

Before Marlow could reply, the carriage driver had something else to say. 'Don't you worry your pretty head about yon lass. She's a quick-witted one is that, and I'll tell you some'at else, lady . . . that there bobby, as big and forceful as he is, *he* won't hold her!' He shook his head and chuckled aloud. 'A whole army wouldn't hold that one! Oh, I've seen the lass before, many a time . . . here at the docks and wherever a busy crowd might gather. She ain't no fool . . . and she slides a gent's wallet from his person like nothing I've ever seen before. It's a pleasure to watch the lass at work . . . though I keeps my own wallet well and truly safe when she's around, I can tell you.'

No sooner had he finished speaking than there came a shout and the sound of running feet. Emma was astonished to see that the girl had broken free of the bobby and was heading straight towards them, the child tucked tight into her hip and, judging by the broad grin on its face, thinking the whole thing to be a wonderful adventure.

The bobby was in close pursuit, blowing his whistle and growing more red-faced with every step, while the girl ran like the wind, with various do-gooders and would-be heroes grabbing at her as she skilfully dodged them. For a minute, Emma could see the girl's face clearly, and she was greatly moved by it. Why, she's lovely, Emma thought, seeing how strong and proud the girl's features were. Of a sudden, Molly's dark eyes were attracted by Emma. She smiled and winked, then was quickly lost to sight, leaving Emma with a warm feeling, and a sense of admiration.

'Who is she?' Emma asked of the carriage driver, for her curiosity was greatly aroused.

'Dunno, lady,' came the matter-of-fact reply, 'just an urchin . . . and Lord knows, the alleys is full o' the blighters. Cut your throat for sixpence, some of 'em would, but *that one* . . . I dunno. Just an urchin, like I said. We'll not see her round these parts again though . . . not now she's had her collar felt . . . you can depend on that! Don't you give it another thought, 'cause her kind can take care o' themselves, believe me.'

In the carriage, with Nelly seated opposite, her son in her arms and her beloved Marlow by her side, Emma thought how very fortunate she was. There had been times during her life when it seemed all hope of true happiness had gone. Times when she had despaired and been wretched. Times when only the thought of revenge had kept her going. She had not forgotten how those she trusted had deserted her when she was most in need of their help. Nor had she forgotten that her dear father had entrusted his daughter and his entire life's work to Caleb Crowther, who had betrayed that trust. What kind of man was he, Emma asked herself, who would see his own niece transported, and not lift a finger to help? And her father's hard-earned business—what of that? In all these years, there had been no word from her uncle regarding her father's assets. But Emma had learned the art of patience. She could be patient a while longer, because there were other matters more close to her heart that took precedence. She had every intention of confronting Caleb Crowther, because there were many questions she must ask of him. Questions which demanded answers, without which Emma knew she would never truly have peace of mind. But, for now, Emma dismissed these disturbing thoughts from her mind. *Nothing* must he allowed to mar the joy of her homecoming. At last she really was home, with her man by her side, and her family about her. At this point in her thoughts, Emma recalled what Nelly had said earlier, that they 'were packed off from England as branded criminals . . . outcasts in society'. And oh, how true that was, Emma thought now as she relived the awful experience in her mind. Above all else, the greatest horror had been the tragic loss of her first-born. She had her family about her now, yes that was true, thank God, but how truly complete it would have been if only her daughter was here beside them.

Sensing that Emma was lost in some deep private place, Marlow leaned his dark head down towards her. 'Are you happy, my love?' he murmured.

'Oh, yes . . . yes.' Emma gazed up at this man whom she would always adore, and her heart was brimming over. 'If only you knew,' she told him with tearful eyes. 'Oh, Marlow, if only you knew how very happy I am.' When he clasped her hand in his and tenderly brushed his lips against her forehead, Emma gazed down at the quiet face of their son. Even in the joy he brought her, there was a sadness in Emma's heart which would not be denied, for in his dark eyes and in that rich dark hair that was so like Marlow's, she saw another face, that of a new-born daughter. Emma tried to imagine how that tiny girl might have grown into a woman. Would she have the ways and manner of herself, she wondered, or would she be more like Marlow?

Realising the futility of remembering and tormenting herself about what was gone, Emma shook all thoughts of her first-born from her mind. She was glad that Marlow had learned nothing of what had happened, because, at least, he would be saved the heartache which knowing would surely bring.

Somehow, Nelly sensed that Emma was reproaching herself for the past, and, bending forward, she put her hand over Emma's, saying in a soft whisper, 'It's all over now, me darlin' . . . it's all over.'

Emma smiled at her, leaning into the curve of Marlow's loving arm. 'I know,' she said gratefully, 'bless your heart, Nelly, I know.' If only Emma had known also that she had been within touching distance of her 'lost' daughter, and even her first grandchild, how wonderfully complete her happiness would have been.

But is it not written that if we believe and if our faith is strong enough, then all things will come to pass.